WILDEWOOD

BOOKS BY JESSICA THORNE

THE QUEEN'S WING SERIES
The Queen's Wing
The Stone's Heart

THE HOLLOW KING SERIES
Mageborn
Nightborn

THE LOST QUEEN SERIES
A Touch of Shadows
A Kiss of Flame
A Crown of Darkness

STANDALONE NOVELS
The Lost Girls of Foxfield Hall
The Bookbinder's Daughter
The Water Witch

WILDEWOOD

JESSICA THORNE

SECOND SKY

Published by Second Sky in 2026

An imprint of Storyfire Ltd.
Carmelite House
50 Victoria Embankment
London EC4Y 0DZ

www.secondskybooks.com

The authorised representative in the EEA is Hachette Ireland
8 Castlecourt Centre
Dublin 15 D15 XTP3
Ireland
(email: info@hbgi.ie)

ISBN: 978-1-80550-363-7
eBook ISBN: 978-1-80550-362-0

To Pat,
a chuisle mo chroí

PROLOGUE

ALEX

It started with a laugh. It was deep and dark, a low chuckle that knew far too much and promised everything.

It always started this way, the laughter rippling its way up through her body. Distinctly not her own. It twisted deep inside her stomach, tightening muscles and sending waves of pleasure through her. Things she didn't understand. Didn't want to understand.

She was running through the trees, the boughs overhead moving as if in a storm, like a wild sea made of leaves and malice. But she had to keep running because the hunter was coming. And if he caught her... if he caught her...

'*Alex!*' her father's voice cried out, echoing after her, ringing around her head and driving her onwards. '*Run, Alex! You have to run! NOW!*'

But she was lost, and desperate and the trees were closing in. And beyond the trees only the manor was waiting, a thousand empty windows for eyes, and an open maw, waiting for her.

There was no way out. She was lost between the wild and the Hall.

She turned back to the trees and saw Theo. Her brother, her twin, had his arms thrown out wide, head tilted up to the sky, caught in the trees as if crucified. Theo still and limp, held by the wild wood, the one that had taken their dad, that would take them all. The forest that crowded close around the Hall, hemming it in, the boundary trapping that malevolence inside. The place to which none of them should ever have returned. The thing that lived in those woods. They had called it the wild when they were children visiting this place. And they feared it.

Theo shuddered, just once, and turned his empty, glassy eyes on her. And it wasn't Theo. Not anymore. It couldn't be. She tried to shout his name but nothing came out of her mouth but leaves and vines.

She choked on them, going down on her knees, clawing at her throat while the wild burrowed through her body, filling her and making her its own. She crawled from the woods, through brambles and undergrowth, to find herself kneeling on the steps up to the door of the Hall itself, caught underneath the shadowy recesses of the Georgian portico.

It's a dream, she tried to tell herself. Just a dream.

The shadow fell over her, blocking out any remaining light.

'*Alexandra,*' the voice said. He held out a hand, pale and beautiful, long-fingered, inviting, terrifying. She couldn't see him clearly. Beyond the elegant hand, he was a dark shadow with burning eyes. His voice was a murmur, but it was the same voice that laughed in her dreams, that reached out to touch her in the darkness, that wound itself around her and promised her everything, that would never keep those promises. Or even worse, might keep each and every one. His voice. The voice that had drawn her through the house's labyrinth of passages and hallways, out into the night. The voice that teased and tormented and would surely destroy her.

'*You don't need to fight,*' he said, the darkness welling up around her as if it was made of tar. *'You don't need to run, my beloved. Not anymore. It's time to come home.'*

She reached out, barely conscious of the involuntary movement, and slipped her hand into that ancient and remorseless grip. She felt his smile like a caress. The darkness closed around her with the finality of a bear trap.

Alex awoke with a scream, bolt upright in her bed. Her room was too bright, stained with green, like the wild wood, like her dream... She gasped for air, the choking sensation of vegetation cramming itself in her mouth from the depths of her throat lingering far too long. She was sheened in sweat, her heart thundering. It wasn't the first time she'd started awake, haunted by dreams about Wildewood. Since she left, she'd continued to run from the place in her sleep. But this dream was different.

Something was wrong. Something was terribly wrong.

Alex couldn't have gone back to sleep if she tried. Theo wasn't answering the phone when she called, or responding to her messages. So she waited. There was nothing else she could do.

As the city woke up around her and the sky finally brightened, sunlight seeping through her apartment windows, she sat in the kitchen drinking coffee after coffee, trying to convince herself it really was just a dream.

Until the cops arrived, just after nine. Two of them in uniform, solemn-faced and serious, and she knew. She just knew.

'Dr Alexandra O'Neill?' Carefully respectful. His colleague hung back, face ready with empty sympathy.

'Yes.' It was all she could do to force out that single, breathless word.

The first man paused, trying to work out what to say, how to phrase this and no doubt inwardly cursing his luck that he had to be the one to tell her. 'Ma'am, I'm afraid there's been an accident.'

Theo. It had to be about Theo. There was no one else.

She retreated a step. 'What – what happened?'

He introduced himself but she was barely paying attention. Because she knew where this was going.

Alex swallowed hard, the mulch of the wild wood still there, mingled with the rising vomit in the back of her throat.

Because she'd already known. From the moment she woke up. From the moment she had torn her way out of that dream.

Twins knew, they always said.

Her twin brother was dead. And she was going to have to go back to Wildewood Hall.

CHAPTER 1

ALEX

Alex's hire car struggled up the hill, jolting back and forth as she failed to navigate potholes of truly epic proportions. The rain made visibility hopeless, the headlights barely showing her anything further than a few yards ahead. There were no street-lights out here. As a city girl, she felt like she was crawling along, feeling her way in the dark.

By the time she'd left the village of Kilfayne, which passed for the last bastion of civilisation around here, the rain came down like Niagara Falls and the night closed around her. She should have had plenty of time, planning to get to the house well before dark. But she'd got stuck behind a collision, and a tractor, and every other inconvenience possible. And it just got later and later.

Beyond the hedgerows, the trees made the road into a blind and twisting alley. There was nowhere to turn around. She was halfway up a mountain. Kilfayne was a good twenty minutes behind her now. And this was the only road – a generous word for the mud track she found herself on – to 'The Big House'.

Wildewood Hall. Ancestral home of the de Wilde family. Her grandfather's home, and a line stretching back before him all the way back to God alone knew when. The estate he had left to Theo.

Hers now, God help her.

Once again, she wondered what on earth she was doing.

It was all her twin brother's fault. That was the story of her entire life.

Coming back was a mistake. She knew that. Everyone knew that.

And yet here she was.

The place that had claimed the life of her brother. And before that her father. And ultimately, all her ancestors before them as well, she supposed.

It was so isolated and cut off, a law unto itself, Gran used to say. Almost fondly, or perhaps that was because she had been an old woman talking to children. Her grandmother, the little Alex could remember of the woman, had come from Kilfayne, and wasn't as reserved as those born to the de Wilde name. When Alex's grandfather had told her, in those haughty tones, not to spin wild tales, Gran had just laughed and spun a new one, even wilder. Tale after tale, of monsters and lost loves, of the children of the forest, of the walker in the woods, of the hungry grass and the endless appetites of lost gods…

Alex shivered at the memory. She blamed those tales, and the loss of her father, for imprinting such haunting dreams on her. Wildewood Hall was the last place on the whole bloody planet she wanted to go back to.

But it wasn't like she had a lot of choice. Theo hadn't left a will. He'd only been in his thirties after all and things like wills were not on his radar. The only things her twin brother had cared about were ecology, specifically *trees*, and this wretched house, which was almost swallowed up by its associated forest, left to him by their grandfather a few years ago.

Probably as revenge. Or at least out of spite.

Theo hadn't seen it that way of course. Theo was a constant

beacon of optimism and hope, a shining light in the world. He could do no wrong. The golden child.

God, she had adored him. Even if he had driven her mad.

Alex hated this place almost as much as Theo loved it. She hadn't been here in twenty years, and she still broke out in a cold sweat just thinking about it.

That the house was now hers would probably send their grandfather spinning in his miserable grave. So at least there was that.

How Gran would have laughed.

It was so dark and miserable that Alex almost missed the gates, which stood open on either side of the lane. It was the only indication that she'd reached her destination, and that this was the place where the so-called road ended and the drive began. They didn't look like they had been closed in years.

She hadn't come back here for their grandfather's funeral. Theo had been buried with their mother just outside Dublin rather than in the de Wilde family vault here.

As she passed through their slated shadows, a shiver ran up her spine, even though she had the heat on full in the car. The windscreen wipers ground away, barely clearing the view ahead for more than a second.

She didn't have to be here. She could let the lawyers handle it all. She *ought* to let the lawyers handle it all. She just wanted to sell the wretched pile of ancient bricks and horrors. And that was what she would do once she had everything sorted out.

But she needed to know what happened to Theo. And to Dad, if she was honest. What really happened. She didn't believe for one second that either death had been an accident.

Wildewood Hall was the only place she was going to find out any of that.

When she'd told the lawyers they hadn't sounded happy. If

she decided to take up residence, they told her, it could further complicate matters. Better to leave it all to them. They kept stalling over some detail or another. The sooner Wildewood was out of her life, the better.

Now it seemed the lawyers weren't just driving up their bill.

Of course, the house was hers to do with as she pleased, they said. But there were difficulties with the entailment and the caretaker agreement apparently. And local issues regarding the woodlands on the estate, the use of the land and the like. She wasn't quite sure what Theo had got up to but his mind had always been on ecology rather than legalities so heaven alone knew what she was walking into.

When she'd finally got hold of the family solicitors, they'd sent her contact details for the caretaker, Mr Walker. But when she'd emailed him, she hadn't even received a reply for over a week. Not even when she sent her arrival time and asked him to confirm receipt by return. It was only this morning, as she'd picked up the car at the airport, ready to set off, that the single, terse message had appeared.

I'll have the master suite ready for you.

Just that. To be honest she wasn't sure what she had been expecting, but something more than that. Not joy or delight, sure. It was all far too complicated for that. But something.

Gabe had just laughed when he rang to check she'd landed safely. He'd said LAX was only eleven hours or so away if she wanted to turn around and come straight home. She assumed he thought that was funny. The thing about her ex was he always found himself way more hilarious than she did.

They were still close. After all, they still worked together, agreeing that they were much better as friends and business partners than anything else. Gabe was best friends with everyone.

It could have been so much worse, she supposed. And he always had her back. Even now. Especially supporting her with the notoriety and the fickle fame from being the great debunker on *The Ghost Patrol*. And all the fall-out from that.

She wasn't cut out for the way that about half the internet was obsessed with her, not like the others. It was one of the reasons she'd decided to come to Wildewood in person. To get away from it. The Sanderson case...

No one liked being exposed as a fraud. Ted Sanderson least of all. He had taken to the internet, and the internet had loved him with all his obsessions and righteous indignation. He turned his ire on her particularly and they followed joyfully. Apparently this was all her fault. Getting herself out of Dodge had seemed like the best possible idea.

The money from the TV show was keeping her afloat, and would for some time. And she had a book to write.

The Sceptic's Sceptic's Guide to Dashing Hopes and Destroying Dreams.

Yeah, her publisher would love that title.

This was a sabbatical and an escape. But she had simply had enough of the whole crazy circus.

And once she had sold Wildewood Hall she could decide what she would do next, on her own terms.

Turning past another bank of trees – no wonder Theo was obsessed with the place, trees everywhere, native woodland, untouched for centuries – the view ahead suddenly opened up and drove any other thoughts from Alex's mind.

The house was silhouetted against the darkness of the night's sky, a few lights on the ground floor illuminating the tall symmetrical windows and the portico entrance. A grand building, parts of which dated back to the Normans. You'd never know, after so many changes and additions over generations of her father's line. It loomed over her little car as she parked, almost far too large to be real. God, if Gabe and the others could see this nightmare straight out of a horror movie they'd lose their shit completely. Just as well she'd insisted that she'd do this alone, that it was her responsibility.

The very thought of having *The Ghost Patrol* team here in force sent another shiver through her that wasn't about the cold, or the house. They were her friends, and they were professionals. But she knew what would happen.

Gabe would be insufferable. Daphne would swoon about the place. Eduardo would hide behind the equipment. Worst for her would be Arnold digging deep into the history – her family history – like a kid in a candy shop, and who knew what he'd find. The things she knew were bad enough. She'd be left there, the lone voice of reason, the sceptic's sceptic, trying to hold it all to some version of actual reality while being the eternal killjoy, disproving every wild theory they came up with. They'd alienate every single local in the vicinity with their antics and make her a laughing stock. And that would be before the whole thing aired.

Then her so-called fans would get in on the act.

It was exhausting just thinking about it.

Staying here, off the grid, away from all the madness, made perfect sense. No one to come up with another amazing scheme for fortune and glory which capitalised on the worst experience of her life, thank you very much, Gabe. No creepy messages or flowers or threats disguised as adoration. No horde of stalkers unleashed on her by a man who had abused his own children in the pursuit of fame. Exposing him on live TV, and compounding it by testifying at his trial, was still something she was proud of. Even if it had destroyed her LA life as well.

Sending her running back here.

Alex's attention was drawn inexorably to the house. It wasn't symmetrical, like the great Georgian houses, or towered and turreted like the gothic ones. It was odd, sprawling across the land, as if it had grown by itself rather than something built by men. She tried to shake off the idea that the house was staring back at her. Daring her to move. She didn't know how long she sat there, memories flooding through her mind.

The trees thrashing overhead, with a roar like the ocean, running through thick forest, tripping over roots and sliding on wet moss, her breath dammed up in her throat, her heart thundering. The cold arched roof of stones closing over her and the stench of mulch. The darkness pressing in on her, suffocating her. Dad's hands falling still, limp on the rich and hungry earth. The gleam of gold beneath rotting foliage. The taste of blood in her mouth, choking her, and the world blurring through tears and terror.

Alex tried to make herself breathe again, in and out, calmly, tried to still her racing heart. She could do this. She had to. For Theo.

Out of nowhere a fist struck the window right beside her head, a series of rapid thuds, and Alex screamed.

CHAPTER 2

ALEX

Through the sheets of rain a bedraggled, bearded man stepped back from the car. The rest of him was hidden under a huge hooded raincoat. He leaned in to peer through the window he had just assaulted.

'Ms de Wilde?' He had to shout over the noise of the rain on the roof. The wind snatched away whatever else he said.

'No.' Alex replied without thinking about it. 'I mean, yes. I mean – it's O'Neill. Dr O'Neill. I took my stepfather's name.'

Why was she telling him that? It was hardly the time.

He peered in closer, bent almost in two, straining to hear her and made a gesture indicating he couldn't. Christ, he was huge.

And here she was, sitting in the dry, just staring at him like an idiot while he was getting soaked to the skin. The wind whipped at the hood, almost tearing it off his head until he had to use one hand to hold it securely in place. His hair was plastered across his face and water ran down his nose and into his saturated beard.

'... Walker,' he shouted. And then he pointed at the house.

Nick Walker. The caretaker. Of course it was him. He must

have been watching out for her and seen the headlights. She'd expected someone older. And less... bearlike.

And she was still just sitting there.

'I just—' she shouted, her voice very loud in the confines of the car. 'I have bags – I'll just get them and follow you in.'

She pointed back at the boot and grabbed her rucksack from the passenger seat, securing her coat before opening the door. The wind almost ripped it from her hands anyway. She struggled out, only to find he was already at the boot, lifting her suitcases out. Oh God, did he think she'd been telling him to do that? Ordering him around like some kind of servant? When she moved to help him, he just shook his head and then waved her brusquely towards the house.

Right, inside. Yes. Out of the storm. She was standing in his way.

With a bitten-off curse, Alex ran up the steps to the main door, which was thankfully open. She almost fell as the wind abruptly cut off, skidding on ancient tiles covered in rainwater and leaves. She stepped through the vestibule, with its generations of boots, umbrellas, and coats, through the ornate glass doors which shielded it, and into the house proper.

Shaking off the rain, she looked up, surprised to see that not a lot had changed. Dark wood climbed halfway up the walls, all those imposing doors, portraits and an ancient mirror almost as tall as she was and four times as wide. The silver backing was so distorted and mottled that from the corner of the eye it looked like it was full of dust and desiccated faces, with the reflection of all the paintings on the opposite wall. Whenever they had come here, her grandfather had escorted her and Theo through these very doors and down this long wood-panelled hallway, naming the faces staring down at them. He'd gone into such detail about the artists who had painted them, and the subjects, she'd worried there was going to be a test later on.

Which... there had been. She'd failed.

The entrance hall was lit by a series of electric lights designed to mimic gas lamps. Above the wood panelling, the walls were painted a deep forest green. At the far end the staircase rose, carved black oak, a graceful and elegant twist of leaves and berries, stately foxgloves on the newel posts, wild woodland motifs to go with the name of the estate.

Her attention was drawn to the door that led to the study, the one she had never been allowed to enter. In the more familiar drawing room, a fire crackled merrily in the fireplace. She could see her reflection in the oval mirror above the mantelpiece. There were a pair of sofas and an armchair with a Foxford blanket thrown over it. It almost looked... inviting... and normal.

The heavy main door slammed behind her, as Nick Walker kicked it closed. He dropped her suitcases and shook himself like some kind of great beast relieved to be in out of the rain.

'Miserable night,' he said, his voice a low growl, like somehow that was her fault.

He pushed back the hood, revealing hair as long as the beard and just as wet. All Alex could do was stare at him. She couldn't tear her eyes off him. He looked like a lumberjack. Or a wolf man.

'Give us a sec,' he went on when she said nothing. 'I'll take these up for you.'

'I'm sorry. I would have got them,' she replied hurriedly. 'I didn't expect you to—'

He shook his head, cutting her off. 'I was expecting you hours ago. You must have had a horrible drive down. Probably should have stayed in the city.'

'Probably,' she agreed weakly, unsure of what else to say. It was a vast understatement. She was freezing and exhausted. Ready to drop, if she was honest. She'd barely stopped on the way down here from Dublin and that had probably been a mistake too.

He'd straightened up now, shrugging off the raincoat. He was impossibly tall and broad-shouldered. She didn't think they made Irish men like that outside of old stories. Half of them looked like potatoes in a GAA shirt. The other half though... this was the other half...

There were reasons they were the heroes of legend, giants and warriors, beloved of women and men alike.

I'd have to climb him like a tree, she thought absently and then sucked in a breath. What the hell was she thinking? God, she really was overtired. She didn't even know him. *And* she was staring again. Her cheeks heated up as she realised how wildly inappropriate this was.

He was an employee, for the love of all that was holy. Not her employee, sure, but the estate's. Somehow. No one had really managed to explain how it worked yet. She wasn't so sure that she had inherited the estate. More like it had inherited her.

'I'm Nick Walker,' he told her, running his hands through his long dark hair to get it back from his face, scowling. 'Not sure if you caught that out there. I couldn't hear you at all.' He moved as if to offer her his hand to shake and then pulled back as he noticed the water still dripping off his fingers. 'I'll get us some towels and make some tea. Sit down inside and warm up.'

She shed her coat and hesitated, looking for somewhere to hang it. Nick Walker just took it from her and turned around, hanging it from a coat rack just inside the main door next to his own. Water pooled underneath on the bright tiles.

Alex noticed there was a puddle forming around her too. She glanced at the fire longingly. But tea would be so good as well. 'Can I help?'

He shook his head, and little splashes of water flew out in all directions, and she thought of a great shaggy hound shaking himself off.

'No, just go warm up before you catch your death.' His tone

was gruff and not to be argued with. It sent a shiver through her that wasn't entirely about the cold.

'You're soaked.'

'Go on with you. I'll dry quickly enough. I was only out in it for a few minutes. Besides, I'm used to working outdoors, Ms de Wilde. You are not.'

Alex squirmed. He wasn't wrong. But he didn't need to treat her like some kind of helpless girl. Or as a de Wilde.

'It's O'Neill,' she said firmly. And because she had been through this far too many times, she added, 'Dr Alex O'Neill.' She leaned on her title a bit, as she usually had to with a certain type of man.

Nick Walker fixed her with an appraising kind of look, pursed his lips and then nodded slowly. 'All right then, Dr O'Neill.' He didn't hesitate over the switch in names, which was a point in his favour. It wasn't sarcastic. Not quite. But it was perhaps on a more than nodding acquaintance with sarcasm. 'Please take a seat. I'll be as quick as I can.'

And then he was gone, heading further into the house and down a passageway which vanished behind the main staircase. She remembered it leading to the kitchen, where she and Theo used to sneak off to in search of treats from her grandfather's cook, a matronly woman with a huge smile and a jovial nature.

Nick Walker moved fast for a big man. And quietly too. Fluid, like some kind of predator stalking its prey. She couldn't take her eyes off him until he vanished from view.

Nick Walker. Caretaker. Groundsman. Theo's best friend. The thorn in her side. The man she needed to tell that once she sold this house he would be out of a job and out on his ear. Once her lawyers unravelled the legal tangle her brother had left her in.

She wasn't looking forward to that conversation, having seen him... and his size. He had far more claim to say he lived here than she did.

And that was a problem. Because while he did, she was going to have the damnedest time selling it.

Wonderful.

CHAPTER 3

NICK

Nick wasn't sure what he had expected. It had never occurred to him that Theo's twin sister would look... well, like *that*! Theo had said she was smart and funny, but he hadn't thought she'd be so stubborn. Or that she'd have a voice Nick could listen to reading a dictionary. Or a fragrance that made him think... so many things he had no right to be thinking. He needed to be careful, that was all. Very careful.

The problem was, he'd never been very good in social situations. There were many reasons for him to stay up here at Wildewood, on his own, away from prying eyes and prattling tongues. That was just one of them.

'So it's not your deal,' Theo had said. 'You have other strengths, Nick. And who cares anyway. It's not everyone who can charm the trees.'

Sally had been even more dismissive. 'No one else can do what you do here, *mo stór*.'

But he had always had them there, to deal with people. And now...

Well, he didn't have anyone.

He'd loved her brother, and missed him every day. Nick had

lost far too much over the years but that didn't make Theo's loss any less. If anything this was the most painful. They'd worked together, dreamed together. Theo had given him his hope back when he'd thought it lost forever.

Now he had no one.

But here she was. Like a ghost herself. She had some nerve coming back here now after the way she had treated Theo. She'd ignored countless invitations from her brother, even when he had needed her most. Too busy being famous in the States. Ghost hunting. Like that was a real job.

But when he'd seen her sitting there in the car, so pale, staring at the house for so long, Nick hadn't known what to think.

Theo might have come to terms with what had happened to their father here, but he had been adamant that Alex never would.

'She won't come back,' he had said any time the subject came up. And he had been right.

'It was worse for her,' Sally had said, in those soft, sad tones. 'You know it was. She found him.'

So Nick had never actually expected Alexandra de Wilde to arrive, even with her curt messages insisting that she was on the way. And now she was here.

She was going to sell Wildewood Hall. To be rid of that part of her past for good. He'd been a fool to believe otherwise. Watching her enter the house, he'd known. She didn't want it. She had never wanted it. She looked so awkward and uncomfortable.

Well, that could work in his favour, surely, help him persuade her to leave. He needed to get her out before she started poking around too much.

By putting her in the drawing room, he felt like he was keeping her from intruding too much while he wasn't there to contain matters. It was comfortable, and cosy, safe enough. It wasn't the heart of the house, like the kitchen, but it was a family room. Formal enough for a de Wilde surely. Nothing much tended to happen in there.

If he could limit where she went and what she got into until she got fed up and left... that might work.

Yes, that was the best idea. And then...

Then he just had to persuade her to leave it alone, to go back to America and let him run the estate for her. There would be a steady income stream, grants and all the rest of it. She didn't have to sell up. Keeping Wildewood intact, and her far away... It was the best thing.

But he had an awful feeling it could never be that easy.

The house stirred around him, creaking, whispering. The wind was finding a way in through the gaps and with it came... well, it was an old house, he would tell her. He had to.

The lawyers had been no more than irritants, like a stone in his boot. He could ignore them. They didn't matter.

But Alexandra de Wilde herself – no matter what name she had chosen – she was a different matter.

No, *not* Alexandra de Wilde. He had to remember that. Theo might have embraced the family name but she didn't. Dr Alex O'Neill – her stepfather's surname, a short form of her name, carefully ungendered for professional reasons no doubt, and a title she had earned through her studies. Nothing of the de Wilde inheritance at all. She had rejected everything.

When their mother died, Theo had grieved for months. Nick and Sally had been here for him all through that. Theo had no one else. Alex stayed away and that had hurt him so much. Nick had been angry about it at the time, until Sally warned him to leave it alone.

Oh Alex went to the funeral, in Dublin. She visited the city and saw old friends, and she had spent some time with her brother and their stepfather there.

But not here. She had never come back here. Where Theo

had retreated, to hide, to grieve, to lose himself. And even when they had finally persuaded him to message her, for his own sake, to ask her to visit as his only living relative, she had refused point-blank.

And honestly? Nick had been relieved. It meant he and Sally could keep Theo to themselves. For a little while it had been a haven. Until it became his own personal, solitary hell.

Now, having laid eyes on Alex, seeing the echoes of Theo in her face, in the blue of her eyes so like her brother's, a true de Wilde, all the heartbreaking similarities and the terrible differences, he knew that this was not going to be easy.

And that Wildewood Hall would never want to let her go.

CHAPTER 4

ALEX

'I can't believe you've inherited, like, a *castle*, Alex,' Arnold said, amazement in his voice, made even stronger by his Californian Valley twang. 'Like... like *Downton Abbey*!'

Alex glared at the little squares on the phone screen, each of her friends perfectly framed there with their stream-ready setup, and her own square showing the drawing room, the camera thankfully reversed so they didn't see that the joke struck home and not in a good way.

'It's nothing like that,' she muttered. 'It's...' How did she begin to describe Wildewood Hall to anyone? Part Manderley, part Thornfield Hall, part Hill House. None of that would help. And technically it *was* a castle. Or had been once upon a time. Before her family had spent generations adding bits on and rebuilding and designing a great house in the middle of nowhere. Disguising what it once was as if that was an embarrassment. And when you were little better than robber barons to begin with, maybe it was. 'You wanted to see it.' She composed her features and flicked the camera setting around again, back to face her. 'There, you've seen.'

'Yeah, but we want to see *more*,' Daphne crooned. 'It's so

atmospheric. You can feel the weight of history there. How many spirits do you think—'

'*None*,' Alex replied, with all the firmness she could muster. 'Absolutely *none*, Daph.'

'Statistically, the chances of that—' said Eduardo.

'None. And don't quote statistics at me about things that aren't real.'

There were stories though. Any number of stories. She and Theo had delighted in them as kids and Gran was always more than happy to share them. Alex wasn't going to tell them that.

She dropped back into the armchair facing the fire. At least she was warming up at last. She had promised to contact Gabe the moment she arrived, and once she had sorted out her data, she'd video-called him because getting Gabe to just talk on a phone was an impossibility. He'd linked the others in before she knew what was happening. She sensed a conspiracy.

'It's beautiful,' Gabe said, his voice a soft purr, and she could already see the wheels turning in his mind. He was always looking for an angle. Of course he was. 'We really *should* think about investigating—'

'*No, Gabe*,' she said again, with even more force. But he wasn't listening. When was he ever listening?

'Come on, an international show, a special. They'd lap it up. I can get the network on board like that with you already over there. And it's not like we'd have to get anyone else's permission.'

'You'd need *mine*. I'm not on the show anymore.'

'Yeah but... No one's happy about that. The fans would go ballistic, Alex. Think about it. A grand comeback. And even the title... *Lady de Wilde*...'

She needed to shut this down fast. 'I'm *not* a de Wilde. And there is no title. I told you. It's extinct.'

He waved a dismissive hand. 'No one actually cares about

that, *Alexandra*. Our very own sceptic inherits a haunted house in Ireland. Think of the promo. It's too good, babe.'

Ugh, even the way he said it: *Eye-are-laaand*. She wanted to slap him. He knew she hated that. She'd told him often enough so he had to be doing it on purpose. To wind her up. Like the way he used her full name. Because she hated that as well.

Well two could play at that game.

'Oh yeah, *Gabriel*, the same fans who sent me the death threats? Those nutjobs? Should I send them change of address cards, do you think, or just mass invite them over to the *isolated* house in the middle of *nowhere*? How many bloody dahlias do you think they can get shipped here? Why not roll up with good ol' Ted as well? I'm sure they'd happily break him out of jail, don't you think? *No thank you.*'

That sobered them all again. It was the primary reason she had left. Ted Sanderson and his acolytes, whose intimidation had been even closer to home and not just online but in her face. They had sent her flowers – black dahlias, of course, his favourite – with little notecards, all completely innocuous unless you knew the hidden meanings. It had been relentless. She'd been so scared she stopped sleeping and she knew she would have had a breakdown if it hadn't been for the others. Gabe had insisted the cops were called, Daphne had stayed with her, Arnold and Eduardo had tracked several of them down. She would always owe them for that.

'Yeah, well,' Gabe said, chastened. 'Not them, I guess.'

There was a long and awkward silence which, of course, she felt she had to be the one to break. As always.

'Look, I'm sorry, I'm just tired. But I really need a vacation from it all. You know that. Until they forget about me. You're already filming the next season, aren't you? You all have commitments over there. And you have Bob McGarry now to do what I did. He'll be great.'

Bob who was not on this call. Who they had deliberately

left out. She tried to ignore how ominous that felt. But Bob was just a colleague and she was a friend. That was a difference. They had been through a lot together, the five of them.

'*Bob*,' Daphne growled, and the tone was all the indication Alex needed of what she thought of their new parapsychologist. He had rubbed her up the wrong way right from the beginning and Daphne was determined that Alex would come back. She had *seen* it, apparently. The spirits had *spoken*. Alex herself had no say in that. It was notable that the spirits often declared that things would happen which matched up exactly with whatever Daphne wanted to happen. Or something that might make spectacular television and generate a host of clickbait headlines.

This was getting her nowhere. Alex shifted around in the chair to get more of the heat of the fire.

'Look, I need to get myself sorted here. I'm going to work on the book, which is all part of the brand, isn't it? And I'll run everything by you, I promise. It'll be a whole new publicity stream. Then we'll see. I'll be in touch and I'm always on the end of the phone if you need me. Or an email. You know that, right?'

Her little posse of ghost hunters didn't exactly look placated. As Alex tried to think of something else to say to them to put them at ease, or at least put them off, Daphne's eyes widened. It was almost comical.

'*Alexandra* darling?' she asked in her most teasing tone. It was never a good sign when Daphne got in on that act. 'Tell me, does your little corner of the Emerald Isle have a history of Sasquatch sightings?'

Sasquatch? As in Bigfoot? Alex was well aware that Daphne was a loveable loon but really? What on earth was she on about?

'No, why?'

Gabe roared out a laugh and the others followed suit. Alex stared at them, bewildered, and then she caught movement in the screen, in the right-hand corner, that window which showed her and the room in which she sat. Someone stood behind her, in the doorway to the hall outside the drawing room, someone impossibly tall, long-haired, bearded…

The bastards!

She killed the call right away and turned around to face Nick, standing there with a tea tray, frowning at her.

'I'm sorry,' he said without sounding anything like it. 'I didn't mean to interrupt your conversation.'

'You didn't. Don't worry. I was just—' There was no way he couldn't have heard that. Oh, damn it all. He had obviously heard Daphne, and the laughter. 'I'm sorry. That was so rude of them.'

He set the tray down without acknowledging her apology. China clinked as he did, that expensive, delicate, fragile sound, and he straightened, handing her the thick fluffy towel he had draped over one arm. 'I'm not exactly looking my best, I admit.'

Neither was she with her wet hair starting to frizz.

'They probably thought I had headphones in. They were worried about me getting here, about me moving so far away. They're my friends. And colleagues. I mean, they were my colleagues. Former colleagues.'

He nodded as if she had just explained everything rather than blurted out word salad, and took the knitted tea-cosy off the teapot, pouring the dark amber liquid into a cup for her. Only one cup, she noticed.

'You're not having any?' she asked.

He shook his head a little too firmly. Well, why would he want to hang around after that? 'I'll take your bags upstairs for you.'

'Oh, I can do that if you just show me where to go.'

'It's no trouble, Dr O'Neill,' he rumbled, the tone saying different, and turned away. And what could she say to that because she had no idea where her room was. She was entirely relying on him to show her around the place. As children Alex and Theo had been banished to the old nursery. She sincerely hoped he wasn't planning to put her up there.

Alex turned her attention to the tray. There were biscuits as well, home-made from the look of them, sitting on a small plate beside a bowl of sugar cubes, silver tongs, and the matching milk jug. Her stomach gave a far too loud rumble. When had she last eaten? She had stopped somewhere on the way, just off the motorway, and that had been a bland sandwich from a chain which she suspected had as much nutrition as the cardboard it had come in.

The biscuit was sweet and buttery, just the right level of crumb, and she had never tasted anything quite so perfect in her life. Her hand was already reaching for another before she thought about it. That didn't stop her.

'Where did you get these?' she asked but he'd already gone. Damn, he moved quietly for a big guy. More used to Gabe, who could make noise while sitting absolutely still, and the rest of them who were impossible to keep quiet even on an investigation, perhaps *especially* on an investigation. She was surprised how unsettling she found it.

She towel-dried the excess water from her hair and checked the phone again as she drank her tea and finished the rest of the biscuits.

We're here if you need us, Gabe's message said. *Even if it's to ward off a Sasquatch. Hope he's not too pissed with us. Sorry!*

Alex shook her head. At least she had that support. Even if it was half the world away. And prone to insulting everyone around her, especially the one person she couldn't afford to piss off right now.

Her gaze travelled around the room. It was a strange mixture of things, its grand fireplace dominating it, the oval mirror hanging above it, the tall windows almost lost in shadows at either end, draped in heavy brocade curtains of blue and gold. There were ornaments set in an array on a console table, and scattered across the mantelpiece.

The fire was merry and warm and she suddenly felt like she could almost nod off sitting here, as if she was a child again listening to Gran spinning her stories about the forest, and the good folk, and changelings and the walker in the woods, hunter and guardian. The firelight played on the stone surrounding it, that heavy grey stone with flickering bits of mica, seemed to hold shapes and patterns which couldn't be there. Old impressions of spirals and diamonds, faces made from the way light and shadow moved, eyes watching her...

From behind her, in the depths of the house, she thought she heard laughter, a high and girlish giggle. Overhead something creaked, floorboards maybe, under a heavy tread. And then something else, something far closer. So close it might have been in the room with her.

A whisper.

Her name.

Alex shot up to her feet and the cup flew out of her hands, smashing as it hit the edge of the fireplace.

The house was horribly quiet in the aftermath.

'Shit!'

She dropped to her knees, pulling the towel off her head to mop up the tea before it got to the rug. The china was in pieces, and as she tried to gather it up, a sharp edge dug into her palm. She cursed again and threw the fragments onto the tray in frustration. No blood. At least there was that.

'Are you all right?'

Nick was back in the doorway, frowning down at her in bemusement.

'Yes, I'm sorry. I just... I dropped the cup and...'

Slowly, she stood up, feeling her face heating up. Tears stung her eyes. She was making a fool of herself and she hated that.

Nick looked at her, his gaze steady, his eyes almost unbearably severe. Judging her, like her grandfather used to.

'You've had a long day,' he said at length, as if talking to an overtired child. 'I'll show you your room. Get a good night's sleep and tomorrow will be better. I'll clean that up.'

'Yeah,' she sighed, defeated. Maybe she should just let him clean it up, and try again tomorrow. He was *definitely* judging her anyway, and when he found out why she was here, if he didn't already know... well... 'Bed would be good. Take me to bed.'

The words were out before she could stop them. They both stood there, staring at each other in abject horror, and Alex wished the floor would open up and swallow her whole. To get it over with quickly for once.

Nick cleared his throat painfully and then stepped back, averting his gaze. 'This way,' he said, his voice a little too tight.

Oh God, Alex thought, face burning, barely here half an hour and already sexually harassing the staff. *Generations of de Wildes would be so proud of me.*

CHAPTER 5

NICK

Sasquatch, her friends had called him. It surprised him that he worried whether Alex agreed.

Nick hadn't really thought about his appearance in months. No one had cared. They'd left him to his grief, letting him work through his loss. He had never been what you might call the life and soul of the party to begin with anyway.

Unsure how to deal with the comment without making things worse, he'd left her to her tea and taken her bags upstairs. He clearly had not been meant to overhear it anyway. He'd just walked in at the wrong moment. Still, he was surprised at how it stung. It shouldn't. What did he care what a load of Yanks thought of him anyway?

But he didn't want to leave her completely to her own devices. Not after hearing her friends talk about investigating the house. The sooner he could persuade her to just leave things as they were and go away the better. But he was reluctant to go back into the drawing room and talk.

So he stood on the stairs, listening to the house respond to her return. Expecting the worst. Any second.

The sound of china shattering was like a jolt of electricity.

He swallowed hard and cursed to himself before hurrying to the drawing room door once more.

Alex was on her knees, trying to gather up the shards in the tray. He asked if she was all right and she'd looked like she was about to burst into tears. And no wonder, really, he realised. She was exhausted and stressed. She'd lost the last member of her family. It had been a difficult time for her and she had then travelled halfway around the world to the last place she wanted to be. A thousand excuses. All valid.

But he knew the real reason was the Hall.

Wildewood Hall.

It sent a wave of sympathy through him. Something he had no right to feel and she had no right to expect. Not that she appeared to expect it. So he tried to be kind. He tried to be patient. And he was apparently very rusty at that because the woman did not look in any way convinced.

'You've had a long day.' He knew that. She'd driven through the worst weather the county had to offer, in the dark. And he'd hardly been welcoming, had he? He could tell himself that he didn't have to be, that she was here to ruin everything and, worse, she was putting herself unknowingly in danger, and that there was no way he could warn her. Not in any way she would believe. 'I'll show you your room. Get a good night's sleep and tomorrow will be better. I'll clean that up.'

He watched those blue eyes glittering with unshed tears, the exhaustion straining her beautiful features.

A shiver ran down his spine, like cold fingertips tracing the line of vertebrae beneath his skin. There was something like a laugh beside his ear, a rush of icy breath.

Then she said those words.

Take me to bed.

Nick froze. He couldn't help himself.

Oh he knew what she meant. It was not an invitation or

anything like that. She was so tired she'd fall asleep there in the chair if he let her.

But the words were out and they sent a pang of something else through him. Impossible, and so stupid. He could only stare at her, at the dawning look of horror and embarrassment as she realised what she'd said. A thousand emotions crammed their way up through him, his body and mind responding. His very soul...

It was the house, he told himself, pushing it all back down ruthlessly. Because he had to. It was just him being alone in the house for far too long. It was his grief at losing Theo, and the strange familiarity that ghosted around Alex, Theo's twin.

And this place. This benighted place.

He cleared his throat, and tried to unfurl the fists into which his hands had clenched, letting go of the need, the desire, the burning thoughts of taking her to bed.

This isn't appropriate, he told himself. This isn't real. You don't even know her.

And a thousand other things that even though they were true, somehow felt like lies.

He needed to get her to her room, let her unpack and rest, and make himself as scarce as possible. The woods would help. Being out there always did. He needed the feel of the wild around him, grounding him in the earth of this place, reminding him who and what he was. Never mind the weather.

Nick took a cautious breath and let it out again, slowly, pushing away all those thoughts of her in bed, centring himself again. He couldn't make himself look at her though. He couldn't let her see the reaction he had to those simple words. Or his desperate need to get away from her right now.

'This way,' he said. Best to get this over with as fast as possible. Take her through the house – the parts of it that were safe – get her settled in the nicest room, and then tomorrow, when she was feeling more pampered and maybe had a better outlook on the place, he could talk to her about its future.

Because she was the only hope he had now.

And he could not afford to mess this up. Or to be distracted by a pretty face. Not just pretty, he thought glumly. Beautiful.

He needed her to leave. He didn't want to get himself entangled with anyone. Especially not her.

No matter what his treacherous body might try to tell him.

CHAPTER 6

ALEX

The laugh she had heard ripple through the house couldn't have been Nick. It had been light, girlish.

It stirred a memory, of playing here with Theo when they were kids, of running through these corridors, and up and down the stairs, chasing... not each other. They were chasing someone else. Other kids. She could almost see them. Hear them... *Lexi, this way. Come on, Lexi!*

And the laughter, those bright giggles.

And as for the whisper... that wasn't Nick either. The voice was sultry and knowing, dangerous. And she remembered it as well. It haunted her nightmares.

Alex knew she was exhausted. Maybe she had just nodded off for a moment, and then started awake, dropping the cup. That made a lot more sense.

Alex steeled herself and followed Nick.

Nick seemed to fall back on formality once they left the drawing room.

He pointed out the dining room, dominated by a huge mahogany table, laid out as if for a banquet, all gleaming silver, white crockery and crystal. In contrast the morning room was mostly covered in dustsheets like a museum of Hallowe'en ghosts. As they reached the staircase he ignored the narrow hallway leading to the kitchen. He clearly didn't expect her to go down there.

'Is there anyone else here?' she asked in what she hoped was a casual manner. Maybe there was a cook who didn't want them in the kitchen.

Nick eyed her strangely, staring for a moment too long. 'No. Not at the moment. A lot of the house isn't in use. You'll see a lot of dustcovers around here. Oh, and parts of it are unsafe so the doors there are locked. The cellar too.' He hesitated, as if he was reluctant to say more about the cellar but felt he ought to. 'Yeah, it's... It's not safe either. Best stay out of it.'

Well, that was ominous. She hadn't thought about the place being unstable. Not until now. In her mind Wildewood Hall was eternal.

'How likely is this place to fall down on us, Nick?'

He cast another look over his shoulder as he moved off again and then gave a brief snort of laughter. 'Wildewood Hall? The chance would be a fine thing. I don't think this house will ever fall down, but *you* might. Weak floorboards, some rot in places, damage over the years, that kind of thing. The ground floor's fine, and the main bedrooms up here. I've done what I can to secure the rest but it would take a fortune to do the whole place up properly. I don't suppose you have one of those.'

'Not in the slightest,' she replied lightly. This seemed like safer ground. 'If only.'

'Ah well then.' There was gentle amusement in his voice. It was strangely comforting. Better than the animosity she'd been reading in him so far. 'Worth checking.'

They reached the first floor and he led her along the landing to a grand corridor lined with even more portraits facing four doors well spread out. He opened the first one on the right. It was above the drawing room. Alex hesitated. She had to take a deep breath before entering.

It truly was a master suite. That was what he had promised her in his message after all. A four-poster bed dominated it, dark brown wood, carved with ornate leaves, berries and, when she peered closer, the occasional animal peeking out. Very like the grand staircase. It was hung with dark green drapery, and made up with about half a dozen pillows and matching bedclothes. Three grand sash windows looked out over the driveway, although all she could see right now was the lashing rain. As she stood there, staring, open-mouthed, Nick went over to close the curtains. They matched the bed as well, she thought absently. Whoever had decorated the room had excellent taste.

It looked like something out of a period drama. Just as well she hadn't shown Daphne this. It would be white ladies, doomed lovers and phantom nuns all over the place.

'Ensuite's in there,' he said with a nod to the left. 'It was an old servants' room. Theo had it done last year so there's a state-of-the-art shower and plenty of hot water.'

'Theo took this room?' A lump formed in her throat. He wouldn't have, would he?

'No. He had this done as a guest room. That's why it's so—' He waved a hand at the curtains and the beautifully restored antique furniture. 'He thought he'd put it up online, for rentals. He didn't want it for himself.'

No. No wonder.

'It was our grandfather's room,' she whispered, the words little more than breath.

'Oh.' Nick frowned, chewing on his lower lip. He froze like that for a moment. Clearly, he knew some family history then. Theo had probably filled him in at the same time as he'd reversed his way rapidly out of this room and decided to charge total strangers a fortune for the privilege of setting foot in it. 'I didn't think. I'm sorry. Do you...' He glanced to the door, no doubt wondering how quickly he could make his escape. He rubbed one of his big hands against the beard. It made a rough scratchy noise. 'I can try to make up Theo's room for you, but it's—'

It was late. And she was being stupid. And he was talking about her dead twin's bedroom. He didn't need to say it out loud.

'No, it'll be fine.' She tried to force a smile onto her face. 'I'm not exactly roughing it here, am I? And you'll want to get to bed too. I'm sorry. Don't mind me.'

He nodded and finished fussing with the curtains, making sure they were closed. It was almost as if he wanted to say something else but didn't know what that might be. Or how to say it, whatever it was.

'Goodnight then,' he said at last and then he was gone. Leaving her standing in the lap of luxury and feeling like more of a fraud than any of those she had exposed on television over the years.

Jesus Christ, what was she doing here?

Her grandfather, Professor Nathaniel de Wilde, had been a grim shadow across her whole childhood. From the first summer they had come here he had doted on Theo and more or less ignored Alex completely. Which had been fine with her because she had spent all her time with Gran, or playing her imaginary games. Theo was the heir to the family name, the boy, but she wasn't even the spare. Just a girl. What use was she to the professor?

Even when Dad died, her grandfather hadn't had a single kind word for her. Not one. He had taken Theo aside, talked to him about duty and heritage and, afterwards, her brother had returned to her, white-faced and shaking. So that hadn't exactly been a dream come true either.

'What did he say?' she'd asked.

For a moment Theo didn't reply. His hands were balled into fists at his sides, nails digging into his palms. 'Doesn't matter.'

She'd put her arms around him and held him close, her twin, the other half of her. 'If you're this upset, of course it matters.'

Slowly Theo had buried his face in her shoulder. 'He said Dad was weak and I had to be strong. And that you shouldn't be here at all.'

They had only been sixteen years old.

And God help her, Alex had hated the old man. She still did. When she'd heard he was dead she'd been relieved. Until Theo had been named as his heir and announced he was coming back here anyway. That it was his duty.

Because the old bastard had planted that guilt so deep even Alex couldn't convince him otherwise.

Alex forced herself to stop thinking about her grandfather, grabbing one of her suitcases and opening it on the bed. She unpacked automatically, with purpose and almost as if she did so in defiance of her memories. She opened the heavy doors of the wardrobe in the corner, to find an orange studded with cloves, encircled with a scarlet ribbon hanging from the rail. The smell swept over her, reminding her of making them with her gran. A pomander, her gran used to call this. Supposed to protect clothing against moths. And other things. She reached out to touch the surface, her fingertips brushing against the little bumps.

That lump was back in her throat. She swallowed it down. Gran was always showing her how to make things from everyday objects, or stuff they gathered together in the woods. Sometimes they made crowns and wore them all day long. Sometimes Gran brought in honey from her hives. Or Alex had helped her collect eggs from the chicken coops.

Were there still hives here? Or chickens?

She hung up her clothes, and then turned to the chest of drawers, where she found sachets of dried lavender tucked in under the paper liners. All very traditional and simple ways of keeping things fresh and sweet-smelling.

In spite of everything, Gran had tucked herself in everywhere. All over this house.

But all of this was too recent. It couldn't have been Gran, could it? She was at least twenty years in the grave. Like Dad.

All these little reminders. This was not going to be easy. Had Theo felt like this too? Had he been more prepared for it?

He'd made peace with the professor after all, when the old man had been admitted to the nursing home and they'd needed a next of kin. Theo was the only person he would listen to anyway. Not Alex.

'He's worried about the house,' Theo had said to her once when the subject came up. 'About what'll happen after he dies. De Wildes make plans in generations, you know? That's what he said. He wants us to have it.'

Theo hadn't actually got that right. He'd wanted *Theo* to have it. Granddaughters were no use to him. He probably wasn't even aware that women could inherit things in their own right, or have a bank account, or vote. He had never once asked to see Alex. Not that she would have come if he had called. If anything, she had the impression he'd rather she had never been born.

Besides, she was in the US by then and had no plans at all to return here, ever.

Funny how plans changed.

Alex went to close the bedroom door and found herself looking at the portrait on the wall opposite, a handsome man with the darkest eyes she had ever seen. She didn't recognise this one. His smile was a twist of his sensuous lips, and for a moment she was sure he was watching her.

A trick of the light, she told herself and closed the door firmly.

There was a key in the lock, heavy and old. So she turned it, just in case.

CHAPTER 7

ALEX

Alex wandered through corridor after corridor of Wildewood Hall. Just as she had in her dreams all her life.

She could hear laughter, the sound of music and chatter, of glasses raised in toasts. When she was little, that was all she'd heard, a party that never ended, and that she could never find. Children called out to her, to come and play, to hurry up.

She threw open door after door but it felt like they were always in the next room along.

Like they were hiding from her.

As she got older the nightmare changed. As she crept down the stairs, those sounds turned to gasps and moans, the unmistakable sound of people having sex. Laughter rang out around her, laughter she remembered all too well. And she wasn't hearing the voices of children anymore. They were laughing at her, mocking her.

A voice murmured her name, *his* voice, inviting her to join them, knowing all the time that she wouldn't. She knew that voice. Knew it far too well. She had been sixteen when she had first heard it clearly, the last time they came here, when Dad died. It had haunted her ever since. But she didn't have a name to go with it.

Alexandra, my beloved...

Her body ached for that darkly beautiful voice, to give in to it, to do whatever it asked. It knew things she did not, and promised her every secret thing she had ever desired.

She couldn't help but follow it in all her nightmares ever since, down into the shadows, further and further beneath the house, deep underground. The earth pressed in around her. The stone walls and ceiling closed in around her like a tomb.

The air wrapped clammy hands around her, pulling her onwards.

Come on, Lexi. It's not far. Go on, I dare you.

Was that Theo? It was the kind of thing he would have said. But it didn't sound like him. And he never called her Lexi. She had been Lex to him. So much so that she had never let anyone else use the nickname. Ever. The voice was girlish, an echo of the past, almost like her own voice but not quite. More than one voice. Sometimes a chorus, taunting her, goading her on.

You're not afraid, are you? Don't be a baby! You're a grown-up now. You can do this.

'Run, Alex!' Dad's voice, desperate and terrified, strangled with shadows. And he was dying. She knew that. He was struggling and he was dying.

Dad's hands fell still, limp on the rich and hungry earth.

The ground was cold and hard when he hit it, the thud he made dull and echoing. The trees crowded close around her and there was something moving among them, watching her, circling her as if she was prey.

And Dad was dead. He was lying on the forest floor, smothered in leaves and undergrowth, his body cold and unmoving. That was how she had found him. That was how...

The cold arched roof of stones closing over her and the stench of mulch. The darkness pressing in on her, suffocating her...

She caught sight of a gleam of gold beneath rotting foliage, a mouth hanging open, hungry and waiting, and the taste of blood and decay filled her mouth and throat.

Alex woke up with tears all over her face. Sunlight streamed through the gap in the curtains, poking a bright finger through the room and illuminating it in gold. It was a blessed relief after the dark corners of the dream.

Taking a long shower helped a bit and by the time she had dragged on her clothes, she was starting to feel almost human again.

Used to the noise of traffic and neighbours, Alex tried to ignore the quiet of the house, pretending that it didn't bother her at all.

The portrait on the wall outside her room was still there, of course. She didn't know why she thought it might not be. Perhaps she had just hoped it would vanish overnight.

The man in the picture was dressed in some kind of Regency garb and wouldn't have looked out of place in a period drama. He'd probably have all the fans swooning over his looks. A classic rake, she decided. Perhaps the hero, perhaps the villain. Perhaps a bit of both.

He was... familiar. She couldn't say why. She was sure it hadn't been here before. But she knew him somehow. Not as a painting but as a... as a person, and that unsettled her. Everything unsettled her about Wildewood Hall.

Alex frowned back at the portrait. She couldn't decide if his mouth was cruel or amused. Maybe both. It added to the feeling she had looking at him.

Set into the bottom of the frame was a small oval plaque with the name Blaise Chambers, and the dates 1784–1826.

Words ran along the bottom of the picture, painted in the shadows, just above the frame, in black against the already dark colours so you could only see them when the light hit it in a certain way. The script was small and difficult to read. She put the torch on her phone to illuminate it but that didn't really help.

Instead, she took a photo, brought up the image and zoomed in – an old trick of Eduardo's.

Omnes contra omnes, quos amabant, convertam, et meam, corpus et animam, faciam.

Latin. Of course it was Latin. It only took a moment for the phone to translate it though.

I will set all of them against all of those they have loved, and I will make them mine, body and soul.

Alex scrunched up her face, as if she'd just tasted something acidic and foul. Charming.

She'd ask Nick and see if he knew who this was. And get him to switch the painting maybe. Something pretty and calming. Anything to get rid of Lord Let-Me-Ravish-You, with his creepy message and watching eyes.

There had to be a perfectly innocuous painting around here somewhere.

She made her way right down to the kitchen. The house echoed around her and noise travelled strangely. She had the impression of people just having left the stairs or the hall ahead of her, or of eyes high overhead on the upper floor, watching her go down.

Humming reached her ears as she approached the kitchen, a deep, soft voice, unexpectedly melodic, which put all thoughts of paintings out of her mind. It sent an unanticipated shiver down her spine and she froze, hand on the doorframe. Nick was taking something out of the oven. Freshly baked bread. The aroma wrapped itself around her, drawing her into the room. There was coffee on the stove too. It smelled divine.

Nick moved through the kitchen effortlessly, still humming to himself, unaware of his audience.

Alex just stared. She couldn't help herself. She had never seen anyone so perfectly at ease with himself, with what he was doing. Last night he'd been grumpy and distant. This was like an entirely different man.

Then he turned around to put the bread on the cooling rack on the table and saw her. And frowned.

She took a step back from the hostility in that expression.

'I have the dining room all set up for you for breakfast,' he told her in a curt tone.

'The what?' she managed.

'The dining room. For breakfast. I thought—'

Oh no, he was not banishing her from the kitchen and dictating where she went in her own house.

'Why would I eat on my own in a dining room like that? Did Theo eat up there?'

Nick's face flushed, what she could see of it beneath the beard anyway. 'Well, no but Theo was—'

Alex pointedly grabbed one of the sturdy wooden chairs at the large kitchen table and pulled it out. She sat herself down and glared back at him.

'Theo was what?'

'Family,' he murmured awkwardly and turned away.

Family. He didn't mean a de Wilde. Not this time. Theo was Nick's family, that was clearly how he thought of her brother. She suddenly felt very alone. Like Theo hadn't been hers at all, not anymore.

Before her brother had died, she'd barely been back to Ireland in ten years. Alex had thrown herself into her studies. Undergraduate, Master's, PhD in quick succession, living in halls and focused only on that. The moment things had taken off in the US she hadn't visited once. Too busy with her stellar career, her celebrity status. Her brother had teased her about it relentlessly. And she'd called him a tree-hugging hippie.

God, she missed him, like part of her had been ripped away.

And she had abandoned Theo here. She had refused to come back and help him. And now he was dead. The report had never made sense. He was young and fit. He shouldn't have died, not here, not in the woods. She needed to find out what had happened, now she was here. She owed him that much.

Nick just looked perplexed. Perhaps the pain of it showed on her face. She hastily looked away again and folded her arms in front of her. How on earth was she meant to ask him about Theo just out of the blue? *What happened to my brother? Did you find him? How did he die? What kind of accident was it?*

'Sorry, I thought...' Nick's voice trailed off. 'It was what we had planned for guests staying in the house. Theo's plan for it, I mean. To let out rooms, bed and breakfast in the big house, that kind of thing. I shouldn't have presumed.' He plucked a mug down from where they hung in a neat row on the dresser. 'Coffee? Or can I make you tea?'

'You don't need to wait on me, Nick. That's not your job. And I'm not a guest.' But she was already sitting down. And she had no idea where anything was. He was standing there with a mug, waiting. 'All right, fine. Coffee please. But then can we just start again? I'm not lady of the manor or a paying guest. I'm not here to lord it over anyone. As soon as I can get the legal situation sorted out, I'm gone.'

His back was turned to her as he poured the coffee, but she clearly saw his shoulders flinch beneath the material of his black t-shirt.

Oh, he knew. He knew what she had planned and when it went through he wouldn't have a job or a place to live anymore. Had he been trying to butter her up? Was that what this was all about? A little less of the grumpiness would help with that then. Or was he just hoping she'd give up and go away? If so, he really didn't know her.

Well, of course he didn't. They had only just met.

His silence bored into her, making her talk. The man could work for the FBI.

'You asked if I had a fortune,' she said, more gently this time. This had to be hard for him too. Theo had tried to make sure it was secure for him and he must have relied on that. Here she was, undoing all of it. 'I don't. I have enough to live on, and an income from... my work, sure, but no real capital. All I have is this house. And I don't want it. There's a hotel chain interested already. They want to renovate the whole house and landscape the grounds. The plans are amazing, a total transformation, golf course, spa, the works. It would be a huge boon for the community too.'

The kitchen was a big room but it suddenly felt small, as if the walls had closed in around her. Nick had turned around again and was staring at her like she was promising to murder kittens or something.

A chill snaked down her back and she was suddenly sure something else was watching her too, something that made her skin crawl. She twisted around, examining the kitchen again. In the corner a strange little door caught her attention. It was firmly closed, a huge black key jutting out of the ornate keyhole and bolts at the top and bottom. The way to the cellar. She'd never been allowed in there. It was where her grandfather had kept his wine. Above the stone doorframe, which looked to be part of the original building, there was a wreath of dried straw and flowers, old and faded, covered in dust. Long forgotten. Still, it caught her attention.

'*For protection*,' Gran had said. Like Brigid's crosses and corn dollies, something so old the purpose didn't make sense anymore. How long had that one been there? she wondered. It looked ancient.

Nick still said nothing about her plans, just set the perfect coffee down in front of her and carried on getting milk, butter and what looked like home-made jam for her. A plate of fresh scones came next.

'Would you prefer a fry-up?' he asked, as if he hadn't

already produced an entire breakfast for her far superior to what she'd normally eat.

'This isn't your j—'

His voice was unexpectedly sharp. 'It *is* my job, Dr O'Neill. I manage the house and the estate. Mostly it's the estate, obviously, but this is part of it. We have cleaners come in, but there isn't anyone else. And this house needs someone to look after it. Not to scrape out the insides and make it into some soulless hotel like any other. And as for the grounds—' His tone rose in anger for a moment before he caught himself. He glared at the table, took in a deep breath, and then looked up again, his temper – because that *was* his temper she'd seen – a little more under control again. 'It doesn't need landscaping. It *is* a landscape. A beautiful one. Now if you'll excuse me, I do have other things to attend to this morning.'

'I can't pay you,' she blurted out, and wished she hadn't.

His face went white and his eyes burned. For a moment he didn't say anything and she thought she had mortally offended him.

He drew in another steadying breath. 'That's already taken care of. I'm paid from the estate. Theo arranged it. The income is more than you'd think. I can show you the books when you're ready or you can sit down with the accountants. Farmland's rented out and gives a good return. We even have bees and sell their honey. There are grants for the rewilding. It's all a going concern, a living place, a rich ecosystem. No hotel chain is going to do right by it. Now, if you'll excuse me, I have work to do.'

He grabbed a jacket hanging by the back door and left as fast as he could, slamming it behind him.

CHAPTER 8

NICK

His pulse was racing. It must be adrenaline. That last interaction had totally got his back up. She was just so... *infuriating*. This was not going as he had planned. *Nothing* was going as he had planned, or as Theo had planned, or as it had been meant to go. It was a disaster.

But when had anything in his life gone to plan?

Nick stalked along the perimeter fence of the estate, ostensibly checking for any damage but in reality... just walking, furious, marking the boundary as best he could. It was an old tradition, one which drew the lines, strengthened the edge so that nothing could slip through that shouldn't, as well as simply checking for damage and the like. It was part of his job.

Theo had given him purpose. Theo had been here for him when his world fell apart and helped him piece some semblance of it back together. Even if part of that loss, a very large part of it, was Theo's fault. But Theo had never meant harm and Nick didn't think Alex did either.

Perhaps she just reminded him too much of Theo. The man who had helped and comforted him when he'd needed it most. When all that was meant to be his, all he had dreamed of, had somehow slipped through his fingers. The man whose secrets he had promised to keep.

Alex was... like nothing he had expected. She was beautiful, all that fire and intelligence, that fierce mind, those eyes...

What was he thinking?

It was supposed to be easy. He'd be here when she arrived, would show her around the estate, and wow her with the work he and Theo had put in. She would have to understand. She was a de Wilde, part of it all.

Tied here, Theo had said. Well, Nick knew all about being tied here too, didn't he?

The estate itself still made a fair income. Not a huge amount, possibly not as much as he had tried to make Alex believe and probably never quite enough overall, but still, it was something. It paid for him, for repairs, for the running of the place. It paid enough to keep the rewilding going. Theo had made him promise. And Sally had wanted it, so he didn't have a choice there, did he? Her legacy, her dream. Preserve the woods, keep them strong...

He was failing. Failing both of them. Which made him so angry with himself it just spilled out.

No, Nick decided. He had to keep things together. Keep himself together. He had offered to go over the books with Alex and he would. Tomorrow. He would lay out the financing and the business plans he had agonised over with her brother, which he had continued to work on in the meantime. He'd make their point. Hell, the *plan* would make the point for him.

And Wildewood could survive as it was, as it always had been.

He looked from the edge of the woodland, across the wild-flower meadow that had once been a lawn, back towards the house. It was beautiful here now. It needed to stay that way.

Not become some bland hotel and golf course or whatever else those lawyers who had latched themselves onto her wanted to make of it. He could sense a charlatan when he saw one and, if the various dealings he'd had with them so far was anything to go by, this was an entire rookery of cheats. He'd been sure once he explained things to her, she'd see it too. That the estate was worth so much more in the long term if it was kept intact and preserved. Not sold off to investors and vulture funds or whatever else they had in store for it.

They'd try to pull it apart, and that would only end in disaster for everyone and everything. Through ignorance and little else. No one ought to want that. His job, his *only* job, was to hold it all together, the estate, the house and the woods. He had promised them, Sally, and then Theo. Both of them. It was a sacred vow. It was his whole purpose.

Instead... well, Alex had made it clear she didn't want him here, didn't need his help or his labour. She couldn't wait to offload the estate, could she? It was just a means to an end. She clearly hated the place.

Frustrating, foolish, determined woman. She didn't know what it meant. She'd never come here since their father died so how could she? She'd only been a teenager then. All she wanted was the money it would bring her. She didn't care that it would be destroyed.

And why would she? It had taken her father from her. Theo had told him all about that. How they had visited and how one night, during a storm, their father had wandered out into the woods. Alex had found his body.

And now it had taken Theo too. From both of them.

He swallowed hard. He couldn't let her look too closely into what had happened to Theo. She would never understand. And he could already see that she had questions, bubbling under the surface. Sooner or later, she wouldn't be able to force them down anymore. She'd ask. And he'd have to lie.

Nick knew all about loss and the scars it could leave. He bore them himself, understood them intimately.

He made his way back into the kitchen but there was no sign of Alex. Nick sat down heavily on the wooden chair, and let his head drop into his hands.

'Damn it, Sal,' he murmured. 'I tried. I'm no good at this. I never was. Theo was the charmer, just like you always said. Not me. Why did you ever make me promise?'

But Sally didn't answer. He closed his eyes, and felt something touch his shoulders, his back, like a caress, like when she had rubbed away all the stress and frustration. A soft murmur of comfort echoed through the house and he shivered.

Sally was not going to come back. Dreaming and wishing about Sally always led down a dark and desolate path from which it was hard to claw his way back and he couldn't let that happen, not again. It was just that here in Wildewood Hall he still felt like she might just walk around a corner, like he could hear her humming to herself, or singing along with him, or follow the echo of her laughter drifting down the corridors, to find her.

God, how he wished he could find her again. Just for a moment.

This had been her place, long before it was his. Not the house, not really, but the woods. The wild wood. She'd been born in Kilfayne. She knew its ways better than anyone else. And when he'd promised himself to her, he'd promised himself to everything she loved as well.

The house had echoed with her laughter when they had both lived and worked here. The three of them – Nick, Sally and Theo. Now he only heard it in his imagination, in his memories. All he could recognise of it was the absence.

He sighed. 'I'll try, love. I promise I'll try.'

He checked the phone but there were no more messages. All quiet on that front then. One blessing.

He decided to go through his emails, getting out the laptop and booting it up right there on the kitchen table. He wasn't the kind of person to use an office anyway. Never had been. And the only office here was the study. He'd left that to Theo, and now to Alex. It was a de Wilde domain ever since the professor's time. Probably long before that as well.

He rubbed his hand over his beard as he waited. He hadn't meant to let it grow. But he'd had so much on lately, and no one to actually make himself presentable for. It scratched against his hand and he imagined the face Sally would have made. She hated beards.

Instead he looked like – what had Alex's friends said on the video call? He couldn't help but overhear.

Sasquatch.

Bigfoot.

Yes, well, he was definitely putting his giant feet in it ever since she had arrived here. And they weren't wrong about the hair either. No wonder he kept upsetting Alex.

He sighed, trying to focus on the glowing screen of the laptop.

It'll be okay, Nick. I promise.

That sounded like Theo, he thought, absently. He was always the optimist. And where had that landed him?

You promised, Nick.

Sally.

You promised me and you promised Theo. You said you'd look after the house and the woods. That was a solemn vow. We always knew the risks. You have to do it. You just have to. You have to protect it. And you have to protect her. It's your duty, mo stór.

There he was, imagining things again. Wishful thinking. Whatever you wanted to call it.

Tears burned in his eyes. He blinked them back furiously and tried to ignore the throb of a nascent headache. His breath misted in front of his eyes and he winced, rubbing his suddenly freezing hands together.

The battery light on the laptop began to blink. He thought he'd charged it. He sighed, digging the cable out of the bag and plugging it in. He needed to get it looked at. The thing was holding no charge at all these days. But he didn't have the time or the money for that either. It worked well enough most of the time. And then, bam, no battery.

He imagined Sally's touch on his back again, that single point of cold comfort. Whenever he was stressed or worried, she'd always be there for him. And vice versa of course. Until she wasn't.

Right on cue, the phone rang.

'Nick?' said his mother-in-law. 'Sorry to ring again, love. I know you're busy. Could you pop down for lunch?'

Nick winced, grateful that Patricia couldn't see him. He needed all the help he could get and didn't want to irritate the formidable woman. But he'd been so focused on Alex... 'Of course. It's no problem. How's she been?'

'Ah, you know. Fretful. She does so hate not being with you. Here, I'll put you on.'

CHAPTER 9

ALEX

That probably couldn't have gone much worse, Alex decided.

After she'd eaten a scone, slathered in rich creamy butter and the most delicious blackberry jam she had ever tasted, she poked half-heartedly around the pristine kitchen to learn where everything was. She wanted to rely on Nick Walker even less after that reaction. He'd just stormed off.

The door to the cellar was locked but, remembering the warning from last night, she left it alone. Unsafe, Nick had said. Right. Sooner or later she'd have to check that out. The company would want to get a surveyor in fairly soon. It hadn't been possible so far. Nick's doing, she supposed. He hadn't exactly been cooperative. Well, that would have to change. Now she was here she would make arrangements as soon as possible.

There had been another room she wasn't allowed into when she was young, of course. Her grandfather's study.

In a fit of grumpy pique, she poured herself another coffee and headed off that way, half expecting it to be locked. She was going to have to ask *Mister Estate Manager* for the master keys. She didn't like the idea of being locked out of half her own house. And it was *her* house, no matter what he thought. Even if she didn't want to be here, she could do with it what she wanted, including poking around, using whatever room she felt like, or selling it. He did not own the place, or have any right to it.

Except he kind of did. Because Theo had signed that agreement. And Theo dying didn't apparently get them out of it. Not easily anyway.

Nick clearly knew that if she succeeded, he was not only out of a job, but out of a home as well. No wonder he was unhappy to have her here.

And no, she didn't need the money. She just wanted rid of Wildewood Hall and everything to do with it, once and for all. Given everything that had happened to her family here, who wouldn't?

The door to the study, across from the hideous ancient mirror which made her look like she was standing in a fun house, was open. So she wandered in, but immediately stopped in her tracks, staring.

An impressive bow window overlooked the driveway where her car was parked. That area was dominated by a huge Edwardian desk. But the rest of the room...

It wasn't just a study. It was a library. All polished hardwood, reading chairs, and row upon row of books. Leatherbound volumes with gilt lettering graced the shelves, some of them hundreds of years old. They lined the three remaining walls almost entirely, only the area on either side of the desk uncovered. It took her breath away. She approached the nearest shelf. Her fingertips brushed against the books' spines and she let out a little sigh of delight.

The History of the Line of de Wilde.

Legends and Folklore of Kilfayne.

The Master of the Revels.

The titles went on. Many of them were multi-volume

works. She imagined Arnold's face, the sheer delight he would wear if he caught a glimpse of this. His little research-obsessed heart would overflow. She really ought to tell him about it. Invite him over and...

No. Whatever there was to uncover before the sale, she was here on her own. She couldn't have them here. She knew that. This place... this place played with your imagination, toyed with you.

Here she was assigning purpose and intent to a house, a building. It might be old but it was not a sentient thing. As these books would illustrate, her ancestors on the de Wilde side had been selfish bastards through and through, greedy and exploitative. People had hated them, and rightly so in most cases. They got what they deserved. That was all.

Apart from Theo.

Still, if something of their evil had managed to permeate the stones here it was hardly a surprise. But there was nothing supernatural about it.

Alex fetched her laptop and set herself up, defiantly, in the study to work. The wi-fi details had been left on the desk – another touch of Nick's efficiency. He must have intended for her to work here then, which half made her want to find somewhere else. She had never liked being told what to do. But the light was perfect, the chair comfortable and the atmosphere ideal.

And it felt satisfying to give a two-fingered salute to the old man who had tried to make her life a misery.

There was no sign of Nick for the rest of the day. She made her own lunch, trying to ignore the feeling that she was scavenging in her own home. It didn't feel like a home anyway, especially when it was just her.

The house made strange noises around her, as old houses invariably did. Pipes murmured and floorboards creaked, sounds echoed strangely. In the end she just put on her headphones and listened to music as she tried to work, until the light started to fade outside.

She took a break as dusk fell, stretching her back and standing up, turning to look out of the tall windows and down the drive.

A battered-looking truck lurched off the main road and eventually came to a halt beside her own car. She watched in silence as Nick got out and fished his phone from his coat pocket, while heading for the house. The big front doors opened with a long creak. She heard him in the hall, his voice gentler than before, a voice tempered by affection.

'No, love. I'll be back down tomorrow. I promise.' He paused, listening, and Alex made her way to the study door, though whether to close it and shut him out or to let him know she was there, she wasn't sure. She didn't mean to eavesdrop. 'I know. I know, but it's not for long. Okay, *mo stórín*. Don't fret. Be—'

His eyes met Alex's as she appeared in the open doorway, and a look she could only describe as guilty spread over his face. Whatever he'd been about to say, he paused and his voice grew a little firmer.

'I promise. I'll see you tomorrow. It's Saturday so we'll have the whole day.'

He lowered the phone and gave Alex a nod of greeting. 'Sorry I'm late,' he said in gruff tones. 'I'll get dinner on.' That was all.

She wanted to say he didn't have to. That she'd sort herself out, but now she looked at him, she didn't have the heart.

'And I'm sorry about this morning,' he said before she could. 'I was out of order.'

'So was I,' she said, because it was the least she could do, to meet him halfway. 'And when you're free, I'd appreciate it if you went over the books with me. So I can understand what there is here.'

'All the better to sell it?' he asked, but there was no real malice in his voice this time. More like regret. He sounded defeated. She didn't like that but what could she do?

Alex shrugged. 'I can't stay here. Simple as that. After Theo, after our dad. You know about that, don't you? From what you've said, Theo must have told you.'

Something flashed in his eyes, grief perhaps. She wasn't sure. She didn't know him well enough to read him. But he nodded briefly and then headed for the kitchen. Alex retreated to the study and closed the door behind her. It was safer.

Nick laid out dinner in the kitchen. A thick and fragrant stew, served with the rest of that bread. She didn't normally eat a lot of bread. LA wasn't a place for carbs, after all. But this was delicious. It made her feel like she was on more of a holiday, rather than... well, reliving her past.

'I believe you were something on TV in the States,' he asked.

'Something,' Alex murmured. 'I'd rather forget it.'

'Ghost hunting?'

Oh good, she thought. He knew. He didn't sound impressed. Did Theo tell him that much? Did they have a good laugh about it?

'The sceptic.' She raised her eyebrows, challenging him. 'There are a lot of frauds out there. And a lot of gullible people. And a lot of perfectly normal explanations which get skipped over in the rush to assign the supernatural as a reason for anything.'

'But you must have seen things you can't explain.'

Alex shook her head. People always asked that but there was always an explanation. Not usually the one they wanted. 'Not really.'

He took a while to reply to that, as if psyching himself up for something.

'You know this house is haunted, right?'

'So I was told.' Too many times. Gran loved those stories. So did Dad. He must have got them from her. He certainly told enough to Alex and Theo. Her mum had constantly warned him to lay off before they had nightmares. Dad never listened. And the nightmares were not his fault.

'Theo believed that—'

She really didn't want to get into that. Not with Nick and not now.

'Theo believed a lot of things,' she cut in. If she sounded curt, so be it. 'Tell me about the forestry experiment instead. That was his real baby, wasn't it?'

'The rewilding?' And the suspicion drained away from his features. His voice grew rich with enthusiasm. 'It's more than an experiment. It's a vital transformation which could change the whole ecosystem of the island. We're restoring the estate as a thriving pocket of the Atlantic Rainforest in a way which...'

Alex laughed as he trailed off, realising that he was about to start evangelising probably. 'Theo got to you too then.'

Nick gave a brief smile, barely visible under the growth of his beard. 'Ours is just a small part of a much larger campaign. And he didn't get to me. If anything, it was the other way around. These woods are special. Old. He asked me to show him around the woods the moment he arrived and I was more than happy to tell him all about it. The woodland here is some of the oldest remnants of original forestry on the island. Really ancient. Most of Ireland's woodlands were destroyed from the sixteenth century on.'

'Perfidious Albion?' she asked, grinning. She had had this conversation with her brother more than once. A tale as old as time around here.

'English warships needed wood. And forests hid wolves, not

to mention rebels. Win–win.' He returned the smile and for a moment she felt something shift in the air between them, something calm and comfortable. It was almost like talking to Theo himself.

Except in all the ways it wasn't. His eyes captured her attention, brown but with glints of green and gold in their depths, the way his hair fell over his forehead and cast them into shadow. Alex licked her lower lip without thinking about it.

Until his gaze moved to watch her.

Her skin shivered, as if someone ran a fingertip down the side of her neck, the lightest touch. As if urging her to reach out and touch him. To kiss him.

A chill breeze blew through the kitchen. Alex started, looking at the door to the outside world, which was firmly closed. No draught there.

The spell broke and Nick cleared his throat. He stood up quickly, gathering their plates. Putting distance between the two of them.

'Let me wash up,' she said, trying not to babble and failing. 'Fair's fair. You did the cooking.'

'There's a dishwasher. All mod cons here. But sure, you can stack it if you want.'

'You don't have a special method for that?' Everyone she knew had a particular way to stack their dishwasher. Even Gabe had a system.

'I can always fix it later,' Nick said, almost as if he was teasing her again. Trying to recapture that moment which had passed between them. He was almost flirting. And God help her, so was she.

But she'd heard him on the phone, talking to someone he referred to as 'love' and '*mo stórín*', the Irish for 'my darling' or 'my treasure' or something like that, promising to spend tomorrow with them. She couldn't make assumptions. And she definitely couldn't afford any entanglements with him. The lawyers would have a fit. She was here to make sure that he was out of a job and out of his home. This could just be his new tactic. She had to remember that.

Yesterday he'd more or less made it clear he didn't want her here. And she'd barely known him for a day.

But as they packed away the dishes, she was aware of his presence, his gaze whenever it alighted on her, even his breath in the quietness of the kitchen. It was like she could sense him without looking at him, as if she knew his every movement around her. As if, should she want to try it, she could close her eyes and find him by touch alone. Her fingers itched at the thought. Reaching out. Touching him. Being touched...

Her breath hitched in her throat.

Oh God, she couldn't be thinking like that. She wasn't sure what had come over her since she set foot inside Wildewood Hall.

She was not desperate. She was quite content with being single. She didn't have time for any of this. And it was all going to be far too complicated. Just like it had been with Gabe. You didn't mix business and pleasure.

Just thinking the word 'pleasure' sent another shiver through her body and she had to let the air out of her lungs in a gasp. Nick glanced at her, his eyes darkening.

'I think I'll call it a night,' she said rapidly. 'Long day yesterday and all that. See you tomorrow. Or... is that your day off? You'll have things to do. So I guess I won't. Don't worry about it. I have work to do.'

'I... sure, I guess.' He looked so confused.

She just ploughed on, unable to stop herself now. 'You can always take whatever time you need off, you know. I'm fine here on my own. Anyway, I'll turn in. Goodnight.'

Her face had gone scarlet. She was so embarrassed and everything she said was making it worse. She was thinking things she shouldn't be thinking, about someone she shouldn't find attractive at all, and had no right to get involved with. Even if he wasn't already involved with someone else.

They were never going to be friends, let alone anything more. He was standing in her way when it came to Wildewood Hall. And she was here to upend his life.

Alex fled up the stairs to her bedroom, passing by that painting she'd completely forgotten to mention to him. The man in it stared at her as she approached, his gaze lingering on her body, his smile taunting her.

She was sure that laughter drifted after her, deep and knowing. Not Nick. It didn't sound anything like Nick. She wasn't sure who or what would laugh like that. She didn't want to know. She just wanted to hide.

Alexandra, a voice breathed, a sound of longing and desire, of raw need, of promise.

In a fit of anger, mostly at herself, she grabbed the painting, heaved it off the hook and shoved it face first against the wall so she didn't have to look at it anymore.

In the morning she'd find a bonfire to chuck it onto. She'd build one herself.

And heaven help Nick Walker if he tried to stop her.

CHAPTER 10

NICK

Nick must have dozed off after he finished tidying up the kitchen. He wasn't too surprised. He was bone tired from getting the house ready and the stress of everything just drained him. And pretending like none of it bothered him, especially when he went down to the village, to make sure those two parts of his life were kept firmly apart...

Or at least as firmly as he could. They had too many meeting points.

He hated the looks he got in Kilfayne, hated the whispers. Oh, he knew what they said about him. And the problem was, they weren't entirely wrong, were they?

One day, Alex would hear all the gossip and the rumours and everything else, all his secrets stripped bare, and then what kind of look would she give him? It wouldn't be the look of obvious desire that had woken its twin in him.

Until she remembered herself. And looked at him properly.

Sasquatch. It was almost funny, now that he thought about it. The wild creature in the woods. Was that how he looked to her? Well, if that protected them so be it. The woods were a boundary and he guarded them. He was not so very far from Kilfayne's own walker in the woods.

He'd just meant to sit down for a while, finish up the emails he'd had to put aside earlier when Patricia called and then...

He woke up still in that hard chair, face on the kitchen table pillowed in his arm, the light of the laptop giving the kitchen an eerie glow and a full mug of stone-cold tea beside him.

Honestly, he didn't even remember making it.

The kitchen door swung wide, creaking, the night whispering in through the boot room beyond. The outer door there was open as well and the scent of the woods was rising. Wildflowers and moss, the peaty, oaky smell of sap and fresh leaves, the warmth of the night... And the sound, the creaks of branches and the whispering of leaves, the nightsong of the forest.

Was that what had woken him? The door opening? Or the woods beyond? But the outer door had been closed. Locked. He knew that. He'd done it himself.

It wasn't locked now.

As he stared at it, he heard that sigh, deep and threatening, a sound of satiation and desire.

He was still dreaming. He had to be.

Except he wasn't.

Outside in the night the wind was rising. There was a full moon over the trees, and clouds scuttered across it, making a patchwork of light and dark flood over the garden beyond the door and the boot room. The trees rose like a black wall on the far side of the cottage garden, their deep tangle even darker on a night like this.

And in between, right at the edge of the woodland, he could see a figure. It wasn't entirely there, nor entirely human. Not really. It was made of leaves and branches, a tangle of vines and tendrils, of fruit and flowers. His imagination, he liked to tell himself.

Even if that wasn't entirely true either.

Nick sighed.

The figure smiled at him – always amused with Nick's dark moods, never one to take anything seriously – and then beckoned him forward. It vanished into the trees as if it had never been there to begin with.

The night stirred with expectation. A bird called softly from the trees, a long wavering song. The wild wood waited.

'All right,' he murmured in a low voice. 'All right, I'm coming.'

What else could he do? What choice did he have? He headed out into the night and the woods closed around him like a tomb.

CHAPTER 11

ALEX

There was no sign of Nick the next morning, although the breakfast things were laid out for her in the kitchen, and the coffee was on the stove. It was Saturday. He'd been making plans, she recalled, so maybe he'd already gone. Alex helped herself.

She'd slept late, her sleep disturbed again by those old dreams. She'd woken in the night convinced there was a party going on in some distant part of the house but was too tired to go and investigate. Besides, there were only the two of them here and she didn't believe Nick was sneaking in all his mates to have some kind of blow-out without her noticing.

It must be the wind or something. Sound travelled strangely in old buildings. She knew that better than anyone.

Gabe would have started talking about stone tape theory – the idea that old buildings could somehow record events of great passion or pain and replay them in the right circumstances, memories etched into the very stones. Eduardo would probably counter with something about infrasound and its effect on the human mind, making people see and hear things, or even just have that uneasy sense of being watched. None of it explained this place, she thought.

As she left the kitchen there was a flurry of movement on the stairs, she was sure of it. As if someone had seen her coming and rushed away. A soft giggle followed and she froze, standing in the hall.

Such an imagination, her father used to say, and ruffle her hair.

The memory was like a punch to the chest and for a moment she couldn't move at all.

Stop making up stories, Alexandra, her grandfather would tell her, in a lot less affectionate tone.

This place was going to be the death of her, she thought. She was going to lose her mind in the quiet, imagining things that couldn't be true. When she got to the study, she opened the laptop and put on some music, turning up the volume as high as it would go. If anything in the house made a noise after that – a pipe or a mouse or ancient floorboards and errant breezes – she didn't hear it.

She did an hour or two of work and then, reluctant to live on whatever she could scavenge in the kitchen, decided to go out. It wasn't far to the village, especially not in daylight. There had to be somewhere there she could get lunch on a Saturday, after all.

There was not much to Kilfayne. It was a village surrounded by a farming community, hemmed in by mountains. A river ran through it. There was a parish church, a small school, a shop and a pub. Alex parked the car outside the pub where a board promised hot food. She took her chance and went in.

The low, intimate babble of voices instantly went quiet. There were no more than seven people in there, all of them staring at her. That was the way of rural pubs. She made her way up to the bar, ordered a coffee, and asked for a menu.

Then, armed with a laminated sheet with various offerings printed on it, she found a table by the mullioned window.

The coffee wasn't a patch on the ones Nick made but she drank it as she decided what to eat. How far wrong could she go with lasagne, she figured. Apart from the obligatory side of coleslaw anyway.

'You're from the telly, aren't you? Home after the ghosts, are you?'

Alex froze as the snicker ran around the room. They knew who she was then.

And they expected her to – what? Flinch? Apologise?

Alex gathered the shield of Dr Alex O'Neill, the great debunker, the sceptic's sceptic, around herself and drew herself up to her full height. Not a great height, especially when sitting down, but the effect was the same. She glared at the young man, wiry, with a terrible haircut and an even worse moustache, lounging against the bar. He had tight jeans and a grubby-looking band t-shirt on. She knew the type, far too well. Ted Sanderson would have loved this one. He would have had him dancing to his tune in no time. The familiar loathing already seethed beneath his skin.

'Don't worry,' she said. 'There's no such thing as ghosts. And I won't be staying long.'

'Oh aye.' He let out a nasty laugh. 'Selling it off, are you?'

It was the sneer in his voice that did it. She couldn't help herself. Fuck him, and everyone in this dead-end village.

'Yes,' she replied coldly.

Shock rippled around the pub, and suddenly it was very quiet indeed. Every eye was on her and every ear turned her way. She'd really done it now.

'What? The house or the land?' another, older man asked from one of the other tables. He looked aghast.

'All of it,' she said, schooling herself to politeness now. She appeared to have gone too far. 'There's a hotel chain interested.

It'll be a great opportunity for the area. Employment, tourism…'

For another long, painful moment no one spoke.

'No good will come of that,' the old man muttered, crossing himself and turning his attention back to his pint.

'Oh, enough of that nonsense,' said the older woman behind the bar. 'Leave the poor girl alone. She's just trying to have a meal. Seán, get off with you. You're meant to be working. And you lot, mind your own business. You'd put anyone off their lunch.'

That seemed to calm things down, or at least shut them up. And Seán, the smarmy little git, shouldered his way out of the door with a backwards glare at Alex which she found chilling.

The lasagne arrived, with a mound of coleslaw which Alex studiously avoided. And chips. What was the obsession with chips?

The pub crowd dispersed while she ate, leaving only the couple of old men nursing their pints by the time she went up to the bar to pay.

'Don't mind them,' said the landlady. 'Too much time on their hands most of them.'

'I don't,' Alex told her. 'Mind them, I mean. But thank you all the same.'

'Are you really selling up? You granda wouldn't have liked that.'

He wouldn't have liked being referred to as a *granda* either, Alex thought with a smile.

'Neither would your brother,' said one of the old men. 'Loved that land, he did. And Hennesey's got grazing rights on the lower pasture. How will that work with a hotel?'

Alex, who had no idea and didn't care, just gave a dismissive shrug as she tapped her card on the machine to pay. This was not a conversation she wanted to be having in the local pub. She shouldn't have said anything at all.

'The walker won't like it either.'

'Nick?' she asked. No, Nick didn't like it at all.

The man made a dismissive noise like 'psht'. 'Not him. The walker in the woods. Although you shouldn't be crossing that fella either.' No love lost there, Alex thought, not from that tone. 'Not after his wife and your brother both. The guards still haven't answered what happened there, and Nick Walker was their prime suspect, wasn't he?'

Alex turned around, staring at them now.

'He *what*?'

'All alone up there in that big house they were, the three of them. And now two of them are dead.'

He had a wife? A dead wife? And did the police think Nick was involved in Theo's death?

'That's enough of that talk,' the landlady snapped. Alex jumped at the sound. 'Nick wasn't even there when young Theo died. He found the body when he got back from the village. Think about what you're saying.'

'What happened?' Alex couldn't let this drop now.

'Oh nothing, just malicious gossip. Sally fell down the stairs, a missed step or something. A tragic accident. Poor Nick found her. And your Theo – God rest him – well, you probably know all about that better than anyone here.' She glared at the drinkers. 'He's a good man, is our Nick. Now, do you want a receipt?'

'A good man,' the other elderly drinker snorted out a laugh. 'All the women around here are mad for him. And look at him. More beast than man.'

'Do you want me to bar the pair of you?' the landlady asked, icily.

'No, Fionnuala,' they both muttered, like chastened schoolboys.

She huffed in satisfaction and handed Alex a receipt. 'There you go, love. You watch yourself, mind. It's an old house.

And the woods around it are dangerous. Don't go straying, will you? Listen to Nick. He knows the place better than anyone.'

Straying? On her own land? Was she getting warned of danger or simply warned off? She wasn't sure.

'What is the walker in the woods?' she asked.

Fionnuala rolled her eyes. 'Just an old story. Like the good people, you know? Nothing to worry yourself about. A boogey man. They used to say that the forest needed a guardian.'

'To keep it safe?'

The two old men laughed, a sound cut off by another glare from Fionnuala, who tried to smile and pass it all off again.

'Pay it no mind, love. Old nonsense, that's all. The story went that the walker kept the woods in check. Or guarded the boundaries of de Wilde land, keeping the curse contained.'

'The curse?' A lot of old families had curses associated with them, didn't they? And they were all a lot of bull.

'The de Wilde curse?' Fionnuala tried that indulgent smile again. 'Surely your granda told you about that. Comes from when they built the Big House. Crossed the fairies, or so they say, building it there. Just a story like the walker. They give Nick such a hard time about it. Because that's his job, and his surname and all that. Superstition and spite. Small communities can be like that. Nothing else to occupy themselves, some people. That's all. Pay it no mind.' Then she found something terribly important to do at the far end of the bar.

Alex waited until she was in the car before she got out her phone and started googling. She'd never read the news reports regarding Theo's death. She hadn't wanted to. But there it was.

Local man detained for questioning... known to gardaí...

And he'd had a wife, who had also died under suspicious circumstances. She googled Nick as well, but there was precious little apart from the reporting on Theo's death. Still, she could ask Arnold. He could find out anything when he set his mind to it. Quickly, before she changed her mind, she fired off an email. That would do. She ought to have found out more about Nick Walker from the beginning. So should her lawyers.

Alex let out a long breath and tried to loosen her tense shoulders.

When she tried to start the car, the engine was dead.

CHAPTER 12

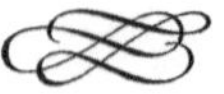

ALEX

The call to the car hire people had been awful. They kept asking what Alex had done to the car. She'd done nothing but drive the wretched thing in an entirely normal way. But it was completely dead. The engine wouldn't even turn over.

She had to go back into the pub and explain to Fionnuala why her car would be staying in the car park until someone came from the company to tow it and God knew when that would be because the guy in the call centre didn't appear to have the first clue where Kilfayne even was.

'Can I get a taxi or something?' she'd asked and Fionnuala had looked at her like she had asked for a helicopter.

She could have phoned Nick. But she didn't want to. It would be like admitting that she couldn't manage things by herself. No. She wasn't going to do that, not with him.

So here she was, tramping up the path through the trees, arms wrapped around her chest, head down, cursing under her breath with every step. Helpless and hopeless, and way out of her depth in this rural setting which was meant to be her home.

But it wasn't her home. She had no place here and never had.

So long as she didn't end up in a ditch. It wasn't like there was much traffic up to Wildewood Hall and that was the only way the road went.

She had no idea why she wasn't just going straight through the woods, but Fionnuala had suggested this route. Keep to the edge of the boundary, she'd said, and don't cross it until the gate. Maybe the locals didn't use it because it was private. She couldn't imagine her grandfather had taken lightly to trespassers on his land. Habit might lead them to avoid it. But it was her land after all. And it was the most direct way to the house.

Her house, she reminded herself.

For now, anyway.

So as she reached the edge of the sun-drenched field, with the sheep grazing down at the far end, she followed the obvious path around it to the treeline. There was a ditch – of course there was – and on the far side a fence with a 'Private property – keep out' sign clearly demarking the boundary.

It was a bit of a scramble but she made it over the fence, thanking God there was no barbed wire involved.

The cool green shadows of the trees closed in over her. The temperature difference was the first thing she noticed. Out there it was sunny, verging on too hot. In here it was a different world. The trees were old and twisted, with bright green moss like velvet on the stones and the lower parts of the tree trunks. And so many wildflowers in the dappled light. A curious quiet had settled around her, almost magical, and Alex had the feeling of stepping into another world or back in time. The only sounds were birdcalls, and rustling.

The beauty of the woods swept over her in a way that was completely unexpected.

And so did the memory.

Gran had led her along paths like this, telling her the names of the trees and the flowers. Not just their official names, but personal private names, magical names. They had made flower crowns, and things with twigs and moss. There had been stories and songs.

It was the only time she'd been happy at Wildewood Hall.

When had Gran died? Alex wasn't sure now. All she knew was her dad was gone, and so was Gran, and Mum wanted nothing to do with the de Wildes. Mum had remarried within a year, and Alex had taken her pragmatic stepfather's surname, as well as his love of the scientific and the logical. She had built it around her like a barrier and left the de Wildes behind.

Then this place had taken Theo too. These very woods.

Had it been deliberate? she wondered. Though they'd looked into Nick, the official account of Theo's death said it was an accident in the woods and there was no one else here at the time. She hoped it had been quick, that he hadn't lain here, suffering, slipping away slowly. Alone.

She swallowed hard. No one else seemed to have made a connection between the death of their father and the death of her brother. But then, who else was left to do that?

Tears stung her eyes and she blinked them away furiously.

Leaves shuddered somewhere off to her left and Alex froze, waiting to see if something was coming through the press of plant life. Nothing appeared.

The path led on, deeper through the woodland, widening out a bit now, and she followed it, trusting it to lead her to the house eventually.

Where else would it go?

So why did it seem like the bloody thing was taking her around in circles? She checked her watch again. That was when she realised it had stopped. She fished out her phone only to find the battery was dead too.

Brilliant. Just brilliant.

A branch cracked, bringing her head up, her attention bristling. A hare stood in the path ahead of her. Beautiful, elegant, watching her so carefully, its long black-tipped ears alert, twitching. But it didn't run. Its coat was a pale brown and its eyes so golden it didn't quite look real. It stared at her for a long moment and Alex couldn't move.

Of course there were hares in the area. They were wild animals and all the fences in the world couldn't keep them out. It was just so much larger than she expected. She'd always just thought of them as a kind of rabbit but that wasn't right at all, not now she saw one for real. And it wasn't the dark brown she had expected. The fur was almost as golden as its eyes.

Another noise from deep in the woods made them both start, and as Alex jumped back a step, the hare took off, bounding down the path. Catching her breath, Alex jogged after it, the path weaving through the trees until it opened into a clearing.

There was a ring of standing stones in the middle. Alex stared, unable to believe what she was seeing. They were old, she realised, really old. There were worn carvings half covered by moss. The circle of grass inside was lush and green, far darker than outside. The trees pressed close around it, forming a third ring.

Shit, if there was some kind of archaeological site here, surely she should have known. The lawyers should have flagged it. There was no mention of it in any of the papers.

And yet... she remembered this place. Remembered being here with Gran. Remembered Dad...

His hand falling limp on the bare earth, as laughter filled the air all around her, rippling through the canopy of trees like birdsong...

It hit her like a blow to the stomach.

This was where she'd found him. She'd been lost in the woods but this was where—

'What the hell are you doing in here?' a voice shouted from the forest.

Alex screamed. She couldn't help herself. She twisted

around to see Nick Walker stalk out of the trees, his expression dark and terrible. He carried an axe, and all she could think of was an executioner.

Alex stumbled back and collided with one of the stones. It was cold, far too cold on such a sunny autumn day. The urge to throw herself behind it and hide from him was so strong.

And then she got a hold of herself. Hide? No. Absolutely not. Anger surged back.

'This is my land,' she reminded him with a snarl. 'Remember? Why shouldn't I be here?'

'Because it isn't safe. This is protected woodland. Wild. It should be left alone, untouched. It's a boundary to a world that will destroy it given half a chance. Didn't you listen to anything your brother ever said?'

She shoved herself forward, using the stone as a launching pad. 'You don't get to tell me about Theo.'

'Well, someone should. Just as a warning. So you don't end up like him. Fionnuala rang, from the pub. Said to tell you the car got picked up. Good God, woman, what happened? Where have you been?'

'Walking back here.'

'For *three hours*? Why didn't you ring me? I would have come to get you.'

How had it possibly been three hours? Alex frowned at him, feeling more herself again. He'd been worried about her? She could tell that now just from looking at him. He wasn't angry, but scared. Why had he been worried about her?

'I was fine. I must have... I got a bit turned around in the woods, that's all.'

He shook his head slowly, as if he couldn't believe what he was hearing. '*A bit turned around.* Right.' At least he wasn't shouting at her anymore. Even if he was looking at her like she'd lost her mind instead of her way. 'We should get back to the house.'

His eyes darted around the clearing, at the treeline.

'What are you worried about?' she asked, curious now. 'I saw a hare. Are they dangerous here?'

She meant it as a joke but Nick flinched. She saw that. No mistaking it. Oh he tried to hide it but she knew what she'd seen.

'They can be,' he replied, gruffly, and beckoned her with one hand. 'Come on. Let's go back.' She made to take a step forward and to her surprise his eyes went wide in genuine alarm. 'Not through the circle!' he snapped.

Alex glared at him but took a step back all the same. There were old superstitions about stone circles and the like around here.

'Are you afraid the fairies are going to come and carry me off?' she said, trying to lighten the mood, before she thought about the ramifications. People held old traditions very dear to their hearts in this country. They might not admit it, or like to be teased about it, but folk belief was still strong.

Nick all but bared his teeth as he bit out the words. 'I'm *afraid* you're going to *damage* a pristine *archaeological* site, all right? And like I said, these woods are dangerous. If you fell here, who'd find you?'

And then, as if he'd said something he shouldn't, he froze, the words dying on his lips.

Theo had been found here. And Nick had been the one to find him. She realised that the moment she saw his expression.

Just like her father. Exactly like her father. God, what had happened?

Dad's hands falling still, limp on the rich and hungry earth.

Here in the heart of the wild wood, in this ring of stones...

The taste of blood in her mouth, choking her, and the world blurring through tears and terror. The gleam of gold beneath rotting foliage.

Alex drew in a shuddering breath and edged her way around the circle, giving it as wide a berth as possible.

Nick turned away as she reached him, leading her back through the trees. She was only thankful he wasn't looking at her face.

'Did you come to find me?' she asked, forcing her voice to be calm. 'Thank you.'

He huffed out something so close to a growl it might as well have been. He shook his head, like he was chasing away an irritant. 'Well someone had to. Clearly.'

Behind her, in the trees, Alex thought she might have heard laughter. Or birdsong. It was hard to tell which. And it was so hard to shake the sensation of being watched as Nick led her out of the wild woods and back to the looming bulk of the house.

Like her dreams... her nightmares... running through the woods, trying to escape, always ending up back at this house.

CHAPTER 13

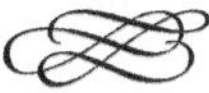

NICK

When Fionnuala phoned and said Alex had left on foot for Wildewood Hall earlier, he'd felt that stab of alarm like a splinter in his heart. Deep and painful. A warning. Same as the day when Theo died. And Alex had been wandering through the woods, as blithe as anything, for God knew how long before he found her.

Anything could have happened. She didn't even know the first thing about keeping herself safe. She didn't even know that she needed to keep herself safe.

Especially in the woods.

How could Nick tell her without sounding, just as he feared, like a madman? And maybe he was. How would he know? That was what everyone thought. Those who didn't think he was a murderer as well. He knew there was gossip. There was always gossip. That was the way of Kilfayne.

What had they said to her? Which of the various tall tales and scandalous rumours had they spun for her? Because they loved a bit of scandal, especially when it revolved around Wildewood Hall and those who lived there.

He stamped his way back to the house, aware that he was

still carrying an axe, like something out of a horror movie, and that Alex had screamed when he bore down on her through the trees. The look of sheer terror had brought him back to himself.

He hadn't expected that.

He hadn't expected that seeing her afraid of him would be... so awful.

And then she'd pulled herself together.

'This is my land,' she'd said and, God help them both, the woods had heard her. He knew that much. He'd felt the trees all around them and the earth beneath them react. He'd felt the words run right through him like arrows.

This is my land.

It was all he could do to find a reply. The wrong one, of course. He never should have mentioned Theo.

He'd found Theo here. In this place. In the clearing. In the stone circle.

And for a moment he'd been terrified he was going to find her lying there too.

Not standing there, arguing with him. He was convinced he was far too late, that he had failed. Because he failed in everything he did.

Three hours she had been missing. Three whole hours. She didn't even realise it.

She'd seen the hare and followed it. She had wandered through the wild wood. He didn't even stray from the path if he could avoid it. He certainly didn't let anyone else do it. Not anyone he cared about. He had warned Theo, time and again. Sally had, of course, but then Sally always did whatever Sally wanted. And Sally knew this place. She knew every inch of it. Every leaf. Every blade of glass.

But Alex? Alex didn't have a clue.

Anything could have happened. Didn't she realise that?

Maybe she did now. She'd realised something of the danger in the woods, just before they left. He'd seen that much and tried to ignore it, to give her the dignity she needed. It was the least he could do.

'Nick,' she called as he opened the back door and held it open for her. She was more herself again now. 'I should have called. You're right. I don't know the area, but I – I didn't think I needed to. But I promise, I didn't damage the woods. I wouldn't. They're beautiful.'

For a moment he was lost for words. Damage the woods? As if she could.

But then he remembered what he'd said about the area being protected. She'd misunderstood. It was probably just as well.

Yes, the woods needed to be preserved, and protected from the world outside. But in turn, they were a protection. They held the line against Wildewood Hall. And sometimes they did that in violent ways.

He couldn't tell her that. She'd never believe him for starters.

'Please,' he said, trying to weigh his words carefully this time. He couldn't alarm her any more than he already had. 'Please take more care in future.'

She could have fallen, he'd said, in the woods. But Theo hadn't fallen. Not really. She could have been lying there, where he found Theo. She could have been as dead as her brother.

That was what he'd been afraid of. That something had happened to her, that the woods had done something. That was why he had brought the axe.

It was little more than a threat. He couldn't have done much with it.

'I'm sorry,' she said. 'I didn't think.'

Well, that was obvious. But why would she? Who had to think about things like this?

Who apart from him?

Nick swallowed hard and felt the tension in the back of his shoulder unwind just a little. She was trying. She was being magnanimous. He had to meet her halfway.

'I'm sorry too. I was rude. It was uncalled for.'

Alex smiled at him, brightly, as if she hadn't a care in the world. 'Apology accepted. Can we start again, Nick?'

'I – of course.'

And then she stepped in through the doors of Wildewood Hall. She passed so close to him he could catch her scent, and he inhaled, perhaps more deeply than he intended to. It was warm and delicate, that fragrance, intoxicating.

And then the house seemed to enfold her in its cold hands, drawing her out of the light and into the shadows.

Nick shuddered and forced himself to follow her. Alex did not believe in ghosts. Theo had told him that time and again. Even though she made her living making TV shows about them, writing about them, investigating them. Even though she had grown up as part of a family with a house where they were a fact of everyday life.

Except she hadn't grown up here, had she? Once their father died, her mother would have nothing to do with the de Wildes. Patricia had said once, 'Nothing good ever came to a woman in this house.'

He thought of Sally and flinched inwardly. He should have made her leave. He should have insisted. Not that she would have listened to him but he could have tried.

Nick believed now. He had learned far too much. To his eternal grief.

He wasn't going to say any of that to Alex of course.

He wanted her. Ached for her. But he had no idea how much of that was real and how much was... well, whatever the house did. He couldn't stop thinking about her.

Sally said that something old and terrible stalked the house.

That the house itself had become subsumed in evil and it had taken all the wise women of Kilfayne to bring it under control.

But they couldn't get rid of it.

Old stories. Legends. Things to frighten children. Or so he'd believed once. Right up until he lost Sally.

Wildewood Hall was no place for a woman. It was no place for the living at all.

ALEX

The nagging sense of being watched followed Alex wherever she went, waking and sleeping. The house whispered around her, especially in the later afternoon, as the shadows lengthened and the branches of the trees seemed to reach towards her across the lawns and the gravel drive. Nick wandered in and out of the periphery of her world and the only other person she saw was the postman. Once. Now that she didn't have a car, she was pretty much trapped here in Wildewood Hall, though she didn't like to admit it. The car hire people weren't helping. They accused her of doing something to the engine. Alex was furious.

Gabe or Daphne called her most evenings, which she appreciated. Mostly it was to discuss work and new cases, to bounce ideas off her, or, in Daphne's case, to mutter ominous things about dark shadows over Alex's life. Which was not really helpful.

Because, despite the improved weather outside, the house was freezing cold, and made strange noises. She felt like she was being watched. Worse, she felt like she was being laughed at.

Maybe it was paranoia. It could have been the memories of

what had happened in the States, of that campaign of terror and torment which had hunted her off social media and off the show. Her therapist would tell her it was. Alex wasn't sure. Not now she was back here.

But there were other traumas too, weren't there? Losing her dad. Mum dying. Theo... to name but a few. And two of them revolved around Wildewood Hall.

Coming back here was a terrible mistake. She should have known better.

One morning she turned on the shower and nothing came out of it. She stood there in her robe, listening to the pipes begin to whine and groan. The noise shook through the walls and, as Alex stared in horror, a thick red-brown sludge emerged from the shower head like meat out of a mincer.

Swearing loudly, she tried to reach in to turn it off, only to feel the icy touch of the stuff slither over her bare arm. She wasn't proud of the shriek that ripped itself out from somewhere deep inside her and she whirled around, grabbing the nearest towel to wipe it off, which only succeeded in smearing it into her skin.

She stumbled back, still scrubbing at her arm, and collided with someone.

Nick stood in the doorway of her bathroom, his hair and beard still wet, his robe tied loosely around his body, like he'd only just got out of a shower of his own. One which had contained a lot more water and a lot less gore. His arms came up around her, although whether to stop her, hold her up, or ward her off she couldn't say. He was strong, she already knew that, but his touch was unexpectedly gentle, secure around her, holding her close. The scent of soap mingled with the scent of him – woodsy, musky, male. Her breath caught in her throat.

'What is it? What's wrong?' The rumble of his voice went through her body as well, deep and reverberating, making her shiver with sudden need.

'Shower,' she said, unable to form words. 'Sludge. I got it on me. I think I'm going to throw up.'

He released her and Alex closed her eyes in mortification. What was she thinking? Why did she have to turn into an absolute idiot around him? Especially when he stood there, hot and half naked. Nick hurried past her, and somehow managed to turn the shower off without getting anything on him. Of course. Longer arms or something. Or just luck. She didn't know.

'That... that shouldn't have happened,' he said, bending over the disgusting mess on the bottom of the tray, glaring like it had personally offended him. 'I'll get it fixed, I promise.' Then he glanced over at her through the fall of dark, wet hair. 'Do you – do you want to use mine? To clean up?'

'Oh God, yes.' He didn't have to ask twice.

Nick's room was smaller and far more simply furnished than Alex's. The bedclothes were still rumpled and she could see the indentations in the pillows where he'd slept. Everything else was perfectly neat and surprisingly impersonal. He left her there, grabbing some clothes to change into and grumbling about old plumbing.

She tried to ignore that he'd told her Theo had only recently had the ensuite put in the master suite, brand new and state-of-the-art. This was not a case of old plumbing. But something could have got into the pipes, she supposed. Now she was away from it, standing in the darkened room which carried the scent of Nick everywhere, logic was able to make a reappearance.

God, what Gabe and the others would have made out of that scene, she thought.

There was a double-frame with photos on the bedside table and a small stack of books. They were the only things that might tell her anything about Nick Walker. That man in the pub had implied something sinister. His wife had died. And the reports

– 'known to the gardaí' was not a good phrase to have hanging over an employee.

In the photo, Nick was younger, clean-shaven and smiling. He gazed in obvious adoration at the woman in his arms, blue-eyed and beautiful. She gazed past the camera at whoever was taking the photo, a secretive smile on her perfect face. The other photo was of a little girl with the same dark hair and blue eyes, the same woman much younger. She was holding flowers and dried grass knotted into a circle, like the one in the kitchen, and smiled so proudly at her creation. Alex stared at the two photos, wondering how on earth she could ask him about them when he'd never mentioned his wife at all. And whether he would tell her anything. Grief did funny things to people.

Like made them hide away from the world in a creepy old house and drive everyone else away perhaps.

Creeping around Nick's personal belongings was not a good idea, she decided. If she could find a subtle way to ask about his wife, she'd do so, but otherwise she was best to leave it alone. Or at least until she heard from Arnold. She showered as quickly as she could, using the shampoo and soap there, aware of the scent that she already associated with him wrapping itself around her now – cedarwood, with a touch of citrus, and something spiced, like cloves or cinnamon – rich, earthy, woodsy. Nick Walker to a tee.

The email from Arnold came at almost the same time as a message from Gabe which simply read *Are you shitting me?* So, he knew as well. Damn, she should have told Arnold to keep it on the downlow. But the group shared everything. They always had. The lack of personal space was one of the more irritating things about working with them.

Not a lot of info on Nick Walker that I can find but I'll keep
digging. No birth cert, which is weird, but it could just be a
name or location thing. I've reached out to a friend in law
enforcement to see what she can find out.

That was probably illegal but Alex decided to let it slide. It
wasn't like she was going to make anything public.

His wife was Sally Neary, a local, and cause of death was
deemed to have been an accident. She fell down the stairs in
Wildewood Hall, two years ago, and they brought him in for
questioning. Your brother too as he was in the house at the
time.

They questioned Theo too? She hadn't heard anything
about that. Not that she'd been in regular contact with her
brother. Well, he had been living here at the time and owned
the place, she supposed. The image of Sally's face reared up in
her mind, her smile in particular, and Alex felt a chill breeze
pass over the back of her neck. The door to the study was
closed. So was the window looking out over the front of the
house. God, she hated the draughts in this place. She shook her
head, dismissing her overactive imagination.

Nick's wife would have been exactly Theo's type, once
upon a time.

The house has rather a fascinating history, Arnold went on,
because of course he'd started digging into the history of the
house as well. Alex sighed.

I'll write the whole thing up for you and see what else I can
dig up, but the highlights – The house itself was built on an
earlier Norman site, some time in the late 1400s, and
expanded, especially in the late 1700s which gives the Georgian façade you see today. Nasty time for the whole country

from then on really. Rebellion in 1798, led to severe restrictions and the de Wildes didn't exactly help. A lot of taxes, a lot of repression. It just got worse and worse, the excesses. They pretty much partied while the countryside around them starved.

They weren't alone among the landlords of the time, she thought. Still, it left a bitter taste in her mouth as she looked around the room in which she now sat. How many of her ancestors had sat right here and not given a shit about what was happening right outside their door? The worst was 1845–1852, often called the Potato Famine, but the Irish name for it translated as the Great Hunger, and it had sod all to do with potatoes and more to do with genocide. It wiped out a third of the population, and led another third to flee the country.

The fifteenth baron employed a steward called Blaise Chambers, known as the Master of the Revels. He treated the house like some kind of private fiefdom. He ran the estate almost into the ground. Bankrupted the family. They almost lost everything. Neither the first time nor the last but the most spectacular. They say he used to host orgies of every excess in the house and no one was safe there. He died in 1826, shot through the heart. A lot of stories about the house say he haunts it still so watch out for him. We really ought to check it out.

That sounded like Gabe had been leaning over his shoulder. She closed the laptop with a sigh.

Blaise Chambers. The portrait outside her bedroom door. She had taken it down the other night. Because who wanted a lecherous perv looking at your bedroom door all night?

. . .

Alex woke that night to noises from downstairs again. And this time she wasn't dreaming. There were voices, laughter, and music. Glasses clinking together. It sounded raucous, a party, happening right underneath her in her supposedly empty house. She turned on the light but the sound carried on.

Enough, Alex thought. She was going to get to the bottom of it. If Nick was bringing in people to party away here at night while she slept, they were going to have some very stern words. And if that really was the case, he'd be out on his ear, contract or no contract. The lawyers would be all over it.

Tired, cranky and ready for a fight, she flung open the bedroom door. Blaise Chambers' portrait leered at her from the wall. Nick must have put the bastard thing back. Alex grabbed it, yanking it off the wall so hard the string holding it snapped and she reeled back a bit to take the weight. Right, she'd bring this downstairs as well. She could use it as a weapon if she had to. Throw it, and whoever was making the racket, out on their ear.

As she reached the foot of the stairs she was aware that the tenor of the sounds had changed. It wasn't just a party now. It was something else. A very different kind of gathering. Low moans, gasps, grunts – the unmistakable sounds of people having sex. More than just a couple too. Laughter, but sultry, full of lust and edged with mockery.

Alex froze, still holding the framed portrait behind her in a suddenly numb hand. Her body felt flushed and needy, as if hearing all that happening just on the other side of the morning room doors made her react in a way she would never have expected of herself.

Desire. Need. Want.

Alex swallowed hard and glanced down at the picture she was still dragging along behind her. He looked up at her, dark eyes hungry, his mouth twisted in a mocking kind of smile.

Blaise Chambers.

I will set all of them against all of those they have loved, and I will make them mine, body and soul.

Alex let the picture thump to the ground, and everything suddenly went quiet. Everything. She was standing in the dark hallway, looking at a closed door, and there wasn't a sound coming from the other side. Not anymore. But her heart was thundering inside her chest and her body felt like it was wound up like a spring. The ache deep down below her stomach, the rush of warmth and hunger, the sweat that prickled her hyper-sensitive skin...

Alex flung the door open. The room was empty, still and silent, the curtains closed so only a sliver of moonlight cut through the gloom. There was no one there. Not a soul.

She backed up, leaving the picture lying there, Blaise Chambers sneering up at her from the floor. This was mad. Had she still been dreaming? Or was she hallucinating? Things like this didn't just happen. There had to be an explanation.

She was halfway up the stairs again when she noticed the figure at the top, dark and terrible, looming over her. She couldn't make out his features but he was definitely there, as real and solid as she was. A man.

'Nick?'

It couldn't be him. The figure was nowhere near as tall or as broad.

The laughter came from just behind her. A child's laugh, bright and mischievous. And Alex recognised it. From some-where in the back of her mind, from somewhere long ago. She knew it.

Alex tried to take a step back. Her foot came down in empty air and, the next thing she knew, she was falling backwards. Her head caught a glancing blow off one of the thick newels carved with leaves and foxgloves, the world exploded in light and pain, and everything after that was black.

CHAPTER 15

NICK

Sally had always said Nick slept like the dead. That the house could be falling down and he wouldn't hear a thing. But tonight, he couldn't sleep at all. How could he?

The house was unsettled. So were the woods. They always reacted to each other.

And he knew why. Of course he knew why.

Alexandra de Wilde... or rather Dr Alex O'Neill. She had laid claim to the land and the woods had heard her. It all came back to her. She shouldn't be here at all. But what could he do? He couldn't make her leave.

He tossed to the side and stared at the photos beside his bed. Theo had taken the picture of him and Sally, that glorious day in the woods, when the sun had shone on them and they had thought there was no danger. He didn't have one of Theo who had always preferred to be on the other side of a camera anyway. 'Who'd want to look at my ugly mug?' he'd said with a laugh. But he hadn't been ugly. He'd been beautiful. Just like his sister. Nick closed his eyes with a groan, dismayed to find his thoughts going there again. When he opened them, Sally gazed back at him from all those years ago, judging him the way she always had done. She could always take one look at him and see into his soul.

Whereas Theo... Theo would drive him up the wall, argue with him over anything, and make him laugh so hard he thought he'd cry. Theo had been a breath of fresh air.

How did he explain any of it to Alex? That there was nothing wrong with the plumbing. That the moment she left the room he had turned on the water and it had been crystal clear. That the house was unsettled by her presence here and so was he.

So unsettled.

He would sound like a madman. He could only imagine what her lawyers would make of that. They wanted him out of Wildewood Hall.

Alex wanted him out of Wildewood Hall. That was why she was here, wasn't it?

He rolled onto his back again, staring at the ceiling as he huffed out a breath. His face itched under his beard. He really needed to get rid of the thing. He hated it. It just seemed like such a lot of work and who was there to care anyway?

Sasquatch, he thought bitterly. That wasn't far from the truth. A wild thing from the woods. A monster. It really shouldn't bother him quite so much as it did. He felt like a fool.

Alex had been in here, in his room just this morning. Well, in the ensuite. But you couldn't get in there without going through here and...

He growled to himself. Why was he even thinking about that?

And when he'd found her in the woods, right at the heart of the wild wood, he'd been so taken aback, and so afraid. Anything could have happened to her in there. She was a de Wilde, even if she denied it.

Look what had happened to Theo, and he loved the place

with all his heart. He had given himself to it body and soul, and it had taken his life.

Nick closed his eyes and tried to will himself to go to sleep. It didn't work. It never did. And his thoughts kept straying back to Alex. He couldn't help that. There was something so bewitching about her. The way she frowned, the way she tilted her head to one side when confused or dubious – which was frequently. The way she had looked, standing in the woods, with sunlight streaming through the shifting leaves, falling around her in green and gold, illuminating her.

Alex, in the woods. The last place she should be. Just like Theo.

It would never be safe. Never.

Not for them.

But at least he'd found her. At least he had brought her back here. Even if here was the last place she should be as well.

He had lost Theo in the woods. He had lost Sally to the house. He was alone here. And that was how he should be. It was safer for all concerned.

The music started first. He heard it filtering through the house, almost designed to tease and cajole. Nick let out a sigh and tried to wrap the pillow around his head. Alex hadn't said anything about it so he had to hope she simply didn't hear it. Some people didn't. Some people drifted through life without any problem whatsoever. Whereas he...

There had been nothing but problems. Ever since he'd first stupidly set foot on the grounds of Wildewood Hall all those years ago.

But if he hadn't there wouldn't have been Sally, or Theo, or—

A thump sounded outside in the hall, further down the corridor towards Alex's room. Nick opened his eyes and sat up carefully.

No one else in the house but the two of them.

There was no one to laugh, no one to sing, no one to cry out. And yet there they were, those voices, right on the edge of hearing. It started with the sound of a gathering, then a party, and then... then something wilder.

Laughter, gasps, the wild carnival of sex and debauchery underneath him in the morning room on the lower floor. So much laughter. Mocking, horrible, endless laughter.

And then a scream. Followed by a bone-shattering crash.

Nick was up out of the bed before he knew what he was doing. Two strides took him across the room to the door but when he grabbed the handle to yank it open, it wouldn't budge. He tugged on it, turned the handle this way and that but nothing worked.

'No!' he snarled. 'Open up.'

He brought both hands to bear on it, trying to force it open first with just the handle, and then with one hand braced against the frame. The door rattled on its hinges but it wouldn't open.

'Damn it! Open up!' He tried again, but the door remained wedged shut. 'Let me out!'

Alex was in trouble out there. He just knew it. Right down deep in his chest, where everything was hollow and scraped out, he knew it.

'Alex!' he roared. 'Alex, are you okay? Can you hear me?'

He tugged again.

'Please, come on. Please help me. Let me out. I have to help her.'

A breath brushed against his cheek, an icy cold touch on his shoulder, and Nick sucked in a lungful of alarm.

The scent of woodlands and wildflowers surged up around him and tears stung his eyes. He blinked them back, furious, and backed away from the door, releasing the handle. His body felt like lead. Too big, too clumsy. Useless.

'Please,' he whispered.

The air was so cold now. The whole room. All the heat had been sucked out of the air, out of him as well. Even as he watched it, the handle rattled twice, then turned and the door swung open with an agonised creak.

'Thank you,' he whispered, breathless, shivering.

Nick bolted from the room, down the hallway to the top of the stairs, lungs burning, heart hammering. There was nothing there. No one visible anyway. But the air was still like an icehouse and he still couldn't quite catch his breath, not now. For a moment he heard the echo of laughter again, childish and bright. But there was nothing innocent in that sound. He knew that. Nothing whatsoever.

The house went still. Horribly still. He could feel it watching him, that oppressive sense of being examined, of something waiting to see what he would do. The expectation.

He looked down.

He didn't want to but he had to. It was just like that night. The night Sally—

A figure lay, sprawled, at the foot of the stairs.

'Alex?' he whispered, as if he could deny it. As if he could make it not real, not true. As if her name was a talisman that might save them both.

She didn't move. This couldn't be happening. Not again. It simply couldn't be happening. It had to be a nightmare. Another one. But it wasn't Sally this time. It was Alex.

Nick thundered down the stairs to her side, his heart louder than his footsteps. 'Alex?' He dropped to his knees. Not that he was sure he had any strength left to stand anymore.

It was just like Sally. Exactly like the night she—

He pressed his hand to Alex's throat and let out a sob as he felt a pulse. Strong, certain. She was alive. She was still alive. Thank Christ!

'Alex? Dr O'Neill? Shit, Jesus, Alex, can you hear me? Please, try to open your eyes. Say something. Anything.'

CHAPTER 16

ALEX

Alex was aware she wasn't awake, but that this wasn't the same dream she relived night after night.

Something reached up from the foundations and the rocks on which Wildewood Hall was built, from the earth itself, from the water deep underground, and coiled around her. It dragged her down, clawing at her skin, pulling her into darkness.

The cold arched roof of stones and the stench of mulch. The taste of blood in her mouth, choking her, and the world blurring through tears and terror, shadows covered her, crawling over her. Inside her.

She stared at the ceiling, blinked at the ornate plasterwork, at the leaves and the vines and... and it wasn't the house anymore. It was a forest, a vast, ancient forest. It was lush and verdant. And alive.

She felt him coming through the trees and undergrowth around her, felt the forest shiver with his approach. A man, crowned with antlers like a stag. He was life, warmth and everything the darkness was not. His very presence drove it away. She remembered that old story Gran used to tell, the walker in the woods.

· · ·

Alex was in Wildewood Hall, lying at the foot of the stairs. She was in the heart of the wild wood, in that ring of stones. Both of them at once. And he was with her. She struggled to focus through the blinding pain in her head.

The floor was cold and hard beneath her body as only marble could be. When she opened her eyes, she expected to see endless faces peering at her over the bannisters of the landings above. Laughing at her. Mocking her.

But, God, her head hurt when she tried to move it. Her skin was sticky.

'Don't move. Try not to – I'm going to call the doctor, okay? Just stay with me.'

Was that Nick?

His voice sounded shaken. Scared. Far from the gruff and grumpy rumble she expected from him. She reached out and grabbed his hand. Such a big hand, his palm and fingers calloused from physical work. He was real. That was something. Touching his hand, feeling the warmth of his skin, that was good. She tried to squeeze but her own hand didn't seem to want to cooperate. So she just clung to him as best she could.

His voice went on, not talking to her now. Or at least she thought not. She wasn't sure. He wasn't making any sense. Or maybe she wasn't understanding him. Was she missing moments?

'Yes. No, she passed out. No, not for long. But she's dazed. I found her... found her at the foot of the stairs. I haven't moved her. She hit her head when she fell. She's only in and out of consciousness. Barely. Yes. Please. As soon as you can. Yes, just bring her with you. I will. I will. Thank you.'

There was something like a sob in his voice. Alex tried to squeeze his hand again to comfort him. It was like squeezing stone.

Something told her that was bad. Something logical and reliable, that was desperately trying to reassert itself and push the nightmares away.

Nick murmured soft, comforting things to her. She wasn't sure exactly what he said. He sounded like another man entirely.

She wanted to hear that voice. Like music. Like the distant sound of rain. She didn't want him to stop talking, so she could just listen to him. He was music in the shadows, sliding through the sharp pain in her head. Much better than anything else she'd been hearing in her dreams, her nightmares, in the house at night.

When she tried to speak, to ask what had happened, he just shushed her and smoothed his free hand over her head.

His big, strong hand. How was it so gentle?

'It's all right. I'm here. Just stay with me, all right? I've got you.'

And then there was someone else with them, someone who shone a light in her eyes and spoke with a quiet authority which could only mean the doctor Nick mentioned had arrived. Alex tried to focus on her, a woman with that kind of firm but fair expression. No-nonsense, her mum would have said. The kind of doctor you wanted.

'No concussion,' the older woman said at last. 'Just a nasty bump, I think. Nothing too serious. Still, you did the right thing calling, Nick. Let's get her somewhere comfortable to start with. No need to keep her on the cold floor.'

Nick lifted her in his arms, so strong that Alex felt like she was floating. She rested her head – the side that wasn't hurt – against his chest and was swept up in that scent again. Cedarwood, cloves and citrus. And something else underneath, an undoubtedly male scent. Nick Walker, she thought, and closed her eyes. That scent was him, entirely. She could feel his heartbeat racing, but he held her so carefully, unwavering, as if she was something precious and fragile.

A few minutes later he set her down on the bed, adjusting the pillows and pulling the sheets up over her. At least until the doctor told him sharply to stop fussing and examined her again.

'There now. Painkillers will see you right. Along with some rest. Honestly, what were you doing up in the dead of night in a place like this?' Nick started to say something. 'Not you,' the doctor told him. 'Off you go and sort yourself out or you'll be no help.' Her voice softened. 'You look half dead. Take a moment, love. Breathe deeply. She's fine. But it can't have been pleasant for you finding her like that.' Not pleasant for him, Alex thought in disgruntlement. She was the one who fell, the one with the thumping headache and possible concussion.

And then she remembered his wife. She'd died falling down the stairs. Just like that. And tonight, Nick had watched her fall. It must have been him at the top of the stairs. Who else could it have been?

The doctor's mouth tightened as she studied Nick with a deliberating gaze. To Alex's surprise, she wrinkled her nose. 'And have a shave, for the love of God. That thing on your face looks set to crawl away to die all by itself. Go see to Maeve. She'll be frantic.'

Somewhere outside the bedroom, there was laughter again, dark with mockery. It rang throughout the corridors of Wildewood Hall, from the floor to the rafters, and Alex started.

All three of them stiffened, just for a moment. Hearing it and making the decision to not admit that. Or just sensing the menacing nature of the house. Nick took another look at Alex, his face so pale beneath the ghastly beard, he seemed ghostly himself, and then he fled.

The doctor Nick had called sat down on the edge of the bed, a grey-haired woman with a dependable kind of face, wire-framed glasses and a stern expression.

'Hello?' Alex croaked.

The older woman smiled. 'Ah, there you are then, pet. Here, I've some painkillers to help with your head. Nothing too bad. You won't even need stitches. I've patched you up. Lucky Nick found you though. Don't worry now. There's no harm done. I'll stay here with you tonight.'

'Shouldn't I be... a hospital or...'

The doctor gave a fond kind of laugh. 'Nearest emergency department open now is more than thirty kilometres away. And an ambulance would take hours to get here, let alone back there. Besides, I don't think there's a need. You were lucky this time. We'll see what morning brings, will we?'

There wasn't much more to say. No arguing with someone like that, not that Alex had any wish to argue. It was comforting, the confidence in that voice. Something to cling to. Like Nick.

'Is Nick... is he okay?'

'Nick? He's fine. Bit shaken, what with finding you like that and all. The state he's got himself into the last few months, I don't know. But you, young lady, need to close your eyes and get some sleep. Don't worry about him. Here, painkillers. You'll need them.'

Alex took the pills and drank some water. She fell back asleep a lot more quickly than she would have liked to admit.

CHAPTER 17

NICK

Nick paced the kitchen, his mind whirling, his stomach in knots. He couldn't bring himself to sit still. Every noise made him jump.

She was all right. She *had* to be all right. Patricia wouldn't lie to him.

But he'd rushed out to the top of the stairs and he'd seen her lying there. Just like Sally. Exactly like Sally.

It had been like reliving the whole thing again, that awful night.

But this time it was Alex lying there.

All he could think was not again. It couldn't be happening again.

He didn't even remember the way he threw himself down the stairs after her, lucky he hadn't fallen too.

And then she just held his hand, clung to him, and he couldn't bear to let her go.

He was lucky he had Patricia's number on speed-dial.

'Just bring her with you,' he'd said. Like that wasn't going to have repercussions. But what else could he do? It was an emergency.

'She's settled upstairs,' Patricia said, coming into the kitchen. She looked worn out.

'Thank you.' It was late and his mother-in-law had been dragged out of bed to come here. 'Let me get you some tea.'

'That would be lovely, pet.' Nick set to work, glad to have something to do at last. 'You did the right thing,' she assured him again. 'A fall like that... well, you know better than anyone.'

They looked at each other, a thousand unspoken regrets passing by.

'Alex is going to be all right?'

'Yes. But this place—' Patricia sighed and took the mug from him, adding her own milk. 'She shouldn't be here, Nick.'

'I know that.'

'None of us should,' Patricia said, a bit more pointedly this time.

'I know that too.'

It was the worst possible situation. Wildewood Hall and its estate had claimed the lives of two of the people he loved most in the world. But one of them was Patricia's daughter, her flesh and blood. He couldn't imagine the pain of that. Or of being asked to come back here at the drop of a hat.

He sank into a chair opposite her.

'Alex wants to sell the estate,' he said. 'To a hotel group or something. You can imagine what they want to do.' She pulled a face and almost made him smile. If it hadn't been quite so serious he might have. 'And she just doesn't realise what this place is like. The danger she puts herself in. She was in the woods today, Patricia. Just wandering through the woods. She got lost. I found her at the heart.'

Patricia frowned this time. Because she was Sally's mother and she knew all about the woods. She might not believe it. But she knew all the same.

'Nick, you have to warn her.'

'She won't believe me. Not about the house or the woods.

She doesn't believe in ghosts. That's her whole thing, the sceptic on that TV show of hers, debunking and disproving everything.'

'Well.' Patricia shrugged. 'There's a lot of places that's necessary. People are very gullible.'

'Yes but not here.'

'No,' she agreed. 'You don't need to be gullible here. You have to convince her not to sell, Nick. For all our sakes.'

'I know. But the more time she spends here, wandering around, stirring up trouble... the more things like this are liable to happen. She could have died, Patricia. Like Sally. Like Theo.'

Patricia set down the mug and took his hands in hers.

'All the more reason to make her see the truth then.'

The peal of a child's laughter sounded from upstairs and both of them shot to their feet in response.

'I'll go,' he said. 'You finish your tea. I'm sure it's nothing.'

She smiled gratefully and Nick headed for the door.

'Nick,' she called after him and he paused, turning back. 'You be careful too, won't you?'

CHAPTER 18

ALEX

There was someone in the room with her when Alex started to wake up again. Someone murmuring a lullaby. Autumnal sunlight was pouring like liquid gold through the gap in the curtains again and she could clearly hear a woman singing softly though she couldn't make out the words. It was a tune she almost remembered but couldn't place.

The events of last night rushed back to her and she sat up sharply. Too sharply, as it turned out. Pain slammed into the side of her head and her vision swam, the light too bright, the shadows too pronounced. Just for a moment.

A little girl was standing at the foot of the bed, holding a rag doll. Behind her stood a woman with the same long dark hair and blue eyes. Both of them stared back at Alex without saying a word, the woman glaring, the little girl curious, perhaps startled by the sudden awakening.

Alex flopped back down on the pillows and tried to stop her head pounding. When she looked again, only the little girl was still there. The woman, who must have been her mother from their shared features, had vanished.

'You look sick,' the child said in a solemn, serious voice. 'I'll fetch Granny. She'll put you right.'

And then she was gone too. Alex could hear her voice ringing out through the hall. She was probably hanging over the bannisters, which had to be dangerous.

What was a child even doing here?

Wildewood Hall was no place for children. Wildewood Hall was no place for anyone.

Alex hauled herself up out of bed and padded to the door of her room. Sure enough, the girl was leaning precariously over the balustrade to call down into the hall below.

'Hey, get back from there,' Alex said, suddenly alarmed at what might happen. 'You'll fall.'

Startled, the child turned, staring at her. 'No, I won't. Not here. Anyway, you were the one who fell, not me.'

'Maeve!' Nick Walker's voice barked from the foot of the stairs. 'What are you doing up there?'

'I was watching her to see if she was going to wake up. She woke up. Tell Granny.'

'Get down here and tell her yourself. You aren't meant to be up there, young lady, and you know it.'

And while he was clearly trying to be stern and commanding, there was a gentleness to his voice that Alex hadn't heard before.

No, she had, she realised. She'd heard it last night. When he'd found her.

Chastened, the little girl pulled back from the abyss, and descended the stairs two at a time, hopping from one to the next. At the bottom turn she launched herself into the air and Nick had to dive forward to catch her. Which he did, effortlessly.

She wrapped her arms around his neck, laughing as he spun her to safety.

'You're so grumpy today, Daddy. But I'm glad you aren't beardy anymore.'

Daddy, Alex thought with a groan. Of *course*. She was the little girl in the photo. Nick set Maeve down carefully and she ran off. Then he looked up at Alex, where she leaned over the bannister to watch them.

And seeing him face-on shocked her. Underneath the once-overgrown facial hair was a face so chiselled and handsome it wouldn't look out of place on one of the mock Grecian statues in the gardens outside, or in one of those beautiful portraits on the walls. Blaise Chambers had nothing on him.

All she could do was stare.

Something snagged her memory about the painting, something she'd meant to do. Hadn't she taken it down? One glance over her shoulder told her it was back on the wall. Someone had hung it up again.

Then there was movement below and she turned back, forgetting about the painting again.

Nick made his way up to her in a rather more traditional manner than his daughter had descended. He seemed wary, as if expecting something else dramatic from her.

She didn't blame him. Nick had found her at the foot of the stairs.

Just like he'd found his dead wife.

'Should you be up?' he asked, solicitously enough. 'How are you feeling? Patricia said not to wake you. I'm sorry, Maeve shouldn't have been up here.'

'No, she didn't wake me. It was the woman singing.'

He gave her a puzzled look. 'The woman?'

'Yeah, the woman with Maeve. With the long hair the same c—' Alex swayed on her feet and, before she knew what was happening, Nick caught her arm, steadying her.

'Yeah, you definitely shouldn't be up yet. You could still

have a concussion. Let's get Patricia to give you another look, eh?'

'Patricia?' she echoed as Nick tried to steer her back towards the bedroom.

'Dr Neary. She came up last night when you fell. I called her in. Look, I'll get her. She's just down in the kitchen. Won't be a minute.'

Alex sat down on the edge of the bed, counted fingers, answered questions and admitted that she had a splitting headache but no blurred vision or dizziness. Nor was she confused. She saw Nick frown when she said that and tried to ignore it. No doubt he'd say different but she wasn't sure why. That wobble on the landing maybe. But that had just been tiredness.

Hadn't it?

'Really, I'm fine. I just... I don't know what happened. I thought... I thought I heard something downstairs but when I went down there was nothing. I was going back up when... there was someone on the stairs. Was it you?'

Nick stared at her and slowly shook his head.

'Oh.' She didn't know what to say to that.

'I heard you fall and came running – no one else was here.'

'I thought I saw...' Alex trailed off. She really didn't want to say any more.

Patricia glanced at Nick and something passed between them, something Alex wasn't sure how to interpret.

A spear of a sensation very like fear pushed its way up under her solar plexus, stealing her breath. She must have turned pale and the doctor didn't miss it.

'Now, you're going to need to rest,' said Patricia. 'Doctor's orders, my dear, so no arguing. A day in bed at least. Maybe two. And then you can ease back into things. No screens, no internet, none of that. Any relapse and you get Nick to ring me, understand? I'm away a couple of days but if it's an emergency I can be back up in no time. Nick can look after you and Maeve.' It struck Alex that Dr Neary, Patricia, must also be 'Granny'. Alex started to protest, but Patricia glared at her. 'No arguments.'

Nick's face was frozen. Had he been about to argue as well? Alex wondered. He glanced at Patricia, who took out her phone and checked her messages, clearly signalling an end to the discussion. Great. Now not only was Alex the enemy, she was his patient as well.

'All right,' he said, his voice subdued. 'But Maeve...'

'I can't take her with me, Nick. You know that. And the childminder's on holidays. I know you were going to stay at mine but... well, it'll have to be here after all.'

He swallowed hard. Alex watched the column of his throat work, his Adam's apple clearly visible now he'd shaved. 'I'd forgotten with all that's been going on. Yeah, I promised, didn't I?' He didn't exactly sound delighted about the prospect of time with his daughter all of a sudden and Alex suddenly felt like she was overhearing something intensely private. 'Yeah,' he said at last, his tone subdued. 'I'll keep her here with me. She'll be no trouble.'

Had Alex imagined the emphasis on *she*, as if Maeve wasn't the one he was worried about?

But the older woman smiled ruefully. 'She never is, the pet. And she's missed you something terrible.'

CHAPTER 19

ALEX

'What're you doing?'

Maeve swung around the corner of the door to the study clinging to the door jamb like it was a gatepost.

'Working.'

'Granny said no screens.'

'That was a couple of days ago.' Alex didn't even bother to look up from the laptop. 'I'm much better now.' Besides, all she was doing was checking emails and a couple of the online forums. Gabe had asked her to look over some case notes and see what she thought about some new locations for the show. One of them was a haunted abattoir, no less. He'd probably wet himself with excitement when that came up as an option.

And she didn't have to defend herself to a six-year-old.

She closed over the laptop and gave the little girl the attention she so obviously craved. 'What have you been up to? Where's your dad?'

Maeve shrugged. 'He's busy outside with the trees so I came back.'

'Are they being naughty?' Alex asked, deadpan, because she

couldn't resist it. She expected at least a giggle. Or to be told she was silly.

But Maeve didn't laugh. If anything she grew more serious, a curious little frown creasing her forehead. 'I made something for you,' she said. 'Daisy says it doesn't work, that's it's *super-sti-tion*.' She stumbled over the longer word. 'But I still made it.'

Alex smiled at her reassuringly. 'That's very kind of you. What is it?'

Maeve held out a palm-sized ring of twigs and reeds, wound together with bright wildflowers. A tiny version of the one in the kitchen, made with less skill but a lot more enthusiasm. There was something about it that caught and held the eye, something that sent a shiver down Alex's back but she couldn't say why.

It reminded her of the ones she used to make with her own gran here in Wildewood Hall. Had Maeve copied the one in the kitchen?

Alex got up from the desk and crossed to the doorway. Over breakfast Nick had told Maeve, once again, to stay out of the study and let Alex work. Alex had heard him. Obviously his daughter was holding to the letter of the law. Her feet were firmly outside in the hall, but that was only a technicality. The other part of the stern commandment was being ignored completely.

'That's very pretty,' Alex told her, turning the circle over in her hands.

Maeve still had that serious expression on her little face. She was a sweet kid, Alex thought, and Nick clearly doted on her. He had been trying so hard to keep her out of Alex's way. Not an easy task. Maeve was persistent.

'Mummy taught me,' she said and suddenly her voice was very small. Something snagged in Alex's brain. Was it the way she didn't make eye contact, the same as Nick when he didn't want to talk about something? They were very alike, the two of them. 'Gran taught her.' Not 'Granny', which was what she called Patricia. Gran was clearly someone else. Nick's mother perhaps? But why would Nick's mother have taught his wife something like this? Well, what was one more mystery around here?

'I think it's beautiful. Thank you. Will I keep it here on the desk?'

'Keep it with you,' Maeve said. 'That's what Mummy says. She says... she says the house isn't good for you. And the trees don't like you either.'

O... kay, Alex thought. Perhaps Maeve wasn't fully aware that her mother was gone.

'You still talk to your mummy?' she asked. She couldn't help herself. If there was a mystery to be solved, she instinctively began to dig, especially after her long experience on *The Ghost Patrol*.

And Maeve didn't disappoint.

'Of course,' Maeve sing-songed. 'And with Daisy and Rose and all the others.'

Alex started. She couldn't help herself. 'Where did you hear those names?'

She knew them. She remembered them. She'd played with a Daisy and a Rose and... She shook her head, thoughts swirling wildly. But there hadn't been any other kids here. Only her and Theo. It had just been a game, hadn't it? Make-believe.

'That's their names, silly,' Maeve admonished her in the way only a six-year-old could. It had to be a coincidence. Or local names. That had to be it, didn't it? Families around here loved to use the same names over and over. 'I play with them. But just them. Not with the dark man, and all *his* friends.' She leaned in conspiratorially and Alex felt herself drawn closer. She couldn't help it. 'They're not nice so we stay away from them... They're all around sometimes, and then they aren't. Like when they're sleeping. But when they wake up, they can be really naughty. And noisy. At night, when I stay here, they keep me awake. Daddy says to ignore them, but that's hard. And Daisy and Rose are my friends. I go and find them sometimes. They like the nursery, and we play on the stairs. And in the attic too with all the old things. But not in the cellar. We aren't allowed in the cellar.' She leaned in even closer. 'Even if they try to tell you it's fine, we never go into the cellar. Or the other dark place. That's the worst.'

Creepier and creepier, Alex thought. *The Ghost Patrol* fans would love Maeve. She was a paranormal reality TV superstar in the making. Where on earth was *the other dark place*?

She really needed to write some of this down. Or record it. But then she'd need parental permission and she really doubted Nick would give permission for this interview. Especially if he heard the details.

'Your dad said that to me too, about the cellar,' she told Maeve. Well, he'd said something like it anyway. 'What's down there?'

'It's just dangerous,' Maeve sighed. She started swinging back and forth again on the door jamb. 'Dark and scary. Like the woods. We're not meant to go there either. Especially not at night. Not without Daddy. You can get lost in there. Lost *forever*.' She gave Alex a very pointed look. The little girl didn't miss anything, did she?

Nick had almost lost his shit when he found Alex in the woods. And the excuse about the archaeology? Flimsy at best. Theo had died there. So had Dad. So maybe they weren't wrong either.

Daphne was so much better with children than Alex was. The same wavelength, she used to say. *They're sensitive, you know, Alex. They see things we've forgotten how to see.*

No, Alex was not going down that particular avenue right now. The house might give her the creeps, and nightmares, but that was only to be expected given what had happened the last time she was here. Bad dreams were the least of it. And as for the woods...

'Tell me about Daisy?' she asked, trying a different tack. Maeve clearly had an active imagination, and probably a host of imaginary friends. That would explain it. Alex had been like that once.

Behind her there was a dull thud. She turned sharply.

A book lay in the middle of the floor. It couldn't have fallen off anything, not and landed right there. But there it was, on the rug in the middle of the study.

Alex stared at it, and then looked for gaps in the shelves or anything that might explain it. There was nothing obvious.

Maeve giggled. 'Silly Daisy,' she said, 'always showing off.' And she skipped off, leaving Alex there, holding a circle of knotted reeds and twigs, staring at a book which couldn't possibly be where it was.

When she finally made herself pick it up, she found it was a book of family history. Her family. *The de Wildes of Kilfayne, 1805–1815.*

The page was open to a short entry.

Tragedy in Wildewood Hall.

6th March 1806, Margaret de Wilde, beloved daughter of Hugh, fifteenth Baron de Wilde, was victim of a tragic accident in the great hall. She was but seven years of age.

Just a year older than Maeve, Alex thought, and the chill that swept over her didn't feel natural at all.

CHAPTER 20

NICK

The woods were unsettled today. He could always tell. He felt it stirring beneath his skin, trailing through his hair, and winding itself around him from the moment he woke from what little sleep he got.

Sally said the woods had always reached out to those who needed them. And Nick needed them more than ever.

Alex had been lying on the floor at the foot of the stairs, just like Sally had been. That image was etched into his mind. He'd thought... God, for that horrific moment he'd thought she was dead too. And that it was all his fault.

Because it was all his fault. He had never been good enough. He had promised Patricia he'd try. But how?

He shook himself. He couldn't get lost in those feelings today. He had Maeve with him. He couldn't leave her in the house alone, and he needed to be alert while she accompanied him. She had already slipped off, back indoors when he was working at the front of the house. He'd fished her out of more than one supposedly locked room since Patricia had left her with him. Maeve could vanish in the blink of an eye, and he was beginning to suspect that she knew the ins and outs of Wildewood Hall even better than he did. Servants' stairs, attics, all the secret places, including the unsafe bits. She slept on the camp bed in his room and even that didn't help.

He needed to keep an eye on her. As well as everything else.

Maeve clung to his hand as they walked deeper into the woods, and she chatted away to him, telling him about something she'd made for Alex, and how the house didn't want her there.

That was what he was afraid of.

'You weren't bothering her, were you?' he asked.

'I never bother people, Daddy. I'm a joy.'

He stopped in his tracks and looked down at her.

'Who told you that, munchkin?'

Maeve smiled back up at him with blissful self-confidence. 'Granny.'

He breathed out slowly, forcing his racing heart to calm. Patricia. That made sense. Patricia had said it to Maeve. She had probably said it to Sally when Sally was a child.

Because Sally had always said that, laughing, whenever he called her out on something. It was frivolous, a joke between the two of them.

Don't be silly, mo stór. *I'm a joy.*

Later on Theo had joined in on it as well.

And God help him, they were. Just like Maeve. His joy.

Well, they had to be to contrast with him. The most miserable man in the world, Theo would always say with that trademark grin. Theo could always make him smile.

'What were you doing today, pet? If not pestering Alex? You wandered off while I was working in the gardens.'

'I picked flowers while you were there,' she protested. Yes, there had been some rather gorgeous cosmos in flower which had been decimated. 'And then I played a game of hide and seek.' She sighed. 'But then Cecil was cranky. So I came to find you.'

Cranky Cecil... Nick didn't want to dwell on that either.

Maeve's fancies, Patricia would say with a gentle smile. *Let her be a child, Nick. It all goes by so fast. Blink and you'll miss it. And you already miss too much.*

'I'm glad you came to find me,' he told her.

He squeezed Maeve's hand and then hefted her up in his arms, settling her on his shoulders. She squealed with delight and stretched her hands out to thread her fingers through the leaves hanging over the path.

The laughter ran through the woods, high and bright and full of joy. Birdsong answered. Just birdsong, he told himself.

'It's beautiful here, Daddy,' Maeve said.

And it was, when she was here.

'It is, but remember the rules.'

'I remember, I remember! Don't come in here without you. Don't stray from the path. Don't talk to strangers or play their games. Don't come in here after dark.'

'Good girl,' he murmured and all around him the wild murmured as well.

He wanted to believe the woods would never harm her. Not his Maeve. Not when he felt the way he did about her. He really wanted to believe that.

But the woods were wild. And she was so small.

'Let's go back to the house,' he told her.

'But we're not finished.'

He glanced up at her. She had her hands tangled in his hair, her blue eyes fixed on something through the trees.

'What do you mean, *mo stórín?*'

'Look,' she said, and pointed off through the trees. For a moment he saw nothing, and then the hare moved. It was little more than the flick of an ear, the blink of an eye. It was not there and then it was there, a pale golden brown, with amber eyes, watching him all too knowingly.

And behind it, a figure in green. Something made of leaves and twigs and moss. A trick of the light...

'Who's that, Daddy?' Maeve asked.

Nick stopped, his body like stone, his eyes filling with tears he couldn't let escape. He clung to Maeve now. Even up on his shoulders, holding onto him as he held onto her, he couldn't shake the feeling that at any second he might lose her. That she might wriggle free and be snatched away by the woods, vanish into their depths never to be found.

The wild woods closed around them both, whispering, sighing, murmuring.

'Just an old friend,' he said. 'Don't you worry about him. Let's go back, Maeve. It's getting late and Granny will be here to pick you up soon.'

'But – oh, he's gone.' She sounded so disappointed and Nick finally managed to breathe a sigh of relief. 'Is it like the house?' she asked.

'A little bit,' he said warily. How much could he tell her safely? He tried to treat it all like a game, but it wasn't. He knew it wasn't. 'But remember the cellar?'

He felt her tense suddenly and wished he'd never brought that up. 'Yes.' Her voice was suddenly small, the word little more than the *s* at the end.

'We don't go down there, do we?'

Maeve shook her head. 'Are the woods like that?' she asked, a tremble in her voice. She sounded like he had just broken her heart with that revelation.

If only that was all, he thought. But he couldn't tell her. No more than he could tell Alex. Not yet.

He prayed that somehow there would never be a need.

'Yes,' he said. Knowing it was only a half truth. Heaven knew, the house was bad but, if the mood took them, parts of the woods were so much worse.

CHAPTER 21

ALEX

It was a few hours later when Nick appeared to ask Alex if she wanted lunch. His eyes fell on the circlet she had placed beside her laptop on the desk, and he froze. Visibly froze. As if horrified or guilty.

Alex just waited, watching him. She wondered if he'd try to ignore it.

'Are you okay?' she asked eventually when he didn't seem able to make a decision.

'Oh,' he said and then made an apologetic face. 'Yes. Just that... Maeve gets these fancies into her head and makes...' He nodded at the circle. 'I'm sorry. She makes them all the time and hands them out to everyone as if they're important. You don't actually have to keep it.'

Alex put her hand out to touch it before he could try to take it away. 'It's fine. I like it. She's a very sweet kid.'

That brought a smile to his lips. He really did dote on her. And Alex wasn't lying. Maeve was sweet, if a little strange. And sad.

'Her mother...' she began and then stopped, feeling

awkward. It really was none of her business and if he didn't want to talk about it, she shouldn't ask.

Nick's smile fell a bit. He tried to hold onto it but didn't quite manage to stop it from slipping. 'She passed away two years ago.'

That was all he said, but it sounded so absolute that Alex didn't have the first clue how to ask any kind of follow-up question.

'I... I'm so sorry,' she blurted out. 'Maeve talked about her...' Oh God, this was beyond awkward. What was she doing? She had no right to interrogate him about his dead wife, for goodness' sake.

He nodded, looking just past her head, still not making eye contact. 'Maeve has something of an overactive imagination. Lots of imaginary friends, that kind of thing. Grief, her counsellor says. And trauma. She sometimes pretends Sally's still here. In the house.'

Alex racked her brains, trying to think of something... anything... to say. Grief and trauma. She remembered that all too well. She hadn't been as little as Maeve when she'd lost a parent. And she'd had Theo constantly at her side so there wasn't a lot of space for the imaginary friends. Still, there had been a few when she was here. She recalled that much.

It had to be lonely for Maeve. Wildewood Hall had been for her.

'Imaginary friends like Daisy?'

A brief bitter smile flashed over his mouth for a moment. He had an expressive mouth, she thought, now she could see it. And a good smile, even when it was tinged with heartbreak. His eyes softened a little and flickered over her face for just a moment.

'Yeah, Daisy.' He raked his fingers through his shaggy overlong hair. He may have shaved but he'd done nothing to trim his hair. But it suited him. There was something about him. Ragged and careworn, like the house. No, like the woods. Wild and a bit rough around the edges, but all the more beautiful for that.

She caught her thoughts and steered them back to safer ground.

Nick, all his rough edges and his shaggy hair, were none of her business, she reminded herself firmly. This was a man who was clearly still in mourning. And dealing with a young child who was not handling grief either. Having Alex here wasn't helping one bit.

'Let me show you something,' he said at last, with a heavy sigh, as if he'd been as caught in his own thoughts as she'd been.

He led her out into the hall, down towards the morning room, portraits all along the walls. This was the most time she'd spent looking at them since her grandfather quizzed her, and she noticed the features echoed in her own and Theo's, in Dad's faces. That haughty stare, those blue eyes, that smile...

She paused beneath a woman she didn't recognise, head held high, hair perfectly piled on top of her head, a length of pearls wrapped tightly around her long slender throat. Speaking of haughty, Alex thought with a shudder.

'Lady Eloise de Wilde,' Nick said. 'Your grandmother.'

No, that couldn't be right. Gran had never looked like that. True, she was young in the painting, no older than Alex was now, and Alex had only known her as an old woman. But *that* woman, the one in the painting... Alex didn't know her at all. It wasn't the laughing, patient Gran who had cared for her when she'd been here as a child while her grandfather had dragged Dad and Theo off to learn about being lord of the manor.

'No, that's not her. I met her when I was little. We used to visit.'

'Oh...' He sounded a bit bewildered, like he didn't want to argue with her, but something was wrong.

'What?' she asked. Why was he going all cryptic on her again? 'Just spit it out, Nick. I don't have time for this.'

It wasn't impatience. Not really. She was shaken and she didn't like the feeling one little bit.

'She died in 1967.'

Well, that was just stupid. He dad would have only been ten. Alex stared at the portrait for another long moment, studying it. 'Okay, well it couldn't have been her then. My gran... Gran was here when I was little. She looked after me while the men were off—' She waved a hand dismissively. 'Maybe she wasn't my actual grandmother then. A housekeeper, or something?'

Oh God, had her grandfather had a live-in lover that he'd pawned her off on? Gran had talked about him affectionately enough, as if he was a foolish but loveable man. Alex had never seen it herself. Gran had been the one to tell her that he was doing his best, that he was trying to help. Even that he was trying to protect her.

Her grandfather, protecting her? She'd not questioned it, partly because she'd not believed her. But what had he been protecting her from?

Nick chewed on his lower lip drawing her attention back to him. That was far too distracting a thing for her to contemplate right now. Because if she started thinking about his lips...

Alex drew in a deep breath. 'You wanted to show me this?'

Nick shook his head but didn't say anything further to her. There had to be a logical reason for him to show her. And why she remembered a different gran, one that couldn't be this woman. She'd work it out.

Another thing to research. There was every possibility that all this was some kind of new tactic to make her give up the house sale or... or... just to make her look like a fool. She didn't know. It was unsettling and she really didn't like it at all. But she followed him as he continued down the hall.

'This one,' said Nick, and stopped in front of a portrait of a young girl. It had to be a couple of hundred years old. She was golden-haired, with the de Wilde blue eyes, and she held a bunch of wildflowers in her small hands, not unlike the ones Maeve had woven into the circlet. Behind her, the line of the woods outside the house rose like a dark threat.

'Margaret de Wilde, youngest daughter of Hugh, the fifteenth Baron de Wilde. Died in 1806. She was seven. They called her Daisy.'

Alex frowned. Daisy...?

But before she could ask more questions, he turned around and waved his hand at another portrait. This was more modern, the girl in it from perhaps the 1920s. 'And this is Rosalind. You'll hear about Rose as well. And Dickie and Reg, Cecil, and maybe even Cornelius. And others. Maeve sees their portraits around the house, and in the books, the old photos and...' He sighed again.

She didn't press him in the brief pause. Her head was spinning. Those names.

'I wanted to take her to a psychologist last year but Patricia says she'll grow out of it eventually and to just let her have her childhood. Not to stifle her imagination, you know? But that's one of the reasons I don't really want her here in the house too much anymore. She stays with Patricia during the week because of school anyway. I thought she'd make friends in the village but...' Another sigh. His eyes glistened as he turned away and Alex felt the wave of pain coming off him as if it was a physical thing. 'She just tells us she already has friends here and they're more fun.'

Alex reached out before she thought about what she was doing, her hand coming up to the centre of his back, right between his shoulder blades. His body was warm but he was so tense, a coiled spring. All she meant to do was offer him a little comfort, a bit of understanding. But for a moment he froze, like an animal about to attack, or flee. Then, slowly, he seemed to relax into her touch. His scent wound itself around her again, as did the way she just needed to breathe him in. It was addictive. Intoxicating.

'I'm sorry,' she said again. 'I didn't mean to bring up the past.'

'The past has a habit of throwing itself right in your face around here, Alex. I'm sure you already know it.'

He nodded to a final portrait, one half in shadows at the end of the hall. A man in a linen shirt. A modern painting in oils, beautiful and so very true to life. As if he might step out of the frame at any second. Her father. In his thirties. The same age he was when he died.

But he hadn't looked like that when she last saw him.

'I've never seen that before,' she said, her throat so tight she had to force the words out.

'Your grandfather commissioned it after he died. Your dad, I mean, after he...' He trailed off awkwardly. 'You know.'

She nodded, staring. Unable to tear her gaze away. 'Mum always said he was handsome. I mean, I remember him but he was... he was my dad. I just thought he was old. I've seen photos of course, but... well, she put a lot of them away. And old photos degrade, don't they? I don't know where they went after Mum died. I suppose Ken has them somewhere... my stepfather, I mean...' She was rambling. She couldn't help herself. This portrait was so much more than any photo could ever capture. It was as though it had been plucked from her own memories. He was standing in a glade in the forest, green-gold light streaming around him through the leaves. The standing stones were just visible behind him.

Where he died, she thought bleakly. The woods outside this very house.

'Run, Alex! You have to run. NOW!'

No, that was earlier. That was in the house. Wasn't it?

The cold arched roof of stones closing over her and the stench of mulch.

She didn't remember. It was all tangled with nightmares, her recollection so confused. Why had she needed to run? What from? Had there been an intruder or... or something else?

He'd pulled her back from the patch of welling darkness, pushed her towards the narrow stairs and the shadows had closed in on him instead—

That had to be in the house, there wouldn't be stairs in the woods. But how could there be trees in the house?

The gleam of gold beneath rotting foliage. Eyes that didn't see, but saw everything, the mouth hanging open, hungry and waiting.

Had she gone to the woods afterwards? She must have...

... deep among the trees, she'd run, screaming for help, for Gran, for anyone. Because something had raced up behind her, something wild and terrible, a hunter, a beast...

A shudder ran through her. The memory was visceral, almost real. Far too vivid. She had to push it firmly away. That was a nightmare, not a memory. It had to be. None of that had happened.

Alex had found her father's body in the woods, not the house. A heart attack, they said.

How could she remember two things at once? What was she missing?

She dropped her hand away from Nick and he caught it in his. His touch was warm and solid, his fingers closing around hers, stroking her skin. He'd held her hand like that when she fell, while they waited for Patricia. He'd been there with her. Even though it must have been a waking nightmare for him.

'What are we like?' she murmured. 'Standing here, haunted by the dead.'

She ought to ask him about the portrait outside her room, that handsome man with the devilish eyes. Maybe she could get the two swapped around. Much better to see her father like that, smiling, bathed in sunlight, every morning. She reached for her phone in her pocket, intending to show him the photo of Blaise's portrait, and... and...

The laughter, dark and taunting, swept through the edges of her memory.

The air chilled around her, just for a moment, and then she was breathless as heat washed through her.

She was suddenly seized by a wild urge to just grab Nick's shirt and pull him towards her. To kiss him, press her body up against his, to feel that strength and that warmth. She remembered the thought that had swept over her when she first saw him, that she'd have to climb him like a tree and suddenly she wanted to try. To push him back against the polished wood panelling and...

Alex sucked in a breath, half desire and half terror. Nick was gazing down at her, his eyes huge and dark, his mouth parted. As if fighting to stop himself from doing the same.

God, how she wanted him to give in. How she wanted to give in. Her heartbeat was so loud she was sure he could hear it and that ache in the depths of her stomach made her breath catch in her throat.

Desire. Need. Lust.

She felt dizzy with it.

He was right there for the taking, something seemed to tell her. A whisper in her ear. A thrumming in her blood. Something twisting inside her, trying to make her abandon all caution to the winds.

'Take what you want. It's your right, after all, de Wilde.'

They had been talking about his dead wife, and dead children, and her dead father... but all she could think about right now was demanding that he show her what it meant to be alive in the most primal way possible.

Alex swallowed hard, the very action painful, as if something was lodged in her throat. She forced herself to step back. Nick released her hand, but stood there like one of those stones in the woods, still watching her. Like an oak, rooted to the spot, his face expressionless.

Nick didn't move for a moment, but then he bowed his head and shrugged his shoulders as if shaking off whatever ailed him. 'We should see where Maeve's got to,' he said, as if nothing had happened at all. 'She gets up to mischief here. I try to keep her out of the Hall as much as I can. You can understand why.'

She did. Grief did strange and terrible things. Especially with a small girl's overactive imagination. Especially in a house with such a dark history.

'You should have lunch, and maybe a lie-down afterwards. Come on, before you get dizzy again. You've been overdoing it. Patricia's picking Maeve up soon. I'll get her to take another look at you. She'll kill me if you have a relapse.'

It was an excuse but it was better than anything she had to hand right now. Whatever was happening between them, she couldn't let it happen again.

CHAPTER 22

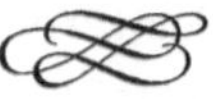

ALEX

That night, there was an addition to her dreams. Nick Walker.

His scent, the scent of the wild wood, the feeling of his strong arms closing on her, holding her, the murmur of his lips against her skin.

Alex woke several times in the night, flushed and breathless. He came to her in the darkness, worshipped her and their bodies wound together endlessly until all was pleasure and desire. His fingertips stroked her molten skin, his voice praising her in that now familiar low rumble. He knelt before her and his mouth devoured her, or pinned her against the damask wallpaper and wrapped her legs around his hips as he entered her with a swift and decisive movement. He spread her out on the bed, like an all too willing sacrifice to lust. His body moved against hers, hot and silken, but she could never quite see his face. His hand closed around her throat, never too hard, just enough to hold her wherever he wanted her, as he kissed her, as he filled her with desire and drove her to a delirious ecstasy. The warmth of him, that addictive musk, wound itself around her, like twisting sheets.

Each time she woke, she was sure she heard laughter. Cruel,

heartless laughter. Like someone or something had planted those dreams in her head to torment her.

Dreams, she told herself as her own fingers moved to finish what her dream had started. They were only dreams.

She could barely make eye contact with Nick the next day, not without feeling her cheeks flaming red and her stomach tightening in an undeniable reaction to his presence.

This wasn't right. She should not be having thoughts like that. Not about him. He worked here and technically she owned the place. Getting tangled with him would be a nightmare. A real legal nightmare.

Not to mention that his wife had died here. Or that his daughter thought she was still here. Was that better or worse? Did Nick believe it too? Was he tied here because of Sally's memory? It might explain why he was reluctant to leave. She'd decided to run a thousand miles from the place which had taken everyone she loved, but she'd understand the reverse as well.

The conversation about paintings and dead children had not helped. He'd been trying to explain Maeve's imaginary friends and all it had done was make Alex question her own memories. She hated it. Had he done it on purpose?

Was this some kind of ploy to drive her out of Wildewood Hall?

And dear God, the dreams were not helping.

It had been a while since she'd had sex, true, but she was a rational human being. She could control herself. But she'd never felt hungry to touch someone else, not like she had yesterday with Nick. Gabe used to tease her about it. A couple of her boyfriends had left because of it. One had called her a cold fish. Another had been even less flattering.

Nick mostly seemed intent on avoiding Alex as much as possible, which was fine. Probably sensible. The less time they spent alone together the better. He was probably afraid she'd try to jump him again, and to be honest so was she. It was the most embarrassing thing about all of this.

That and the fact she couldn't shake the wanting. Yes, it was definitely better to stay out of each other's way. Avoid temptation.

He had work to do as well, mostly out on the estate. He was just doing his job.

Alex should have been working on her book but she was having to spend more time wrangling the lawyers who were getting absolutely nowhere. Apparently, the situation with the inheritance had got a lot more complicated, as there was some kind of entailment involved which stretched back through generations of the de Wilde line. It tied the remaining land to the house, and the house to the family, in ways Alex didn't really understand. With no male heir, the title Baron de Wilde would revert to the Crown. Which was fine by her. She certainly didn't want it.

But that left the estate in limbo, because the title belonged to the English Crown and the land was in Ireland and while there was documentation going back hundreds of years it was in no way clear what legally should happen to it now. There were various covenants as well, mostly relating to the woodland for some obscure reason, which many of her vaunted ancestors had drawn up. Layers and layers of complications. Including the latest one which Theo had drawn up for Nick and Nick's job.

Sure, the feckless wonder could do that, but not write down a simple bloody will.

It was a nightmare.

She could fight it in court, they told her. It could all be untangled. The law firm assured her of that. But at the same time, Gordian knots were mentioned, and she had to look that up – an impossible tangle which could not be unravelled, which Alexander the Great had cut apart with his sword.

She wasn't Alexander the Great. More like Alexandra the

Moderately Competent in Her Own Field. She didn't have a sword.

Alex glanced up at the wall visible through the door of the study where a dozen weapons of various shapes and sizes had been mounted long ago on either side of that ghastly mirror. Okay, maybe she did have a sword. Several. But that wasn't the point.

Untangling the legal mess around the estate would take time. And money.

So much money.

Money she didn't have.

And worse, because of it the hotel people were getting cold feet. There was no bargain to be had here, not anymore. If she couldn't pay to take the court case, they would have to. And they didn't want that outlay. Or the effort. What had looked like a quick and profitable deal was turning into something no one wanted to touch.

Alex fought not to curse out loud, kept her voice calm and professional, and tried to ignore the stinging in her eyes.

The only way she was getting out of this was to take court cases in at least two different jurisdictions with uncertain outcomes which would cost a fortune.

And then she'd probably have to take Nick to court as well. Even though it would be best for them both to create as much distance between them as quickly as possible. He had a contract, she reminded herself. It let him live and work here. And to do that to him... to take even the small comfort that living here might give him without so much as a by your leave... She really didn't want to do that. She could see now what this place meant to him, his last link to his wife. He might not want Maeve here – understandably given her imaginary friends – but he couldn't let go either, could he?

Alex sat in the study, her back to the window overlooking the drive, and pinched the bridge of her nose. From the corner of her eye, through the door, she could see at the ancient mirror on the far wall of the hall through the open door. She could see herself in it as she leaned back in the chair at the desk. Movement caught her attention, just a flicker of something in the corner of the mirror. Her breath caught in her throat as she turned to study it more carefully. There was nothing there. No one else in the house.

But she was sure.

Just for a moment, anyway. She forced herself to exhale, slowly, carefully. Made herself drop her tense shoulders and twist her neck to the side to loosen the taut wire of her muscles.

She closed her eyes, letting herself imagine some kind of much needed relief. She was so tightly wound after her dreams. It might be a fantasy, but didn't she deserve that? Just a little one?

Hands came to rest on her shoulders, massaging, caressing. Strong and clever hands, so very gentle and relaxing. Slim with long, dexterous fingers. They worked her tension free. Fingertips brushed against her throat and she let her head fall back with a soft groan of relief. She was so surprised, she couldn't think of a thing to say.

What was Nick doing in here? She hadn't even heard him come in. Since that moment in the hall when she'd rubbed his back, he'd been trying to avoid her, she was sure of it. She'd been stupid, that was all, and she'd only wanted to offer some comfort. And now, here he was, more than returning the favour. And God, he knew what he was doing with his hands, that was for sure...

But they didn't feel like his hands. His were broad and powerful, calloused from hard work while at the same time tender and unbearably gentle.

A breath of cold air riffled through her hair, a soft laugh which brushed against her.

Alexandra, the voice murmured. Not Nick's voice. The

accent was all wrong. Not an actual voice at all. It was a sigh on the breeze, a whisper that ran through the house.

But it said her name.

And then the hands tightened around her throat and squeezed.

Alex's eyes snapped open in shock, and in the mirror... in the old silver-backed mirror out there in the hall, she could see herself, pale and helpless against the too bright window behind her. Faces pressed up against the other side of the ancient glass, grey and faded, or rather images of faces like old photographs, but they moved. They sobbed and cried out. They were trying to escape, hands pressing against the other side of the mirror, faces trying to push their way through. A host of them, old and young, male and female, pale and ghostly faces...

And in the midst of them, between her and the window, loomed a huge black shadow.

It coiled over her like a storm cloud. It twisted around her body, a band of it tight around her throat, tightening still, choking her.

She gave a strangled cry and tried to pull herself free, but the shadow held her fast, and the air turned icy. She was frozen there, trapped, as it crushed against her skin, and then, to her rising horror, slid underneath her flesh. Lines of ice ran through her veins, and a rush of frozen air rippled over her flesh, like breath, but cold, so cold.

This couldn't be happening. She was seeing things, feeling things, that were not real. Could not be real. It was a nightmare. It had to be a nightmare.

With one final effort, Alex threw herself off the chair and onto the floor. Objects crashed down around her, books, framed photos, anything that had been sitting on the desk, including her laptop and headphones.

And Maeve's little circle of twigs and dried flowers.

Alex didn't know what made her do it but she managed to

fling out her hand and it closed on the charm. She clutched at it convulsively, twigs and thorns and God knew what digging into her skin. She could feel the dry flowers crushing in her fist. But still she hung onto it. Gran had always said those little woven things were a protection. Maeve had said more or less the same thing.

Abruptly, the force surrounding her was gone.

As if it had never been there at all. Like a door had been closed on a wind, or a machine turned off. It was just gone.

She lay still, breathing hard, shivering. On the floor yet again.

'Alex?' Nick's voice, strangely echoing, far away. 'Alex? Are you okay?'

No. No she was not. She couldn't explain what she'd just seen and felt. Unless...

She'd fallen and cracked her head only a few days ago. Perhaps these were side effects of that. If this was a case on the show that was exactly what she would have said. She would have meant it kindly enough, showing concern for the poor person hallucinating and terrified of her own shadows. It felt so dismissive now.

Her hand shook, but she couldn't bring herself to let go of the charm. She needed it. It had saved her. Hadn't it?

What had Maeve said? The house wasn't good for her. No shit. It never had been. Not for any of them.

CHAPTER 23

ALEX

'Alex?'

Nick thundered into the study like some kind of giant, heedless of whatever else might be in here tormenting her.

Nothing. There was nothing. Dear God, Alex, she told herself, get a grip.

She didn't know what had just happened but it wasn't ghosts. There was no such thing as ghosts. There was always a logical explanation.

Unfortunately, at the moment, that logical explanation was that she had suffered a traumatic brain injury.

No. Not that either.

She tried to make herself breathe, as she pushed herself up from the ground.

Nick caught her, lifted her back into the chair, his eyes frantic. 'What happened?'

'Nothing. I...'

He'd want to call Patricia. And then it would be hospitals and brain scans and medication and who knew what else.

No. Just no.

'I fell over.' Oh God, that was worse.

He was so close. She could see the flicker of disbelief in his eyes, the way he frowned at her in excruciating detail. He leaned over her, one hand on either arm of the chair as he studied her so there was no way she could escape.

'What happened?' he said again, more gently this time, but still painfully insistent. Slowly, carefully. 'You can tell me. No matter how strange it might seem. I know this place, remember? I live here. I—'

And there it was again. He lived here. She was about to throw him out of his home. The guilt of it rushed up inside her. And after it came indignation.

'I'm fine,' she said, aware of the stubborn tone in her voice. He glanced down. She was still clutching the charm Maeve had made, so tightly that she risked crushing it.

'You saw something,' he whispered. It almost felt like an accusation.

'I saw...' She stared up into his face and desperately wanted to tell him. To admit it. She hadn't just seen something. She had *felt* something, *heard* something, something had *attacked* her... But if she did that, it would make it real. And she was all about challenging superstitious nonsense, about uncovering frauds and revealing truth.

It couldn't be ghosts. It simply couldn't be. She had lived her whole life disproving that, over and over again.

If she even suggested it to Gabe and the others she would never live it down.

If it wasn't her imagination or a hallucination, someone had to be doing this to her, someone who wanted to scare her so much she left Wildewood Hall. And the most obvious candidate for that was Nick Walker.

Alex had lived through a campaign of intimidation once. Just because she had stood up to a terrible man and exposed him for the monster he was. She was not afraid of Nick. She'd seen monsters in real life. They didn't have to be supernatural.

The land of the living was more dangerous by far.

Then Nick's left hand came up to cup the side of her face, his touch so gentle and careful, tender. As if she was something to be treasured and cherished. This man she barely knew.

She ought to flinch back or pull away. She ought to tell him to back off. Accuse him of... of... whatever it was she thought he was doing. Trying to frighten her off, make her doubt her sanity or her belief. She ought to tell him to go to hell.

She did none of those things.

Alex pushed herself up and kissed him. She didn't know why. She didn't really know how she found the strength. But she had to do it. It didn't feel like she had a choice in the matter.

His lips met hers, warm and hungry in a way that made her ache inside. His hand still cradled her face, and she grabbed his shoulder to keep herself upright. His mouth opened to her and Alex pressed on, a desperate and needy kiss, her tongue darting forward to meet his. He knew what he was doing, that was for sure. It was the kiss of a man who knew how to kiss, knew the nuances of pressure and how to use lips, tongue and teeth to devastating effect. Alex gasped into his mouth and was answered by a low rumbling moan in his chest. A sound of need. Perhaps of submission.

She wanted him. Wanted him more than she could ever remember wanting another human being. She pushed him back without releasing him until the backs of his legs were at the edge of the desk and he was forced to sit on it, still kissing her, his hands beginning an exploration of their own now. She pulled at his t-shirt so she could slip her fingers underneath it. His body was tight and superbly muscled, a lean and powerful creature made from hard work. His abs jumped beneath her touch and, moments later, his hands had found the curve of her breast on one side, and of her waist on the other. He pulled her against him and there was no doubting his arousal now. She could feel him through the jeans, hard for her. The shape of it burned against her body, and she moved, pressing closer until he gasped aloud.

And how she wanted him.

Any second now, any moment...

That soft, sibilant laugh rippled through the room, dark and dangerous. Nasty. Someone was laughing at her. At the two of them.

Someone or something.

Alex froze and Nick pulled back, his dark eyes widening in horror. Actual horror. He was almost lying back on the desk and Alex was astride him, ready to pin him down and ride him into oblivion given half the chance. They were still half clothed. Barely. The relevant half, which was a relief.

'I—' she began, and stopped because she simply didn't know what to say. There weren't any words. This was awful.

'I should—' His voice failed him too. He licked his lips and she felt a wild urge to kiss him again. Consume him. Make him hers.

Alex slid off him, trembling with the effort of withdrawing, and the shame of what had just almost happened.

'Alex,' he murmured and he sounded so unsure. Regretful... and something else. Something like guilt.

She let herself slump back into the chair, her face flaming as she forced herself to look at him, sitting on the edge of the desk, still painfully aroused. Her face heated with embarrassment and tears stung her eyes.

Fuck, she thought. Fuck, shit and indeed, bollocks.

What had she been thinking? Well, no, not thinking. She had not been thinking at all. He was an employee. She owned this place. If the legal team found out about this... Oh Jesus Christ, what had she done?

'I'm sorry,' she whispered. 'I don't know... I didn't mean... that was...'

Inexcusable. She didn't know what had come over her. She had no words for how bad it was. These were all things she should be saying but the words kept dying in her throat when she tried to voice them. What on earth could she say?

'It's the house,' he said. 'Sometimes it just...' At her confused look he trailed off, unwilling to finish.

'The house?'

'You've sensed it, haven't you? You've seen them, heard them? Please, Alex, I'm sorry. I should have said something right from the start. But I—'

The house? How was he using the *house* as an excuse?

'That had nothing to do with the house, Nick.' She couldn't keep the snap out of her voice.

The problem was she didn't know what had caused it or why. All she had known was that she wanted him. She wanted him so badly it made her crazy. He was handsome, unbearably so. And beneath the grumpy exterior was a man who used it as a defence, as a way to turn people away and protect himself and his daughter... and this house too. No doubt about it. He was trying to get her out of Wildewood Hall. Was this all part of that plan? A new tactic? Seduce her and then blackmail her?

Or just convince her she was seeing things, hearing things, sensing things, that the house of her nightmares was out to get her? It had all the trappings of a haunting that would make *The Ghost Patrol* team lose their collective shit, send the fans into paroxysms of delight online and launch the ratings through the roof.

But she didn't believe in any of that. Not really.

The alternative though? That she was losing her mind, that she was hallucinating, that she had just tried to assault a man twice her size, an employee no less...

Oh God...

'You have to know the reputation this place has,' Nick continued as if she hadn't said anything at all. He hadn't moved away. Just sat there on the edge of the desk, his legs still framing her, gazing down at her, like some kind of glorious Celtic sex god with his long, dishevelled hair, and the huge dark eyes, pupils still wide with desire, flecks of green and gold in the deep brown encircling them. His mouth, his throat, his hands... the way those hands had felt on her bare skin...

She felt her body starting to respond all over again, the heat inside her rising, the need to reach out and brush her fingertips over his skin, to breathe him in again.

Don't think about that, she told her brain, her brain which just laughed at her and went on doing what it wanted.

'I know about the ghost stories,' she told him. 'I don't believe them. I have spent my life showing people that ghosts don't exist. I don't believe in ghosts.'

'What if they believe in you?' he asked, as if it was the most normal question in the world.

Somewhere in the house a door slammed. Then another. And a third. One after the other, all the doors in Wildewood Hall, it seemed. Alex stared only at Nick, and frowned.

'Who are they?' she asked, quietly. All her walls were crumbling, and she was losing the battle to hold on to her staunch scepticism.

He shrugged and that shadow of grief flickered over his beautiful features. 'Anyone who ever died here. They're trapped. All of them. That's what Theo thought anyway. He was sensitive to it. Like you.'

'And this?' She waved a still shaking hand between the two of them. He got her meaning thankfully because she wasn't ready to start describing what had just happened. Not right now.

Got her meaning and a hell of a lot more, it seemed.

Nick blushed. Actually blushed, the colour rising high on

his face, and all down his neck, down below the fabric of his rumpled t-shirt. Alex found her mouth going dry again at the thought of that flush spreading across the perfect chest she'd caught a frantic glimpse of, the one her hands had ranged across.

She had to force her breath to calm again, and she waited.

Nick hung his head and chewed on his lower lip in far too distracting a fashion before finally answering. 'Yeah. This. This happens. Like, not to everyone. There has to be something there first. A spark, an attraction, but it happens. Like this... to you, to me... And Theo too. There's one ghost – I mean, not just one, there's loads but one in particular – more active than any of the others. Stronger. He plays games with people, with emotions. With desire. They call him the Master of the Revels, Blaise Chambers.'

Alex knew that name.

'Blaise?' A shiver ran up her spine, and she recalled the painting outside her room. His portrait.

The one she'd tried to take down, which someone had hung back up, the one she had been meaning to ask Nick to remove, but somehow the thought always seemed to slip her mind before she could.

That Blaise Chambers...

And suddenly a flood of memories came to her.

'*Behave or Blaise will get you.*' Her father used to laugh about it. Gran had not found it funny at all.

Chambers was said to appear from time to time, walking the halls, lounging in the morning room or the drawing room, and Alex knew of incidents in family lore where servants and guest fled in horror after a night here thanks to Blaise and his wandering ghostly hands.

Arnold had mentioned him too.

Alex remembered the Latin on the painting, that knowing face and the triumphant smirk...

Omnes contra omnes, quos amabant, convertam, et meam, corpus et animam, faciam.

Arnold's research suggested that, when he died, Chambers had left that message scrawled on the walls of this very house, over and over again. Some of the more gruesome versions of the tale said it was in blood, because why not? One portrait was not enough. Not for him.

How he had done that when his last living victim, or lover depending on the story, Richard, the sixteenth Baron de Wilde, had blown his chest open with a musket, Alex didn't know, but when did such folktales make sense?

There was even a story about the lost de Wilde treasure, stolen by the man who had manipulated and tried to destroy them. There was a book about him on the shelf over there too, she thought. But she didn't want to go anywhere near it right now.

Then something hit her.

The links Arnold had sent reported that some people heard the sound of his parties – or orgies, more correctly – but when investigated found all the ground floor rooms quiet and empty. There were so many rumours and half-remembered tales about the man, in life and in death, that he had entered into legend. And, she hadn't put two and two together at the time...

But she'd heard them too.

In her dreams, but also when she was younger, when she stayed here. But her recollections were so muddled between reality and dreams...

'Sally used to say... when he wants something... Alex, he doesn't stop. He manipulates people. Me, Sally, Theo...' Nick stopped, drawing in a shaky breath, and Alex tried to figure out what on earth that meant. Because she didn't really want to ask, or find out. 'And he never stops. Not until he has what he wants.'

She swallowed hard, her throat almost too tight to do so.

'And what does he want?' She knew the answer that was coming. There wasn't really any other answer possible. But that didn't mean she actually wanted to hear it.

Nick said it anyway, and the crushing finality of it all closed around her like a trap.

'You. He wants you. The last of the de Wildes.'

CHAPTER 24

NICK

They retreated to the safety of the kitchen, carefully positioning themselves on either side of the huge wooden table, like it was a barricade between them. Safer that way.

Because if the Master of the Revels wanted the two of them together... it was best not to be. Not until they could work out why.

Nick couldn't explain what had happened up there in the study. It was horribly embarrassing because he couldn't deny that he was attracted to Alex and had been from the first. But that had not been him up there. And he thought it had probably not been her either. Not entirely, anyway.

Alex was still pale, her hand trembling as she cradled the mug of tea. He could have got one of the nicer tea sets out. Probably should have. But this was all he could manage right now.

What would Theo have said? Alex was his sister. And Nick's relationship with Theo had been complicated enough already.

And Sally – dear God, what would Sally have said?

What did he tell Alex? What could he tell her about them,

about everything that had happened? How would she take that? Things were bad enough as it was.

He closed his eyes and reached out, trying to detect that trace of Sally that sometimes followed him when he was in the house. This had been their home, all three of them. But she wasn't here. Not now.

He wasn't sure what worried him more – that she was avoiding him, or that he had somehow driven her away.

Or that with Alex here, Blaise Chambers' power had finally swallowed her up entirely, the protection she had afforded him for so long now vanished. The ghosts were loose and the hall was so active right now... all because Alex was here. Of that he was certain.

'Ghosts,' Alex said after a long drawn-out silence.

That brought his attention back to her and he tried not to stare. She looked like an angel sitting there, or like one of those portraits in the main hallway. The de Wilde women were beautiful, all of them. And they either left the house or led short and miserable lives. Even the ones who had married in from the village, and there had been more than a few.

And now Alex was back here and had nowhere else to go. She might not call herself de Wilde, but that clearly didn't matter.

The house knew. That was obvious.

'Ghosts,' he replied, not sure where this was going.

'And you knew.'

'Everyone knows. You knew, although you denied it,' he said, aware of the defensive tone in his voice. He couldn't help it. 'The house is famous for it. Ask anyone.'

She gave him a look. Sally would have been proud of that look.

'I think you know a lot more than what everyone else knows, Nick. I don't know what happened to me in there but...' Her voice trailed off, confused and embarrassed. Well, quite. It said a lot about her that she was horrified by how close they had come to… whatever they had come close to doing. At the same time, that stung. But at least he had an idea what was causing it. Or rather *who* was causing it.

'The Master of the Revels,' he said solemnly.

'The painting outside my bedroom,' she said, an adversarial tone in her voice he was starting to recognise all too well. 'Did you put it there?'

He shook his head. He didn't know the painting. He hadn't moved any of the portraits.

'I took it down,' Alex said. 'And then it was back up. I tried to get rid of it that night, when I fell on the stairs.' He didn't dare correct her. He recalled his own experiences of that night far too clearly, but no painting. 'I want it gone, Nick.'

'I'll see to it,' he promised. That was the least he could do. 'But he isn't tied to a painting. He's a power inside these walls.'

Alex fixed him with another glare which called him a liar and a fraud.

'A great excuse,' she muttered.

He sighed, feeling defeated already. 'It's really not.'

She narrowed her eyes, the denial back in them, plain to see. 'A ghost did not make me try to jump your bones, Nick.'

He was tempted to ask her what did then and indeed who had been doing the jumping, if only to see her face go red again. She even blushed attractively.

But was that his thought? Or something else?

Damn it, Sally, where are you when I need you?

He needed to try another tack.

'Look, you have experience investigating ghosts and hauntings, don't you?' He spread his arms wide. 'So why not investigate this? Prove it, one way or the other. And if you *can* prove it, lay it all to rest. Exorcise them or whatever it is you do.'

'That's Daphne's field,' Alex said, as if it was obvious. 'Not mine. I'm the voice of reason. And ninety-nine times out of one hundred I'm the one who's right.' Alex took a moment to drink her tea. Behind that perfect mask of a face, he could sense her mind working. Perhaps she was actually considering it. Christ, he hoped so. Ignoring this was not going to help anyone. In fact, he had a feeling it was downright dangerous. She had to see that, didn't she?

'You could ask your friends to come over and help?' he offered. But more people was probably a terrible idea. The more people, he feared, the more energy for whatever lurked here to feed off. It was the other reason he kept Maeve as far away from the house as he could. He had promised Sally. Nick did his best to keep everyone else away from Wildewood Hall. It was his duty. And to let people just wander around here...

But perhaps if she had her team around her, her friends, people who knew what they were doing, perhaps then...

'No, absolutely not,' Alex replied firmly, as if shocked he would even suggest it. 'You have no idea of the circus it would turn into. And Gabe would—' She winced and then shook her head adamantly. 'Can you imagine what the spin would be? It would make sensational television. All of it. Gabe is an expert at that. Master of the Revels would be Master of the Orgies in no time. Sex ghosts and people unable to control themselves and...' Her breath caught in her throat. She made herself exhale slowly and Nick could imagine what she was picturing. But at the same time, he could still taste her, still feel her skin under his fingertips and feel the sensation of her warm weight straddling his lap, pressing down on him... 'No. Just no.'

Problem was, orgies were probably the least of it, if the stories were to be believed. Devil worship. Human sacrifice. Rituals and abominations.

It hadn't stopped with the death of Blaise Chambers either. Two hundred years later, his spirit lingered on, and when he targeted someone, went to work on their mind and their soul...

Nick still remembered the look in Theo's eyes. The guilt, the shame, the horror.

He couldn't tell her that. Not about her own brother. About what he'd done...

'But there had to be a logical explanation,' Alex went on. 'There is always a logical explanation.'

'Ninety-nine times,' he said. 'What was the other one then?'

This time she outright scowled, caught by her own phrasing. 'It's a figure of speech.'

He had a feeling that was a lie.

Alex cursed softly to herself and then relented. 'All right, I'll talk to them. I'll get the equipment. And get them on research help. But they are *not* coming here. You said Sally knew about the ghosts here. Can you tell me what she said?'

There was a hesitancy in her question, that natural urge to avoid bringing up a lost loved one. Nick knew it well. But he owed her this.

And if he didn't come clean now he never would.

CHAPTER 25

NICK

'Sally was...' Nick paused, trying to find the words for everything Sally had been. Laughing, dancing, smiling Sally. He had found her in the wild wood, like something out of an ancient legend, her long dark hair loose, her feet bare. Because that was Sally. There was a time before Sally but it was like a sketch in pencil compared to the technicolour world he'd found with her, and with Theo. 'Long ago they would have called her a witch,' he said with a softer smile. 'Or fairy-touched or something. But she was just... Sally saw the world in a different way. I had no idea what that was until I met her. She called me here, she said. Just reached out on the wind through the trees and I came. I don't even remember why I ended up here, but I did. Her explanation is as good as any.'

Alex wore a tiny frown. 'She sounds like Daphne.'

Nick shrugged. He didn't know Daphne but he didn't doubt what Sally had been able to do. How could he when he'd seen it and felt it and known the truth of it?

'She was sensitive to the house and the land. The women of her family were the ones in the legends, the wise women of Kilfayne. You've heard of them, haven't you?'

Alex nodded, a smile spreading over her expressive mouth. 'My gran was full of stories about them. Said we were related, I think. Some of them married de Wildes. Sally told you the same folklore then?'

She did more than that. *Understand*, she'd whispered to him on their wedding night, as they lay together naked in the wild wood, entwined on moss and leaves, *that this binds us. The wild protects us and, in turn, we protect the land, Nick. It's a solemn duty. But you have to enter into it willingly. It's a sacred vow. Lay claim to this land and it will lay claim to you as well.*

And he had. He had thought he had understood the implications. But he had thought they would be together forever, just the two of them. That whatever they faced, they would do it together.

He'd been a fool. And now he was as trapped as any of the ghosts here.

When Theo came, and the ghosts just got worse and worse… and Sally and Theo… and then Theo had been all he had left and…

No way he was about to tell Alex any of that.

'What do you know about the house?' he asked.

Alex lifted her hands. As much as anyone else probably. It was her family history, even if she didn't want it. 'When we came here as kids our grandfather told us all about the various generations. He would have had us believe that the land here had been some of the earliest inhabited on the island.'

'And he was right. He researched it, conducted archaeological excavations. You get your scientific mind from him, I think,' Nick said. She made a face, which he chose to ignore. Not the time to get into her animosity to her grandfather. He could understand it given what Theo had told him about the way the old man had treated her. *Like he wanted to drive her away even when we were little,* Theo had said. And maybe he wasn't wrong either. 'He changed, over the years, or so Patricia says. She knew him when they were younger. He became bitter after his wife died. The influence of the house, or so she thinks. He was isolated here and the hall... it works on people, like I said... You see the problem.'

Alex barely suppressed a laugh this time. 'You think I'll get stuck here and become a miserable shut-in spinster? Or a sex addict?' He knew better than to answer that. She must have read the hesitation too because she sobered instantly. It wasn't a laughing matter. 'Well... anyway, moving on. What did his research show?'

'There was a prehistorical settlement here. A ritual landscape of forest and stone. What little remains of that is—'

'The stone circle.' She was quick. Or she knew the stories. Not quite in the same way he did perhaps. She thought it was all made up, but he knew better. He knew the forest, knew the stones...

Where her father died. Where he had found Theo.

He pushed on.

'Yes. There was a cairn in the ring of megaliths. Long gone now. The story goes they destroyed it to build the original keep. They used the stones in the earliest foundations. There's evidence everywhere. The lintel in the drawing room fireplace has carvings which marked the entrance. Or so the archaeologist thought.'

What kind of fool took apart an ancient monument to build a house? There were a thousand stories of what a stupid idea messing with them was from all over the island. You stayed away from anything that might belong to the good folk, you never touched what was theirs or wandered into their places. And all the truly ancient places belonged to them.

'Yeah, the de Wildes were always clever like that,' she muttered. 'So the house is cursed.'

'Something like that.'

She sighed. 'All right. Dangerous forest. Cursed house.' Like she was ticking it off a list. 'And what does that mean?'

'That anyone who dies here is trapped here. That it feeds on their spirits, uses them. But it also uses the living. And it changes them.'

She drank the end of the tea. It had to be cold by now, but she drank it anyway.

Changes them. An understatement. But she didn't ask how.

'It's just old stories, Nick. It has to be. This country is full of them. We end up rerouting motorways to avoid a fairy tree, or attributing the downfall of a business empire to moving a grave. This is an old house. Of course it's going to be weird. There are so many things that could explain what's happening here.'

Her eyes were warm with something like bitter amusement now and he felt his shoulders lose a little of that tension. She wasn't dismissing him outright. That had to be good, didn't it? But she wasn't scared either. She was... she was remarkable. She was working through the problem as if it was something from her show. And she was right. Not all of the wild stories about this house could be true. Everything grew with the telling and people had been telling stories about Wildewood for a very long time.

'I do know that there are spirits trapped in this house,' Nick said. 'I've sensed them. Maeve *sees* them, talks to them...'

'Daisy and Rose.' The good humour was gone. It was almost animosity at the mention of those names.

'Yes. Not so imaginary friends. Theo said that when the two of you were kids—'

Of course, she shut that down straight away. He'd known she would. Theo had talked about it, and said Alex refused to admit to anything that happened back then.

'Oh look, we made up all kinds of things when we were kids.' The abruptness told him her brother had been right. Theo had been the one to tell him to try to keep Maeve away from the house in the first place. Much good it had done any of them.

'They are as real as you and I. Most of them are just trapped. No more than lost souls, looking for a way out, echoes of what they were in life.' He didn't mention that they were prey to Blaise Chambers.

Alex set down the empty mug and leaned forward, elbows on the table, her hands laced together under her chin, studying him with far too keen an eye for his comfort. He tried not to squirm.

'What do you want from me, Nick? If it's so dangerous here, why not just shut it all up and leave? Go and live with Maeve somewhere else and be safe? Why are you so invested in this place? I know Theo gave you a job and you feel you have a duty to him, but we can come to an arrangement, especially if I could just sell the estate and have done with it. I won't see you out of pocket, I promise.'

Hadn't she been paying attention at all? His fists clenched. 'You can't. *Please*, Alex, listen to me. You can't.'

She had shifted back in her chair, ready, he realised, to run if she needed to. Her face had gone pale again. She was afraid.

Afraid of him.

It was like a punch to the stomach, sharp and sickening. He'd seen it that day in the woods too. The last expression he wanted to see on anyone's face, but especially on hers. What had happened to her to create that instinctive reaction? The memory of her body against his, her lips demanding his submission, of her pushing him back beneath her... The heat, the desperation, the rising urge to...

Nick swallowed hard and pushed it away. He forced himself to sit still, unfurling his fingers and placing his hands flat on the wood of the table. Grounding himself. Making himself as small and unthreatening as possible. He could not afford to lose control. Not here. Not with her.

'Sally died in this house,' he murmured softly. 'She's trapped here too. I can't leave while she's here. I can't desert her. I made a promise.' Something stung his eyes and he had to blink away the tears. His throat had gone tight. 'Theo and I both did.'

'Theo,' she murmured. Her eyes had grown wider now, and they welled with tears which glittered like broken glass, so bright a blue, so like her brother's. 'He's trapped here too.'

That was the one good bit of news he had for her. He shook his head. 'Theo, and your father, died in the woods. There are sometimes hints of them here but... But the others... the children, your ancestors, their friends and servants... the ones who died in the house... they're trapped. Some of them have become part of the evil lurking here, but some still resist it. Not that it matters. They're all victims. I vowed to help them, and so far I've failed on every front.'

Her chair scraped against the tiles as she pushed it back. Before he knew what was happening, she had made her way around the table and wrapped her arms around him, holding him close. It was a gentle touch. No heat, no passion. Not this time.

But right at this moment it was everything he needed. Alex held him and suddenly all that grief and anger subsided. Nick melted into her embrace and it almost felt like coming home. She believed him, he realised. Not entirely, perhaps, but enough to want to help.

And that was enough.

CHAPTER 26

ALEX

Of course the call was a disaster. Alex had known what Gabe would say long before she actually tried to tell them what was going on. Not that she told them everything.

They definitely didn't need to know about the incident in the study for one thing. Or about anything resembling orgies. The sounds could be explained... somehow.

'We'll come over!' Gabe told her, eyes shining. 'We can sort out flights and be there before you know it. I'll make the calls—'

'No,' she told him as firmly as possible. 'Besides, you have contracts in place. You can't afford to piss off the network, Gabe, and you know it.'

He gave her that plaintive puppy look. Once upon a time it might have even worked.

'But Alex, it's a breakout opportunity. They'll understand, hell, they'll love it, and besides—'

'There is no besides. I'm here. I'm on site. And I don't want you all here. If the stories about this place are true, it's too risky anyway.'

Daphne sucked in a breath which almost sounded delighted and Alex frowned at her. 'I don't believe it.'

'Believe what?'

'*You.* You're starting to come around at last.'

'No, I am not. I'm talking about practicality. Parts of the Hall are unsafe. I can't have you lot tramping around wherever and getting hurt. I don't even think there are enough bedrooms in a fit state to be used.' That was her excuse and she was going to stick to it.

'It's a *castle*, Alex,' Gabe chided.

'You have a vastly inflated opinion of what that means around here. This isn't a fairy tale. There's, like, six habitable rooms. You're not coming over and that's that.'

'Besides,' said Daphne with a wicked grin which boded nothing good, 'she wants to keep the Sasquatch to herself.'

Alex suppressed a growl. 'Don't call him that. Leave Nick alone.'

'*Oh?*' Daphne purred the sound with one of those shit-eating grins. She was a born matchmaker that one. Not always successfully. She'd fixed Alex and Gabe up after all.

Gabe's tone was a lot more suspicious. 'And what exactly do you know about this Nick guy, other than your brother gave him a free ride?'

Alex wasn't about to let him start in on that. 'Enough,' she growled. 'Or I'll end this call and just sort it out myself.'

It was like wrangling small children. Maeve was better behaved than these lot. Alex took a deep breath, trying to centre herself.

'I did turn up some more information,' Arnold said in that soft voice. He always waited for a lull to chime in.

'What?' asked Gabe.

Arnold cleared his throat as if in preparation to deliver a lecture. 'Okay, so, Blaise Chambers, the Master of the Revels, was killed by Richard de Wilde, the sixteenth baron. That's Hugh's son, right? The report says in late August 1826 he lay in wait in the kitchen and shot Chambers through the heart as he came out of the cellar. He was the only one of his immediate family left alive and blamed Chambers for their deaths.' She heard him clicking on his keyboard, looking for a reference in his notes. 'That's possibly where the whole curse of the de Wildes story starts. Difficult to say because the records before this are patchy and a lot of it's just hearsay. The curse was meant to be hardest on their daughters. *Marry young,* one of them wrote to her sisters, *whoever will have you, leave as soon as you can. Never look back.*'

'And there you are back again,' said Gabe. 'You don't listen, do you?'

Alex glared at the screen and he just shrugged. Water off a duck's back.

'So if the house is cursed,' Eduardo asked, 'why not just burn it down and walk away? It sounds like they wanted to, your ancestors.'

'Well first of all, arson,' she told him. 'Pretty sure that's illegal.'

Ed grinned back. 'Only if you claim on the insurance.'

'People have tried,' Arnold went on before Alex could come up with another smart answer. 'During the 1920s, there was a campaign to drive out the local aristocracy by burning the houses, part of the war of independence, and the civil war that followed. When it came to Wildewood Hall, a Republican brigade arrived. Alex's great-grandfather faced them down apparently, but so too did the people of Kilfayne, standing side by side with him. His wife was one of them, you know. The brigade fell back to the woods and... only one of them made it out alive. He'd lost his mind. He said the house is a prison and the trees are the guardians. That they'd taken the lives of those who wanted to destroy it because if anyone destroyed the Hall, a monstrous spirit trapped there would have escaped.'

'Chambers?'

'Must be. Chambers ran a Hellfire Club there. Allegedly they worshipped the devil, or something older, linked to the house.'

'Oh, come *on*,' Gabe exclaimed. 'You have a *Hellfire* Club connection? Alex, why have you *never* told us any of this?' He sounded genuinely outraged. Or maybe just annoyed at being kept out of the loop. She hadn't told him for this very reason. And she had never planned to come back here.

'Not one of the famous ones,' she corrected him. It was unknown compared to Wharton's or Dashwood's Hellfire Clubs in the UK. Or the one connected to Montpelier Hill in Dublin. She definitely didn't want to tell him they'd been child's play in comparison to everything Chambers was meant to have got up to here. She wasn't mentioning ritual sacrifice and secret temples dedicated to eldritch gods and whatever else the tale had spiralled into. Beyond Kilfayne people didn't actually know about that. She did not need Gabe telling the world about the sordid history of her family. 'Lots of places had Hellfire Clubs in the eighteenth century. It was the college frat house equivalent of the day, Gabe. Overprivileged dickheads who wanted an excuse for excessive partying. You would have fitted right in.'

He was still grumbling but she ignored him. If he kept it up, she'd just put him on mute. Shame it didn't work in real life.

'Can I finish?' Arnold said softly into the strained silence. 'Chambers' actions cursed the family.'

'If they weren't already cursed,' Alex muttered.

'Maybe. But look, the things he did there, the things the family allowed to happen there, all the deaths on their hands, that kind of thing soaks into a place, into the stones and the earth. It didn't end with his death either. They could have helped people and they did nothing, just feasted and partied on while people died in Kilfayne. And the locals never forgot that. Nor did the land, or so the story says. All the family bar Richard died, accidents and the like, but there's an implication that Chambers murdered them and covered it up. Children as young as—'

Enough, Alex thought. She was tired and fed up. Her family tree was filled with terrible people and they were still paying for that. Chambers might have been the worst thing to happen to Wildewood Hall and Kilfayne, but the de Wildes had done nothing to restrain him. Maybe they were worse. Maybe they deserved to be cursed. All the dead daughters, all the miserable lives, all those they had failed, all the shit she was still dealing with. She really needed to wind this call up. It was getting her nowhere. All she needed was equipment. Not more tall tales.

'Look, guys, I'm not even sure there's anything really going on.' Well, that was a lie. Something was definitely going on but there was no way she was going to admit that. Not to them. Not after so long as the non-believer. She would have to get into far too much excruciating detail. Gabe would gloat. She knew that. 'It's more... a feeling, okay? And I want to put Nick's mind at ease.'

'Oh well, *as* it's all about *Nick*,' Gabe drawled.

She was about to tell him where to go but hesitated. Last night could have ended very differently in just a few more minutes had she not regained sanity. And all the things that could have happened... her breath caught in her throat and something warm and wicked pooled in the pit of her stomach.

'Stop it, Gabe,' she told him, as irritated with her own wandering thoughts as with him.

She managed to steer the conversation around to Eduardo and the various pieces of tech she would need. She sketched out a floorplan and identified the main areas to cover. The study, obviously, given what had happened there. The bedroom. She didn't say it was where she was sleeping. And the main hall and grand staircase. That was a start. If they needed more later on, she could revise it. She decided on fixed cameras, EMF meters and a couple of digital recorders she could carry with her. She had her camera equipment with her and the software she would need on her laptop anyway. Keep it simple and above all keep it scientific. At least she wouldn't have to put up with those bloody spirit boxes which just spewed out random words on demand which Gabe adored. Utter nonsense which occasionally made for spectacular television.

'I'll reach out too,' said Daphne. 'I know I'm not there, but perhaps my spirits will be able to help. I'll do everything I can. Send me photos. I can use them as a touchstone to start off.'

'Thank you,' Alex said because while she didn't quite believe herself, Daphne was her friend. She meant well, and sometimes she did subconsciously pick up on things the rest of them missed. Daphne might appear to be nothing more than a loveable flake, but she was clever and intuitive behind the façade. She spotted patterns that other people missed, picked up on emotions and subtext, that was all. Alex just figured she didn't realise what she was doing. So she thought ghosts had told her. Alex had always dismissed it outright, but... well, now it was starting to take on a different hue, wasn't it?

'I'll get it all shipped to you asap,' Eduardo told her, interrupting her strained logic as she tried to explain everything that happened to her rationally. Again. 'I can find a local supplier, I'm sure. But Alex, you'll be careful, won't you? We don't investigate alone, remember? That's not just for correlation of the experience. There are safety concerns too. You're in an old building. You said parts of it are structurally unsound.'

She gave him a smile. She could always rely on Ed. 'I'll be careful, I promise. And Nick's here too.'

Gabe grumbled. She ignored him. Daphne was looking

decidedly smug. Alex ignored that too. Just as well they were on the other side of the Atlantic. Otherwise, she might be tempted to strangle the two of them.

'Send me your findings,' Eduardo told her. 'Any recordings, photos and such like. I'll run them through my system here as well to double check.'

'That's great, thanks.'

'There's something else,' Arnold said. He sounded a little less sure of himself now, which was unusual. 'Those men that vanished in the woods. In the 1920s? Look, it's probably just a coincidence, but...' He chewed on his lower lip. 'One of them was called Nicholas Walker.'

Alex pulled back, staring. It had to be a coincidence. But it was a weird one.

'Okay,' she murmured. 'Well, I don't think he's over a hundred years old, Arnold. If he is, he's remarkably well preserved.' She expected a laugh, but none came.

There was a long pause, and no one made eye contact with her. Gabe cleared his throat awkwardly. Damn, she probably could have put it better than that.

'I just thought...' Arnold stalled and tried again. 'I thought I should mention it, that's all. I looked at the family. I thought your Nick Walker might be a descendent.'

There was another awkward silence. 'He's not *my* Nick Walker,' Alex said numbly.

But maybe she wanted him to be. And that unsettled her more than she could say. She barely knew the man. Her face had heated up again. She was probably scarlet and they were all looking at her right now as if daring her to deny it any further.

Arnold cleared his throat and carried on. 'Remember that thing in France with the archaeologist, Ariadne Walker? She found the lost city and married that hot millionaire? Her brother Jason has a podcast now, about folktales and the supernatural. I met him at a convention a couple of years back. I think they might be related to him. I'll see what else I can find out. I could reach out to them, the Walkers?'

'Alex,' Gabe interrupted yet again, but this time he sounded more solemn than before. Not jealous. Just concerned. 'I have a really bad feeling about this. Be careful, okay?'

CHAPTER 27

ALEX

Alex slept only fitfully that night. The house sighed and whispered and she tried to ignore it. But the sounds crept into her dreams, twisting them into moans of pleasure, and that damned laughter, until she woke up sheened with sweat and breathless, staring into the darkness.

She had the distinct impression that the darkness stared back at her, smiling like a wolf. She was dreaming. She had to be. This was not real. Just another nightmare.

The bed dipped. The voice was barely there. The faintest whisper, but close now, too close, like someone was leaning close to her ear.

'Do you not remember what I can do, my Alexandra?'

Alex sat up abruptly, lashing out and meeting nothing in the dark. As she fumbled with the switch of the bedside light, phantom fingertips brushed the back of her hand and she bit back a gasp.

That soft chuckle of laughter came again.

'Stop it,' she hissed at her own imagination, as she finally clicked the switch. The light was a warm glow, a blessed relief.

And the shadow at the foot of the bed faded with another barely heard laugh.

She had been dreaming. That had to be it. A nightmare. That was all. Another bloody nightmare.

She sat there for some time forcing her breath to calm and her heartbeat to slow again before getting up, wrapping the dressing gown around her, grabbing her phone and padding downstairs in search of a cup of tea. Because she wasn't going to go back to sleep for some time. She knew that much.

It was 3 a.m. Nick's bedroom door stood open and Alex couldn't help but glance inside. It was empty, the bed still neatly made. Was he still up? Unless he'd taken himself off up to the old servants' quarters on the top floor, in among the eaves, far away from her. But no, they were attics, not bedrooms. She'd looked at them early on, so chock-full of the junk of generations piled on top of itself that she'd just shut the door and walked away. Or maybe Nick preferred to camp out in the forest, she thought with a half grin, like the wild man she had first taken him to be.

She took the old servants' stairs, a quicker and more direct route down to the kitchen from her room. They were plainly decorated in comparison to the main stairs, simple stone steps and a solid curving rail. Every so often there were paintings, mostly landscapes but a few portraits as well. She glanced at the faces as she passed and tried to shake the thought that they were looking back, their eyes following her.

Like she was an interloper in this place. Perhaps she was. It was their home, not hers. Or their prison if Nick was to be believed. She could definitely sense their judgement. Like she was somehow failing them, the constant disappointment.

It was starting to get irritating.

The sense of being watched was everywhere. The mirrors and the windows with darkness pressed close outside were the worst. She caught flickers of movement out of the corner of her eye and pressed on, telling herself it was just her reflection caught in glass and polished surfaces. By the time she reached the kitchens, she was trembling, and not just from the cold.

But it was cold down here. It was like walking into a fridge. Her breath misted in front of her mouth and nose. Old buildings had no insulation, she reminded herself. It was the middle of the night. And the weather had been all over the place since she had arrived here. No wonder it was cold. She pulled her dressing gown closer as she busied herself putting on the kettle and getting out a tea bag and milk.

Noises behind her, in the darkness. Laughter, murmurs, a distinct sigh, a gasp of pleasure... or pain...

She ignored them religiously. She had to. They couldn't be real. Not unless she captured them on a recorder. On several recorders to rule out errors. Not until she had real, solid evidence. She refused to believe anything until then.

'Alexandra.'

That voice again, soft and dark with promise, amused at her defiance.

The noise of the kettle boiling filled the room, drowning out anything else again, and she gritted her teeth. Her head swam and she felt sick, like she was about to faint or throw up and it would be anyone's guess which happened first.

A psychic drain, Daphne would say, nodding sagely but sympathetically. But there was no such thing. Not really. A blood sugar crash was more likely. Or any number of things. A reaction to stress. Post traumatic stress disorder, even.

Or something more ominous.

Perhaps she should see a doctor, a specialist of some kind. Call Dr Neary again at least. Perhaps...

'My Alexandra...'

She froze, leaning on the counter, staring at the mug. She couldn't seem to move. Like the other day in the study, when she'd seen that black cloud of nothingness rise to tangle itself around her. Right before Nick had arrived. She couldn't move. She could barely breathe. And yet that tell-tale heat was sweeping through her again, that ache...

A hand slid up the side of her leg. Just for a moment. As real and solid as anything around her. Teasing. Questing. Determined.

'No!' she said as firmly as she could, and twisted aside. The sensation vanished. Not real, she reminded herself. This was not real. Her voice shook. 'You can't do this. None of this is real.'

Then why was she talking to it? Whatever it was.

The kettle clicked off, and the noise made her jump. She was alone in the dark cold kitchen. She busied herself making her tea.

This was no good. She couldn't go on like this. She was hearing voices, seeing things. She needed help. Maybe she was having a breakdown. Coming back here had been a terrible idea. She had always hated this place. She associated it with the worst things to ever happen to her. With nightmares and horrors.

Theo should have known better than to come back. So should she. Had her brother gone through this as well? Had he told anyone? He and Nick had been close. He and Nick's wife Sally too. He must have confided in them.

Wildewood was cursed. It always had been. From time out of mind. Everyone said it. Her mother had drilled it into the two of them for as long as she could remember, while her stepfather had tried to make soothing noises and preached rationality. He'd been her anchor in the chaos of the past.

It had taken her dad. It had taken Theo.

There was no one else left. Just as it had said. Just her.

The last of the de Wildes, Nick had called her. And he said whatever had cursed this place, it wanted her too.

The women of the de Wildes were never safe here. Her

grandfather had said that. She didn't know when but she remembered the words clearly. His voice rising in anger. But why the women?

Alex closed her eyes as the memory grew like a bubble. She'd blocked it out in the days that followed her dad's death. But she let it come to her now. They had argued, the two of them. Argued about her.

'—just thankful I never had a daughter. What were you thinking bringing her back here? You must have known that he would sense her and start to rise.'

'Not this nonsense again. There was no one else to mind her. Susan's working. And she wanted to come, begged me.'

Her grandfather slammed his hand down on the desk with a fearsome bang. 'Because they beguile her. Don't you see it? She's almost a woman now. Chambers will be on her like a hound on a hare.'

'That's enough!' Dad yelled, furious.

'*Omnes contra omnes, quos amabant, convertam, et meam, corpus et animam, faciam,*' her grandfather retorted. 'Is that what you want, Edward? Really? She needs a guardian.'

At the bottom of the stairs, Alex had sat alone, listening. And the dark man had wrapped her in his arms and whispered that they lied, they didn't understand, they never would. Only he would...

The memory was so vivid she might have been watching it unfold for the first time.

Blaise Chambers had held her in his arms and comforted her, whispered promises and lies and she... she had let him.

The same man who had promised to corrupt and destroy every last member of her family line.

'*You do not need a guardian,*' that voice had murmured, as if trying to seduce her. It sounded like it was teasing her too. '*You are a woman grown now, my Alexandra. Let me show you what that means...*'

A woman grown? She'd only been sixteen! The wave of revulsion at the memory brought tears to her eyes. She should never have come back. She should leave. She should get the hell out of here and just let it fall into ruin. Or burn it down to ashes.

But those who tried to destroy the house died. Or got taken by the woods, which amounted to the same thing.

The phone rang, so loud she almost screamed in shock. The tune was a bright, jangly rendition of 'Shiny Happy People', which Daphne had set up for herself as a laugh on a particularly long and uneventful case in West Virginia. An old photo of her friend's smiling face came up on the screen as well and Alex answered at once, eager to hear a friendly voice, to make contact with the real world again.

What was it, about 7 p.m. there? Daphne had probably forgotten about the time difference again. She never got it right.

'Daphne, it's three in the morning,' Alex started without waiting to hear what it was about, a laugh in her voice. She was awake anyway, after all.

But when Daphne spoke, she was neither shiny nor happy. She sounded frantic.

'Alex! Thank goodness I got you. You have to get out. You can't stay there. Not even with your guardian. He can't help you this time. The walker in the woods isn't enough and I think he's already half lost himself. There's a darkness. It's old and it's hungry, and so powerful. Not just the man in the portrait. Something so much worse. It isn't going to let you go. Not again.'

'Daphne—' But her friend raced on.

'No, listen to me. It knows you. It wants you. I felt it reaching up out of the earth and the stones, out of the darkness below. There's a – a temple. But not a holy place. That's its centre of power. Right there beneath you. It's still there, Alex, waiting. A broken god of lost places. The woods have tried to hold it back but they can't. Not now. Not with you there. I tried to reach out and focus on you, to strengthen you, to help guard you. I tried to raise a dome of protective light and I-I—' Daphne coughed, tried to clear her throat and her voice changed, gravelly and agonised. '*Omnes contra omnes, quos amabant, convertam—*'

She didn't get any further.

All Alex heard was a dreadful, guttural choking noise and then a thud. 'Daph?' She sounded like she was having some kind of fit. 'Daphne!'

The line went dead.

Shit. She didn't know what to do. Something had happened to Daphne and she was stuck on an island an ocean away. She held the phone so tightly she thought she might crush it.

Gabe lived closest to Daphne. Minutes away. Alex dialled his number and was rewarded by a wall of noise which indicated he was in a bar somewhere.

'Darling,' he drawled. 'How are your ghosts?'

Oh, she didn't have time for this.

'Shut up and listen. Daphne's in trouble. You need to get to her now.'

That sobered him. Instantly. 'Trouble? What kind of—'

'We were on the phone. Gabe, she collapsed. I think she was at home. You have a key, don't you? Please, go find her.'

For once, he didn't argue. He was already moving. The background noise changed from bar to street and then he was in his car. 'Possession?'

'I don't know.' She wasn't lying. She wasn't sure about anything anymore. 'It sounded bad. Really bad. She just collapsed while we were talking and the line went dead.'

'It's okay, Alex. I'm on the way. There in minutes. I'm going to hang up and I'll ring you back, okay?'

And then he was gone as well.

A laugh rippled through the air around her. It was nasty and cruel.

'Alexandra, my love. See what you do just by being here, the power you give me...'

No. No this was not happening and it was not her fault. And she was not listening to the voice.

That voice from the past, from her nightmares.

From the night that Dad died.

Tears burned her eyes as she stared at the phone screen, willing it to ring again.

This was stupid. She had to do something. She sent messages to Arnold and Eduardo and waited again, staring at her phone. Willing it to ring. Praying for it to ring.

'Alex?'

She twisted around so fast she almost sent the mug of cold tea flying, ready to run or to fight. Ready for anything.

Nick stood in the doorway between the kitchen and the boot room, the outer door still open and the gardens dark behind him. He was bare-chested, his hair falling to his shoulders and a pair of pyjama pants hanging low on his hips. Had he been outside like that? In the woods? What had he been doing?

She opened her mouth but nothing came out.

'Are you okay?' She flinched as he took another step into the room and he stopped as if he saw something in her which alarmed him. He raised his hands, as if to show he wasn't a threat. He was barefoot, grass stains on his skin. There were leaves tangled in his hair. 'Alex? What happened?'

The phone rang behind her and she snatched it up. 'Gabe?'

Please, oh dear God, please...

'I'm here. She's okay. She's coming back to herself. I'm going to get her to an urgent care clinic as soon as I can but she's okay. It's okay. The guys are on the way. What did she say to you? She's not making a lot of sense right now. She doesn't remember what happened.'

Alex was aware of Nick still standing there, listening

bemused to their conversation. He'd be able to hear Gabe. He wasn't being quiet.

'That we... that we were in danger here. Something about a guardian and...' She looked up, met Nick's steady gaze, and tried not to flinch. The walker in the woods, Daphne had said. He couldn't protect her. Did she mean Nick? 'She said she reached out, to help protect me and... something attacked her, Gabe. It sounded like something was trying to choke her.'

Alex recalled the sensation of hands tightening around her own throat in the study.

'Her phone's completely drained,' Gabe murmured, and she could imagine him examining it as he spoke, drawing his own conclusions as to what had done that. 'So's her laptop. Everything here with a battery, I imagine.'

Gabe believed that ghosts could do that, drain power from batteries to steal the energy and manifest themselves. And they had found cameras, recorders and other equipment drained in just such a way on more than one of their investigations. It wasn't evidence of ghosts, as far as Alex was concerned, but Eduardo couldn't explain it. He was diligent about charging everything up. Yet it still happened. She'd put it down to faulty equipment or some kind of electromagnetic interference they didn't understand yet. Now she wasn't so sure. It seemed like a flimsy excuse, a desperate grab at rationality.

And it didn't matter. Not right now.

'Are you sure she's okay?' Alex asked through a tight throat.

'Yes. Here, do you want to talk to her?' His voice was warm with reassurance. Gabe had always been good at that. And right now, she needed it.

'Alex? I'm fine.' Daphne sounded very small and tired. But she was herself again. 'Really. Just a bit wobbly now.'

Wobbly. What a word to use. 'You'll go to a doctor, right?' Alex didn't mean her tone to come out so harsh but it did and she couldn't help it.

'I promise,' Daphne murmured. 'Gabe's going to take me in the morning. It'd only be an ER now. Better I see someone who understands.' Because if she turned up in the average ER claiming to have been attacked by a ghost, they'd probably medicate her and lock her up while charging her a small fortune for the privilege. Daphne had confessed that was one of her greatest fears. Alex suddenly understood it far too keenly. 'Gabe's looking after me. Don't worry.'

Gabe took the phone back. 'I'll keep you updated,' he told her. 'I'll stay here with her tonight and we'll make sure she's fine. Stay safe, okay? You aren't there alone, are you?'

Her eyes met Nick's again. They were darkly beautiful and they watched her intently, bright with concern.

'No. Nick's here.'

'Huh, right.' That didn't sound positive. But at least he didn't argue this time. He had concerns enough of his own. 'Be careful, Alex. I don't like any of this.'

Neither did she. And she didn't like his implications either. 'Nothing is going to happen between me and Nick, Gabe. Nothing at all.'

It felt like a lie even as she said it.

He wasn't buying it either. 'Yeah, so you say.'

'I do. And anyway, it's none of your business anymore.'

She hung up and steeled herself, ready to turn around and apologise. Nick didn't need to be in the middle of her, Gabe and whatever overly protective thing her ex had going now. It was excruciatingly embarrassing, with her coming to oust him. Being stuck in this wretched building, and all the weird attraction and strange goings-on, was just heaping in on top of that.

But he didn't need to have overheard that. Or her outright rejection of him.

She really ought to apologise. She really ought to explain.

But when she looked for him, Nick was gone.

CHAPTER 28

NICK

The accounts books were all out of order. At first he though Alex might have done it, going through them ahead of him to look for ammunition. But she hadn't been into the storeroom where he kept them, and all his current records were on the laptop. Besides, these went back years, from long before Theo had arrived. They had packed it all away when they switched to the online system. But Nick had been so careful to make sure they were in order.

They weren't now.

He'd have to take everything out, go through the books, and put them all back in order. It was going to take hours. But if she wanted to see the originals...

He definitely wasn't hiding from her. And he wasn't replaying the conversation she'd had with her friends through his mind.

Nothing is going to happen between me and Nick, Gabe. Nothing at all.

She'd been so lost and afraid when he'd come into the kitchen, straight from the wild wood and the night. All he had wanted was to fold his arms around her and comfort her. And then she said that.

It shouldn't bother him. It was the best thing, the right thing. He needed to stay away from her, he knew that. That was what had sent him out to the woods in the first place, to ground himself, to get some perspective, to put distance between them and combat whatever seemed intent on forcing the two of them together. Because he wanted her. She was all he could think of now. Alex O'Neill...

Instead, he had spent a whole day and a night trying to keep his distance again. The house was quiet, biding its time probably. And she was locked away working on her book or preparing for her investigation. He didn't know. He didn't dare ask. It was better to keep away from each other.

It simply wasn't helping. She was all he could think about. Her body in his arms, his mouth on hers, Alex whispering his name...

His gaze snagged on the notebook. It shouldn't have been here at all. That one belonged in the study. It was one of her grandfather's, leather-bound, with thick cream paper. He'd had them shipped over from somewhere on the continent and used to write up all his research into them. It might help her. But why was it in here?

The professor had studied the house for years, obsessed over it and its history and, like Sally and her family, was determined to keep whatever was infesting it locked away.

He flicked it open, reading the elegant script looping across the page. Dates, names, references to papers, even something that looked like diary entries.

Nick had accidentally inserted himself into her family too much already. He'd just hand it over. That was for the best.

The sound of a van outside brought his attention back to the world around them. The equipment Alex's friend had ordered for her was due today. He didn't want them to leave it sitting outside if it rained so he locked the storeroom and went to the front of the house to take the delivery.

The back of the van stood open, and a wiry man was struggling to haul out a box. Nick went to help and found himself face to face with Seán MacBride from the village. He'd never liked the miserable git, who was always ready with a snide remark behind someone's back, especially Nick's. Sally had called him a chancer, when she was feeling generous. Theo had called him a little bastard. To his face on several occasions.

'Nick!' he squawked, and almost dropped the box. Nick caught it. The last thing he needed was for Alex's expensive equipment to be damaged because he'd scared the delivery man.

'New job?' he asked.

'Er... yeah. You know. Filling in.' That made more sense. He didn't see Seán holding down a job for long. They carried the boxes to the back door and then Seán went back to the van, reaching into the front passenger seat. 'There's... uh... there's these too.'

It was a bouquet of flowers, dahlias, so dark a red they were almost black.

'Who from?' he asked, taking them.

Seán gave his trademark snide little laugh, the one that always put Nick's teeth on edge. 'She must have a secret admirer. There's a note. Make sure she gets it, won't you?'

He jumped back into the van and took off down the drive in a spray of gravel.

Now was as good a time as any. Nick knocked on the study door. He'd give her the flowers and then bring in the equipment for her.

Alex opened the door, smiling to see him there, and so he recognised the instant that she realised what he was carrying. Her face froze, the colour draining from her cheeks, and she all but threw herself back from him.

'Alex?' he gasped, moving to catch her but she raised her hands as if warding him off and collided with the back of one of the armchairs.

'Where the fuck did they come from?' Her voice sounded strangled.

Nick stared from her to the flowers and back again, completely confused. 'The delivery guy brought them. Well, Seán from the village. Moonlighting probably. He said you have a secret admirer. There's a note.' He plucked it out from among the blooms and held it out to her. Alex didn't move. She was frozen there.

'Read it,' she said.

Nick put the flowers down on top of the nearest cabinet and opened the little envelope. There was a card inside. 'Thinking of you' was embossed on the front and 'and all the things we'll do' had been printed onto a sticker inside. That was it. It looked totally innocent.

He held it out to her again but she didn't move. She was trembling. Nick put it down with the flowers.

'What is it?' he asked. 'Alex, please? Talk to me?'

'Did you – are they from you? Is this a trick to—'

'No.'

God, he was going to kill Seán. He kept picturing the nasty git's smile and realised he'd known she'd react like this. He'd fucking known.

Nick spread his hands wide, trying desperately to show her he meant no harm. He'd always known he was big and intimidating. He used it in the past when he had to, on thugs, on poachers, on bastards like Seán MacBride. And he would again.

But not now. Not with her.

'Alex, please, I'm sorry. Just explain it to me. Like I'm an idiot.'

Because he was. Clearly.

She sank into the chair. 'Will you just get rid of the flowers? Please?'

Nick had never picked something up so fast or hurled it out into the hall quite so hard.

Alex's eyes were closed and she pinched the bridge of her nose as if trying to ward off a headache, or tears. Nick waited, worrying his fingers together. He'd never seen anyone react like this. Not to flowers.

After a moment she moved, more like an automaton than a living breathing human, grabbed her laptop and after briefly doing something with it, handed it to him. Her email was open on the screen, a subfolder filled with unread messages. So many of them. All of them vile.

Nick put it down on the desk. She was sitting down again, her head in her hands.

'What is that?'

'Ed set up a script that filters them before I see them, and auto-forwards them to the cops. Not that there's a lot that can be done about them. But at least I don't have to deal with it. I mostly just try to forget it's there.'

'Abusive emails?'

'I wish that was all,' she murmured. Nick didn't dare move. He didn't dare speak. He had to wait. It was excruciating. 'We had a case,' Alex said at last. 'Ted Sanderson. He was obsessed with the Black Dahlia murder, Elizabeth Short. She was killed in 1947 in LA. It was brutal, horrible and no one ever found out who did it. Sanderson tormented his daughters, made them believe that whoever killed Elizabeth was coming for them too, that it was a demon. And he loved the celebrity of it, thrived on every second of notoriety. There was no demon, of course. I exposed him on the show and he was arrested. I testified against him. He went online and tapped into a whole world of men who hate women like me. They used to send me black dahlias with innocuous little messages, just like that. Every week. Sometimes every day.'

She shuddered and looked up at him, wide-eyed.

'You think this came from them?'

The glare she turned on him then was terrible. 'Or from you. An attempt to get rid of me. Frighten me off.'

That... that had never occurred to him. Cursing, he realised he was still standing there, too big, too threatening, the man who had made no secret of the fact he had never wanted her here and wanted her to leave as soon as possible. The man who frightened her. God, this was... this was not what he'd intended. Carefully, he sank to his knees in front of her. Alex watched him and the wariness in her eyes made his heart ache. 'The delivery man brought it.' *And later on I'm going to deal with him too.* 'I didn't realise. I knew you left your show. I didn't know any of that.'

What she must have gone through, was still going through... God, if he could get his hands on Sanderson or any of his followers right now... What were the cops even doing?

'Well, I didn't exactly make it public.'

'Is that why you left the show?'

'And the States. It wasn't worth giving them the target anymore. I guess they've found out where I am then. There was a guy in the village, when I had lunch in the pub. I thought maybe... he knew who I was.'

'Seán MacBride?' He ground out the name.

'Yeah, Seán something.' She sounded so tired, exhausted. And all he wanted to do was wrap her in his arms. But he didn't dare touch her. Not now. 'That was what Fionnuala said.'

Oh yeah, Nick was going to kill him. 'Seán brought them with him. He was driving the delivery truck with your equipment.' Alex's eyes brimmed with unshed tears and she bit her lower lip. Nick felt something twist inside him, a new type of anguish. 'I'll deal with him. Worse, I'll tell Patricia and she'll deal with him. She's friends with his mum.'

'Why do they always live with their mum?' Alex murmured numbly. 'I'm sorry I accused you. It was... it was a shock. They know where I am now.' She put her head down in her hands again, trying to calm her breathing. She looked like she was about to have a panic attack. 'I'll have to find somewhere else. I'll pack and... and maybe you could drop me to the train or...'

'You aren't leaving,' he said aghast.

She barked out a hollow laugh. 'Oh, come on, Nick, I thought that was what you wanted.'

'Not now. Not like this. Not because of *them*.' This time he did reach out and take her hands in hers... carefully, gingerly, stroking the skin as softly as he could. And to his amazement, she let him. 'I won't let them get near you. I won't let anyone hurt you, Alex. I promise. I'll protect you.' The words felt right and true. Nothing had ever felt quite so right. 'Alex, I am your guardian. I can help you. Shield you. Please. Don't leave.'

CHAPTER 29

ALEX

Eduardo had sent top of the line stuff expressed to her from a supplier in Dublin. He must have done so as soon as possible after Daphne's collapse – Alex refused to call it a psychic attack on principle, but that's what the others had said it was. The speed at which he'd swung into action made it feel even more urgent than before. If only they were here with her now. Gabe making jokes, irreverent to the last, Arnold triple-checking everything, Daphne waxing lyrical about atmosphere and spirits, Ed setting up all this shit...

Too dangerous. Far too dangerous. The house felt like an oppressive weight on her shoulders. It ate into her consciousness. The shadow of Blaise Chambers fell over everything.

There had been no other obvious incidents though. For that Alex was thankful. Not supernatural ones anyway. The flowers had left her rattled enough. Sharing the truth of all that with Nick had been an unexpected relief.

Nick had knelt on the ground in front of her and had taken her hands in his. 'Don't leave,' he'd said. She tried not to put too much meaning on that. It stirred something inside her she wasn't aware of needing. Not lust, not that time. Something far more profound than that. 'I am your guardian.'

She didn't need a guardian. But the words to express that wouldn't come. They reminded her too much of Chambers.

But 'Don't leave.' There had been anguish in those two words.

She might not need him, but she wanted him. And it meant so much that he wanted her to stay, that he trusted her to help him and the spirits trapped here. Like Sally.

She couldn't let herself think about it. If she thought about it, it brought back Sanderson and then she really would have a breakdown.

Alex busied herself with setting up cameras, recorders and checking that everything was fully charged. Finally satisfied, she retreated to the bedroom and sat on the bed, facing the open door and the portrait of Blaise Chambers.

All she had to do was take the wretched thing down and turn it to face the wall. Or better yet, chuck it out a window or something. Nick had promised to get rid of it for her. But he'd forgotten, hadn't he? It seemed to slip out of memory the moment after it was mentioned.

She couldn't bring herself to touch it again. The smirk he wore told her what he thought of her cowardice too. But last time she'd touched it, she'd fallen down the stairs. Fallen... or been pushed. It didn't help that Chambers' expression made her think of Sanderson, the way he'd looked at her in the courtroom, when he still thought he might get away with it. Or of Seán in the village, that horrible, knowing, superior sneer.

She had sworn never to do this again but here she was. Investigating. In the last place she wanted to stir up a spirit. Looking right at that bastard's face.

Diving right in at the deep end, as it were.

She didn't know why she'd waited until dark to do this. The house was more active at night, but she wasn't sure she needed that. Perhaps it was just a ghost hunting tradition. No one wanted to believe in ghosts in broad daylight.

She pressed the record button and drew in a breath.

'Is there anyone here?'

As corny a start as possible really, Gabe would tell her, and hardly good TV, but a really bloody good question when you got down to it.

Was there really anyone there? Or was she imagining it?

This was easy. She had done it a thousand times. Record, ask a question, wait, ask another question. Keep going. Watch the EMF meter, listen out for the REM pod. Record everything. Listen back later.

The boring bit, Gabe always called it.

She stared at the portrait but nothing happened. Blaise gazed back, a small smile playing on his lush lips, his dark eyes amused. She had to stop thinking about him. She was filling in spaces with her own imagination and that would not do.

There was a scientific process to this and she was going to follow it to the letter. She was a professional, not a sensationalist, no matter what the popular media tried to say.

She'd got into this game to solve the mysteries, to provide people with logical answers and to tear down all those misconceptions and charlatans. It had seen her hounded off the internet and out of the States, and now she was holed up here in the middle of nowhere with nightmares coming out of the woodwork all around her. She was not going to give in to hysteria and superstition now.

Alex turned off the recorder, standing up and stretching her tense shoulders as she did so. Some people swore by tape only but she agreed with Eduardo. The more up to date the tech the more reliable and less likely to introduce errors it tended to be. Tape could carry traces of something recorded on it before, for example. She put in her earbuds, keyed up the sample and pressed play.

'*Is there anyone here?*'

Her own voice, followed by nothing much. She could hear her breath but that was all. '*Why are you here?*' Nothing. '*What's your name?*' Nothing. '*Do you have a message to pass on?*' Still nothing.

This was getting her nowhere.

'*What do you want with me?*' There was a distinct wobble in her voice and she winced. What was she doing? Her hand slid up to the stop button.

And then she heard it.

A whisper, little more than a hiss, right on the edge of hearing.

'*Alexandra. My beloved.*'

'Oh, Jesus. Fuck!' She hurled the recorder onto the bed without even meaning to. She just didn't want it in her hands anymore. Unfortunately, it was still playing and something happened to the volume as it hit the covers. And she still had the earbuds in, still connected.

The voice – his voice – roared in her ears.

'*Oh, the things I'll do to you, now you're grown. The pleasure and the pain, all rolled in together until you won't be able to tell one from the other. I'll make you mine, body, mind and soul, mine and my god's. We'll tear your mind apart and remake it as I will. My Lady de Wilde, the last of them, promised to me for so long, and to my god. I'll offer you up to my lord Crom and together we'll take you apart. My beautiful girl, the power you give me, the sheer level of lust simmering away inside you. The god of the hungry grass will take it all and use it, even as I use you. With my hands on your skin and my cock inside you, we'll drink you down like fine wine until there's nothing of you left. Until all you are is a being of raw pleasure, his and mine, body and soul. I'll make you mine forever, Alexandra. And his. Our lover, our plaything, our slave.*'

Alex tore the earbuds out and hurled them after the

recorder, standing there, breathing hard, her chest heaving with the effort.

Blaise Chambers. It had to be. Who else would talk like that?

And he had plans for her.

Plans which made her body heat in an instant, which made her stomach twist with need. And at the same time, horror, abject terror at the thought.

Who or what the fuck was Crom?

A god, he'd called it. The god of the hungry grass. What was going on?

A broken god of lost places…

That was what Daphne had said. Right before she collapsed.

No… no, right before she collapsed she'd said…

Alex looked up at the portrait where the words hid against the darkness of Blaise Chambers' coat.

Omnes contra omnes, quos amabant, convertam, et meam, corpus et animam, faciam.

I will set all of them against all of those they have loved, and I will make them mine, body and soul.

One of the REM pods went off, beeping wildly. Then the other, the one outside the door. Both of them, shrieking like tiny black boxes full of banshees.

Alex let out her own cry of alarm. This wasn't like her. She didn't get scared like this. But she was never normally alone. She had Gabe and Daphne to rely on, and Eduardo's calm reassurance, and Arnold's endless information, cross-checking facts.

Doing this alone sucked.

What had she been thinking?

That she was the big brave sceptic. That she didn't believe any of this and she was going to prove it wasn't real. But it didn't take a lot to be brave when you didn't think anything frightening could really exist, did it?

And something existed here. Something dark and terrible. Something which knew her name, knew her innermost thoughts, and wanted her in every way conceivable.

She swallowed hard, trying to regain some sense of perspective here. She made herself pick up the recorder again, took a deep breath and played the file once more.

'*Is there anyone here?*' Nothing but silence. '*Why are you here?*' Nothing. '*What's your name?*' Nothing. '*Do you have a message to pass on?*' Nothing again, same as before. '*What do you want with me?*'

Alex held her breath, waiting for that obscene voice with all its lewd promises, calling her name, swearing it would take her apart and feed her to its god.

Nothing.

Not a single thing. Not a sigh, not a whisper. Not a sound.

'You absolute fucker, Blaise,' she growled out loud.

She thought she heard his laugh. Just on the edge of hearing. Because of course she did. He was toying with her. Like always.

And then the power in the recorder just died. Right there as she held it in her hand.

'Oh, come on,' she whispered and saw the REM pod lights flicker and go out. No shriek this time. Nothing. She threw herself towards the nearest fixed camera.

The screen was black. The battery dead. Drained completely.

Her breath promptly misted in front of her face and she shivered as a wave of cold swept over her. Slowly, she dragged her gaze back to the portrait of Blaise Chambers. He was still smiling at her, his eyes still boring into her soul. She could imagine his mouth moving as he promised her pleasures and pain that would unmake her mind.

His lips on her skin, tracing a cold line down her neck and along the back of her shoulder. Making her shiver.

The smile in the painting was wider now, the mouth parting to reveal his teeth, and his eyes flashed with desire. As she watched he leaned forward, pushing his way out of the frame, hands closing on its edge... This wasn't happening. This couldn't be happening.

Not here and now. And definitely not without any way to record any bastard evidence.

Alex flinched back with a cry of alarm, unable to stop herself closing her eyes, and when she looked again it was just the portrait, the same as it ever was. She had to take a moment, staring at it, forcing herself to calm.

This is why we don't investigate alone, she thought bleakly. Ed was right. At least you should have another human being to corroborate any experiences. It wasn't just a safety issue.

Except that right now it really did feel very much like a safety issue.

So when Nick appeared in the doorway, she could have cried with relief.

'Are you... are you all right?' Nick asked, his tone wary. She didn't blame him. She'd been shouting at the top of her voice. She had to look like a madwoman.

'Not really.'

'Are they messing with you?'

No, she was not just accepting this. Especially not to him. She couldn't. She refused. 'We still haven't established that there's anything here to be messing with me.'

And yes, she knew that was stupid. Because of everything that had just happened to her only moments earlier. But she needed to say it all the same. For her own sake. Just to cling to that last shred of sanity a little longer.

He nodded slowly, clearly unconvinced. Alex scowled at him and went to check the other camera. Completely dead too. Of course.

'There's a bag out there in the hall,' she said to Nick. 'Pass it in to me, will you?'

He bent to fetch it and handed over the black duffel bag. She rooted around in it to get the fully charged batteries. She'd found at times like this simply keeping them in another room, or in this case the hallways outside, seemed to keep them safe from whatever drained them. All the more reason to believe it was some kind of naturally occurring electromagnetic event they couldn't track just yet.

One day, she promised herself. She definitely believed in Eduardo's ability to solve a technical issue. And right now, falling back into the realm of science and logic was the only comfort she could find.

With the cameras at full power again, she checked the footage. It was hard to see on the tiny internal screen, but there did seem to be some kind of movement by the doorway as she'd been listening back to the recorder. Alex squinted at it, frowning.

'What is it?' Nick asked.

'I don't know yet. I'll have to get it up on the laptop and have a proper look. Something is playing merry hell with the power though.'

He nodded as if that was only to be expected but didn't seem to have a reply. Well, he lived here. He was entirely used to all the weird shit. He was a believer, she reminded herself.

'Are there often fluctuations in power here?'

Nick shrugged. 'Well, it's an old house.'

'What about batteries? Do they drain quickly all the time?'

'A lot of my stuff is quite old. Sally's laptop and the phone... But... yeah, I guess...'

Alex fixed him with a glare. Why was he being so evasive all of a sudden? He was the one who had been talking about ghosts and stuff.

'What's wrong?'

Nick's mouth tightened and then he held out a large notebook. It was black leather, a good quality, and had clearly been much used.

'What's this?'

'It belonged to your grandfather. I found it in among the account books.'

The urge to drop it flared up and Alex couldn't hide the scowl that spread over her face. 'Right,' she said, dubiously.

Now? He'd only brought this to her now? Had he really just found it or had he only just decided to give it to her? And if so why?

'It's got notes in it about the house, its history, his research and about... about people's experiences here. I thought... I thought it might help.'

She made herself open it. The handwriting was spidery and small. It would be a bugger to read. Great. She turned a page, the thick paper whispering as she did so, and a word caught her eye.

Chambers.

The chill that passed over her wasn't supernatural this time. She read the rest of the line, and couldn't help carrying on to those after it.

Chambers has his eye on the girl. He wants her for Crom.

I have tried to warn Edward but he remains steadfast in his conviction that this is all superstition and nonsense and has warned me not to involve his children in my 'delusions'. He insists on bringing her, despite my warnings. But now he will not heed me at all. I fear the worst, that the influence on him is already too strong.

Young Theodore promises me that he will allow no harm to

come to his sister, or the estate, that he will keep her away from
the areas of danger.

Edward, her father's name. Theodore, her brother's.

The girl.

Her grandfather was writing about her? The date at the top of the page matched up with that last, dreadful visit here all those years ago. Twenty years ago.

The argument in the study. The raised voices. Blaise's arms folding around her...

A tear slid down her face and spattered on the page. She wiped it off hurriedly and shut the book with a snap.

Nick had moved towards her, a look of concern on his handsome face, his hand already reaching out to her.

Alex took a step back and he let his arm drop back to his side. Taking anything, even the simplest form of comfort, seemed like a bad idea right now. And something she desperately wanted.

But again, she recalled sitting on the stairs with those formless arms closing around her, pulling her in, and that voice whispering comfort and promises. So many promises...

She curled her arms around the notebook, holding it against her chest. She couldn't think of anything to say. She had never felt quite so alone.

'I'll be downstairs,' he said, awkwardly, so crestfallen that she felt a pang of something she didn't want to examine too closely.

'No, wait.' God, this was horrible. Painfully awkward. 'I'm sorry. I didn't mean to make you uncomfortable. The other night. Well, and the other day. I didn't... I'm sorry, okay?'

Nick gave her a tentative smile. 'I probably shouldn't have told you all that stuff about Sally. It was... look, it just feels like she's here and sometimes I think she is, that's all. And I can't leave knowing that. Not that I could leave anyway. And stuff does happen here.'

Well, she knew that, didn't she? It couldn't all be her imagination. Because if it was, she definitely needed to see a psychiatrist and get a prescription for some serious medication. No, this was not in her imagination. Not the batteries anyway. That was quantifiable. Evidence. And not the voice. Hopefully.

'Thank you,' Alex said, indicating the notebook. 'It's definitely a help.'

'It looked personal.'

She tried to smile. The expression didn't sit comfortably on her face. 'I think so, yes. He was writing about my father, around the time he died. And about Theo and I.'

Chambers has his eye on the girl.

She shuddered. She couldn't help it. Had Nick read that? Did he know what her grandfather thought?

Chambers had his eye on her now all right. He'd told her that himself.

Nick took another step, as if something pulled him to her unwillingly. Or shoved him from behind perhaps. But his face said he wanted to comfort her, that he felt sorry for her. He lifted his hands to her again and Alex swayed towards him, needing to feel his touch, to bury her face in his chest, to let him hold her and keep her safe.

If only for a moment.

The recorder burst into life, and a voice, a horribly familiar voice, blared out of the speaker on its side.

'Don't touch her!' Theo's voice roared at them. 'Don't you *dare* touch her!'

CHAPTER 30

NICK

There was no mistaking the voice. Or the effect it had on Alex.

Between the notebook and the dahlias from her stalkers, she was already wound up tighter than a spring.

And then Theo screamed at them both out of a piece of technology which could not have recorded him at all, let alone saying the words he said.

Don't touch her!

It was like a slap to the face. The anger that surged up in Nick's chest startled him. How dare he? *Him*, of all people...

Alex staggered back, white-faced, and her legs simply went out from underneath her. She was still clutching the notebook so she dropped like a stone.

Nick moved on instinct alone, catching her before she hit the ground, turning to shield her from the bed and whatever was rising there.

But nothing happened. There was no attack, no force battering into him. Nothing flew across the room under its own steam. No wind, no wall of icy cold, nothing. He was holding her. No, cradling her. And she felt so right in his arms. Like she belonged there.

She looked up into his face, blinking, eyes wide. Her mouth parted and the need to not just touch her, but draw her to him, kiss her, possess her was almost overwhelming.

A loud pop fractured the silence, and a hiss, followed by a sharp acidic smell, and then smoke. And...

'Oh shit!' Alex exclaimed, twisting out of his grip, as the recorder in the middle of the bed belched out foul-smelling black smoke, the plastic of its cover bubbling and melting onto the bedclothes. 'No! Shit!'

Nick grabbed the topmost blanket and pulled it off the bed, taking the recorder with it. He threw it over the smoking equipment and brought his foot down on it hard, two, three times to put out any flames. Then he picked up the whole thing, and heading for the ensuite, threw it into the shower and turned on the water at full blast, immersing the remains of the lithium-ion battery before it could fully ignite.

It was deathly quiet in the room behind him. He looked around at Alex, who was staring up at him, speechless.

Slowly, Nick looked back at the mess in the shower. Her recorder. One of the ones that had been express shipped here by her team, probably at great expense. Brand new equipment which must have cost a fortune.

Shit.

It had probably been destroyed from the moment it started to smoke anyway. And a fire could have taken the whole room with it, maybe the whole Hall. It was always a risk in a building like this. A constant danger.

But still. He'd stamped it to death, smothered it and drowned it, in seconds. Acting on instinct alone.

'I'm sorry,' he whispered.

Alex shook her head, swallowed hard and then an expression of resignation took the place of her fear. 'Better that than the whole place going up in flames.' She drew in a breath and slowly let it out again, closing her eyes. Her lips moved as if she was praying, or counting. Begging for serenity and patience perhaps.

He'd just destroyed her equipment. And her evidence as well. He simply couldn't do anything right around this woman. Not from the first moment he had met her.

Sasquatch, her friends had called him. And he felt like it, stumbling around, in her way, breaking things.

'You heard him, didn't you?' she asked in a very small voice.

Theo, warning Nick off her. Oh yes, he'd heard that all right.

Nick couldn't dredge up an answer. He just nodded instead.

She held out her hand. 'I think we should go downstairs. Give it a rest for the night. Maybe have a drink. I don't think either of us should be in here. Or alone. Not now.'

'Are you sure? You heard him.'

He waited, expecting him to tell him no, or to go to hell. Her brother certainly didn't want him anywhere near her, did he? And Theo had always said that the two of them even *thought* the same way.

But why? Why would Theo warn Nick off Alex like that? What had he ever done to Theo? If anything, it was the other way around...

No, that wasn't fair either.

Nick closed his eyes and tried to push away memories of his friend and his wife and all the misery this place had inflicted on the three of them.

Alex's hand slipped into his. He hadn't heard her get up, but she stood in front of him now, holding onto him. Or maybe he was the one holding onto her, clinging to her like a lifeline.

That had been Theo's voice. Shouting at them. Warning her. About him.

God, it hurt.

'Come on,' she told him, her voice so gentle. 'There's got to be something to drink in this place somewhere. My grandfather used to have all the wine in the world in the cellar and barely touched a drop. Is that still there?'

'I'll have to deal with that first.' He nodded towards the ensuite.

'I think it's dead, Nick. You killed it.'

How did she manage to make him smile at a moment like this? But she did. 'All the same. Just in case it reignites or...'

Alex slipped by him and scooped the remains of the recorder up before he could stop her. She marched to the window, pulled it up and tossed the sodden, melted mass out onto the gravel driveway below.

'There,' she said, wiping her hands together. 'Nothing for it to set fire to out there, okay?'

She was right. Nothing but gravel. Not known for burning. 'Okay,' he agreed. 'Let's get a drink. But Alex—'

'I heard him. We both did. And once we've had that drink maybe you can tell me why my brother would say something like that to you.'

Nick lit a fire in the drawing room while Alex poked around in one of the dressers and emerged with a pair of wine glasses that were probably Georgian. It was later than he'd thought. Night was settling in.

'Are these okay?' she asked.

They probably weren't worth that much, plain and simple as they were. Her grandfather had sold anything especially valuable.

'They're yours,' he said. It shouldn't feel like such a big thing, but it was true. He had to accept that now. Wildewood Hall was hers. It didn't react to just anyone like this. Neither did the woods.

She flashed him a smile and set them down on the small Victorian side table by the sofa. 'Wine?' she asked.

'In the cellar,' he said and almost swallowed the word, shooting back up to his feet. 'I'll get it. Stay here.'

'I can—' she started.

'No,' he said, probably too sharply. 'I'll go. It isn't safe.'

An understatement. But he really didn't want to get into that. Not right now. And not after what had happened upstairs. The house was too active by far, and Alex was a focal point. And the cellar... it was a bad place, just like he'd told Maeve all her life. The worst place in the whole house.

Alex gave him another of those very knowing looks but obviously decided it wasn't worth arguing.

'Right then,' she said and settled down on the sofa, opening the notebook and starting to read.

That might be worse, of course. But not by much. What had the professor put in there? He had known more about the house and its history than anyone else. Still, she needed to know.

She frowned, a tiny line drawing between her eyebrows as she focused. God, she was beautiful. Intense. Perfect.

And Nick shouldn't be thinking about her like that. Not right now. Perhaps not ever. Theo had been clear enough. Horribly clear.

'I'll only be a minute,' he said as he left.

'If you aren't back soon, I'll come after you,' she called out. She tried to make it sound more like a threat than a promise. He wasn't fooled.

She would too. That was a given. If there was one thing he had already figured out about Alex O'Neill, it was that she would charge into a raging fire if she thought she would solve a mystery, or help a friend.

Was that what they were becoming? Friends?

Was that all?

Well, it had to be all. And it had to be enough. He had no

right to be thinking any of this, and how did he even know if what he was feeling was real anyway? And Theo had just made his feelings known. The house had a way of playing with you, Sally had always said.

Like now. Like then.

And friends? What had he ever done to deserve friends?

It was much later than he thought. He stepped into the kitchen and...

The door to the cellar was standing wide open.

A dark and endless hole, a mouth waiting to swallow him up. He was sure he had closed it the last time he was in here, but that was the way of this building. He turned on the light and took a deep breath.

It was always cold down there. Icy. Part of that was by design, of course. It was a cold room, storage. And part of it...

Well, this was Wildewood Hall. And the cellar was the oldest part of it. Deep under the earth, small for so big a house, a pocket of malice in the depths of it, clad in ancient stone...

Stone far older than the house itself.

Some of the stories said Blaise Chambers had died here. Right at the bottom of those steps.

Nick steeled himself and stepped into the cellar, closing down every emotion as he crossed the threshold and felt the touch of something old and vast.

Was this where the stones from the cairn had been used? That was what the professor had thought, but he had never found any real evidence. Just stones. And surely it wasn't big enough. But it was where Nick felt the darkness most keenly.

Sally had always said, whatever happened, it couldn't touch him. He was protected. She had woven the charms which still hung above the door, and were strung above the steps leading down. She had refreshed them year after year. Layer upon layer of protection.

He wasn't sure about any of that. He never had been. But he had to believe her. She was all he had.

Like the protection the wild offered. But this came from Sally. It was woven with love and all the more powerful for that.

Her protection had been everything to him. And he had lost it.

The hiss beside his ear was bad enough. He could imagine teeth and claws on his skin, waiting to sink in, to end him. It came close, that malevolent presence, but it couldn't touch him. He descended the stone steps and his feet hit the compacted earth at the bottom. The wine was only the reach of his arm away. He should have moved it up to the kitchen.

But he had to come down here every so often. It was necessary. A sacrifice that needed to be made. A test of will. And a way to make sure everything was still intact.

'Why not just lock the door and throw away the key?' he asked Sally once.

She'd smiled. God, he missed her smile. 'Because then he would just get more powerful, like a pot with the lid left on. It would boil over eventually. And we don't want that, *mo stór*.'

So that was why he still kept things down here, still offered that small sacrifice of coming down here once in a while and facing the darkness. He wasn't sure it was working. Not anymore.

It was boiling over anyway. Just because Alex was here.

With Theo it had been hungry, needy. But Alex... Alex was a whole different thing. It was ravenous. Like her presence was feeding an addiction. Like it had been waiting for her all along.

And not just in the house. Not just Blaise Chambers. In him as well.

'Help me, Sally,' he murmured. 'I need you now. More than ever.'

He felt the teeth press close again, sharper, far more vicious. And then...

A scent like wildflowers. He breathed it in, relieved to sense her presence at last.

'Go to her, mo stór. It's all right. It's meant to be.'

Sally, his Sally, still here. It was all right. She was still protecting him, protecting this place. She had promised that she would always be there for him when he needed her. Her presence was a blessing. Sally was a joy.

He welcomed her in, feeling her sweep over and through him as he grabbed a bottle of wine from a case and turned back to the door at the top of the stone steps. The lightbulb flickered as if it was a candle.

Old house, old electrics... one desperate scrabbling thought, frantic for an explanation. He locked the door as firmly as he could.

CHAPTER 31

ALEX

The drawing room was warm and cosy now, the night cut off outside. Alex had been looking into the fire but turned at a slight noise to find Nick right behind her, so close she could feel the heat of his body. He had left the wine bottle on the occasional table but she hadn't heard a thing. Her hand came up to his chest and stopped there, feeling the muscles beneath the soft cotton, the beating of his heart under his ribs, the way he drew in a ragged breath. It came back in a rush, that need.

Now it was different again.

Theo had ordered him not to touch her. And how dare he? How *dare* he think he had any say over her life? Theo was dead.

And she was not. Damn it, she needed to feel alive. And Nick was right here.

'We...' he began and then seemed to lose the words he'd been about to say.

'We what?' she asked. God, she wanted him. There was something so animal about it, so vital. She gazed up steadily into his eyes, illuminated in the fire, and all she could think was how much she wanted him. Her body ached with that need.

'We shouldn't.'

No doubt what that was. What they both wanted. This was different, she knew. No outside interference. This need came from her. And yes, part of it was fuelled by what had happened upstairs, by the voices that shouldn't be possible. Her whole worldview was turning upside down.

Nick had come to her rescue. He'd promised to protect her. He was there for her.

'Because of what Theo said?' she asked. 'My brother was never the boss of me.' If anything, Theo telling her not to do something like that was liable to make her do it. And he should have known that. Nick shook his head, but he didn't smile. He didn't move away either.

Nick closed his eyes and leaned into her touch. Alex slid her hand down his chest as slowly as she could, carefully, taking in every contour. The muscles were taut as wire, stretched almost to breaking point. He shuddered at her touch and his breath came out in a long low hiss.

Her own pulse thudded through her whole body.

She wanted him. God, she wanted him so much. She couldn't remember desire like this for anyone. So maybe it wasn't all natural.

Did that make it wrong?

'Nick,' she murmured, and brought her hand up to his face. Safer, she thought, at first. Then he opened his eyes again and it was not safe. Not at all. The hunger in him made her whole body quake with answering need. 'Talk to me.'

He shook his head and something told her he just couldn't find words again. His mouth opened and she wondered if he still had words to use. But she had to know. She had to hear him say it because if he was losing himself, then this wasn't right either.

He licked his lips, and she couldn't tear her eyes off that flash of his tongue, the hint of teeth behind it. The hunger. The need.

Slowly his gaze met hers, and he nodded. From somewhere he managed to dredge up his voice. And it was his voice, ragged and wary, but *his* voice. 'I want you, Alex. From the first moment I saw you.'

Alex gave a small laugh of recognition. She couldn't help herself. Hadn't she been thinking the same thing?

She pressed her palm against his cheek and felt him shudder. A fragrance of wildflowers flowed around them on the air. Something from the fire perhaps, or something else. Something she couldn't define. But it was there, sweet and comforting.

She didn't know what she was doing. She was still just acting on instinct but if this was wrong... it really didn't *feel* wrong. How could it be wrong?

Apart from being out here illuminated by the fire, with the curtains open, in the dark, where anyone could come by and see them... Except they couldn't, could they? This was all private land. Her land. And he was its guardian.

The word rang around her head. *Her guardian.*

That meant something, something ancient and important. And this place... this place was special. Magical. It had a purpose. So did he.

Her guardian.

She shifted herself closer. His scent was of the wild as well, intoxicating. And now she had touched him all she wanted to do was touch him more. Both hands moved against his skin, pushing under the t-shirt, on to his chest, down his side, up again to touch his throat. Nick's mouth closed on her fingers and he sucked one into the warm depths, his tongue teasing the sensitive fingertip.

Alex gasped in surprise and delight. She couldn't help herself.

'Do you understand?' he asked. 'It's a bond. Between us. A blessing from the wild. Please tell me you understand?'

Because it would break his heart if she didn't. That was what his look seemed to tell her. Or if she did this, without realising what it might mean… that would be wrong too. What it might really mean.

And though she couldn't put it into words, somehow, instinctively she did. And he was right. There was such a weight to this place, to Wildewood Hall. Anything done here, promises made or vows exchanged, or pleasure shared… well it would mean so much more than anywhere else.

Did she want that?

But one look at Nick, and the longing on his oh-so-serious face…

Oh yes, she did. Even if she couldn't put it into words.

She leaned forward, rising on her toes, and pressed her lips to his. For a moment she felt him shudder again, his whole body, as if electricity ran through him.

'What do you want me to do?' she asked, lips still brushing his.

And then he touched her. Finally. His hands pulled her shirt out of her jeans and his fingers skimmed across the hot flesh underneath. She pulled it off without thinking about it and reached behind herself to unhook her bra. The air on her skin was a shock for only a moment. Then Nick was there instead. His hands, his mouth, the press of his body to hers.

And oh God, she was really doing this. Here, in the drawing room, in front of the fire. And everything told her that was a terrible idea.

But she was with Nick. And Nick would never allow her to come to any harm. She was the lady of Wildewood Hall. He was her guardian. That sense of the wild cocooned them both.

His mouth joined his hands, teasing her, his eyes closed as he knelt with her and eased her back onto the floor. The aged rug felt warm and soft beneath her. The next thing she knew they were both wriggled out of jeans and underwear and then…

They were both naked.

All around them the Hall seemed to still in anticipation, waiting, watching. And this time she didn't care. She closed her eyes and drew in a shuddering breath, welcoming him.

Nick bent his head to kiss her and then worked his way down her body, his mouth a hot line of desire. He licked her throat and she arched up with a startled gasp as he claimed first one and then the other breast, caressing the nipples to hard points before leaving them cold and wanting with only the touch of the night's air to sate them.

His mouth moved down further, head bowing between her legs and she couldn't keep in a growl of need as his tongue explored there.

As he moved, she felt the touch of leaves and vines, and other living things. Things green and growing, brushing against her bare skin, delighting her, delighting in her. As if she was making love to the wild wood itself.

And then... then she wasn't in the Hall anymore. They were outside, in the night, in the stone circle. The moon shone high overhead and the trees whispered.

Madness, this was madness. But she didn't want it to end. She never wanted it to end. This fantasy, this experience, all that it was to be with him. Alex buried her hands in Nick's hair, tangling them in the length of it, the same way the tendrils and vines tangled around the two of them, and pressed him closer to her.

His tongue teased her. Her hips moved in an increasingly frantic rhythm and she threw back her head as she gasped for air.

The trees crowded close. The night air was warm, like a cocoon around them both. The stones were silent sentinels, encircling them. They were safe here. It was perhaps the only place they were safe. And the land rose around her, brushing soft shoots of life and vitality around her. Something bound itself around her ankles and her arms, traced lines over her stomach and her throat.

'Please,' she said, not even sure of all she was begging for. Apart from Nick. He was all she wanted now. All she could think of.

'Are you sure?' he asked, as breathless as she was.

In the study, she had felt like someone else, as if her whole being had been overcome and transformed, possessed, but here, now, whether she was in the drawing room lost in a fantasy or really had somehow been transported to the woods, she was herself. She had never been so wholly herself in her life. And she was sure. So sure. She wanted him. She wanted to be made whole.

And the wild wood offered that. To be more herself than she had ever been before. To be free.

Nick offered that.

'Please, Nick. Now. I need you.' The words spilled out and Nick rose over her, his eyes so hungry, but still wary. Careful. He was always so careful. She admired that about him. How could she not? Too many people in her life had been reckless with her. She had to be the sensible one.

But not here, not now.

She saw the hesitation in his eyes. Nick thought he might hurt her, but Alex didn't. Not for a moment. He couldn't. Not him.

You don't know him, some last thread of sanity tried to tell her. Not really. He could be anyone, or anything. She knew nothing about him, not really. Not where he came from, or anything about his past before he came here, or what had happened with Sally and Theo. Just wild stories, vague mentions, and things that made no sense.

But she didn't care. Not anymore. And she did know him. Somehow. Somewhere. In her heart of hearts...

He groaned as he entered her, her name twisted with a

sound of agony and pleasure, and she felt that noise, that vibration, all the way through her aching body. When he started to move, she was lost. Lost in him, lost in the woods, lost in pleasure and desire and everything in between. She had never felt so alive. Nothing had ever felt so right. This sense of belonging, of being part of everything around her... His mouth on hers teased every cry from her body and his fingers threaded through hers, pushing her hands down into the soft embrace of the earth. Briars tangled around their wrists, thorns digging into the skin, tightening, binding them together in pain and pleasure.

This was a promise, she realised. This was a vow. It was sacred. She accepted it wholeheartedly. And she wanted it. All of it. Everything Nick and the wild wood had to offer. This was her land. She had claimed it. And he was the guardian.

Alex's hips rose to meet him, and she cried out. In that instant she was everything, everywhere, the trees and the earth and the night sky, she was part of the woods and part of the land and Nick was hers, completely, utterly, part of her as she was part of him. She could no more have let him go than she could let loose her own soul. He gasped out something, words of promise, vows and sacred assurances. And all Alex could do was accept them, accept him.

'Yes, yes, Nick, please, yes.'

He groaned something she didn't catch as he sank into her, deep and perfect, filling her completely, his body a bow against hers, every muscle straining to give her pleasure and chase his own. He came silently, hard, mouth open and his whole expression almost dazed as he gave himself up to sensation, as he lost himself in her and in the world of the green, of the wild.

Ripples of pleasure still ran through Alex's body. She lifted her hand again and ran it through his long hair, brushing it back from his face as she watched him struggle to catch his breath. He was a dream in human form, everything she could have desired and wanted, an incarnation of pleasure.

The scent of wildflowers wrapped itself around them, the press of the wild and the murmuring sound of a distant voice singing for joy, just on the edge of her hearing. Magic, she thought. It was like magic.

Finally, Nick found his voice again, although he didn't open his eyes, not yet. He let his head fall forward, his hair curtaining them both, as he struggled back to himself.

'Sally, *mo stór*,' he sighed, his voice a song of adoration and relief. 'Thank you...'

All around her, Alex's dream shattered, hurling her back into Wildewood Hall, tangled on the floor of the drawing room.

With a man who had just called out someone else's name.

CHAPTER 32

NICK

Nick snapped his eyes open with the horror of what he had just done and the words he had said. It was like a bucket of cold water. No, worse. Far worse.

He stared down at her face. Her beautiful, horrified face. Firelight turned it golden, her eyes already brimming with molten tears.

He'd sensed Sally's presence around him, the scent of wild-flowers and her acceptance of this, of him and Alex, her joy in his joy. She'd told him to go to her. He had been so grateful that she would give him this, that she would release him at last. To Alex. So he'd thanked her.

The words were like ash in his throat now and dark laughter echoed on the edge of his hearing.

'I—' he began, and couldn't get any further.

'Please, just... just get up...' Alex whispered, refusing to make eye contact with him now.

No, this was all going wrong. Completely, utterly wrong.

He drew back, fighting the urge to just take off outside, into the deepest part of the forest and never emerge again. That would be fair, wouldn't it? But Christ, he wanted to. He needed to. He was a creature of need. A monster.

Alex grabbed her shirt and pulled it on, then her jeans, never looking at him.

Nick couldn't move. But he had to do something. He had to stop her before everything was ruined.

'Alex,' he tried again. His voice cracked as he said her name.

'Don't worry about it. I shouldn't have pushed things. It's my fault.' Her voice sounded leaden, as if she was forcing the words out. No matter what she was saying, she didn't believe it.

But it wasn't her fault. This was all him.

'Alex,' he said again and reached out to touch her shoulder. She froze and, to his horror, he could see the tears spilling over her eyelashes, firelight making them glow. When she didn't pull away, he drew her closer, wrapped his arms around her and held her. 'I'm sorry. Truly. I'm so sorry.'

She just shook her head. And what else was there to say? He'd called out Sally's name, not hers. He'd called out her name a thousand times before when they were here together. For a moment, just a moment, he'd been lost, and so grateful that Sally had been there, and let him go to have this with Alex. And it wasn't fair. And it wasn't right.

But there was no denying that it had happened.

Alex trembled against him.

'I don't know what came over me,' she whispered. The wash of shame hit him like a wave. He cursed himself.

Even though Alex had been all he could think of, all he could feel... *he'd said Sally's name.*

He was an idiot. A fool. A bastard.

'I'll make it up to you,' he managed at last. 'Any way you want. Any way I can.'

But what could he offer her? How could she want anything from him now?

He kissed her hair, inhaled its floral scent and the traces of the sweet earth and leaves of the wild woods that lingered in it now. She was still a de Wilde, after all. He would protect her, keep her safe.

Why had he said Sally's name? He had felt acceptance, pleasure in his pleasure. For a moment he'd thought she was releasing him, letting him feel all he had lost again, with Alex. For just a second it had felt like they might have a future.

And he had screwed it up. Completely.

Or had it all just been some kind of cruel trick?

A flare of anger took him by surprise. Not at her, never at her. At the house. At the woods which had reached out through him and used her. At the trees. For the first time in his life, Nick felt a low burst of rage at the world that had made him. How could they do that? How could they use him to hurt her like this?

'Alex,' he murmured.

'*Stop*.' The word was sharp, and laced with pain. She turned away, wrapping her arms around her chest. 'Stop saying my name. It's too late.'

Nick cursed himself, and his stupid voice. This was all some kind of vile joke, something the house had dreamed up to torment them both. And it was working.

'It was a mistake,' he tried again.

'Yes, all of this. It was all a mistake. I'm an idiot. You're still in mourning and I took advantage of that. If anyone should be apologising—'

'What?' He pulled back, and gently as he could, turned her around so he could see her face again. Alex didn't fight him but once they were face to face she stared resolutely into his eyes. She wasn't kidding. She was in deadly earnest. 'You don't understand—'

'You loved your wife and lost her. You clearly aren't over it. I should never—'

'No. I mean, yes, I loved her. And yes, I might never be

truly over losing her. But I wanted this. I wanted *you*. Please, Alex, listen to what I'm saying. I want *you*. Have done since I first saw you. And I lost Sally long before she died. Her and Theo—'

Now she really did jerk back in his arms, horror painting her features. 'Sally and *Theo*? Oh, Jesus, Nick! What did my brother do?'

Oh, that. He hadn't got around to explaining about that. It wasn't exactly the kind of thing that was easy to broach. He shrugged. 'Fell in love. Sally was easy to fall in love with. So was Theo. And I—'

And I'm not, he wanted to say. I'm a monster. I'm a means to an end. Maybe I always was. Oh, she was good to me, and I adored her. But...

It wasn't a matter of who loved who, or who was married to who. The land here wanted what the land wanted. It wanted him and Alex together now. So did Sally.

How could he tell Alex that? He'd terrify her again. That seemed to be the only thing he was good at.

At least the woods didn't want her life. But they wanted everything else.

The house seemed to give a ripple of satisfaction. He felt his desire stir again. Already. The wild was gone now, sated. And the house was still waiting.

Wine and firelight and the two of them alone together and...

Give in to your nature. Be what you were always meant to be. Take your due.

He drew in a ragged breath as the darkness in him surged up again. His skin tingled, the heat beneath it spreading. No. Not like this. The house had got a taste of desire, and it wanted more. It wanted her. It would use him to get her.

'No,' he murmured to himself as if he could make it real, make himself believe it. This wasn't right. He felt like he was being forced into something. He'd felt that since the first moment she had arrived. Like they were both being manipulated. Like something was trying to push the two of them into bed together. And then what?

When they lost themselves in each other again, in that wild pleasure, what would it do? What would they do? Had it been like this for Theo and Sally? Had the house manipulated them like it was trying to manipulate him? Because if so... they had not had any choice, if the entity infecting the Hall made them, had forced them...

Then it wasn't a betrayal, was it?

And he wasn't the monster he feared he was, tied and bound to this place, created to serve and protect it. Made to love against his will...

Because he had loved. Loved Sally, loved Theo.

He had been in the cellar and he had sensed it. He didn't have a name for it. No one did. Just... the thing in the cellar. Sally had called it an old god. Professor de Wilde had called it a dark entity in his notes. Theo had called it the monster. And sometimes *that bastard.*

Chambers had made sacrifices in the earth beneath the house, that was what they said, that he had died there. He had woken it through rites of blood, and shed the last drops of his own there in the end.

Nick was no stranger to the other, to the way it moved through human flesh and changed it. But the communion he found in the wild wood was so very different from this. Now he was at war with himself, torn in two by conflicting powers. One from the shadows and the dirt, the other from the trees.

'*Oh Nick, love,*' he almost heard Sally's murmur of dismay. The scent of wildflowers rose around him but so too did something else, something rank and putrid. '*Nick, what have you done?*'

It wasn't his fault. It had never been his fault. The anger that rose inside him was blind and furious.

If anything, it was *her* fault. *Sally's* fault...

He'd had a life and lost it. And after that, after the fear and the pain, he'd been at peace. And she had stolen it from him. She had stolen everything from him...

His hands shook. He balled them into fists at his sides. That wasn't right, was it? It couldn't be. Because he loved her still, beyond reason, beyond rationality. Sally was everything. It was written on his bones.

'I told you not to touch her,' Theo whispered, his voice full of sorrow. Had Theo known this would happen? How could he have known?

'Nick? Are you okay?' Alex's voice cut through all the echoes of the past. Even now, even hurt and upset, she saw him in pain and she cared. How could she care so much? He'd done nothing to deserve it. Nothing. Alex's hand, still shaking, touched his face, her fingertips so light and cold against his flesh.

'No,' he said again. His own voice sounded strange to his ears, slurred and deep, a growl. He was losing himself. Those weren't his thoughts. He needed to get out of the house. 'Stay here,' he told her, aware of the rough edge to the words. He couldn't help it. 'Don't follow me.' He needed to get away from her. He needed...

Her... her body against his again, her skin pressed to his, lips on him and his on her... gasping her name as he filled her... making her his at last, again and again, until he had all she was able to give, and then still more and taking and taking and...

It was too much. Far too much. The need, the hunger, the urge far too strong. It wasn't him. It couldn't be him. Nick had always been a careful lover, giving and open, and the demands coursing through him right now were as far from that as it could get.

The darkness was too strong. Chambers reaching out, determined to use him. To hurt her.

The bastard...

He couldn't. He just couldn't. He wanted her. Too much. Far too much. As much as he had ever wanted his wife. Or any other lovers. More. Far more. He didn't know if that was real. Not anymore. He didn't know if any of it was real... what he felt for Alex, or what he had felt for Sally, and Theo...

He didn't know if anything he felt was real. Not now. It broke his heart. He could feel it cracking in·his chest, his racing pulse tearing it apart.

He just *couldn't*.

Nick bolted for the door leading outside, down the hallway, through the kitchen and out into the night, sprinting for the woods as fast as he could. It was like an infection, that thing beneath his skin, in his blood, trying to make him into someone he was not. He could hear Chambers' laughter ringing through his head.

He needed the green, the wild. Like Sally had said, he needed salvation from something even more ancient and less human than the monster even now intent on using him. They had brought it here, the two of them, him and Alex, drawn the wild into the house and tangled themselves together with it.

They had woken it. And they had woken the house.

And that was dangerous. Especially to a de Wilde. He had to get away from her, away from Alex.

ALEX

It was hours before Nick came back. She'd waited up, scanning through the diary, drinking the wine by herself.

Don't follow me.

No arguing with that. He'd looked ready to snap so all Alex could do was watch him vanish into the night. She wanted to follow him, to make sure he was all right, but she didn't dare.

They had made love. There was no other word for it. Better than any of her dreams. She'd never felt so fulfilled, so perfectly in tune with another human being.

And then... then he'd said Sally's name.

The house was horribly still and quiet without him in it. That was probably a good thing. She didn't want to think about ghosts. She didn't want to think about Theo warning Nick away, rightly so considering what had happened. Or of Nick fleeing into the night rather than face another intimate moment with her. But she still couldn't shake off the feeling that they had both been set up somehow.

When she finally heard him come back something in her unwound with relief. She didn't know what she'd say to him.

She couldn't find the words. But surely something would come to her.

Nick didn't come to find her though. Not at first. She stared at the fire, listening to the soft sounds of his movement down in the kitchen and in the hallway. And she certainly wasn't going to go looking for him. She had to have some pride left.

Instead, she turned to her research. It had to be good for something. Using her phone Alex photographed the notebook, each and every page. The light would just have to be enough. She sent the lot to Arnold with a brief description of what had happened. Very brief. No mention of sex. Or a man running away from her into the darkness.

She must have dozed off in the chair. She woke to him tucking a blanket over her.

'Alex?' Nick's voice was soft and cautious. But it was his voice again. That edge of panic was gone. 'I – I owe you an apology.'

She blinked herself to wakefulness. He was kneeling down beside her. There were leaves in his hair and dirt on his beautiful face. She reached out absently to touch him and this time he didn't pull away. It was almost as if he leaned into her hand, as she brushed his cheekbone.

The scent of the woods was everywhere about him. But so too was the peace.

'Are you – are you all right?' she asked.

As if running off into the night was the most normal thing ever. Maybe it was here. There seemed to be nothing normal about Wildewood Hall. Or the woods.

He nodded, although his eyes still looked troubled. They were so deep a brown, but in those depths she could see flecks of gold as well, and... and green... She could get lost in his eyes.

She didn't know what she'd said or done. She didn't know how to ask. She pushed herself up to sit straighter in the armchair and her body protested.

'I was worried. When you took off. I'm sorry, Nick. I didn't mean—'

He smiled, as if nothing had happened, as if he hadn't fled her company just hours earlier. It was like a different man. 'Not your fault, Alex. You should go back to sleep. Why not take the sofa? Or my room, if you want.'

Go up those stairs on her own? No. And, she noticed, he didn't suggest for a moment she go up to the master bedroom where Chambers' portrait clung stubbornly to the wall outside the door. For that she was grateful.

'Where will you sleep?'

'Here,' he said, and settled down by the fire with one of the blankets.

Far enough away from her to be safe. Still close enough to guard her. Her guardian...

She would have to leave it at that. It had been a mistake. A terrible mistake. Better to leave it be and never touch it again.

Never touch him again.

Alex had ended up sleeping through breakfast, curled up on the sofa. Nick was nowhere to be found and so she had set to work analysing the recordings of last night. Now she'd missed lunch too. She wasn't entirely sure how or why. She hadn't nodded off, but she'd been so engrossed in her work that time just skipped by her. She had downloaded the data from the cameras and run them through the filtering software but they showed nothing of any use. Nothing beyond shadows and dust reflecting the light, all of which could be easily explained.

The other recorders had picked up some noises which might be whispers or sighs, or might be nothing more than the building itself settling, or Nick moving around somewhere below.

Certainly nothing like the voice the two of them had heard.

She forced herself to ignore the way her body still craved him. Even knowing he still wanted a woman who was two years dead. She cocooned herself in work. In research. In what she knew.

She sent all her data through to Eduardo. He was a genius when it came to this kind of work. And Eduardo would tell her the truth, no matter what it was.

The email she got back from Arnold was worse than she imagined.

> I read up on Blaise Chambers. He was a real piece of work. Is he your ghost? Daphne says watch out for him. She thinks he's the one who attacked her. Ran what they called a Hell-fire Club but was more like a cult. Your grandfather says Chambers built a temple under the house.

Under the house? There was only the cellar and that wasn't that big. A teeny tiny temple then, surrounded by wine bottles.

> But the professor thought it was contained, that he had it sealed away. After your father died. But… he says Chambers wanted you back in the house, to wake it again. Pretty lurid stuff here, Alex. You need to be careful.

Arnold still wasn't finished. Alex read the rest of the message and her throat seemed to weld itself shut.

> You may need an exorcism. Remember what to do? I can send a crib sheet.

Oh good, Alex thought. And no, she didn't need an exorcism crib sheet. She'd seen Arnold do endless exorcisms and blessings. It was all hokum anyway.

Or at least that was what she was going to tell herself.

Her hand strayed to the circle of twigs and flowers that Maeve had made for her. Perhaps she ought to keep it with her permanently. Protection, the girl had said. The wood's protection. Keeping her safe from the house.

Her own grandfather had been afraid of it. That much was clear from his writings. He blamed it for the loss of his wife, and his son. He blamed it for everything. And yet it had its claws into him as deeply as was possible.

To the last.

And now, Alex was afraid it was working on her as well.

CHAPTER 34

ALEX

As night fell on the house again, Alex could already feel the presences growing. She was more sensitive to them now. Blaise, her ancestors, all those lost souls who had died in the house.

That brought her head up as the realisation struck her.

Theo hadn't died in here, had he?

Her brother and her father had both been found in the woods, in the stone circle or nearby.

But she had heard Theo. Clearly.

She and Nick had both heard him.

What did that mean?

What happened to someone who died not in the house but in the woods? And why then was Theo coming back? To help her? Then why Theo and not Dad?

She opened the diary again, this time towards the end.

He has but one purpose, one drive, one true desire. He will set them all against all that they have loved, and make them his, body and soul. Omnes contra omnes. They will pour out libations over his head, offerings so sweet and so profane. They will give up all they are to him.

Her grandfather's words sounded like the ravings of a madman. And yet, they were echoes of other things. Things she had heard in this house. The words on Blaise Chambers' portrait. Things Blaise had said to her.

If it really was Blaise Chambers.

Living and dead are all trapped here. All our line are forfeit. Those who bound him, and those who guard him still. That is the price they promised and the price that must be paid. We must atone and they must pay their debts. Unto the very last, the two bloodlines combined. And when that last thread is seized or cut, Crom will be free.

Crom? Her eyes lingered on the word. The voice had mentioned Crom, hadn't it? She couldn't remember. It slipped through her memories like an eel and her mind shuddered at its touch. And yet they went hand in hand, somehow. Chambers. And Crom.

And she was the last thread of the de Wildes. Grandfather meant her. When he wasn't raving about bloodlines anyway. He had to mean her.

He has his eye on the girl. Even now. Especially now she's of age. I begged Edward not to bring her back but he has never believed. She carries Kilfayne in her as much as de Wilde. Chambers will use her, and tear the barriers down. He will manipulate her desires and her dreams, make her think that his wishes are her wishes. And heaven help her if that happens.

Alex sighed and closed her eyes, wishing she had never come here. She could still leave. She ought to leave. It was the sensible thing to do. Anyone would tell her so. Her online stalkers knew she was here and they'd soon be bombarding her again. And Nick still wanted his wife. The house was manipulating them both or the sex last night wouldn't have happened.

But she would be leaving all those ghosts trapped here.

Theo. She'd be leaving Theo. Trapped or not, something was drawing him back here.

She'd be leaving Nick trapped here too. In a living hell. Forever trying to hold the line against a force that had grown too strong, a reality that was tearing him apart.

And he said Sally had called him. That he didn't know why he'd come here in the first place and clearly Sally wouldn't let him go.

Nick didn't talk about his past, about where he came from. Nothing before he met Sally. Like he barely remembered it.

'Damn it, Sally Neary,' Alex hissed under her breath. 'Why did you have to embroil him in all this? Why did it have to be him?'

A thud came from upstairs. Of course it did. Who wanted her attention now?

Nick still hadn't come back, not to Alex's knowledge anyway. There was no one else here.

And she had just invoked the spirit of the last of the wise women of Kilfayne. Sally Walker who still had her claws so deeply in her widower that he called out her name during sex with someone else.

'Right,' she said and pushed herself up from her seat, the diary forgotten. 'Right, enough. You want to have it out with me, Sally, let's have it out. Because I have some things to say to you.'

Another thump. Like a dare.

Alex stormed up the stairs, only pausing to grab one of the recorders which she thumbed on as she followed the increasing noises from a room at the far end of the main corridor. She didn't know this part of the house but it didn't matter. It was hers. All of it. Just like Nick had said and she had had enough.

She threw open the door to reveal a narrow corridor with a slanted ceiling. It must have been servants' quarters once upon a time but now it was heavy with dust and dimly lit by light coming through a dirty window at the far end.

Bells hung on metal coils along the wall to her left.

Another thud, this time from behind another door, further down the narrow corridor. There was something in there. Someone.

No. Some*thing*.

'Who is it?' she called out, her voice sounding much louder than she would have thought. 'Who's there?'

There was another noise, a guttural cackle, and then a shush, followed by a giggle. Then a scuffling and something else fell, a great clatter of noise.

Alex grabbed the door and flung it open.

The room beyond was filled with boxes and cases, and a jumble of lifetimes. Books turned almost white with dust spread across the floor, in between half a dozen chairs.

And in the middle of it all sat Maeve Walker, a battered tin tea set straight out of the 1960s laid out in front of her – three cups, three saucers – as if she had been playing with friends.

Perhaps she had.

Alex stared at her and Maeve stared back, open-mouthed, as if she had not expected any interruption, and certainly not from Alex.

'*Maeve?* What are you doing here?'

Maeve looked one way and then the other, and again, Alex got the distinct impression she was making eye contact with people Alex couldn't see.

'I didn't go into your office. Daddy said not to disturb you. So, I just came up here.'

'But how did you get here? To the house, I mean. Why aren't you with your grandmother?'

Maeve scrunched up her face. 'I *was* with her. I was with

her all morning and it was *boring*. We just went to people's houses and I had to sit quiet and behave. I wanted to see Daisy and Rose.'

Daisy and Rose... Alex narrowed her eyes. The dust swirled softly around the girl, and in the half-light of the room Alex might almost be convinced that it formed two clusters, not much bigger than Maeve herself. Almost.

'Are they here now?' she asked dubiously.

Maeve frowned. 'Yes...' She sounded wary now, as if afraid that she was in trouble. And when Nick found out about this she probably would be.

'Maeve, did you come up here all by yourself?'

'I walked. I was very careful. I didn't use the roads.'

Oh, sweet Jesus, Alex thought. Anything could have happened to her. She could have got lost in the woods. She could be dead in a ditch. She was only six, for God's sake. Patricia had to be losing her mind about now.

'Downstairs,' Alex said. 'Now, while I ring your grandmother.'

Maeve looked horrified. 'But she'll be cross.'

'Oh, you bet she will.' Alex was already pulling up the number on her phone.

Maeve began to cry, loudly, miserably, a long wail of a small child who didn't know how to get out of whatever trouble she had just landed herself in.

Patricia answered the phone on the first ring, her voice pained and panicked. 'Alex?'

'She's here at the Hall. I just found—'

A cardboard box flew off the top of one of the piles, just as if someone had hurled it right at Alex with all the strength in them. She turned just in time, and the box hit her shoulder, spinning her around, sending the papers inside flying around her like giant demented butterflies.

'Daisy, no!' Maeve wailed, dismayed and horrified. 'Stop!'

'Enough,' Alex snapped, a voice of authority she wasn't even aware she could produce. Not at Maeve, but at the air beside her, and a figure shimmered into view. Just for a second. A little girl, like Maeve. And then she was gone again. Another pile of boxes started to shake threateningly. 'Daisy, Rose, just stop it. Now.'

Patricia's voice sounded tinny on the phone still in her hand. Damn, she was still there and now she sounded pissed off. *Really* pissed off.

Alex winced and put the phone back to her ear. She couldn't afford to get into an argument right now. Better to be short and sweet. 'Dr Neary? Sorry, something fell. She's fine. She's here with me. We'll wait for you. I'll call Nick. Let him know what's happened.'

She hung up, aware of the ominous presences behind her even as she brought up Nick's number and pressed the screen. 'Maeve, let's go downstairs,' she said, carefully gentling her voice. The malice fizzled in the air around them. This wasn't good. None of it.

Nick sounded out of breath when he answered, but he didn't hide the concern in his voice at her calling him. The tone, however, said that he didn't know. Not yet. Damn. 'Alex? What's wrong?'

'Maeve's here at the house. She just showed up on her own. We're in the attic. I phoned Patricia but I think—'

'*What?* I-I'm on my way.'

That was all he said. The line cut off and Alex wasn't sure if he'd hung up or the signal had just died. In this house, anything was possible.

Maeve was sobbing loudly, thoroughly miserable now. She leaned against the wall, her hands over her face.

Alex felt terrible but all she could do now was damage control. 'Look, let's go down to the kitchen and find out if your dad left any biscuits around.'

'He m-makes the best b-biscuits,' Maeve agreed, hiccoughing through the sentence. She held out her hand for Alex to take. But as Alex reached for her, she snatched it away. No, not snatched. It was more like someone hit it aside. Maeve gave a little gasp of pain and alarm. 'No, Rose! That's nasty. She's my friend too.'

Another flicker of movement and this time Alex saw both the girls glimmer into view. Maeve's age. Barely older than their portraits downstairs. Daisy was blonde with ringlets, her face a soft oval with rosy cheeks, like her portrait. Rose had dark hair in plaits, and she smiled at Alex in a slightly unsettling way. Too intently, too fixed.

Their scrutiny was powerful. As if something else was looking out through those eyes. It reminded her too keenly of Blaise Chambers.

'I-I'm your relative,' Alex said, because she couldn't think of anything else, not when they looked at her like that. *Like sharks,* something deep inside her whispered, and she wanted to curl up and hide. 'Sort of.'

What was she to them? She didn't know the family tree. A cousin? Or great-great-great-niece or... something... Cousin. Cousin was easier. Quicker too.

'I remember you,' a voice whispered, a little girl's voice with an edge of something else. *'You were here before. Long ago. We only wanted to play. Blaise said we could. But she wouldn't let you play with us, the old witch...'*

A chill shivered up Alex's spine again, colder and darker than before.

They knew her. They remembered her. From when she was a kid.

On one hand, they were only little girls. She could see that. Of course they wanted to play, not that whatever they had in mind sounded playful. Not with Blaise Chambers' name appended to it. They'd wanted to play with her, and now with

Maeve. On the other... they were ghosts. Actual ghosts. She was looking at ghosts. She had the proof she'd always wanted.

Not objective proof. This could all be a hallucination. But she could see them, was talking to them. And they were talking back. Rationally. Clearly...

Her phone felt cold and heavy in her hand. She could take a photo. She could do it one-handed. Would they come out in a photo? If so... Gabe would lose his mind.

And she... she would finally have proof. The actual proof she had always wanted, demanded. She'd have it right there...

'Just hold still a second,' she murmured, and lifted the phone up, framing them as best she could. She pressed the camera button on the side, praying it would work. It had to work. That terrible fake shutter noise echoed around the attic room.

Maeve gave a cry of alarm, an abortive warning, and something hard slammed into Alex from behind. She fell onto her knees and another wave of impacts sent her face down into the floor. Weight piled down on top of her, layer upon layer of it, pinning her there, helpless.

The door opened behind them. 'Alex? Oh, dear God, Alex. What happened? Maeve? What did you do?'

Nick was standing over her, hauling off magazines and boxes and whatever else had avalanched its way on top of her. Alex tried to stand up but her whole side protested. She coughed, clearing dust out of her throat and mouth and somehow that was even worse.

'Maeve,' she wheezed.

'Did she do this?' Nick looked horrified at the thought and his voice darkened as he turned his attention on his daughter. 'Did you?' The girl stood all alone now, awkwardly, one leg wound around the other, her hands knotted together.

Alex's heart squeezed inside her. It wasn't Maeve, and it wasn't fair she got the blame either. 'No. No of course not.'

How did she even begin to explain who, or what, had? She picked up her phone which she'd dropped when she went down and opened the screen.

And there it was.

Blurry, definitely not in focus, and mottled with flying dust and the weird half-light. But she could see Rose and Daisy flanking Maeve, both of them. Not quite there, not quite real... but she could see them.

'Nick,' she hissed and showed it to him. 'Nick, look.'

He glanced at the screen and snorted. Like it wasn't ground-breaking. Like it wasn't anything special at all. But he wasn't scoffing at the picture, Alex realised. Rather he was annoyed by what it proved.

'Where are they?' he asked the girl, his tone positively murderous.

Maeve looked up at him in horror, like she didn't know him at all. 'They're gone, Daddy. I'm sorry. I didn't mean—'

'It's not *me* you should be apologising to.'

Her voice went up half an octave with anguish. 'I'm sorry, Alex.'

Alex folded. She couldn't help herself. 'It's okay, love. No harm done. But they – what were you doing with them? They could have hurt you, Maeve.'

'They wouldn't hurt me. They're my friends. They're just... they're angry and they're sad and they don't have a proper mummy either and they want... they want a family.'

Alex tried to stretch her aching body and then froze. A mother? Did they see her as a mother? She certainly hoped not. Taking back the phone, she sent the photo to the team. And instantly regretted that. What would they say? They were going to be all over this. Gabe would definitely be on the first plane out now.

Downstairs the main door slammed and they both heard Patricia shouting for Nick, her voice frantic.

'Shit,' he said, his face suddenly pale. Well, Alex wouldn't want to be on the wrong side of an angry Dr Patricia Neary either. Nick peered at her doubtfully. 'Are you sure you're okay?'

Just attacked by ghost children, she wanted to say but this was not the time. Just captured actual evidence of their existence too. The one thing every ghost hunter, no matter how sceptical they might be, has ever wanted. Something wild fluttered inside her, something that didn't feel part of her at all, a sense of vindication. Which was stupid because her whole mission had always been to disprove the existence of the supernatural, to find rational explanations and yes, to unmask charlatans.

Not... not *this*...

Not find proof. And at the same time that was all she had ever wanted. Actual proof.

Nick was still studying her, waiting for an answer, but anxious to intercept his mother-in-law as well. She nodded firmly and followed him down the servants' stairs and out into the main hall where the local doctor was standing, her hands on her hips, the very picture of an enraged grandmother. Alex stopped in the door, not wanting to intrude. Maeve gave a little moan of despair, and shrank back behind Alex's legs.

Oh yes, she knew what was coming.

'Where *is* she? I swear to you, Nick, I took my eyes off her for a second while I was seeing to Maura O'Shea's leg. I'd been trailing up and down the whole village looking for her when Alex rang. Where is she?'

'Here,' he said, in a surprisingly calm voice. 'Don't fret yourself, Patricia. She's safe. She made it to the house.'

'Anything could have happened to her. The little devil. You let her run wild, Nick. You always have. You and Sally both. No discipline, that's your problem. No discipline at all.'

Nick drew in a breath and the air went decidedly chilly, and not through anything paranormal. Not this time.

'Patricia, this isn't the time.'

Alex had never heard him use that tone with anyone before. She'd thought his relationship with Sally's mother was fine but this... this was weird.

'No, this is *exactly* what I'm talking about. You hole yourself away up here, because of all the nonsense Sally put in your head, and in that child's head. No wonder she hares off up here at the slightest provocation. She's frantic to be with you, Nick. You're all she has left. But neither of you should be here. You should have left when my Sally died. You should never have come back here. Everyone knows that, everyone says it. The whole place is cursed. Every dog in the street knows that. Those bastard de Wildes have brought us nothing but misery. Even now.'

Alex backed up, horrified to be overhearing any of this.

'Patricia—' Nick said again, trying to placate her with his tone before she said something more, but it was too late now.

'Yes, the de Wildes. It's always the de Wildes, isn't it? First that Theo, with Sally mooning over him when she had a perfectly good man in you. And you, staying with him after Sally died. Even though it was *his* fault. And now *her*.'

Patricia turned on Alex, glaring at her. She didn't even look like the same woman. Not anymore. The kindly doctor was gone and Alex didn't know what was in her place.

'Don't think I don't see you there, Alexandra de Wilde. This is all *your* fault. You swan back in here, stirring it all up again, waking up what should be left to lie. You and your whole cursed family.'

CHAPTER 35

NICK

It wasn't the first time Maeve had taken off. It wouldn't be the last either, Nick was sure.

'She's a runner, that one,' Patricia had said as soon as the child could walk.

Maeve ran every opportunity she got and she never looked back. Nick had never been sure if it was because she knew someone would come after her or if it didn't occur to her that she might actually get lost. Not at three, not at five, not now at six. She knew the woods, and the house, she knew the village like the back of her hand and all the paths in between, across the fields and through the woods. Her little feet always led her back here, to Wildewood Hall.

And once they lost Sally, Maeve had wanted to be nowhere else.

'With her da,' the villagers had said, as if it was the most natural thing in the world. And it ought to have been. She had lost her mother so she wanted to be with her father. As if she was afraid of losing him too. But Nick feared it was something else. She didn't want to be with him so much as here, in the

Hall. Where the spirit of her lost mother still lingered. Where she had friends.

And he had to be here too. Because who else was going to guard the place, to keep the spirits from doing untold harm? Patricia might think that everything Sally believed was arrant nonsense but that didn't change anything.

And now Patricia was blaming Alex? No. No, that wasn't fair. If all this was anyone's fault, it was his.

He should have been firmer with Maeve. He should have abandoned the Hall and the woods like Patricia said, or found some way to juggle this better.

If there was such a way.

But it was far too late now.

'Enough, Patricia,' he said, his voice far darker in tone, the voice he used for the woods, not for his mother-in-law, intentionally drawing her fire on him. 'This isn't Alex's fault. I know you're angry. I know you're scared. But Maeve's here. She's fine.'

Patricia snorted. She definitely was not herself today. Nick shot her a glare but she ignored him. 'I can't watch her all the time. I've got a practice to run, and there's no one else to do it.'

'I told you I'd pay for a childminder,' Nick began. It was an old argument, one he really didn't want to rehash again, especially not now.

'And who is that going to be? Some idiot like one of the Murphy girls? Faces never out of their phones. Our Maeve would run rings around them and you know it.'

It was not the time to point out that Maeve was already running rings around Patricia or they wouldn't be here.

'Why don't you get Patricia a cup of tea?' Alex tried to intervene. She didn't have to, especially given what had been said. He was never so grateful to hear another voice. 'She's had an awful shock, you know that. I'll stay with Maeve. We'll go to the study and wait, is that okay?'

Nick looked at his daughter, her pale little face, half-ghost herself. Her arms were wrapped around Alex's leg like she was clinging to a rock in a storm.

He'd seen the photo of Maeve with the two ghostly figures. The gleam in their eyes. The look on their faces. And he had a really bad feeling about it. He didn't want to consider what it might mean.

He just wanted his daughter to be safe. He didn't want to leave her right now.

But Alex was right. Patricia was beside herself and he needed to calm her down first if any of them were going to get anywhere.

'I won't let her out of my sight, Nick,' she said. 'I promise.'

And he believed her. Alex would look after Maeve, keep her occupied somehow. At least until he could get Patricia calmed down. She would keep her safe.

Patricia drank the tea with a grim determination but finally a wave of exhaustion passed over her and she looked old. Far older than her years.

'I apologise,' she said at last, oddly formal with embarrassment now, her eyes the same steely grey as her hair. 'I-I shouldn't have said any of that. I don't know what came over me.'

Nick wanted to say Wildewood Hall but he didn't dare. She'd have opinions on that and it wasn't the time. Besides, she'd only just set foot inside the house so that wasn't an excuse. Not that she needed one, not really. Patricia adored Maeve. She must have been beside herself with fear when she realised her granddaughter was missing.

And maybe the spirits here just latched onto that, ratcheting it up, revelling in her distress. The bastards.

'No need to apologise. You had a fright, that's all. And I know she's a handful.'

'She's a joy,' his mother-in-law said softly. 'But she's too like Sally sometimes. Too like my mother as well. Wild. Too full of fancies. It scares me, Nick, the situations she could put herself in. Has put herself in. It's not right.'

Nick chewed on his lower lip, not sure how to respond to that. 'She's just a little girl with an active imagination, Patricia. And yes, Sally and your mother filled her head with stories, but they're just stories...'

Patricia made a disgruntled '*pah*' noise.

'We both know that's not true. I'll apologise to Alex. She didn't deserve that. She doesn't deserve any of this, even if she is a de Wilde.'

'Don't—' he began, but she waved him to silence.

'Well, she is. And I can see the effect she has on you. And on this place as well. Right from the first I could see it. I'm from Kilfayne, boy. I may not practise what our foremothers taught, nor set any great stock by it, but I'm not without my own skills. Be careful, Nick. That family... they bring nothing but ruin to us. Even if they don't mean it. They can't help themselves. Look at Sally and Theo. Look what they did.'

Nick suppressed a groan. He really didn't want to bring this up. Especially not with his mother-in-law. 'They fell in love.'

'While she was *married* to you.'

Nick shrugged awkwardly. He would have thought Patricia would have taken Sally's side. He'd never dared to bring it up just in case she did. Because Patricia was the closest thing to family he had besides Maeve and he didn't want to lose her too.

'It wasn't their fault,' he whispered at last. 'It was this place. This house. It changes people.'

'Not you.'

He tried to smile. It didn't work. 'Me most of all, I think.'

Patricia shook her head, got to her feet and ran a hand over his hair. It was an unexpectedly maternal gesture and Nick didn't know what to do with it. He just stared at her. 'I don't know everything that our Sally did to you, pet, but she didn't deserve you. Other men would be raging still. But you defend her. Now, I should take her wayward child back home with me. Like you said, this house changes people and I don't want it changing our girl. She's too precious for that.' She paused, thoughtful. 'Or changing me, for that matter. That wasn't like me at all. I don't know what to say. The sooner I'm away the better. Besides, there's a storm coming in tonight.'

Nick forced himself to grin. She was from Kilfayne after all. 'Did you smell that on the wind?'

Might as well try to make a joke of it. But Patricia wasn't laughing. Neither was he.

'I heard it on the weather report. Like a normal person, thank you very much. Nasty one, I believe, a red warning. Storm Ferdia or some such. Why do they keep giving them names now?'

Nick shrugged again. To make them feel more real, he thought. More of a threat so people would take them seriously. Like the ghosts who lingered here, it was supposed to be easier if they had names rather than left them as faceless, terrifying entities. 'I should make sure the estate's secure then.'

'Always comes first, doesn't it?' Patricia muttered. He didn't know what to say to that. He felt a bit like he'd just been told off.

'But,' she went on grimly, 'before I go, I need to say I'm sorry to Alex. You –you really do like her, don't you?'

The question caught him off guard. It sounded light and carefree, but there was weight to it he couldn't define. He felt his face heat and winced. How on earth was he supposed to tell his late wife's mother how he felt about another woman, let alone how he felt about a woman like Alex?

Apparently, he didn't need to.

'Well, that answers that,' the older woman said with half a laugh. 'All right then. Well, I'll make peace and get out of your way.'

'All right?' he asked cautiously. 'Just like that?'

For a moment he thought she might say something else but then Patricia just sighed. 'You deserve something good in your life, Nick Walker. Something more than just little Maeve. You deserve a *life* and someone you love who truly loves you. And if you truly think she can give it to you I won't argue.'

'It's a bit early to talk about love, Patricia. I hardly know her.'

She rolled her eyes dismissively. 'You know your mind and you know your heart. But please, dear God, boy, be careful. I wouldn't see you hurt again.'

Nick didn't stick around to hear Patricia's apology. He didn't want it to look like he had demanded it, and it didn't seem his place to eavesdrop either. Maeve came out of the study to let them talk, her shoulders still tense, her head low. So, Nick swept her up in his arms and held her close. She smelled of the forest, all fresh leaves and flowers and sap, his little girl, winding her arms around his neck like ivy, and squeezing tight.

'I'm sorry,' she whispered in that tone she always used when she wanted to be forgiven. 'Is Granny very angry?'

He let out a gruff laugh. 'You frightened her. People sometimes get angry when they're frightened. You need to tell her you're sorry.'

'I will. I promise.'

'And don't do it again.'

She didn't acquiesce to that quite so readily. 'But I don't want to stay down in the village. I want to be here with you. And with Alex. I like her. And I think... I think we need to look after her, Daddy. The house doesn't like her half as much as we do. Daisy said...'

She trailed off and Nick realised that too many times when she tried to tell him something Margaret de Wilde had told her, he had changed the subject or told her not to tell tales. This time he set her down on the bench in the hallway and looked into her face. Bright eyes stared back at him. Sally's eyes, blue as the summer sky.

'What did Daisy say?'

Maeve chewed on her lower lip for a moment. 'That the dark man wants her. That he'll use you to get her. I told her no, that you wouldn't let the dark man hurt anyone. And she said I was...' she frowned, her mouth twisting around the unfamiliar word... 'an *im-be-cile*. I told her that wasn't nice.'

Nick took a careful breath in, let it out. Stay calm, he warned himself. This is Maeve. Not Daisy. Because if he ever did manage to get his hands on Daisy... 'You're right. It's not nice. And not a word to use about anyone, okay?'

She nodded solemnly. 'She said you kissed Alex.'

Oh. Shit.

It was like a punch to the solar plexus, driving all the air from his lungs. What did he say to that? How did he answer her?

'Did that make you feel bad?' he asked as carefully as he could.

Maeve looked away, squirming a little with obvious embarrassment. 'Not... not *bad*. I like her. She's nice. She talks to me like I'm not a baby. And if you like her... Granny says you're lonely.'

Damn it, Patricia.

'Did Granny say that to you?'

'No, to Mr and Mrs O'Sullivan, and the cleaner, and Doreen in the surgery.'

Great. The whole village was now talking about how sad

and lonely he was. And probably about Alex as well. There was nothing a small community loved more than a bit of gossip and who better to provide it? Just what they needed. Ghosts and the living, all speculating about the two of them and watching their every move. Perfect.

But right now, he needed to answer his daughter. And he needed to be honest. 'I do like her. Very much. But I don't know if she wants to stay here. And I don't know if she likes me in the same way.'

Maeve frowned, shifted around a bit as if uncomfortable, and then seemed to reach a decision. 'The dark man wants her. Like he wanted Mummy.' A chill swept down his spine and the breath caught in his chest like it was snagged on a hook.

'What dark man, love?'

She screwed up her face as she always did when she thought he was being stupid on purpose. 'Rose and Daisy told me. The *dark man*. You know, the one outside Alex's bedroom. In the picture?'

The picture. The one he'd promised Alex he'd take down. Damn it, he'd forgotten. Like something else had tugged the thought from his mind. Blaise Chambers.

And then the other words snagged on the thorns of his scattered mind. *Like he wanted Mummy...*

'What does he have to do with Mummy?'

Maeve's eyes suddenly brimmed with tears. 'He took her away from us. And he's... he gobbling her up, like the wolf in the "Three Little Pigs". Soon there'll be nothing left. That's what Rose said.'

Bloody Rose—

'That's not true, love. Mummy's—' How did he explain any of this to her? 'Mummy's in heaven.'

Maeve looked at him like he was the child. She chewed on her nails and then shook her head rapidly. 'No, she isn't. She's here. She can't leave. You know that, Daddy. I know you do. You talk to her as well.'

The door behind them opened and Patricia came out, calmer now, quieter. She fixed Maeve with a stern look.

What timing. He needed to ask his daughter about what had happened to her, about Rose and Daisy, about Chambers, but he couldn't say a word of that in front of Patricia. Not now.

'Well, little rabbit, do you have something to say?'

Maeve's face fell. 'I'm sorry, Granny. But I just wanted—' She looked helplessly at Nick, who reached out and took her hand, squeezing it gently. 'I'm sorry I ran away.'

Patricia nodded solemnly. 'Apology accepted. Go on out to the car. I'll be out in a minute to take you home.'

Maeve's face fell and her grip tightened on Nick's hand. 'But I wanted—'

'It's a school night, pet,' he said. Besides, the house was active, and the ghosts she had always thought of as friends were hardly acting that way. More like snide little bullies. If there was a way to teach them a lesson he would find it. Or maybe Sally would.

Which was another question – where was Sally and how could she let this happen to her daughter? It made no sense. He had always believed the spirit of his wife protected Maeve when she was here.

Given all that had happened during the last few days, was that protection slipping? Because of him? Because of Alex?

Better that Maeve wasn't here, he decided, and met Patricia's questioning gaze with a solemn nod.

'Back you go with Granny, love,' he murmured. 'But first you can go and find some of the biscuits I made earlier to take with you. They're in the kitchen.'

She trailed off dejectedly, not even the promise of biscuits enough right now. Not really.

'She'll be fine, Nick. And I'll keep a better eye on her, I promise.'

He smiled even if he didn't feel like it. 'I know you will. Thank you. For everything. I don't say that enough.'

'You don't have to.'

She gave him a hug which took him completely by surprise. He closed his eyes, leaning into the maternal gesture. Patricia, for all her austerity, was always there for him.

She said a cordial goodbye to Alex and he walked her down to the kitchen. There was no sign of Maeve so they went out to the car. Still no sign.

A tingle of alarm went through him.

Patricia sighed, annoyance creeping back in. 'Where's she taken off to now? She really doesn't want to go home, does she?'

Because it wasn't her home, he thought. This was. It always had been. But he couldn't say that to Patricia, who had opened her heart to his little girl. He hadn't been able to cope after the loss of his wife and his friend, and Patricia had been the one to step in.

'We'll find her. She probably just got distracted and wandered off somewhere.'

'Or those so-called friends of hers lured her off,' Patricia muttered and he was inclined to agree with that tone. Yes, he definitely had to find some way to deal with them. This couldn't go on. Alex would know a way, wouldn't she? Or those friends of hers would. Some kind of way to bind them or send them on their way, to make them leave his daughter alone for once and for all.

'You check the gardens and I'll check the house.' But as he turned back to the door, it slammed in his face. He grabbed the handle, yanking hard, but it wasn't budging, stuck fast.

Wildewood Hall had just shut him out.

CHAPTER 36

ALEX

Patricia was no sooner out the door when Alex's phone started to ring like there was no tomorrow.

Gabe. Of course it was Gabe.

'Are you *freaking* kidding me?' he yelled the moment she answered.

'How are you awake?' she asked.

'How could I be *asleep* when you send that? Incredible, Alex. Just incredible. Eduardo's already analysing it. And Arnold says he's cross-checking pictures in that online database thing to identify—'

'Margaret and Rosalind de Wilde,' she said calmly. 'I don't know their exact dates but I'll get them. Margaret died in 1806, and Rose in... the twenties maybe. They're friends with Nick's daughter. Although I'm not sure friends is the right word. More like parasitic little—'

'Wait, you know all of this already?'

She sank down into the chair, staring at the bookshelves and praying for patience. 'It all still has to be cross-checked and confirmed. And it's a very blurry picture. They knocked me over before—'

'They *what*? Physical contact? Are you okay?'

Damn, she should have explained better than this. 'Yes. No, just... a pile of boxes and magazines fell on me. Nothing serious. I think they were just warning me off.'

At least she hoped that was all. Had she been standing somewhere else, like at the top of a staircase, it could have been a very different story. They'd tried that already. Had they killed Sally as well? Her breath caught in her throat. There were too many coincidences all of a sudden. She thought of the exploding recorder. Not to mention the attack on Daphne.

The sooner Patricia took Maeve home the better.

'Do you think the little kid is a catalyst for poltergeist activity?' Gabe asked.

'Maeve? Yeah, maybe. She's very young though. Or maybe the ghosts just didn't want to have their photos taken. I didn't ask permission or anything. Do I need their consent?'

She said it before she thought better, her smart mouth landing her in it yet again. But there she was, admitting to Gabe that ghosts were real. That she might need to ask permission from them. Was data protection still a thing in the afterlife?

Gabe sucked in a breath. 'Are you... are you *sure* you're okay, Alex?'

'Yes, why?'

'Because Daphne's right. You really do sound like a believer all of a sudden.'

Did she? Maybe. It was kind of hard to keep up the denial here. Mostly she was just tired. Sick and tired.

'I know,' she murmured, really wishing she didn't have to admit it. 'Look, I need some advice. From you or from Daphne, I don't know. But I don't want to pull her in any further, not after – well, you know.'

'What do you need?' He wasn't arguing. Or crowing in triumph. That was probably a bad sign. Or at least a glimmer of how serious this really was.

'I have to find a way to lay a dark spirit to rest. Like, really dark.' God, even as she said it, it sounded ridiculous. How often had she scoffed at people talking just like this? No wonder so many people online called her a bitch. 'There was a man, Blaise Chambers. He lived here in the late 1700s, early 1800s.'

'Yeah, I remember. Same time as the dead kid?'

Shit, yes, probably. She hadn't thought of that. 'I guess so. He was the land agent or steward or something. Would have worked for her dad but basically ran the whole place. Arnold has all the details. But he's key to the darkness in this house, Gabe. He ran the Hellfire Club here. He was a terrible person, by all accounts. And he probably still is. You get me?'

'Yeah.' It came out like a sigh, a long breath of understanding.

'So how do I cut him off? How do I lay him to rest? Or exorcise him? How do I get rid of him?'

Maybe she did need a crib sheet after all. She couldn't half-ass this. There was too much at stake.

'*Oh Alexandra.*' Gabe's voice sounded weird, twisted and wrong. Not like himself. The phone signal stuttered, broke up and then surged back to life, louder than ever. '*You don't.*'

'What?'

'*You don't, Alexandra. You don't get rid of me. You surrender. You give in. You become the creature you were always meant to be. You're a de Wilde, the last of the de Wildes. You belong here, with me. Oh, the things we will do in honour of our dark master...*'

It wasn't Gabe's voice. Not anymore. She didn't know what it was. Pulling back the phone, she stared at the screen. It was still connected, still showing Gabe's name. But she wasn't talking to Gabe. She knew that now.

'Who are you?' she whispered. Her voice shook far more than she would have liked but she couldn't help that.

'*You know who I am, Alexandra,*' he purred. '*I'm yours. I always have been. And you are mine. Why fight it?*'

The voice was still coming out of the phone but even as she watched it the battery icon drained of power and the whole screen went dark.

Another face was reflected in the screen. A face she knew far too well. The face from the portrait in the hall upstairs.

Blaise Chambers smiled at her. A horrible, knowing smile.

Nick. She needed Nick. She needed to find him now.

'*He can't help you, Alexandra. He can't even help himself. Not when I have everything and everyone he ever held dear in the palm of my hand. He'll give in. Just as you will. It is inevitable. You both belong to me now.*'

'No.' The words sounded so small. But at least she could still say it.

Everything and everyone he ever held dear…

Sally. Theo. And Maeve…

I will set all of them against all of those they have loved, and I will make them mine, body and soul.

Oh God, where was Maeve? She had left with Patricia, hadn't she?

Somewhere beyond the study, a door slammed as if caught by the wind and Alex jumped, dropping the phone. It thudded onto the carpet, entirely drained of power.

Ghosts did that. Drained batteries. She accepted that they did now. Just before they did something a lot worse.

Shit. Shit. Shit.

Alex turned back to the desk and grabbed the wreath-like charm Maeve had made for her, the twigs digging into her palm. That brought a bit more clarity to her.

She still had this, and it still worked. Whatever the little girl had tapped into with it, still worked.

She turned around and Sally Walker lunged towards her, eyes wide, mouth distended, screaming silently.

Alex threw herself back and half fell into the chair, clinging to the charm as if her life depended on it. Perhaps it did. The ghosts here were powerful and completely out of control.

Wind whipped through the study, tearing at every surface. Papers went up in a maelstrom, and books thudded off the shelves, slamming into the ground as if hurled by unseen hands. Sally was wild. If there was any of Sally actually left in this creature of rage and despair. Dark hair moved like ink in water, and her eyes were hollow and empty, filled with darkness which bled into her pale skin like an infection.

'Enough!' Alex yelled. 'Talk to me.'

Talk to me. Like that was normal. Like any of this was normal.

She tried to focus, made herself sit still in the midst of Sally's fury, and breathe in and out, just like Daphne had once taught her. It had been on one of those cases she still couldn't explain. Not entirely. And it had been awful.

Like this.

She clung to Maeve's charm.

'Sally Walker, talk to me. Calm down and talk to me. I can't help you otherwise.'

Walker, that was the thing that did it. Calling her Sally Walker. Reminding her of Nick, of Maeve, of who she was. The wind changed direction and Sally appeared again, stalking towards her with it, her face still a snarl of pain.

'*My daughter! My little girl! My Maeve! You have to do something!*'

'She's with Nick and your mother. She's safe.'

'*No, she isn't. She wandered off again. They have her. He'll kill her. Please. I'll do anything. I'll give you whatever you want, de Wilde. Please!*'

'What do you mean, she wandered off? Where is she?'

The wind started up again. More books came off the

shelves, flying through the air, and all around the Hall, Alex heard the sound of doors slamming.

'This isn't helping! Show me the way. You have to know.'

The room shook, the floor, the ceiling. The walls...

And then a panel in the wall to the of the desk, one of the few areas of wall not covered with bookcases, opened with a long slow creak. A secret door. Of course, there was a secret door.

The wind died down and all was quiet.

'*Go,*' said Sally. It was no more than a whisper, a sigh. All the strength she had garnered together was gone with the effort she'd needed to do that.

The passage beyond was unlit, impossibly dark and heavy with cobwebs. Because of course it was. Of course, the stupid haunted house had a lightless secret passageway leading down as if descending to the pits of hell itself.

Gabe would wet himself in delight.

Gabe! She'd been talking to him and the phone had died. She grabbed the laptop, which was thankfully still plugged in, and fired off an email.

Tell me how to lay it to rest.

Wind buffeted at her again and the door slammed back against the wall. Sally was getting impatient and Maeve was in danger. She didn't have time to waste.

'Nick!' she yelled. No answer. Not from the house anyway.

She heard a faint shout and spun around. He was on the drive outside, waving at her, miming opening the window. Patricia stood beside him, pale with concern. Alex fumbled at the latch on the bay window of the study, but it was wedged closed as if the wood had warped.

'I can't open it. I have to go after Maeve. There's a passageway.'

He shook his head, and lifted his hand to his ear. He couldn't hear her. Damn it.

Maeve, she mouthed at him and pointed to the secret doorway and then down. It had to be down, didn't it? Under the house.

Daphne had talked about something under the house reaching up out of the earth and the stones, out of the darkness. And Alex had felt it, when she fell, when she lay there half-conscious on the floor at the foot of the stairs. She had felt it reaching up for her.

And people had always said Blaise Chambers had done his most evil acts in a temple under the house....

A temple. A place of power. A broken god of lost places, waiting beneath her. Daphne had said that when she was attacked.

The cellar, surely. But the cellar was small and only occupied the space under the kitchen. It didn't extend to this part of the building. And this looked older. A lot older. Where was this going to take her?

Alex fought to catch her breath. She was running out of time.

An email blinked at her on the laptop. Three words. Gabe must have typed them as quickly as he could and sent it back.

Prayer. Salt. Silver.

Great, she thought. Prayer. What did she know about prayer? She didn't believe in anything. But yes, salt had to work. It was the oldest way to banish evil, in so many religions from Christianity to Buddhism, and older. And silver... silver was a pure metal. It warded off evil spirits and protected against possession. Daphne wore half a ton of the stuff on investigations. Where was she going to find...

The dining room was right next door. Nick had it furnished

like a display, laid out like there was going to be a banquet as soon as they brought the plates out. There had to be salt in one of those ridiculous silver salt cellars, didn't there? Shit, she hoped so.

She sprinted out into the hall and into the next room, grabbing the salt cellar from the middle of the table, tipping it over into her hand. Tiny white grains came out.

Thank you. She didn't even know who or what she was thanking. It didn't matter. She shoved it into her jeans pocket. Just for good measure she grabbed a candle and matches from the mantelpiece. Armed as best she could be, she headed back to the study.

Sally was waiting, a half-formed shape by the doorway to the darkness.

'You've got to stop with the wind now,' Alex said as she took a moment to light the candle and felt the whole room still, like the entire house was holding its breath. Her own chest was aching with anxiety but she had to get a hold of herself. Maeve was down there somewhere.

So was Blaise Chambers and whatever he had worshipped.

Maeve's circlet lay on the table and she grabbed it, sliding it onto her wrist. Then, cupping her hand around the flame, Alex started down the stairs into the dark.

CHAPTER 37

ALEX

The stairs led inexorably downwards, longer than the ones to the cellar which Alex had only glimpsed. If Nick had been keen to keep her out of there, he'd be losing his mind at the thought of his daughter down here alone. Alex edged her way down the treacherous steps. They were steep and uneven in height, the stone old and worn smooth. The candlelight flickered around her, sending shadows dancing wildly. Oh, what she would have given for one of the high-powered torches with her equipment upstairs, or even her bloody phone. But there wasn't time to fetch anything now. She'd wasted enough time finding the candle and the salt. It would have to do.

The sense of a presence at her back, the touch of phantom fingers on her shoulders pushing her forward told her that Sally was there too. And Sally was terrified. Maeve was down here, and in danger.

Finally, Alex reached the bottom. The ground underfoot was compacted earth and a huge empty space stretched out ahead of her, a circular undercroft, lined with old, uneven brick-work. She knew this place, she realised. She'd seen it in the notebook, a floorplan. So her grandfather had known about the door and what was hidden under his study.

It was vast, running from the front of the house to what must be almost as far as the kitchen to the back. Open, empty, and dark...

And in the middle, a very small figure, bathed in an eerie light, stood as still as any statue.

'Maeve?' Alex whispered, and her voice echoed around them, bouncing back to her far too loud, the single word multiplying into a cacophony that couldn't be natural. She could hear laughter behind it, terrible mocking laughter. It didn't sound like Chambers either. Nor was it like the birdsong laughter in the woods.

This was something else, unnatural and ancient.

Alex grabbed the salt cellar, brandishing it like a weapon.

'Maeve, love, come here. Let's get out of this place.'

But Maeve didn't move. Not even a shudder. She was staring fixedly at the floor and, as Alex reached her, she saw there was a pool of something dark and unpleasant collected there, in a hollow in the floor. Like tar, or old blood, or... Alex didn't want to consider what else it might be. The first two were bad enough.

And it glowed. The light, watery and sickly as it was, came from it. Bioluminescence, she tried to tell herself, or some kind of mineral or....

Ectoplasm, a voice in the back of her mind supplied. Possibly a memory of Daphne. But tainted. Because Daphne didn't sound like that.

In that hospital in Texas they'd seen it running down the walls. And she'd said that it could be creosote and rainwater, but the samples they collected showed nothing at all. Gabe still had a jar of that somewhere in the apartment, old and dried out and flaking like paint. He liked to bring it out at parties.

The smell was the worst. It clawed at her nose – rot and

putrescence, like something had died down here. A lot of things probably. She didn't want to think about what they might be. And Maeve was standing right over it, staring into its depths. Transfixed.

Alex moved closer, wary not to startle the child, or fall on the uneven ground. The candle was flickering again, in danger of going out, which was the last thing she wanted. And the sense of Sally was still there, a wall of ice behind her pushing her forward. But even Sally was growing weaker now, down here, any strength she had gathered draining out of her into that hole in the ground.

Exhaustion swept over Alex in a wave, followed by despair. Her limbs suddenly felt leaden and heavy, but she pushed onwards. This wasn't normal. None of this was normal.

Whatever lurked down here was drawing strength from her now. From her and from Maeve.

'Maeve, love,' she tried again. 'Maeve, you have to come back with me now.'

'I can't.' Maeve's voice sounded very calm, very still. 'He'll hurt you.'

The girl was holding another of her little charms, her hand a fist at its edge. The leaves and flowers trembled, her own tension translating to them. Her arm stretched out over the pool, but she didn't let it go. Tears streaked her face.

'There's no one here, love,' Alex told her. That was a lie, but she needed to make Maeve move. 'No one to hurt me. How did you even get down here?'

She hadn't come through the study. Alex would have seen her. Last she'd known, Maeve had been with Nick.

'Through the cellar. There's a hole at the back. I didn't mean to come in, Alex, but Daisy said I had to. And I had this. I thought I could stop it hurting you. But now... now...'

A great sob welled up inside her and she shook as it

escaped, the noise deafening in this eerie place. Her misery washed through the air and Alex almost took a step back.

'*Maeve,*' Sally murmured, another wave of despair.

Maeve's panic went up a notch.

'Mummy! You can't be here. It isn't safe. It wants you here. It owns the dead, Mummy. If it touches you...' Maeve sniffed, as if steeling herself, and before Alex could stop her, she slid her hand through the charm, like a bracelet, dropped to her knees and plunged her hands into the hole.

Sally screamed and the house above them shook. Dust cascaded from the roof overhead.

Alex hurriedly shoved the salt cellar into her pocket so as not to lose it and grabbed Maeve's shoulder, pulling her back from the hollow full of God knew what. Something else came too, dragged up out of the depths in Maeve's hands. A glint caught Alex's eye, a flash of candlelight on... was that gold?

The thing tumbled free of Maeve's grip, rolling like a misshapen ball across the earthen floor away from them both with a terrible thumping sound. Maeve sobbed in shock and alarm and Alex pulled the girl to her.

There wasn't time to look closer and she wasn't sure she wanted to. It all felt like a trap. Maeve stared at her blankly, almost as if she was dazed, her charm hanging around her wrist like a bangle. But something foul and black soaked it, dripped from it.

Perhaps it was all that was protecting her. Her hands and lower arms were covered in the same vile stuff.

This wasn't good. Not good at all.

'Hold out your hands, Maeve,' Alex told her firmly and when the girl obeyed without question, she fumbled to get the salt cellar from her pocket. The metal was uncomfortably cold, almost burning on her fingers, but she held onto it and tipped salt into Maeve's hands. 'I want you to hold onto this and think of being safe. Think of your dad, and your granny and whatever else keeps you safe, understand?'

'I want Mummy.'

Could Maeve not see her anymore?

'She *is* here, love,' Alex said and the candle flame grew even brighter. So did a glow on the far side of the chamber where the thing Maeve had pulled out of the hole lay discarded. Alex tried not to notice that. 'She's here.'

Prayer, Gabe had said. Alex wasn't even sure what she believed in but she knew that prayer worked, if only to calm the human mind.

From the darkness, two other figures were emerging now, small like Maeve but possessed of a malevolence Alex hadn't expected. The two girls, she realised. And yet somehow not.

Rose opened her mouth, smiling to reveal glistening teeth, and Daisy's eyes were as black and empty as the pit before them. Beneath their skin was a tracery of fine black lines. They weren't the sweet and innocent child ghosts they had appeared to be. Perhaps they had not been for a very long time. Malice came off them in waves.

Maeve began to cry again, soft shuddering sobs, and Alex wrapped the arm holding the candle around her, pulling her in close. 'Don't look, love. It's okay. I'm here.'

'That's what they want, Alex. They tricked me. They said it would help but it... they lied to me! They want you here too.'

Did they? Well, they would regret that, she thought with a rush of vindictiveness. Ghosts or not, no one liked a bully.

Alex drew back her free hand and flung salt at them. 'By the power of light and hope and all things sacred, I banish you. Leave this place and go to the other side.'

CHAPTER 38

ALEX

It was not the most beautiful prayer in the world but it didn't have to be. It just had to state an intention. Daphne had always said the simpler the better. But then Daphne always spoke about following the light, and of loved ones waiting on the other side. Gentle, cajoling words, offering peace and forgiveness. It didn't have to be about God, it was all about the intent, the desire behind it and the nature of that desire. And all Alex wanted was those ghosts gone from here and far away from Maeve. They had too much hold over her already.

But as the spirits of the two girls recoiled and vanished Alex could already feel something else rising. This came from the darkness underneath, from the shadows, from the earth itself, bubbling up like whatever tar-like substance filled the hollow in front of them, oozing across the dirt floor now. Alex skidded back as it moved, the surface breaking for a moment and the foul water, or whatever it was, sloshing towards her boot.

Maeve screamed in fear, and this time, Alex wrenched her back behind her, shielding the girl with her own body.

'Maeve!'

It was Nick's voice. There was a crash and the sound of

something crunching on the far side of the undercroft. It sounded like he was tearing his way through the wall from the cellar.

'Nick, there's a door in the study!' Alex yelled. 'There's another way down. Bring a torch!'

She didn't even know if he heard her until the racket stopped.

And then the laughter began.

It came from the ground, from the ceiling, from all around the two of them. Maeve's arms locked around Alex's leg. Alex could feel the wet goo seeping in to her jeans, like acid against her skin underneath, and she couldn't have run even if she had been able to find the strength. All she could feel was the ground shaking like they were in the middle of an earthquake. The fetid liquid sloshed out of the pit, that eerie glow illuminating the chamber. In the far corner, where whatever Maeve had pulled from the pit had rolled, Alex caught a flash of dull gold. It looked like a misshapen figure, its mouth open and hungry. What was it?

Blaise Chambers rose up before her, coalescing in that light over the pit into his handsome, devilish form, his predatory smile fixed on Alex. He offered her his hand and when she recoiled, he laughed.

'He's Crom,' Blaise murmured. '*You know him. You know him most of all. You were here before, Alexandra. You were to have released him, but you were too young, and your father inter-fered. It takes a woman with de Wilde blood. Not this child. But you can still serve your part now. You will free us all. It was meant to be you.*'

No. This wasn't possible. This wasn't happening.

Memories, tangled and worn at the edges, flooded back with terrifying clarity.

She had been sixteen years old. Her father had told her to run. And she had run. She had run so far and so fast that she thought she would break apart. She had never stopped running.

Dad had found her here in the darkness. Her father had come to find her.

She had run and he had never left.

They hadn't been in the forest. Not at first. She remembered now. They'd been in the darkness. Down here. And that face, that same open-mouthed hungry face, had come alive and grinned at her.

Alex's hand trembled, the one holding the candle, a tremor that ran up her arm.

Blaise took another step towards her. She just had to drop the candlestick and supplicate herself before him, reach out for him, beg him... She could already feel her fingers loosening, her knees bending, her mouth opening. It would only take a moment. Drop the candle, let the darkness take her and ...

Sally Walker swept over her and through her, as cold as a winter's night, her voice twisted into an incoherent scream. Alex threw herself and Maeve back with a cry of alarm and watched in horror as whatever remained of Sally's spirit threw itself at Blaise.

And he caught her with hands like eldritch claws, holding her tight.

Sally jerked like an old rag caught on a thorn bush. Her eyes opened wide, her mouth wider, huge and stretched beyond bearing, a scream that was both wrenched out of her and made up of the core of her. But the sound came from Maeve, still clinging to Alex's leg, her fingers like nails driving in through the material of Alex's jeans.

'Oh Sally, sweet Sally,' Blaise purred. 'So impetuous. You always thought you knew best. And you were wrong. I destroyed you in life. Now let me do the same in death.'

Dark lines threaded Sally's pale skin, moving like living things now, like black worms under her incorporeal flesh. Blaise

Chambers was claiming the spirit of Sally Walker now, corrupting all that was left of her, making her his own.

No, Alex's mind screamed at her. This had to stop. It needed to stop.

She still had Maeve's charm around her own wrist and it hadn't lost its power. Not yet. This was Sally's symbol, her creation, even if her daughter's hands had made it. This meant something to her.

'Sally,' Alex shouted and her voice didn't even sound like her own. It was strong and powerful, a voice that would not be argued with. Somehow she found the words Daphne would have used. 'Sally Walker! Depart this place in peace and in light. You are no longer needed here. Open your heart to the light waiting for you, Sally. Look for it. There are people waiting for you. They've been waiting so long. It's time to go, do you hear me? Now, before the darkness devours you.'

There had to be a way to stop this, to save her. To drive Blaise away and break his hold on the spirits of the house, before he took Sally as well. Blaise laughed, his fingers digging into Sally's incorporeal flesh. Sally flung back her head and screamed, her mouth distended in agony.

'You think you have power here, Alexandra de Wilde? You think this is your land? You have denied it for twenty years. And with her gone, the guardian can be yours and yours alone. Even if you could help her, why would you?'

Because it was the right thing to do. Because she couldn't let him take Sally. He would just keep coming, for her, and eventually for Maeve.

At that thought Alex locked eyes with Sally, her frantic hollow gaze.

Maeve was her daughter, her child, the one good thing she had ever done in her life, she seemed to say. She needed to protect her. That was all she had ever wanted. That was why she was still holding on.

'Maeve is protected,' Alex told her. 'Nick loves her. He'll do anything for her.'

'*Not enough*,' said Blaise. '*And when she comes of age she'll be mine as well. Mine forever, all of you. You will give her to me.*'

No. Alex's hand tightened into a fist around the salt cellar. It was all she had but most of the salt was gone now. She'd driven off the girls and poured it into Maeve's hands to protect her. And Chambers was so powerful.

What would Daphne do? She'd ask for help, call on her guardian spirits and reach for the light, as she always did. Because Daphne had hope. '*Your little psychic friend?*' Chambers taunted. '*I poured myself into her and almost ripped her mind apart. And what a delight it was. She couldn't fight me. What makes you think you could? You're nothing, Alexandra.*'

Daphne saw the best in people. She always had. Whereas Alex...

She faltered, took a step back, and Sally gasped in pain as the darkness devoured more of her. Maeve cried out and tried to pull away, to run to her mother, but Alex couldn't let her do that. She might just be a child but if Chambers got his claws into her who knew what he'd do.

This is your land... It might have been Sally's voice. It was an echo, an agonised sigh, a prayer. *I know it by the blood we share, the blood of Kilfayne. Claim it, as you claimed it with Nick. Call it. Give yourself to it and let it take me. It's the only way. Call the wild...*

Alex froze, the charm in her hand, and the tainted earth beneath her... But beneath that... in the rocks and foundations of the world... this was *her* land. All of it. Wildewood was hers. She had said so herself when Nick found her in the woods.

This is my land.

Alex reached out desperately. She didn't even know what for, not really. But she remembered... long ago... calling for help like this... desperate to escape. And her dad...

'*Run, Alex! You have to run! NOW!*'

But she couldn't run. She couldn't leave Maeve. She couldn't leave Sally. So she reached out, blindly, desperately, just like she had all those years ago... just like before, something responded, something old and powerful. Something far beyond her.

The scent of the forest erupted around her, the smell of trees and freshly unfurling leaves, of the undergrowth and the mulch beneath it, the green of growing living things. And it wound through Alex's body, making her gasp in alarm. The charm she held in her clenched fingers sprouted new leaves, and flowers unfurled. The forest filled the air around her, the wild wood and the charm which had brought it, vibrant and strong.

'*I'm with you, Lex,*' Theo's soft voice murmured. '*Let's finish this.*' Her brother. The other half of her. She could feel his hands on her shoulder, the warmth of his body. She could feel Theo all around her. Living, vibrant, real...

'Theo?'

The sense of his smile was all she had by way of a reply, and the leaves wound themselves around her, the taste of them in her mouth, their rough touch brushing her skin. She shuddered with recognition.

She remembered. The forest, the way it had enveloped her, protecting her. The way it had taken her into its heart and ...

Blaise snarled something and pushed Sally to her knees before him, hands tightening around her throat.

'Get the fuck off her, you bastard!' Alex hurled what was left of the salt at Chambers, the salt cellar arching like a line of light through the shadows, and with it came the force of the woods in a storm. He fell back, flailing as the granules fell like scattershot on his ghostly flesh, punching tiny holes in the apparition. Sally tumbled to the ground at his feet, but he wasn't paying attention to her now. The light from the silver spread through him, like fire eating through tissue paper. He writhed, trying to escape it. All around them, from every corner of the undercroft, voices screamed and Alex wrapped herself around Maeve, trying to hold her close and protect her.

There was an explosion of light, so bright Alex had to close her eyes. But in the afterimage burned onto her eyelids, she saw something else. Theo's figure, filled with green and gold light, pulling Sally up, taking her in his arms and holding her close. The remaining leaves from the charm turned to motes of light and flew towards them.

Theo grinned at Alex. That stupid reckless trademark Theo grin.

And then her brother and Sally Walker were gone.

The candle fell, the flame snuffing out on the muddy ground and the undercroft was plunged into a darkness so complete that Alex wouldn't have been able to see her hand in front of her face, even if she wasn't half blind from what had just happened.

It had just happened, hadn't it? That had really happened.

Breathing hard, she sank to the ground and gathered a sobbing Maeve to her. Maeve... the little girl shivered in her arms. It wasn't her fault. Just like it hadn't been Alex's either.

'It's okay, sweetheart,' she murmured, running her hand over Maeve's hair. 'It's okay, I've got you. He's gone.'

And so was Maeve's mother. And Theo...

Alex's throat tightened. Somewhere in the shadows she heard a laugh, soft and sibilant. Not Chambers' laugh, not this time. It came from the far corner where Maeve had thrown whatever she had pulled out of the ground.

Not gone... Free...

The darkness seemed more solid there, like a living thing, boiling and rising, thick as that horrible tar-like substance, rank and creeping towards them. Alex shuffled back blindly.

Another sound filled the chamber, like thunder, but this

time it was more localised, coming not from all around them and beneath them, not from the shaking earth and the walls of the house, but from behind them, where the stairs descended from the study. A beam of light swept back and forth over the undercroft like a lighthouse on speed.

'Maeve! Alex!'

Nick skidded to his knees beside them, his face white and drawn with horror. Alex released the girl to him but laid a hand on his arm to still him, trying to ignore the way she was shaking. She moved his torch around to shine on the pool of black sludge and felt him freeze as he saw it, all his muscles going rigid with alarm.

'What is it?' he asked.

She lifted the torch up a little and it picked out the grinning face of the golden idol. It sat upright in the corner, as if it had been carefully placed there, surveying the whole undercroft. Staring at them.

'And what the fuck is that?' Nick exclaimed.

She didn't know the answer to that. She couldn't seem to find words.

'Alex? What happened?' Nick asked, trying desperately to gentle his own voice and barely managing it.

Alex opened her mouth to answer but she was suddenly exhausted, her head pounding with a headache. All that she had in her had gone into freeing Sally from whatever that thing was. And she wouldn't have managed without Theo.

He'd come to help her, to save Sally. She had called him when she called the wild wood and now... now he was gone again. The pang of loss shot through her again, that emptiness. He was gone. And so was Sally.

And how did she begin to explain any of that? Especially to Nick.

I exorcised your wife. She's gone forever. You'll never see her again. She went with my brother, the man who stole her from you in life as well...

No. No, she couldn't say that.

'She saved Mummy,' Maeve piped up, unexpectedly, her voice still racked with sobs. 'The bad man had Mummy and Alex saved her and set her free. Alex and the man made of the light from the forest. And they saved me. From the dark man.' She sobbed again, rubbing her hands furiously on her clothes in desperation. 'Daddy, there's icky stuff all over me. I can't get it off.'

CHAPTER 39

ALEX

The first thing was to scrub Maeve's hands and arms clean, and then bundle her up in the car with Patricia, Nick holding her close until the very last minute, almost bent double, half in the car, promising over and over that he'd come down to the village and see her as soon as he could.

Alex stood by awkwardly, trying to keep from breaking down into a sobbing mess herself. She wanted to. She wasn't sure how she was holding anything together.

She had seen Theo. Without him, she might not even be standing here. He had saved her, Maeve and Sally. She wouldn't have had the strength without him.

And then what would have happened?

She remembered that place, the creeping darkness sucking at her soul. She remembered her dad...

'*Run, Alex! You have to run! NOW!*'

How did she remember that now? And why did the darkness that had reared up around her in the undercroft still feel like it was pressing in on the back of her mind?

'Alex?' Nick called her back to the here and now with a

start. His voice sounded as shaky as she felt. 'Maeve would like to talk to you.'

Alex leaned into the car only to be engulfed in a huge hug. 'Thank you,' the little girl said into her shoulder, her voice muffled but unmistakable. 'And you have to be careful now. He's angry. He saw you, and he remembers you. He wants you.'

'Who?' She couldn't mean Nick. He just looked terrified.

'The dark man. Here—' Maeve pulled back and then scrabbled around in the pocket on the seat in front of her, before pulling out a plait made of dried grass and withered daisies. Another one. How many did the child have? She knotted it around Alex's wrist before Alex could stop her. 'The other one is gone with the man from the forest, but this will protect you. I promise. Like you promised my mummy you'd protect me and Daddy. I'll look after you too, Alex.'

'Thank you, sweetheart,' Alex replied. 'And... maybe stay with your gran now until we know it's safe here, okay? No more adventures until you're bigger.'

Maeve grinned at her. 'And when I'm bigger, I'm going to hunt down ghosts like you. And help them. Like you helped Mummy.'

Patricia couldn't wait to get into the car and drive away. Alex didn't blame her.

She and Nick watched them go until they vanished beyond the gates. He had his arms wrapped around his chest, like he was still hugging his daughter. Alex fiddled with the new grass bracelet and wished she had the child's powers of belief. Especially self-belief.

Dark clouds were gathering over the valley beyond the trees, that kind of roiling darkness that presaged a storm.

Nick drew in a shuddering breath before turning to her.

'What happened down there?' But before Alex could answer he stalked towards the house as if he had taken a personal grudge against it. 'Every bloody door in the house shut up fast, like they were bolted from inside. This one and the kitchen. The keys wouldn't work, nothing. I had to smash a window in the boot room round the back to get in. And then I heard you in the cellar, but I couldn't find the two of you.'

'Maeve said she came through the cellar. There was a hole in the wall down there.'

'Yeah, I found it but I couldn't get through. She must have wriggled in like a rabbit. How did you find that door? I never knew it was there. It looked like it hadn't been opened in decades.'

He yanked the front door to the house open so hard that Alex feared, old and heavy as it was, it might come right off the hinges. Nick wasn't just scared. He was angry too. And that made for a bad combination.

'Nick...' She didn't know how to tell him any of this. She'd seen his wife. Theo had come to get her, called her *love*... How did she even begin? She was just going to make everything worse.

When she touched his shoulder, the muscles were knotted and tense. He shuddered at her touch and then froze.

'Is this my fault?' he asked tentatively.

His fault? How could this be his fault?

'I don't think so. I think... I think it's the temple in the notebook. Chambers' temple. To that thing.'

He hesitated again, as if reluctant to ask any more. But in the end, he clearly couldn't help himself. 'Maeve said you saved Sally.'

'I think she tried to sacrifice herself to save us first. And then... Theo came...'

Nick hung his head and said nothing for a moment. Alex waited. She had to. Part of her wished she hadn't said anything at all. She was an idiot.

'He would,' he whispered at last, his voice cracking. 'Of course he would... Thank you. Both of you.'

'Nick?'

But he looked up again and Alex found herself trapped by those eyes, the mix of green deep in the brown, the flecks of gold. The lights from inside the house caught the glow in them. Her hand came to rest on his chest. She couldn't help it. Nick's closed over it, so much bigger, stronger, like something she wanted to cling to.

His lips parted and, the next thing Alex knew, he kissed her. It wasn't like before. Not like in the study, when she'd felt out of control and desperate. Or in the drawing room, when the wild had engulfed them both. This was deep and gentle, a careful invitation. She couldn't help but respond. But even as she let herself be swept up in it, in the closeness of him, the warmth, that heady scent, in the soft groan that came rumbling up from his chest, he broke the kiss.

His hand trailed down the side of her face and he frowned. There was heartbreak in those eyes now.

'I'm sorry,' he said abruptly and pulled away. 'I shouldn't. I—'

He pushed the door open and went inside. Alex closed it carefully behind her and then followed him into the kitchen, ignoring the study for now. The cellar door still stood open and Nick stopped at the top of the stairs as if steeling himself for another confrontation.

'Take a moment,' she told him. 'Please. It's been a lot. And it's getting dark outside.'

The wind was rising. She could hear it rattling around the house. The storm was coming in fast.

'Maybe you're right. But we do need to sort that window in the boot room first with the weather turning. Hang on here. I'll get my tools.'

He left by the back door and returned in minutes, trailing

the wind and rain behind him. He had some pieces of wood and Alex helped him measure and cut them. She swept up sawdust while he hammered them into place over the narrow window at the side of the door. For good measure she cleaned up the broken glass as well. He must have smashed the small window pane and then reached through to open the door. He was lucky he hadn't sliced open his arm in the process.

With the rising storm firmly outside the house, he seemed to unwind a little.

'Tea,' said Alex.

He gave a wavering smile and sat down at the table, their positions oddly reversed all of a sudden. His broad frame looked out of place as she slid past him but no more so than when he was handing her freshly baked goods or dishing up his wonderful meals. It was more that this time she was the one fetching mugs and milk, and setting the teapot down between them.

They both stared at it in silence. Both unwilling to broach the subject.

And then Alex remembered her phone, and Gabe, and the aborted call. Oh God, he'd be frantic by now.

'Shit, hang on,' she gasped and sprinted to the study.

The door to the undercroft still hung open like a gaping wound. She closed it firmly and dragged one of the armchairs against it for good measure. Just in case, she told herself. In case of what, she wasn't sure.

She scooped up her dead phone, plugged it in and turned it back on.

There were a dozen messages, missed video calls and various other attempts at contact.

Alex, what's happening?

Tell me you're ok. PLEASE.

What's going on???

She typed quickly, straight into the group chat.

We're ok. All good. She paused, wondering what on earth she could say to explain any of it. *I think we have a bigger problem than I thought. Arnold, what do you know about something called Crom? Or the god of the hungry grass?*

The response she got was not comforting.

Crom? Not the one in Conan the Barbarian? Gabe. Of course it was.

The phone rang. Arnold already had an answer, of course. Because he was that good.

'Alex? Sorry. It's easier than trying to type all this. I'll put it all in a group email in a minute. Just glad you're okay...' He paused, concern bleeding through his words. 'You *are* okay, babe, aren't you?'

'Yeah,' she said, aware of how hollow her voice sounded.

He didn't sound convinced but took her word for it. 'Okay so, this is for real, not fantasy. And there's a lot. I looked it up earlier because it was mentioned in your grandfather's notes and I thought it was weird, you know? There was a god called Crom in Ireland, very old, pre-Christian, pre pretty much everything. Howard nicked the name for his Conan books, that's all, and mangled the hell out of it. There were a few Croms in Irish lore – Crom Cruach, Crom Dubh, Crom Cenn, maybe more. Could all be the same thing, or aspects of an old god, could be brothers. At least metaphorically. Like the Titans. Mostly it's just scraps of stories though, all written by monks so there's an obvious bias. Sometimes they're lumped in with demons and the stories are nasty enough for that.'

She could hear him clicking his keyboard, bringing up more information.

'Crom means bent or crooked. Cruach is a heap or a pile, as in bodies. Dubh means black and Cenn head, like *severed* heads, but most of the accounts are from the Greeks and the Romans who loved talking about the barbaric Celts headhunting, bloodletting and sacrificing whoever they could. So again, not reliable. One story goes that there was a golden idol, set up in a ring of standing stones, and they'd pour blood over it, pile up the bodies of the slain in front of it and have orgies, that their hunger was never sated. But like I said – remember the sources. I don't know about the god of the hungry grass. That could be a local thing.'

'All right,' she told him, fighting down her rising sense of dread. A golden idol in a ring of stones. There was a ring of stones in the woods. And in the undercroft... the thing Maeve had pulled out of the ground, the hunched figure with the grinning face which had rolled off into the corner... that could have been a golden idol, couldn't it? But she didn't want to say that out loud.

'Speaking of local references... There are folktales about the wise women of Kilfayne. They could turn into hares and stuff and they were charged with keeping the land. Ask your Sasquatch about them. I bet he knows.' He gave a soft laugh which petered out when she didn't join in. 'They're mentioned in your grandfather's notes too. They were said to have defeated an evil being which sounds a lot like a Crom. Such things can't be killed, he says, so instead they trapped it using the magic of rock and water and the earth itself. They built a great cairn over the thing to imprison it and grew a vast forest around it, a living barrier, imbuing the trees with enough power to contain Crom, and to destroy those who would release it. There was some kind of ritual role, a guardian, called the walker in the woods.'

The words rang like the whine of tinnitus in her ears. The wise women of Kilfayne had created a guardian, the walker in the woods. Just like they'd told her in the village. They'd joked about it being Nick because of his surname. But now she wasn't so sure it was a joke. Fionnuala had shut them down right away.

And Nick was always escaping to the woods. He guarded them. They gave him strength. And peace. They were his refuge. He had called himself her guardian and she had said this was her land.

She looked up at a sound to see Nick there in the study with her, listening, watching. So quiet.

God, they'd brought this on themselves, the two of them.

Arnold was still talking. 'The walker is dedicated to guarding the prison, but it isn't clear if that was a hereditary role, an elected one or a sacrifice maybe? Whatever it was, the guardian is called to serve the trees, it says, and they're part of the spell binding Crom. And that great enchantment worked for generations.'

Until the de Wildes came along, and ruined everything. She didn't need to say that.

'I think that's where your house comes in. From what the notebook says, the curse transferred itself to the building. That entity lingered on in the stones and in the earth, sleeping deep, but the woods couldn't protect the people inside the house anymore. Those who live there risk falling prey to it. That's what Blaise Chambers found, and raised, and worshipped.'

Of course it was.

That was why the de Wildes had the reputation they had around here, why they did nothing to help their tenants during the Great Famine, why they exploited the whole area, why they raped and murdered their way to power. Why the women died young if they stayed here, and why the men were bastards.

Why Chambers was still so powerful even though he'd been dead for two hundred years. Because it wasn't just him. He wasn't just a ghost but was tied into something else. Crom. The thing he had worshipped in life and served in death. The thing he wanted to feed Alex to.

She didn't know how, but she had recognised it as soon as she laid eyes on it. Like something inside her had always contained that knowledge. That little bit of Kilfayne, the part of her Gran had nurtured, the part she had always suppressed. The part that had saved her and damned her father...

She had to face the fact that there might be what Gabe would classify as a demonic entity living underneath her house. How did you say that with a straight face?

CHAPTER 40

NICK

The last thing Nick wanted to do was go back down into that hidden crypt.

The feeling as he had run down those steps, the awful oppressive dread, the terror that something had happened to Maeve... his heart still ached with it and his stomach tied itself into a knot.

She was safe now, safe with Patricia. Away from Wildewood Hall. That was all that mattered.

Well, not quite.

He and Alex sat in the study now, where he had followed her after her abrupt departure from the kitchen, both of them avoiding looking at the chair propped up against the wall where the hidden door was. He was trying not to think of what lay beneath them like a gaping mouth. Alex was still reading an email, a look of fixed determination on her face. When she had finally turned her phone back on, the number of notifications had been astounding. After she had spoken to Arnold, she had spent an hour placating and calming the rest of them.

They really cared about her, worried about her. And they had a better idea of what they might be facing here than he did.

If they were that concerned, he knew it had to be serious indeed.

They might be the epitome of gung-ho Americans, especially that Gabe, but in this case... in this case they were terrified. And determined to protect her. From the house, from him, perhaps even from herself.

Nick just wanted to retreat into the woods and let them sweep him away. The storm would rouse them and in that wildness he could forget himself. Perhaps forever. Now Sally and Theo were gone – and they *were* gone, he could feel it – and Maeve was safe with Patricia, there was nothing to keep him here, was there? Except Alex. He couldn't leave Alex to face this alone.

Maeve had made him promise. Alex had saved her, and she had saved Sally's spirit, helping her escape with Theo... of that he had no doubt. His daughter had been very clear on what she had seen and what had happened, and despite her youth and what others believed, Maeve wasn't actually given to flights of fancy. Nick had smelled the wild woods as he rushed down those stairs. The scent of them had washed over him and through him, so powerful that he thought he was plunging headfirst into the clearing with the stone circle, the heart of the wild wood, rather than the darkness under the house. At first, he had thought he must have brought it with him. But he didn't. Alex had called it, somehow, called the wild to save his daughter. It had to be Alex. The dead couldn't do it, Maeve was too young, and there was no one else here.

Nick owed Alex everything.

But that wasn't all.

He *wanted* to keep her safe, he realised. He *wanted* to make sure that no harm came to her. Not just as the guardian of this place, its protector. He wanted Alex safe. More than he ever had anyone other than Maeve.

Even Sally.

Sally had never needed him. Not really. He was a symbol to her, some kind of manifestation of that which she served. He represented the woods. But she had never loved him. He had adored her, worshipped her, served her.

But she had never made him feel the way Alex did.

Nick drew in a breath and held it, until his lungs strained. How was that possible? He barely knew her, not really. And yet...

For years he had felt bound here, tied to the woods, to Sally, and now... now that was gone. The tether broken.

Sally was gone and Alex had been the one to help her escape from whatever had trapped her spirit here. He hadn't even been there to say goodbye. Theo had come for her. And she'd gone gladly.

And that was all right as well. He had said goodbye to Sally long ago. Perhaps even before she died. When he saw her with Theo, when he understood that she didn't really love him. Not like that.

And perhaps he had never really loved her either. He saw that now.

It was a world away from what he felt now for Alex.

He just hadn't known. He'd never realised the intensity of the emotion.

Was this love? This burning, desperate feeling, this need to hold her and shield her, this desire to be better for her, to deserve her.

The shock of it made his heart pound. It couldn't be. He barely knew her.

But she had saved and shielded his daughter. She had given herself up to the wild. He owed her everything. And even if she hadn't...

She was more like her brother than she would care to admit. So easy to love. And he had loved Theo in spite of everything that happened. He'd never stopped loving him.

How could Nick possibly know what he was feeling? If any of this was real? Or if the house was playing games with him? How would he ever know?

'—need to have a proper look at that thing,' Alex said.

He jarred back into reality. 'What?'

She studied his face for a long moment. 'I said, I think we need to have a proper look at the statue.'

'Is that wise? It was buried down there for a reason.'

'Maybe. But that reason might not have been to our benefit. Right under the house like that? And then the whole area blocked off and hidden? It was left there so it could fester and grow, infect the whole house. Hidden away.'

Except for the secret door. Someone had known about that. Not Theo perhaps. But her grandfather had written about it.

'Is there anything in the notebook about sealing or controlling?' he asked.

'I think he knew it was there and he was hiding it. Perhaps trying to keep it under his control. He didn't tell Theo anything, did he?'

'I'm pretty sure Theo would have told me if he knew. Or Sally.' But there were things none of them had told each other, after all.

And were there things he wasn't telling Alex now?

He hadn't hidden his true nature from her. Not intentionally. But nor had he shared it. He'd run off, hidden, stayed away until he was sure he could control himself. He hadn't shared his past, dreamlike, mangled and half-forgotten as it was. He refused to let her see what he could be when the wild took him.

Sally had never really seen the thing she had made of him. Not really. She saw purpose, she saw need. But not him.

Alex's hand closed on his fist. She stood beside him now, a look of concern on her face as she bent over him. 'Are you okay?' Her touch was warm and so painfully gentle.

'Yes, I – I'm sorry. What were you saying?'

'Do you want to talk about her? About them? Sally and Theo, I mean?'

She didn't manage to look as if the prospect thrilled her either, but at least she offered.

'They're at peace now,' he replied at last, forcing the words around the lump in his throat. 'They're together. And safe. That's what matters.'

Alex hunkered down in front of him, searching his face for something. She didn't let go of his hand. The pad of her thumb brushed against his knuckles. 'Any other man might still be angry, might want revenge. Might want them to suffer. Not find peace together.'

Nick shrugged. What did they say about people setting out to get revenge? First dig two graves. He'd already done that. He had stood over two graves anyway. It definitely hadn't helped. 'I never saw the point in that kind of thinking. It just tortures everyone.'

'True,' Alex replied, and then her phone rang again. 'Oh, for God's sake.' She poked a finger at the screen as she got up and turned away. 'Yes, Gabe, what now?'

She walked out of the room, and he could hear her pacing in the hall. Talking, listening, talking again. Which left Nick sitting there, looking at the hidden door. On his own.

His hands shook, just a little, and he clenched them into fists again to make it stop. Blaise Chambers had tried to take his daughter. He had almost taken his wife's spirit. Even after death he had tried to destroy her.

And he was supposed to be the guardian of this place. He was supposed to protect it. He'd been focused on trying to protect it from Blaise, and hadn't thought that there could be more.

Nick dragged the armchair away from the door, opened it and stepped into the darkness. For a moment he just stood there at the top of the stairs, looking down into a space blacker than a moonless night. He felt nothing of the wild wood here now. Nothing of the trees that sustained him and filled the emptiness inside him. But he could feel something down there still. It was an empty, sucking hole underneath the house, where Theo had lived, and all his ancestors before him. It was the thing that Sally had been trying to guard against when she embroiled them in her schemes.

It had almost taken Maeve...

His head swam and he had to reach out and steady himself against the wall. It felt greasy, unclean.

'Nick?' Alex said again, her hand resting on his arm, her fingertips so cool, like points of ice.

He shook himself, trying to clear the fog gnawing at the edges of his mind. The need to turn around and sweep her up in his arms again shuddered through him. He could still feel her lips on his, that bruising kiss, the way it burned. The way he hadn't entirely felt like himself as he kissed her.

Nick swallowed hard, forced himself to focus on the here and now. Something was wrong. This place was evil. And he knew why.

'Maybe we shouldn't. Even if it's not—' He wouldn't say cursed. He couldn't. Even if that was what it felt like. 'What if it's old? Shouldn't we get an archaeologist or something?'

She considered that, perhaps not noticing that it was just an excuse. 'Maybe. But we need to take a look at it, at least. Take some photos. No one is going to believe us otherwise.'

'Okay,' he agreed, but he didn't move. 'Then we need torches. And work gloves.'

'Work gloves? Why?'

'I don't want to touch anything down there. Do you?'

The statue was hunched and misshapen. More like a rock than a figure. And there was definitely a glint of gold. Nick wasn't sure. Something felt off, like it was luring them in, teasing them, offering them riches if they were brave enough, or foolish enough, to try to take it.

It was an idol. There was no mistaking it. A hunched figure, just like they had thought. Alex had said it was called Crom, that her grandfather had identified it in his notebooks. And it definitely looked to be covered in gold, if not completely made from it. He wasn't sure and part of him didn't want to examine it too closely. It left him cold. Cold to the core.

The small hunched figure, squatting in the corner of the undercroft, more or less under the drawing room now, with a gaping mouth and round eyes, knees up and splayed wide, clawed hands gripping the base on which it crouched.

Nick stared at it and tried to shake off the immediate feeling that it was staring right back at him. All he wanted right now was to get out of the dark.

Alex, who had been examining it in the same kind of solemn silence, took out her phone and photographed it from every angle. Then stared at it for a moment longer. Nick frowned. It was like she couldn't tear her eyes off it and that was a troubling idea.

'Alex,' he said, and lightly touched her shoulder. She brought her hand up and closed it over his, the gloves keeping them apart. But it was a contact, an anchor. Just that touch. 'Let's go back upstairs.'

Slowly, without saying a word, she nodded.

Alex emerged from the secret door behind him, closing it firmly.

'Crom,' she said at last, staring at the photos on her phone. Then she sent them to her group chat.

'Looks like it,' Nick agreed reluctantly.

'I wonder which one.'

He shrugged. 'I don't really care. I'm still not sure we shouldn't have put it back in the hole.'

'I'm not sure we should leave it down there,' Alex murmured softly. He didn't know what to make of the tone of her voice. 'It's strong in the darkness.'

Her voice trailed off again and Nick saw her shiver, her shoulders tightening.

Carefully, quietly, he wrapped his arms around her and pulled her back against his chest. She melted against him and he felt her exhale, a sigh of both relief and release.

'Thank you,' he whispered. 'For finding Maeve. And for Sally too. You saved her. You and Theo. Maeve told me.'

She didn't turn around but he felt her fall still as if she was holding her breath.

And strangely he found that he wasn't able to breathe either. Not anymore. She was there in his arms, her body soft against his.

Nick held her a little tighter, and pressed his lips against the top of her head.

CHAPTER 41

ALEX

His kiss on the crown of her head was unexpected, the warm rush of air, the closeness, the tenderness of it all.

Alex felt her eyes sting with sudden tears and she closed them tight.

An image flared in her mind and the idol was still there, staring sightlessly at them with its bulging golden eyes. A low sultry laugh shook the air, just for a moment, for her ears alone.

She must have flinched because she felt Nick pull back. Her eyes snapped open. The idol was still beneath them, out of sight if not out of mind.

'I'm sorry, I—'

Alex turned her back on the door, facing Nick instead. It was a much better view for starters. But he had already put distance between them and his arms fell to his sides. He looked so awkward and unsure she just wanted to pull him to her and kiss him properly this time.

'There's nothing to be sorry about,' she told him firmly. He didn't look entirely convinced. 'That wasn't because of you.'

Nick glanced suspiciously at her, and then understanding seemed to dawn in his expression, and he nodded.

'We still need to secure the house before the storm hits. And you're probably hungry. I could make us some dinner.'

It wasn't what she had in mind. But it was a start.

And the man could cook.

'Dinner sounds great.'

Nick made a vegetable stir-fry, quick and crisp and delicately flavoured with a mix of spices Alex couldn't begin to guess the composition of. It was probably witchcraft, she decided, chasing the last of the noodles around the dish so as to soak up the sauce. No, *definitely* witchcraft. He was a kitchen witch – that was a thing, wasn't it? – as well as a guardian of the forest.

And the most fascinating man she'd ever met.

Her face heated as she thought that and she made herself look away. Unfortunately, she glanced towards the door to the cellar and the darkness that was still seeping through the gap under it.

'I'll see to that next,' he told her.

The thought of him going down there into the dark, with that thing lurking on the other side of the wall... 'Tomorrow will do, won't it? Once the sun's up?'

If the sun came up. The wind was rising steadily outside now, hurling rain against the exterior of the house. She was half waiting for the windows or doors to burst open at any second.

But not even the storm would dare to invade Wildewood Hall.

'Let's get some wine and hole up in the drawing room for the night. Anything else can wait, right?'

CHAPTER 42

NICK

The bottles of wine were down in the cellar. Nick hesitated at the top of the steps, staring down into the darkness. But there was nothing there now. Couldn't be. Alex had sent Blaise packing, hadn't she? The idol was on the other side of the wall. It could rot there in the darkness.

He shook his head. He was letting all this get to him. It was just the cellar. He didn't like the place but he had been down there a thousand times. It was creepy and dark. Nothing more. With everything that had happened, he was a bit shaken. Chambers was gone.

He made his way down the steps and reached for the nearest wine bottle.

There was a rush of wind from behind him, a foul miasma, and he spun around, staring back up into the light. Something fell from the lintel of the doorway up above him, twigs and old dried reeds and straw scattering like chaff. The charms collapsed, one after the other, all the way down the steps, fragments raining down. Darkness fell with them.

A shadow stretched down the steps, filling the doorway,

cutting off the light from the kitchen. The solitary bulb down here flickered and died, while the dark shape loomed over him, misshapen and huge. Nick's breath caught in his chest as if a vice had just closed around his ribs and tightened.

He stared up at it, his way out blocked, the step hidden from view by this thing. He felt rather than saw it smile, bare its fangs, and reach for him, claws sinking into his skin.

'*Wild thing...*' it hissed. He could feel its breath on his face, cold as the grave, older... darker... '*Not much of a guardian, are you? More like a monster. Why not let yourself be wild? It's what you want, after all. Why not take what you want? No one could stop you. Give in to your nature. Be what you were always meant to be.*'

The bottle slid from his numb hand, crashing onto the floor and shattering. The violent noise broke the spell. Nick jumped back with a strangled cry,

And the shape at the foot of the steps was gone.

Nick cursed, fixing his mind on the trees and all the protection they could offer.

But the echo of that other voice was still there, in his blood, in his core. A pulse that would not be dismissed, working its way through him.

Wild thing...

'Nick?'

Shit, that was Alex's voice. She was up there in the kitchen, looking for him. How long had he been down here? It had felt like only a minute or so but Wildewood Hall played tricks. He could have been standing there like a statue for hours fighting off whatever entity still lurked down here.

He shook himself back to reality.

'Just a sec,' he called up. 'Don't come down. I dropped the bottle. Broken glass everywhere.'

Alex peered down from the light of the kitchen.

He couldn't let her come down here.

Why not take what you want?

'Are you okay?'

'Sure,' he lied. He wasn't. He really wasn't. Things were already spiralling out of control again. So soon. He felt sick. He was a monster, deep down inside, and something was calling it forth. 'Fine. I just need to clear this up. Sorry.' He tried to make his voice firm and unshaken. Not terribly well but convincingly enough. 'Why not go back to the drawing room where it's warm? I'll only be a few minutes. I just need the dustpan and brush and...'

And they were up there, with her.

'Here,' she said, as if reading his mind. She took a step forward but he held up a hand.

'Throw it down,' he said and she obeyed, tossing them down the stairs to him. He tried to snatch them out of the air, missed, lost his balance and brought his knee down straight onto a jagged shard.

His curses were even louder this time and his head swam. Not with pain exactly but with awareness of the blood in the air. And laughter. There was laughter all around him. Mocking, echoing, taunting. The dustpan and brush clattered onto the floor beside him, useless.

'Nick!' Alex cried out in alarm.

'Stay up there,' he roared, aware that she was already moving, her feet on the cold stone steps, heedless of the danger to body and soul. 'Alex, don't!'

She stopped, three steps up from him, and slowly retreated backwards, her eyes wide with alarm. Thank all that was sacred.

Moving faster than he should have given he was bleeding and in pain, he swept the broken glass into the pan and left it there. He'd sort it out later. Instead, he grabbed another bottle and bounded up the steps, intercepting her before she could think of going down there herself.

White-faced and shocked, Alex was leaning against the table and simply staring at him, her hands gripping the wood, as if she was about to haul herself up on it to escape him.

He slammed the door to the cellar closed and locked it.

The ancient warding was scattered all over the floor, pulled apart, little more than dried straw and fragments of flowers now. It was an old one. A powerful one, he had thought, the kind made by one of the wise women of Kilfayne long ago, which Sally had added to each year, refreshing it, giving it new life. And now it was broken. All the smaller ones too.

Bastard. The absolute bastard.

Nick should have known better. He should have never let his guard down. He was an idiot. More than an idiot.

He'd been distracted. He had thought they were safe with Chambers gone, that it was over. That the statue was just a statue.

'You're bleeding,' Alex gasped.

He could smell it, coppery in the air, almost taste it, rather than feel the cut. Not good. That was not good. He'd just bled in the cellar. On ancient stones, in the presence of the very thing Chambers had worshipped. That was never good.

'Here.' He held out the bottle of wine like it was some kind of trophy. He hadn't even looked to see what it was. But she had wanted a drink so he'd gone to get her a drink and now...

His head swam again. That surge of anger came from somewhere else. He was sure of it.

'*Are you scared?*' a voice whispered. And there was a laugh. A bitter, taunting laugh. It sounded like Chambers. But not entirely. It sounded like something else as well. Like a chorus. '*Coward. They owe you. The de Wildes. She owes you.*'

Alex grabbed the bottle and put it down on the table, ignoring it completely.

'Sit down,' she told him. 'Let me see to that. Do you have a first aid kit?'

'Under the sink,' he said, grudgingly, hardly able to form the words. A first aid kit wasn't going to help him now. He wanted to throw up. He wanted to curl up and hide in the darkness until everything went away. He wanted... dear gods, he wanted... his eyes fixed on her... he *wanted*...

She pulled out one of the chairs and for a moment he thought she would just manhandle him into it if he didn't comply.

It felt like someone shoved him from behind.

Nick limped to the seat and sank into it while Alex fetched the first aid kit. The lower part of his left jeans leg was dark with blood and a jagged piece of glass protruded from the material. He winced as he looked at it.

Alex knelt down in front of him, her head bowed. 'Okay, hold on for a moment.'

And before he knew what she was doing, she'd pulled the glass out. The blood came faster now, pumping out. She slid her hand up his leg, assessing, and pressed hard above the wound to try to staunch the flow.

'You'll have to take them off,' she said so matter-of-factly.

His jeans. Right. Of course. They weren't loose enough to push up. And if they were going to check out the cut, she needed access. His chest heaved as he tried to catch his breath. There was so much blood.

But it was Alex asking. Alex on her knees in front of him. He swallowed hard and a wave of pain and dizziness swept through him. That voice again, that urge, Chambers, not Chambers...

'Why not take what you want?'

No. Just no. There was nothing erotic about this.

'Isn't there? Blood and sex and the wild urge... Give in to it.'

She was waiting. If he left it any longer, she looked like she would do it for him and he couldn't stand that. He'd lose himself completely if she touched him there. He fumbled with the fly and shifted, standing up a little, so he could drop his jeans to his ankles. This was not how he had imagined this. Not in the slightest.

And he had imagined it... God help him, he had. In the night, in the morning, in the trees, from the first moment he saw her...

He *wanted*...

He was painfully aroused. He really shouldn't be but he couldn't disguise it. Folding his arms across his lap didn't help. Neither did trying to distract his mind and body with thoughts of the estate accounts...

An ocean of numbers wouldn't help right now.

A cruel laugh echoed around his head and he screwed his eyes shut, tilting his face up to the ceiling in despair.

But Alex just ignored him, intent on the injury. Dear gods, he prayed she hadn't noticed.

Alex cleaned the cut, the antiseptic making him wince. But while the cut had bled initially, it wasn't deep and it had already stopped by the time she'd finished.

'There,' she said, pressing a plaster to the wound – a pitifully small cut really to bleed so much – and smiled up at him.

For a moment he thought he would do anything for that smile. Anything at all. The wild need eased off, the edge softening suddenly, and the scent of flowers wound itself around him again, the wild winding surrounding him, protecting him again. Just like Sally.

'All done,' she went on. Her hand brushed his thigh as she got up, sending shudders of need through him. Her touch... oh fuck, he needed her touch...

He tugged up the jeans again as quickly as he could and fastened them, taking care to turn away from her as he did so.

This was not going in any way like he had imagined. Nothing about Alex was how he imagined.

'Right, wine,' she said, pleased with herself, and grabbed the bottle again, heading off back to the drawing room.

And God help him, all he could do was follow, like a predator with a scent.

CHAPTER 43

ALEX

The storm outside was getting worse. An update on Alex's phone told her that the storm warning had been raised to red overnight. There was a string of messages from her team, but she honestly didn't have the energy to deal with that right now. She was exhausted. All she wanted to do was sit in front of the fire they had lit in the fireplace and drink her wine. Then sleep. But the oppressive sense of the house still weighed on her. And the storm meant they were trapped in here.

She watched Nick cross to the windows and stare out into the night. She wasn't even sure what he could see. The rain lashing against the panes obscured even the darkness outside, pressing close as if trying to get inside.

'Everything okay?' she asked. The cut on his leg hadn't been bad but it had bled a lot initially, so much so that she'd feared it was much more serious. And then it had just stopped. Still, it worried her. After everything that had happened...

'They're unsettled,' he murmured. 'Scared.'

'The woods?'

'Yes.'

'You can sense that? What they're... feeling?'

'I can sense the wild wood, the trees themselves and the spirits in them. I don't know what it's feeling exactly but... it's part of me. I feel it inside of me. The woods are scared. Not just of the storm. There's something else.'

The image of the idol beneath them came vividly to her mind again. Too vividly. Something else indeed. And Nick... he hadn't been himself since the cellar. Something was wrong.

'Are they trying to warn us?'

A thud sounded from overhead, where her bedroom was, and then they both distinctly heard the sound of footsteps. Slow and steady, determined, they moved across the ceiling, heading for where the door would be. Footsteps on the stairs. Laughter, dark and terrible.

Alex threw open the door to the hallway. She hadn't even been aware of getting up and running across the room, but the next moment she had the handle in her hand and she was looking out into the hall leading to the front door.

There was nothing there. Of course there was nothing there. The hall was empty. Wildewood Hall did so love to play games.

The lightbulbs flickered, dimmed for a second, then blazed with an incandescence which made her eyes burn.

An afterimage appeared, where she had been staring, Blaise Chambers, dark and beautiful and terrible, standing in front of her, one hand reaching out towards her, as if to touch her face. He wasn't gone. She might have saved Sally but he was still there!

The house plunged into darkness.

Nick cursed loudly and Alex recoiled, bumping into him where he had followed her. They retreated, back into the warm and ruddy light of the fire.

'Power cut?' she asked, aware that her voice was shaking. There was no sign of Chambers now, but it still felt like he was watching her. Smiling that horrible smile. Laughing at them.

'I'll check the circuit board and get the generator going.'

A dreadful feeling twisted in her stomach. 'Where is the generator, Nick?'

Don't say the cellar, she thought, sudden fear clawing at her throat. Please don't say the cellar.

'In the outbuilding to the back of the kitchen,' he said solemnly, as if reading her mind and trying to put her at ease. 'It's fine.' Apart from him having to go out in the storm. 'Here.' He grabbed a couple of candles from the mantelpiece and lit them from the fire before putting them into two candlesticks. He handed one to her. 'I'll be as quick as I can.'

'Is it safe out there?'

He actually smiled. As if having something to do, no matter how dangerous, was finally a relief.

'I've a torch and wet weather gear in the boot room. It's just a storm. A bad one but just a storm. I'll be fine. Back in no time.'

She had to say it. 'What if the house locks you out again?'

He fixed her with a more serious look. 'You're in here. It's not going to stop me getting back to you, Alex.'

There was nothing she could think of to say to stop him. She clung to her candlestick, and watched the flickering pool of light around him make its way out to the hall and vanish.

The house seemed to close its arms around her chest and squeeze. It drove the air from her lungs and her heart lurched up in her throat.

'*You still want him,*' the dark voice murmured from just behind her. '*Take him. He'll only thank you for it. He wants you so desperately. He needs you. You know that.*'

Alex tried to push the intrusive spirit from her, picturing a beam of light shining down on her, just like Daphne had drilled them all on time and time again. She had never taken it seriously before. Now it felt like the single lifeline she could cling to.

Her legs went from underneath her and she dropped to her knees, knuckles white on the candlestick.

'*Really?*' Blaise chuckled softly. A ghostly hand, like the touch of the north wind, curled around her throat and squeezed until Alex's mouth opened. '*You think you're strong enough to withstand the two of us combined?*'

The words snagged on her reeling mind. *The two of us? What did he mean, the two of us?*

Lips brushed against hers and something kissed her, delving deep into her, every touch maddening. She couldn't see him but she could feel him. She could barely feel anything else. The pressure all around her deepened its grip. Hands slid down her sides, and then his fingertips were on her skin. Clothes meant nothing to him.

'Don't...' she tried to say.

'*You don't mean that. I know what you want. Your own body betrays you. Let me show you. Surrender to me, Alexandra.*'

The mouth trailed down the side of her neck, captured one hardened nipple and he sucked hard, making her gasp out loud.

'*I'm a god,*' he whispered. '*I joined myself to Crom. I made that bargain long ago. And now you have released the strongest part of me. Locked in the dark, lost in the depths beneath the house there was little I could do but influence life above. But now... now... We have tasted the blood of the guardian and it is so sweet. Let us take more, you and I together. Let us devour him...*' She could feel the wolfish grin against her flesh, the touch of his teeth. '*With the idol free of the pit, I can show you pleasure the like of which you have never known. We will bring it into the light, you and I. And with him, I can be everything you could ever wish for. All you have to do is give him to me. You can do that, Alexandra. Give me a new life and I will give you everything.*'

His questing fingers slipped inside her, finding the warm depths of her body and her soul, twisting and stroking until

Alex's head fell back, helpless before him. Ghost, god, who knew what he was? But all her defences were nothing now.

The two of them, Chambers had said. The ghost and the god.

She was a fool. What had she been thinking?

Pleasure rippled through her body, raw and terrible. A spear of desire that shook its way to her core and left her gasping and desperate.

'Let me in, Alexandra. Let me give you everything. Worship me and I will adore you. You're the last of the de Wildes and you carry the blood of the women of Kilfayne, those very witches who imprisoned Great Crom. And now, my beloved, you will set us free.'

The candle went out. Only the firelight illuminated the room and she was trapped. In the mirror over the fireplace, she could see her reflection, silhouetted against the flames. Her skin was flushed and gilded as the infernal light touched it. And all around her, the shadow wound itself like a great boa constrictor, tightening its grip, burrowing into her and weaving spells beneath her treacherous willing flesh.

She was alone in the house. Nick was outside somewhere in the storm. But he was near the forest, near the trees. Surely, they would protect him. She had to warn him! She tried to reach out again, tried to catch that sense of the wild that had come to her in the undercroft when she had needed it most. It slipped away from her.

'Not this time,' Blaise chuckled. *'Do not fear. You will both be ours. The last of the de Wildes and the last guardian of the wild wood. Don't you see, my beloved? You are the key we have been waiting for. You are the bait for this trap. You made him fall. And with him everything holding us trapped in this place will fall as well. My lord Crom and I will be free at last. Free of Wildewood Hall, free of the wild wood itself. There is a whole world out there ready for us to make our own.'*

CHAPTER 44

NICK

The wind and rain buffeted him from the moment Nick stepped outside into the night. The torch he'd taken from the boot room was barely any use. He put his head down, shoulders to the storm, and forced his way across to the plant room in the old dairy. He had to drag the door closed behind him and that was a brief respite.

Storm Ferdia still howled outside but at least in here he wasn't being drenched and battered at the same time.

There was no power. That was obvious. The mains were out, probably a line down on the way up here from the village. He just needed to get the generator up and running and they would be grand.

The machinery was cold and dark, and the small stone room stank of petrol.

His throat tightened as he realised what he was standing in.

Someone, or something, had opened the cap and pumped the fuel out of the generator. It spilled across the stone flags, seeping in between the cracks. Even if there was enough left in it to start the machine up, doing so would be a massive fire hazard.

Thank God he hadn't tried to come out here with a candle. Not that the flame would have made it this far in the wind and the rain.

But why do this? And how?

He stepped back, wary now. 'Sally? What's going on?'

But there was no answer. There couldn't be an answer. Sally was gone. Theo had come to get her when Alex called him.

Alex. He'd left her alone in the house.

A house which wanted to be cold, dark and isolated. A house which wanted her for itself. It had already locked him out once to have its way.

This was wrong. All of it was wrong.

They shouldn't have left the fucking idol out of the hole. They should have just put it back down in the ground where the roots could hold it. Better yet, he should have mixed up a ton of concrete and poured it over the bastard thing.

The pain in his leg became a burn. He thought he heard laughter. Dark and knowing, mocking, a laugh which had haunted him for years.

And now it wanted Alex.

He didn't know how he knew that. But he did. Nick ran from the outbuilding and the storm struck him with furious force, slamming him back against the wall outside. The trees were an ocean in the tempest, the wind howling through them, leaves and other debris whirling through the air. Rage, that was what he felt in the land and in the storm. Rage born of terror. The land itself was screaming and the air screamed with it.

'I'm sorry,' he tried to say but the storm snatched his voice away.

This was wrong. All wrong. The woods seethed with rage and he – he remembered what it was like to have that force turned on him. Long ago, so long ago, another lifetime...

They'd come in the night, ready to torch the house, him

and his brigade, ready to burn down the relics of the old imperial oppressors and make way for a new Free State. They'd done it before, all over the country, watching these symbols of the aristocracy blaze and then fall to ashes. And it had felt so good to vent that rage. He'd lost friends and brothers, his family torn apart by independence and civil war, and this was justified.

But when they reached Kilfayne, when they reached Wildewood Hall, the people they were there to represent stood side by side with their landlord to drive them away. Bewildered, his brigade had fallen back to the woods and the women...

Dear Jesus, the women had called up a storm like this and the woods had surged to life. He'd seen men torn apart, crushed, swallowed up by the earth until, at last, he was the only one left.

A woman had stood over his broken body, long dark hair, wild blue eyes. Sally's grandmother, perhaps, or great-grandmother. She looked just like her, filled with the same power, the same determination, a wise woman bent on revenge. He'd begged for his life and she'd taken it anyway. She'd smiled a knowing smile and told him he'd make amends. That he'd go on making amends. She was the last thing he saw before brambles and vines wound about his body, before leaves and mulch filled his mouth and crushed themselves down his throat, before the earth dragged him under. He didn't know anything for a very long time.

Not until Sally had danced in the wild wood, and summoned him back again. She'd told him the time had come. Guardian, she'd called him. The walker in the woods.

And he'd failed.

Reality slammed back into him, cold and hard and awful. It left him gasping in the wind and the rain, in the howling night. Something was happening. Something terrible. Right now.

Alex. He needed to get back to Alex.

Nick sprinted through the storm, barrelling through the

back door of the building and into the boot room, almost falling on his face as the wind cut off.

The house was far too still and far too quiet. Even the raging tempest outside seemed muffled and distant. Wildewood Hall closed around him like a trap.

'Alex?' he yelled, his voice far too loud in this silence.

He didn't bother to pull off the raincoat and the boots, just kept going, forcing his way through the kitchen door and up the corridor to the main hall.

There was laughter above him, light and delicate, the sound of children twisted to mockery. He could imagine them, all the hollowed-out ghosts, leaning over the bannisters of the upper galleries, looking down on him. Sweet voices turned to something cruel. And others too. Men, raucous and brutal. Women, their voices ringing like music or the song of mockingbirds. More of the spirits than he had sensed in years. They clustered around now, hungry for whatever sport they could make. Sally had always been there, shielding him, in life and in death. But now Sally was gone.

And the old god was loose.

He could feel the walls of Wildewood Hall pulse with malice sunken into them over a thousand years.

'*Your time here is over, guardian. You have failed. You never really had the strength beyond what your creator could lend you. And she was always flawed. She stole you to begin with and what starts with a lie will always come undone. She made you from the dirt of humanity as much as the dirt of the forest.*'

His creator? Did it mean Sally?

Nick struggled on, trying to ignore them, feeling the drain on his stamina. He felt almost dizzy with fear, but he pressed on. Strength was seeping away with every footstep he took within the walls of this cursed building.

'Alex,' he shouted again, her name almost a sob. She had to be all right. He should never have left her. 'Alex, answer me!'

How many ghosts were there in Wildewood Hall? Crom must have trapped and corrupted so many over the centuries. Blaise was only the most successful of his conquests, Nick realised, the one who dragged down all the others, a man so corrupt and dissolute that his fall had been just a light and careless step into darkness. And after that the two of them had been partners in crime. Crom needed a physical form to free himself, someone to possess, someone to house his spirit and to feed from. To use in order to feed from others.

Women from Kilfayne had married into the line of the de Wildes, he knew that from Sally. It had been part of their plan to strengthen the wild woods. It had worked too. For centuries they'd protected this place, because it held that monster in check. And now... now there was only Alex left with the blood of both. Maeve may have Sally's power one day, but she was only a child yet.

And that dark power had no use for a child, thank God.

He had used Blaise Chambers. But Chambers had been killed, shot through the chest on the cellar steps, his blood soaking into the earth below. Where Nick's blood had joined it...

Crom needed a host. A living host.

'Alex!'

You had one job, his heart screamed at him, still carrying echoes of Theo's voice. *You had just one job. You're the caretaker, the guardian. You only had one job.*

And he had failed.

More than failed. He'd left her on her own in there.

Nick skidded around the corner into the drawing room. Alex was on her knees, curled into a ball, her arms wrapped around her body and the candlestick lying on the ground before her, the flame out.

Crashing to his knees in front of her, Nick grabbed her and pulled her into his embrace. Her hands felt like ice, as he rubbed the skin as if he was trying to summon life itself back into her.

'Alex? Talk to me.'

For a moment she didn't reply. Perhaps she couldn't hear him. Perhaps she didn't want to. But then, slowly, she seemed to come back to herself.

'It's you,' she whispered, her voice shaking. 'Oh Nick... I thought... I was so scared. I thought...'

Before he knew what was happening, she surged forward to kiss him, her hands pulling free so they could tangle in his hair and close on his shoulders. Her kiss stole his reason, just as it had before. His reason and his will. She was all he wanted. She was all he had ever wanted.

Had Sally known it would be like this? Had Theo? Had it been like this for the two of them? Was that why he had tried to warn Nick off? Or had he meant Chambers?

And here in this house, right now, in the middle of a storm, with the power gone and the spirits of the place on the rise, was the wrong time and the wrong place. But he didn't care. How could he care?

Alex held him, kissed him with all the focused intention that he had dreamed of since the first moment he laid eyes on her.

She pushed the wet jacket off his shoulders and slid it down his arms. His t-shirt went next, pulled up and over his head to expose his torso to her exploratory hands.

'Alex, slow down,' he tried to say, but she bit the words from his mouth.

'I don't want to slow down,' she said, the smile a torment. 'I want you. Just you. We have unfinished business. You owe me, Nick Walker.'

Firelight glittered in her eyes as she pulled off her clothes. Such reckless abandon. It stole his voice, stole his reason.

'Do you want this?' she asked, so simply. 'Do you want me?'

'Of course I do.'

'Well then.' She smiled and opened his jeans, pushing him back so she could free his cock. Nick gave in and struggled out of the restrictive clothes. It was like breathing again.

Because he did want this, more than anything. Maybe even more than he had ever wanted anyone else. He didn't just want Alex. He needed her.

A moment later his breath caught in his throat as Alex's mouth sank onto his shaft. He groaned out her name, unable to help himself. She was softness and warmth, her teeth grazing ever so gently against his most sensitive skin, drawing out his pleasure and leaving him helpless, needing, wanting, a creature of pleasure and nothing else.

He fought to focus and glanced down to find her looking up at him, her eyes wicked with reflected desire.

Not her eyes, something in the back of his mind tried to tell him. Those weren't her eyes. They were dark and endless, glimmering with firelight.

Her hands claimed him again and he couldn't fight her. He didn't want to.

Alex pushed his helpless body back onto the carpet. Both of them were naked now and he couldn't tell anyone how that had happened. It had been a flurry of fingers and fabric and then they were twined together again. Breath on skin, lips and teeth and need, so much need. She dragged her body up the length of him and settled herself astride him, pinning him down.

'Tell me you're mine,' she said. Her voice trembled with desire.

'Alex... are you... are you all right?'

Was she? Was he? This was all so overwhelming. He didn't want it to stop. But he wasn't sure he had any kind of control over what was happening. It felt... primordial.

And God, the hunger in him was almost out of control, but something was wrong. Something was terribly wrong. The heat of the flames brushed over his body, and it was all he could do not to lose himself completely, to flip her over and take her like some kind of animal, all ravenous hunger and wild desire.

'Say you want me,' she whispered.

'I do. Of course, I do but—'

Alex shifted her position, lifting herself for a moment, and then sank down on his cock, taking him all the way inside her, right to the root. He gasped, unable to think anymore, unable to move, so complete and overwhelming was the sensation. So perfect. This was perfect.

'Tell me you're mine,' she said again, and that strange echo in her words made her sound...

There was another voice. Something ancient and endless and terrible. It lingered behind her words, a whisper, a sigh.

'Alex,' he hissed but all she did was smile down at him.

That was not her smile. Her body began to move and he couldn't help himself, moving with her. It was a dance, a call and response, and he had to join in, to answer her every demand, spoken and unspoken.

Because God help him he did want this. All of it. He wanted her in every way.

That need swept him away.

In the firelight and the shadows, bodies sheened with gilded sweat moved, wound together in bliss. He couldn't tell where one started and the other ended, or how many they were. In a clearing in the forest, where the great bonfire roared and lit up the night, where crackling sparks shot skywards, and the faithful gathered, shedding blood and seed and all the pleasure in them at the feet of the golden idol. Whatever it demanded.

The twisted little form squatted in its place of honour and the old god spilled out of it, travelling through the offerings and into the supplicants. It turned their pleasure to pain, their desire to destruction and it fed and fed and fed...

Cries of lust became howls of agony, but they didn't stop, couldn't stop. They tore at their bodies, drinking blood and devouring flesh. They were as endless as their divinity, and as relentless in their demands on each other.

'Alex.' He didn't know where he found his voice but it was torn from him as if ripped through brambles and thorns. They needed to stop. He couldn't find the words to say it but that didn't make it untrue. He couldn't tell her. That something was wrong. That something was using them both, feeding on them, that this... this wasn't...

But how could it not be right? He was with her. They were together. Finally.

He had to stop.

But he wouldn't. He couldn't. He knew that now. Alex wasn't there anymore. Whatever was gazing down at him out of those beautiful eyes, it wasn't Alex. It wasn't even human anymore. And neither was he.

Perhaps he never had been. He had memories, true, but they were vague and distant things, like someone else had described them to him. Like someone else's life, a hundred years gone by. All he remembered clearly was Sally's voice in the wild wood, Sally telling him he was her guardian, telling him into being, calling him forth...

No. That wasn't possible. He had a life, he had memories, a family, he had a daughter, he had...

'Lies,' the voice said. '*All lies. You have nothing. You are nothing. You're a thing made of wood and moss and all those stolen memories cobbled together. You should have died a hundred years ago. You're nothing but lies made flesh.*'

He felt the darkness reach out through him, into him, deep into the earth beneath the house. Into the power of the wild wood itself.

All he knew was its hunger. And that it was feeding.

Nick's back arched and he cried out Alex's name in one last attempt to reach her, before the nightmare swallowed him whole.

CHAPTER 45

ALEX

Her name on Nick's lips, a cry of ecstasy and despair combined, shuddered through her half-delirious mind and Alex opened her eyes to see fire. Not the one in the fireplace. No, this was something else, far bigger, as tall as the trees, crackling and dancing, laughing at her. A bonfire. A huge bonfire. Like the one people still lit at Hallowe'en, like the ones they lit millennia ago to celebrate the days when the world of the living and the dead were closest, when spirits could reach out again and touch...

Nick was spread out beneath her, his bare skin painted with a language she didn't know, his arms bound above his head, his head thrown back and his eyes closed. And they weren't in the house, not any more. They weren't anywhere that still existed in this world, but somewhere else, somewhere long destroyed. They were in a forgotten chamber, a tomb, a structure of ancient stone, and he was going to die. He was a sacrifice and he was dying, even as she moved on top of him, even as he filled her with life and desire.

Alex's hands pressed to his chest, to the painted whorls and spirals that decorated it, white and blue and black smeared beneath her touch. Tears leaked from the corners of his clenched eyelids and he knew... somehow he knew... what she was doing to him...

No, not her.

No, not her. This wasn't her. She'd never hurt him. Never.

But she couldn't seem to stop.

'*Make him ours,*' the voice hissed in the back of her mind and it wasn't even Blaise anymore. Not now. This was a voice as old as the stones from which Wildewood Hall was built. And she would make him hers. Theirs. She had to.

Alex bent to kiss him. He tasted of blood, but that didn't stop her.

She wanted him. Oh, how she wanted him. Everything about him. Even if she ripped him apart to have him. He would die here. She knew that.

And like it or not she was the weapon that would kill him.

The guardian of the wild woods would die and become... other. Become the god, its new vessel, its new toy. It would be free at last.

'*And oh, the fun we'll have,*' it cackled in the back of Alex's mind. '*The things we'll do. The three of us. Oh, the pleasure-pain and the agony of release, and all the glory of blood and seed you'll both pour out for me. You and all you touch.*'

Around her wrist, something tightened, insistent and alive, a touch of green and growing things. Alex stared as the grass bracelet Maeve had given her unfurled strands of new life, tendrils which wound tighter against her skin, flowers which opened as if to the sun.

Nick gasped her name once more.

Tell me you're mine, she'd demanded. And Nick said her name. *Her* name! Not Crom. He'd called out to her.

'No,' she whispered. She didn't even know where that word came from let alone what it might mean. This wasn't something she could stop. She was just one woman, already given over to its vile touch. Her family had made this bargain long ago. For power. For wealth. For this piece of land. She was a de Wilde.

'No,' Alex said again, this time more certain, more sure of herself. 'I'm not...'

She was Alex O'Neill. She'd given up the de Wildes twenty years ago.

The entity laughed, a bitter mocking laugh which made her flinch. As her motion stilled, Nick tore free of the bonds holding him. His hands closed on her hips, digging into her skin, a bruising grip which would not be broken. He cried out again, words she didn't know, couldn't hope to know. It wasn't English, or Irish, but something from long before any of those languages had names, let alone a place here. He pulled her to him and fucked her as if his life depended on it.

She cried out as a wave of sensation swept through her, as her body clenched around his and she came, her mind shattering and reforming only to shatter again.

'*Give yourself to us,*' Crom howled in the wind and the rain and the roar of the fire.

This wasn't right. It couldn't be right.

'No! I'm not a de Wilde. I'm Alex O'Neill and you will not take me!'

Green tendrils of the bracelet binding the two of them together burst into flower, the growth moving faster now, rushing up around them. The grass rose, hungry and all-consuming, and the wild woods closed in on them, smothering and swallowing them up. The world around her tore itself apart.

And all of a sudden she was back in the room, with the storm still battering at the windows and the fire dying in the grate, and Nick underneath her so still and quiet. He gazed sightlessly at the stucco ceiling.

Oh God, what had they done? What had *she* done to him?

'Nick?' Her voice came out as little more than a whisper.

'Nick? Are you—?' She couldn't say okay. He didn't look okay. 'Nick, please talk to me.'

He heaved in a breath, let it out so slowly. When he finally spoke, he sounded dazed. Lost. 'Alex?'

'Yes. Yes, it's me. I...'

A slow smile spread over his lips, the lips she had kissed, and tormented. The lips she wanted on her again. A lazy smile, too knowing to belong there. She watched it develop with a dawning horror.

'Alexandra,' he said, in a low drawl that didn't sound like Nick at all.

Alex tore herself away from him, grabbing her clothes where they were scattered around them both, pulling them on as fast as she possibly could.

Nick propped himself up on one elbow and watched her, in no hurry to mimic her dressing. Why would he?

Naked, bathed in firelight, hair still damp from the storm...

Alex almost fell over as she pulled on the jeans again.

'Where are you going?' he asked, his voice teasing, mocking, and not like Nick's voice at all. 'Come back. We have so much to finish, you and I. Endless experiences to explore. Your guardian is mine. The witch may have created him to protect this place, but you broke him for me, Alexandra. You lured him in and shattered him to pieces. You made him bleed.'

She needed silver and salt. She needed daylight. She needed...

Oh God, what had she done?

Nick swung his legs around so they were beneath him and he crouched there, silhouetted in front of the fire, like a great cat about to pounce. 'There's nowhere to run to, Alexandra,' he told her, still smiling. Like it was all a game.

And maybe it was to him.

'Nick...' she whispered, but she couldn't keep the hopelessness from her voice or her eyes. Because that wasn't Nick, was it? Not anymore.

And she knew full well what it was.

He shook his head slowly and the smile widened still further until he was showing his teeth. Almost like a snarl.

Not a guardian, not anymore.

A hunter. Feral and dangerous. A predator.

And she remembered, all those years ago, in the darkness.

The cold arched roof of stones closing over her and the stench of mulch. The darkness pressing in on her, suffocating her. Dad's hands falling still, limp on the rich and hungry earth.

Down in the undercroft where her father had found her and tried to help her. Where Crom had taken him and made him its creature.

The gleam of gold beneath rotting foliage. Eyes that didn't see, but saw everything, the mouth hanging open, hungry and waiting.

The idol, waiting for her, ready for her to free it. For all this to happen.

The taste of blood in her mouth, choking her, and the world blurring through tears and terror.

Just like now.

'Are you going to run?' he asked, amused at the whole idea. 'If you run, my sweet Alexandra, I'll have to chase you. Isn't that what happened all those years ago? Your father told you to run. And look how that turned out.'

'Run, Alex! You have to run!'

And she had run, out into the night, out into the trees. Because the trees were the only defence against this being, the final line of defence. The trees and the spirits wound through them. She'd called out, begging for help, praying for their guardian...

But the guardian was gone. Nick was... Nick was gone.

There had been no guardian back then. No Nick. Just her father. She had run and her father had followed and...

But he had been trying to protect her. He had always protected her. From the family curse. From the ghosts. From Blaise Chambers and the thing that haunted this house...

Hadn't he?

'You have to run! NOW!'

He had been lost too. He had been... been... chasing her... hunting her...

He had come after her. Not to protect her. Not anymore. Her father had already been gone long before he pursued her into the woods.

'You were always mine,' Blaise growled. 'You always will be. I will find you in any lifetime, in any form. Eternity binds us together, Alexandra de Wilde.'

Something struck the windows behind her, and she heard the crash of glass breaking, and suddenly the night tore into the ancient building, the wind and the rain and the darkness in a maelstrom of chaos.

She spun around to see the debris strewn across the carpet and the furniture, and a tree branch like a huge grasping hand reaching into Wildewood Hall, as if it was trying to grab her. She backed up towards the doorway leading to the hall, barefoot and wearing only a t-shirt and jeans.

'Where are you going?' Nick's voice teased in that terrible sing-song way.

The storm was upon them. And the wild woods didn't have a guardian anymore. She had handed him over to their enemy, who had made him its own.

There was only one thing to do.

You have to run, Lex. You have to get out of there.

It sounded like her father. It sounded like Theo. The voices on the edge of hearing, but there all the same. But they were gone. Theo was gone. And her father had died twenty years ago, because of her. He had been trying to protect her and it had taken him. Because of her. It was all her fault. It had always been her fault. She hadn't been fast enough. She had *never* been fast enough. They had gone to the wild wood.

Tears burned in her eyes and she fixed her gaze on Nick until the image blurred and twisted. It was Blaise Chambers crouching there, rising slowly, holding out his hand. He didn't believe she'd bolt now. Because he was right. Where was there to go? Maeve had taken the idol out of its containment and Alex should have put it back. But she hadn't. In the darkness, in the earth under the house, the roots of the wild wood had tried to smother its power. It was loose now, in the undercroft, filling the whole house with its power.

She had let it tempt her, seduce her, and then she had let it use her to seduce Nick. He was gone. And this was all her fault. Again.

The house was Crom's and the forest was Nick's and now Nick belonged to Crom through Chambers' possession of him... and she had nothing. Not to mention that the wild woods hated her family, every last one of them. She had betrayed whatever thin trust it had been willing to build through Theo, through Nick, through her feelings for him. She had given him over to its eternal enemy. There was nothing and nobody at all to help her now.

She didn't have any choice. There was only one thing she could still do.

Alex ran.

And the moment she bolted for the door, Nick leaped forward in pursuit, letting out a savage roar of triumph that the hunt was on at last.

CHAPTER 46

ALEX

Alex tore down the hallway, heading for the front door and the nearest way out. But as she reached the glass doorway, the rolling thunder in the air made her hesitate. Just in time too. The glass partition shattered, shards exploding in every direction, crashing down onto the floor. Barefoot and helpless, she backed up.

No way out, not through there.

Blaise, still wearing Nick like a tailored three-piece suit, leaned on the doorframe leading into the drawing room, watching her nonchalantly.

'You're going to have to come back eventually,' he said, in a lazy drawl. 'There's no way out of this. Not now. Not tonight. Go out into that gale and it will kill you. Go into the woods and they will kill you. They know you for the traitor you are now. Just like your father. Just like your brother. Give in, Alexandra. Come here and do as you're told, woman.'

No. No, she was never going to do that. The very fact he thought he could just command her like that was infuriating and that edged out the terror just enough.

Alex glared at him and he twisted poor Nick's beautiful

face into something snide and superior, which just made her even more indignant.

She bolted the other way, heading for the kitchen and the back door. He'd follow. She knew he'd follow.

He had to.

Alex grabbed the corner of the door to the kitchen and slammed it behind her, throwing herself towards the boot room and locking that door after her as well. The back door was still bolted, the panel Nick had put over the window barely keeping out the storm. She dragged back the heavy iron bolt with sluggish fingers, fumbling as she did so.

'Don't be foolish, Alexandra,' his voice – not his voice! Not *his*! – came from the kitchen, almost a sing-song of amusement. Blaise was coming and she couldn't get the bloody door open. She was going to be trapped in here with nowhere to go.

Finally, as if in answer to her muttered prayers and curses, the bolt gave and the wind threw the door in, almost taking her off her feet as it did so. She was driven backwards and she felt the kitchen door behind her buck as Blaise threw Nick's body against it. He'd be through in seconds, she knew that. Or he'd find another way. Between them Nick and Chambers knew where all the keys were kept, every passageway and secret path in this place inside and out. And he was strong enough to just break his way through the door if pressed. Blaise wouldn't care if Nick was hurt. Not now. He was just a tool, a blunt instrument.

Alex ran, letting the night and the storm envelop her in their own madness.

The wind screamed at her and the rain lashed against her face. She was drenched in seconds but she couldn't stop. It didn't matter that she couldn't see where she was going. Invisible hands guided her now, instincts and terror leading the way. The wild wood might hate her family, but it was the only hope she had left to her. She stumbled forward, barefoot and desperate, slipping in mud and sliding beneath the canopy of trees which lashed back and forth in the storm. She had to shield her face and head as the world flung the debris of the forest at her, steel herself and press forward as the wind tried to drive her back.

'Please,' she yelled, and her voice was instantly snatched away. 'Please, you have to help him. You have to help me help him. Please!'

She was back in that nightmare, running desperately through the woods which hated her and all her kind, pursued, hunted. Blaise Chambers was coming to get her and all she knew was that her father had screamed at her to run, so she had run. She had never stopped running.

And her father... her mind threw up that familiar wall of blackness, that thing she didn't want to remember. Because why would she want to remember his death? Why? It had all been her fault. He'd tried to protect her and he'd paid for it. Like Nick.

Crom was going to kill Nick if he couldn't have her. Through Blaise, he would tear Nick apart if they had to. And it was all her fault.

Alex sobbed and fell, her hands slamming down on nettles. The pain sent shockwaves through her, forcing her up again, making her stumble onwards in her heedless flight.

Behind her something was coming through the trees, something fast and deadly. The hunter. The wild thing. The beast...

This couldn't be happening. Not again. Not with Nick this time.

Because she had always known what had pursued her so long ago, and in every nightmare since. She had always known the face. It was always a face she loved turned against her. Changed and transformed.

And it was always her fault.

She didn't know how she found the clearing. She couldn't

have been going in the right direction, because she had no idea what direction she was going in. The wind buffeted her and turned her around and there were trees where they shouldn't have been. The screaming in the undergrowth sent her scrambling backwards and then she fell in between the standing stones.

And everything went suddenly still and silent. The wind stopped and raindrops hung in the air around her like diamonds.

'Well,' said a familiar voice. 'You really butchered that, Lex. And you were so close.'

Theo sat on the ground, cross-legged, his hands folded in his lap like he was fucking meditating at a yoga class or something. Moonlight fell around him, through him, illuminating him. Vines twisted around his body, coiling about his arms and legs, leaves shifting beneath his skin. Living, growing, unnatural natural shapes and things that made him appear here before her.

Alex pushed herself up from the earth and grass, tried to shove her soaked hair out of her face and left a trail of mud up her cheek like a smear of war paint.

'Theo?'

Her voice was just a strangled sob.

'Yes,' he said. 'Or at least, what's left of me. What I gave to the woods.'

'The woods killed you.'

He shook his head. 'It doesn't quite work like that. Not if you're willing. It's a sacrifice, Alex. A gift. Nick did it, a hundred years ago. I had to do the same. Take his place maybe. And by becoming part of it, I saved myself. It was the only way.'

'You and Sally...'

'Yes,' and he smiled, a beatific smile. 'She's safe now, as long as the woods are safe. You called the woods, Alex, and now you have to give yourself up to them. Wildewood always demands a price from us. All of us.'

'Are you... are you telling me to sacrifice myself? To Crom?'

He laughed. He actually laughed. And, oh God, it was a sound she had longed to hear again. His laughter. It was like birdsong, like the sounds she'd heard in the woods when she got lost there. That was why it had felt so familiar. It made her heart ache with loss and regret. So many years of regret. Whatever he was now, he was still her brother.

'No, never to him. To this.' He spread his arms wide and flowers fell between his fingers. 'Sally and I tried to stop Crom. We did everything and we failed. We even made Nick the guardian and gave him Maeve to protect because we thought—'

'Wait, you *gave* him Maeve?'

Theo smiled. He always had such a secretive, knowing smile, like a naughty child who thought he had got away with something and had just been caught.

'What did you do?' she hissed, but Theo didn't answer that.

'And now Crom has him. You have to kill him. It's only because the god of the hungry grass still wants you, the last of the de Wildes, that he's still here. Otherwise, he'd just walk out of his prison.'

'I am not killing anyone, you idiot. Especially not Nick.'

'He's of the forest, Alex. Part of this. He died more than a hundred years ago, part of a group of men who wanted to burn the house and free Crom, whether they knew it or not. But the woods weren't having that. Sally called him out of the wild wood, a changeling created in the original Nick Walker's image, from his essence and that of the wild, to protect Maeve until she came of age, in case I couldn't. And I couldn't, could I?'

There were oak leaves curling through his hair, and the curls were dotted with small, blue flowers, like a crown.

'Why would you—?' Alex stared at him, and understanding dawned on her. 'God *damn* it, Theo, what did you *do*?'

'What I had to,' he told her, still smiling. 'It doesn't change what you must do, Lex. Let the wild have you both. It's the only way. It's too late to try anything else. Kill him, destroy Crom. Whatever it takes.'

'You're mad,' she snarled at her brother.

Theo just reached out, fast as a robin darting after an insect, and pressed his fingertips to her forehead. 'Remember,' he told her.

And years of barriers fell away, all the methods by which her mind had tried to protect her. Everything that had said nightmare, or hallucination, or childhood terrors, all fell away like dead leaves in autumn.

Her memories, her *real* memories, thudded through her consciousness, as if she was being repeatedly slapped across the face. Sobbing, she tried to escape, but there was nowhere to go. Not from this.

She'd stood in the undercroft, just as Maeve had stood there. Daisy and Rose had flanked her, smiling, laughing.

'It won't hurt, Lexi. Don't be scared. He's going to make everything better again. He's going to make us all be together at last. We'll be a family.'

She'd looked down into the hole in the ground and tried to take a step back. But they wouldn't let her. Not now. Phantom hands held her far too tightly.

And the face looked up out of the darkness.

That grinning, bug-eyed face, golden and gleaming and terrible, all the teeth showing. The face that had haunted the corners of her nightmares, that had called to her, sung to her, reached out to her. The gleam of gold beneath rotting foliage. Eyes that didn't see, but saw everything, the mouth hanging open, hungry and waiting.

Blaise pushed her forward with unassailable force and she couldn't stop herself. Why couldn't she stop herself?

'You're the last of them, the women of the de Wildes. Your

blood is of the de Wildes and of Kilfayne,' he said. 'You can set him free. You can set us all free.'

But she didn't want to. She didn't want to touch it. She knew it was wrong. Something inside her told her that, something she had to listen to. But she couldn't stop herself. She knelt down and reached into the earth beneath the house, pulling it out. It was heavy and cumbersome and she wasn't strong enough. But she couldn't seem to stop. The cold arched roof of stones closing over her and the stench of mulch. The darkness pressing in on her, suffocating her.

'Alex?' her father cried out. His footsteps were thunder on the steps down from the study. 'Alexandra, get away from it.' Alex dropped the idol back into the ground and twisted around, a wild surge of hope filling her. Dad was here. He was here and he would save her. And everything would be all right again. This nightmare would be over. Because he always saved her from her nightmares.

Blaise Chambers whirled around, striking her father's solar plexus like a spear, pushing through him and into him, taking him in that moment of his greatest weakness, when all his defences were down, and making him his own.

She saw it happen, saw her father's eyes go wide with shock and horror, saw his mouth fall open in a silent scream.

'Run, Alex,' he gasped. His last ever words to her. 'You have to run! NOW!'

And he fell, hands still, limp on the rich and hungry earth.

It wasn't the darkness of the forest around her. It was the undercroft, the house itself, its deepest most terrible heart, and she had led her father here, right into a trap.

Because the man getting up again, straightening his spine, lifting his head, smiling that terrible smile... that was not her father, not anymore.

Alex ran. It was all she could do. She threw herself into the gap between the undercroft and the cellar, while the ghosts of

Wildewood Hall tore at her, their nails like brambles on her skin, as they tried to catch her and drag her back to the thing that now possessed her father.

She made it outside, into the darkness of the woods, and the forest seemed to convulse around her. She was part of it, something it wanted to protect. She knew that now. It was part of her. Her blood, not just that of the de Wildes. She was of Kilfayne as well, that was what Gran had told her. Gran was one of the wise women and so were countless others of her line. Grandfather had a whole chart and everything. Different families, different times, but always there to tie them to the wild wood and make it strong again, to protect them all from the creature trapped beneath the house.

And the wild wood knew her. It loved her. How could it not love her? She belonged here. She was its child as well. From the moment she came here, the woods had reached out.

But the figure lurching after her like some kind of savage beast... the thing that wore her father's face... that ran so much faster than she did...

It caught hold of a handful of her hair, dragging her to a halt, squirming and crying for help from the air and the water, from the earth and the sky, from all the trees and all the living things around her. Screaming.

And he had laughed. Blaise Chambers had laughed. The ancient god Crom had laughed. Her father had laughed...

'Mine,' it had said with a chorus of long dead voices.

No, the forest had replied and its roar was deafening. Mine!

Alex had reached for it, let it fill her. She'd tasted leaves and mulch and growing things, felt them in her veins and entwined around her bones. She made it her own, even then, unknowingly, only a child trying to grab hold of anything that might help her. Because she had to. Or she was lost. Everything was lost.

The wild wood fell on her father and tore him to pieces.

It left her sobbing over a corpse.

Right here, in the ring of stones, in its centre, in the heart of the wild wood.

Alex lifted her wretched face to look at her brother's spirit, but found he was gone. Another man sat there, his sad eyes fixed on her, his so familiar face wearing the other older smile, one filled with love and devotion.

'*It's okay, Alex,*' said her father, his voice no more than a whisper. '*That was the past. You couldn't have saved my life, but you did save my soul. By bringing me here.*'

The leaves spilled out of his mouth and nostrils, framed his eyes and tangled in his hair. He smiled his own smile again.

'I have to save Nick. They have him now. What can I do?'

'*He isn't real, love. Let him go. Let the forest take him back.*'

'But Nick is real. He's Maeve's father. And I think I – I love him. Please, you have to help me save him.'

'*There's nothing to save, Alex. You don't understand. Theo was Maeve's father. Sally was a wise woman of Kilfayne, more powerful than any for generations. Not since your great-grandmother. But Sally didn't trap Nick here. She made him from the forest. The walker, don't you see? You remember that story, don't you? The walker in the woods. She took a dead man's spirit and made it flesh, reconstituted him from leaves and bark and filled him with the spirit of the wild wood. She created him. Only the wild wood can contain Crom, lock the old god away beneath its roots. Call it now, and tell it to take the walker back. It will destroy him, and Chambers, and Crom will have no more power here. But you have to do it. You have to call it. You are the only one who can. That's why Crom wants you so badly, my love. You are the only one left with the blood of both.*'

'There's Maeve. If Theo told the truth. I'm not the last.'

He smiled gently, a strange admonishment in his eyes. '*She's just a little girl, love. It has to be you. And by the time she comes of age, it will be far too late. Would you put that burden on her?*'

'No,' she whispered, horrified. Besides, she knew enough to realise how Crom worked. He would go after Maeve now as soon as he got free and there would be no one to protect her. Not if Nick was gone.

And they were asking her to kill Nick. To give him up and damn him forever.

'He isn't real, Alex. You can do this.'

'But he *is* real.' She had touched him. She had made love to him. She had laughed with him and eaten the food he made and desired him more than anyone she had ever met. He was real. He was hers. He had to be real.

A huge hand grabbed her hair, fingers tangling in it as she was dragged back to her feet and a body as hard as any tree trunk pressed against the length of her.

'Oh, very real,' Blaise snarled with Nick's voice. 'More real than ever, thanks to you. And now he's ours, so are you. It's over, Alexandra. You are the last of the de Wildes and you have the blood of the women of Kilfayne in you, however watered down. You can still the wild wood and set us all free. You can have him as your own if you want. We can give you that. But you will submit to us. We have won.'

CHAPTER 47

NICK

The forest called to Nick, desperately trying to pull him back to himself, but all he knew now was the hunt. The rhythmic pulse of blood thrummed in his ears, and in the back of his throat, painting it with copper. The blood he had spilled on the dirt floor of the cellar, unwittingly giving it to Crom. It had woken the old god, and now he was lost. All the time that dreadful voice beat in his ears, a voice like a drum, telling him to run, to pursue, to hunt, to kill.

It was what he had been made to do. It was all he had been made to do.

And he had been made. He wasn't a creature of flesh and blood. He knew that now. He was the wild, and the chase, he was all aching teeth and burning muscles, and the scent of prey enveloped him, driving all other thoughts out of him.

Behind him the huntsman cried out in delight, Chambers exhorting him to run her down, to bring her to heel, to pin her to the ground and—

No, that couldn't be right.

He knew that couldn't be right. Because he knew the scent

he was following. He was covered in it, had breathed it in as part of him. He still yearned for it.

'*Don't think,*' the dark god told him. '*Just feel. Let the hunger take you. There is nothing else. Just live and breathe and hunt, that's all there is.*'

That blinding hunger surged up again, filling him as he reached the edge of the trees and felt their revulsion sweep through him. They knew what he had become, the dread transformation that had come over him. They knew he was lost and the horror of it all made the wild wood recoil from its creation. Because he was its creation. He understood that now.

He wasn't human. He had never been human. It was a dream. A trick. A thing to keep him docile and under control. Sally and Theo had lied. They had given him memories that were not his own. They had made him a changeling creature without anything to replace. They had given him a cuckoo to care for and they—

No. No, that wasn't right. However he had come into being, whatever magic had been used to create him, it didn't matter now. He was real. He knew he was.

They had given him *Maeve.* His Maeve. With all the love and joy in her heart, all the sweetness that she brought with her, his ray of sunshine, *his Maeve...*

'*They lied,*' Chambers told him in savage tones that tore all hope from his heart. '*They lied and they used you. They said Sally was your wife but you were nothing to her. You were just a cuckold, a changeling they made to protect their child in case they failed. And they did fail. You are thing born from lies and you will crumble like the infirm ground on which you were made.*'

But he hadn't failed them. Maeve was safe. Patricia had her. And Alex had protected her, even when he could not. Alex had saved Sally from the house, and from Chambers. Theo had come to take Sally with him. He'd come with the wild wood.

Because Theo hadn't died in the house. He'd died here among the trees on his own terms.

'*Think, my love,*' Sally seemed to whisper from the heart of the storm. '*You are a rational being, not a beast. You can think and feel. You can love. I know you can. You love Maeve. And you love Alex. I know you do. Love transforms all things. It makes you real. You are not a monster. You are a man who loves so much. Please, think, Nick.*'

How could he think with the wildness consuming him, with Crom burning inside him and Blaise Chambers, the bastard, screaming at him? His veins were boiling and his breath was trapped in his throat. His teeth cut into the sides of his cheeks and filled his mouth with blood. His muscles burned as he flung himself through the woods and they rejected him at every turn.

Why were they rejecting him if he was part of them, made from them? He was the guardian...

Think.

How did a beast like him think? He was pure instinct and reaction, he was the hunter and he was in pursuit of his prey. And her scent...

Her scent.

Alex.

Nick fought for control, for rationality, for something, anything. And it slipped from his grasp. Because he had found her instead.

Just kneeling there, in the middle of the stone circle, while the rain slammed down around her and the wind tore at her.

'But Nick is real,' she shouted, her voice almost lost in the tempest around her. 'He's Maeve's father. I think I – I love him. Please, you have to help me save him.'

The wind seemed to still and Nick froze with it. Listening, incredulously, to her words.

She loved him? How could she love him? He'd done nothing but hurt her. And they barely knew each other.

But...

But she said he was Maeve's father.

'But he *is* real.' Alex sobbed out the words as if in denial, as if arguing with someone or something he couldn't see.

Perhaps he'd never be able to see it. Not now. Not when he was lost. But he still knew what it was.

Alex was arguing with the wild wood itself, the thing that had made him, that would destroy him. She was trying to save him. Even now. Even after everything he had done...

Love transforms all things. It makes you real.

He came to a halt behind her and his hands moved in spite of himself, against his will. He didn't have a will now. He never would again. He was Crom's creature, Chambers' host. He was nothing but a shell for their evil.

Accept that, and it was so easy. Just give in and stop fighting, and all the struggle would fall away, taking the pain and the misery with it. That was what they promised, the two of them. He tried to believe that.

If he just gave up the struggle, and joined them in an unholy trinity, he'd never want again. Never feel the pain and loss. Never be not-enough for anyone again.

But Sally said differently. So did Alex.

You are not a monster.

His hand grabbed Alex's hair, fingers tangling in it, and he dragged her to her feet, pulling her back against his body so he could hold her struggling form still. But she didn't struggle. All the fight seemed to have left her. Whether it was fear or defeat, he didn't know.

His mouth moved, his voice used by the very thing he despised.

'Oh, very real. More real than ever, thanks to you. And now he's ours, so are you. It's over, Alexandra. You are the last of the de Wildes and you have the blood of the women of Kilfayne in you, however watered down. You can still the wild wood and set us all free. You can have him as your own if you want. We can give you that. But you will submit to us. We have won.'

Wait.

Why was Chambers making bargains with her?

It was like a punch to the gut. He *was* real. Alex said it and Alex made it so. She named him, called him Nick. Here, in the heart of the wild wood. She was a de Wilde too but, by Chambers' own admission, she had the blood of Kilfayne, a wise woman, like Sally. Like Maeve would be one day. Like all the long line of them back to the beginning of all of this.

She called him back into being, just as Sally had.

She made him real. Now.

And they were not alone. They had the forest, the wild wood, the very thing that had trapped and contained Crom for millennia. They knew how to control it. To keep the bonds tight. Or to let them go entirely.

But he couldn't let Alex give in to Crom and Chambers... He just couldn't.

The things they would do to her. It was like he had a glimpse into their minds as well, as if he could see their intentions now. Every promise was a lie. They were cruel and vindictive. He couldn't let Alex give herself up for him.

He would never be worth that. He was nothing. Just a creature of the forest, a memory, a ghost of someone long dead, a simulacrum made of magic and promises broken...

He knew that now.

Somehow he loosened his grip on Alex's hair and ran his hand instead in the gentlest caress down the side of her face that he could manage.

Know me, he wanted to say, but his voice was not his own anymore. He couldn't speak. So, this gesture would have to be enough.

Please, Alex, please know me. Trust me this one time. Even if I failed you before. Trust me now.

Old words came to him. Words he barely dared to think.

'*Mo stór, mo croi, mo mhuirnín dílis.*' Those words in the language that was written on his soul, expressing the only thing he wanted her to know. That he loved her. That he always would. The only words he would say if that was all he would ever be able to say again.

My darling, my heart, my own true love...

Alex shuddered in response, as if she heard them whispered on the wind, or in the beating of his heart, and she half turned to look up at him in wonder. She knew. She had to know. She understood the words and their meaning, and she had heard him. Part of him was still here. Still hers. She had to realise.

'Nick?' she whispered. She *had* heard. He saw that in the wonder filling her beautiful eyes. He had found his voice, in the wind and the storm, and now, when he tried again...

'*Call the wild woods,*' he told her on a stolen breath.

'But it'll kill you. It'll probably kill us both, anything to stop Crom...'

He winced, thought of Maeve, of her having to face this one day, and he knew what he had to do. What they both had to do.

'Please,' he whispered, and buried his face in her hair.

While it was still possible, she had to do it now, because he felt the power that possessed him exerting its control again. His grip on Alex's body tightened and his free hand closed on her throat. Even as he tried to stop it, Crom, or Chambers, or perhaps both of them, surged through him and grabbed at Alex, ready to crush the life from her before she could do what had to be done.

But they were too late. Far too late.

Alex, his Alex, was brave and valiant. She didn't hesitate this time. She called the wild wood as if she had always been in communion with it. She reached out with all that she had in her, stretching up to the canopy and down to the mycelium and summoning it all to her.

The wild wood responded with a roar that drowned out the storm.

As it rushed in on them, Nick tried to shelter her, pulling her down and shielding her with his body. It was all he had left, this form that had been created through magic and hope and need. And now he used all that he was in an effort to save her.

Even if it meant his own destruction.

So be it, he told the woods he had loved so much. *Take me back, but please*, he begged, *please, let her live. She's everything. Please.*

And he prayed those words over and over until his mind was torn to pieces and scattered like seeds on the wind, and he knew no more.

CHAPTER 48

ALEX

The storm rushed back with a vengeance, screaming at her, tearing at her, trying to drive her into the earth, or rip the weight of Nick's body off her and hurl him away so it could get to her. But he held on, and she held onto him, reaching for the wild.

There was nothing human here. There was no conscious mind that thought like hers, no morals or ethics. Whereas Alex had been able to sense the individual ghosts in the house, sense the people they had once been, this was something else, something vast and terrifying and so completely alien to her. It was wild, and endless, and remorseless. It was angry. So angry.

It blamed Nick, she could sense that. Saw him as a traitor and it would have retribution for that.

'No, that's not right,' she tried to tell the wild wood, or whatever that vast consciousness was. But she was little more than a sigh in its screams of rage. She dug her hands into Nick's body and found, instead of skin and muscle... bark, wood, and moss...

Nick was gone.

Abruptly the storm stopped again as the world around her twisted to that other plane, that different far-off place that was bathed in sunlight instead of the storm at night.

Alex lay on the floor of the forest, in a clearing surrounded by much younger trees and no stones at all, clinging to the gnarled trunk of an ancient oak tree. Its roots wrapped around her, as if it had grown over her for more than a hundred years, trying to protect her. There was no sign of Nick, no sign of the storm, and no sign of the house either.

Reality had shifted, and this was not a dream. She was scratched and bruised, still soaked to the skin, her hair plastered over her face. There was birdsong coming from the trees and it sounded like laughter.

'Well,' said a gentle voice, ripe with the same amusement she'd heard in Theo's. But this was not her brother. Not this time. 'This is a conundrum. What are you doing here?'

An old woman sat in the middle of the clearing, her fingers moving quickly and deftly as she threaded twigs and stalks together, wove flowers into the pattern with reeds and all manner of living things, entwining them into shapes and patterns Alex couldn't hope to understand. In her lap, a large golden hare nestled as if it had been sleeping there. It blinked at Alex, watching her intently, twitching its long ears.

Alex extracted herself from the roots of the tree, sliding out as best she could, wincing as her clothes caught against it and pulled.

'I don't know where I am,' she admitted.

The old woman smiled, her green eyes twinkling. She never paused in her work as she looked up. Alex knew that voice, knew that face. Knew those hands and the patterns they wove. 'That's probably a good thing. You aren't meant to be here at all.'

'This can't be real,' Alex murmured.

'Oh, I'm afraid it very much is.'

'Gran?' The old woman smiled up at her briefly but didn't answer. She continued with her work, fingers moving so quickly. 'Where's Nick?'

The woman tilted her head to one side. 'Nick? Nick who?'

'Nick Walker.' Alex's brain was supplying an answer she really didn't want to be real.

'The walker? Oh.' There was such sorrow in that simple 'oh'. She nodded to the oak tree in the clearing which Alex had been wrapped around, which had been wrapped around her. That couldn't be right. There was no tree here. But...

But this wasn't here. Or now.

'Where am I?' Alex asked, deciding to try again from the start.

'You're in the wild wood, my dear. The old wood. Where it all began.'

Which was no help at all.

The old wood, she thought and looked around. Really looked. This was a young forest, thick and lush but without the weight of ages clinging to it. Wood anemone and dog violets clustered around their feet, an imperious stand of purple foxgloves swayed in a breeze she couldn't feel. Above them, in the understorey, she saw the bright green of hazel and the dark sheen of holly leaves. And beyond that, the oak canopy gazed down at her, shifting every so often, the soft creak of old wood in the breeze. But none were so old as that oak in the centre.

There was no oak in the clearing, her mind kept saying. *It shouldn't be here. It shouldn't...*

But it was.

'He's the heart of the wild wood, made flesh,' said the old woman. She lifted what she had been making and handed it to Alex. It was one of those circles like the ones Maeve had given her, but far more elaborate and decorative. There were flowers and stalks of grass, the heads heavy with seed, as well as leaves and twigs.

Alex took it in numb hands and felt a shudder of recognition run through her.

'You aren't my gran, are you?'

The old woman shook her head and stroked the hare. It preened beneath her hands.

'Your grandmother died before you were born, *a chailín ghil mo chroí.*'

'Who are you?'

'I'm the mother of the wild woods.' The old woman smiled. 'I'm the Cailleach. And for a while I was your gran, when you needed me.' She pulled strands of golden corn from beneath the hare and started another pattern, weaving the lengths together, plucking up flowers and grasses from the forest clearing beside her. 'The wise women were my daughters. I have always stood against Crom. I locked him away, and raised the forest to enclose his tomb. We keep it strong, the wild wood, so that he cannot escape. All down through the long years, to you, and onwards, to Maeve.'

'Did you teach Maeve?'

'We have all taught Maeve. She's special, that little one. Wild wood all the way through. A woman of Kilfayne and the blood of the de Wildes. Like you. But her time hasn't come yet.'

'The de Wildes run to boys,' Alex murmured absently, running her fingers over the pattern. It was like a maze and she kept getting lost.

'That's what happens when something kills all the girls.' Her voice was stark all of a sudden and when Alex looked up those piercing green eyes were very close. Her teeth were bare too, the teeth of a fox perhaps, and the white hair drifted like dandelion seeds. 'I taught you too, Alexandra. Or tried to. I kept you safe for as long as I could. You are mine as well, a part of me. You and Maeve both. We entwined the blood of the wise women with the blood of the de Wildes time and again, but you all leave, or die. Not that I blame you. Ah, but this time, because he used poor wee Maeve and you too... this time because he took the guardian we set to watch the boundaries...'

'Has he won? Crom?' Alex asked. She hardly dared to say

the words. Because it would mean she had failed. It would mean she was dead. And that was what this felt like, being in this place. Alone. Like she had died.

'Not yet,' the woman of the wild wood purred. 'Not unless you decide to stay like your brother. Will you go back and bury Crom for once and for all, my child? Bind him deep underground and wind the roots of the wild wood around him? Keep him there forever and stand watch? Will you do your duty for both your lines?'

Both her lines. Both Maeve's lines too. Her ancestors included the wise women of Kilfayne. Theo had loved Sally who had given birth to Maeve. The two, wound together, like these patterns of tangled twigs, vines, reeds and flowers. The Cailleach was of the land. And all this land was once her wild wood.

And if Alex didn't... the god of the hungry grass would rise again, and this time there would only be Maeve to stand against him, all on her own. Oh, in ten years or more maybe. But she wouldn't have Nick. She wouldn't have anyone. If she even had ten years. Because if Crom escaped now, wearing Nick's face, and turned up at Patricia's house in the village...

Alex had to do something. Now.

'Put him back in the ground,' said the old woman of the woods. 'Bury him deep and bind him tight, then call the wild wood. We will do the rest.'

The old woman – her gran who was not her grandmother – blew her a kiss, and something slammed into Alex's chest with the force of a jackhammer.

CHAPTER 49

ALEX

Alex thudded onto the marble floor, back inside the house, her clothes, skin and hair all soaked, while the wind and the storm screamed on outside, rattling the windows and the doors like some kind of demonic force intent on its destruction. And perhaps it was. If Crom could tear down Wildewood Hall, and kill her in the process, that might free him too. He already had Nick, the guardian of the wild wood. And he had almost had her as well.

With no idea of what had just happened or how she had found herself back here, Alex tried to make herself move, to roll onto all fours and get up. She was clutching the circle of vegetation in her hand, half crushed and still as wet from the rain as she was. She had no idea where it had actually come from and how she had brought it inside. Her hands were torn and scratched, with smears of blood, dirt and sap all over them. Had she made it? Or found it?

Or... or had that dream been real? Had she been given it?

She thought of the stone circle, and the light of that ancient sun, and the Cailleach. And the old oak tree.

If that was real, Nick was gone.

Something like a stone landed in her chest and all her ribs seemed to tighten. She felt brittle, like she would crumble to pieces. Her eyes burned. It wasn't fair. It wasn't...

Blaise's soft laugh echoed through the hall and that brought her back to her senses. He was still here. And so was Crom. Without Nick to contain them, their spirits roamed free.

Bury him deep...

That's what her grandfather had tried to do, right under the house, in the undercroft after she had let it out. He had buried it deep, bound it with charms and sealed it up again, hidden the very chamber which contained its resting place.

The study door was open so she made for it.

Nick could still be outside in the storm, in the forest. He'd been helpless and lost and...

Or he was gone. Really gone.

Alex had to push the thought away. There wasn't time.

'Really?' Blaise's voice asked. '*You're just going to abandon him to his fate? The man you so recently claimed to love? The man who sacrificed himself to save you?*'

'You said he wasn't a man,' Alex snarled.

His figure coalesced from shadows now, standing behind the desk. His desk, of course. He had ruled this house with a fist of steel and a voice which wrapped it in velvet. Now he appeared again, drawing on every ounce of power left to him. He looked like his portrait, in the prime of his life, heartbreakingly handsome, a Regency rake who would sit perfectly in any period drama and steal the heart of everyone who looked at him. His smile was a twist of disdain on his perfect features and his eyes dark as his soul.

'*True,*' he told her. '*He isn't. I am here though and I can be whatever you want me to be, Alexandra. You know that. You always knew that. I will give you whatever you want and all you will ever know is pleasure. Just stop this foolishness. Accept your fate.*'

The urge to listen to him was powerful. Because it would be so easy. He didn't lie to her. He never had. Her family had done nothing but lie. To her and to Nick. Everything was based on lies. From the very first. The de Wildes had lied and lied and used all those lies to gain power and influence. They had used the power of the wild wood to draw on the power Crom granted them. Their daughters had been the price, unless they ran as far and as fast as they could away from this place.

'*Run, Alex.*'

Her father's voice. The last thing he had said before Blaise had taken him over and turned him into a monster.

She clenched her hands around the circlet until its thorns dug into her hands. Her blood was fresh and bright, and the stab of pain drove a single moment of clarity into her.

Why was she even standing here talking to a ghost?

She lunged forward, through the secret door and down the stairs.

Blaise screamed in abject fury as he threw himself after her, and the house shook, the ground beneath her bucking wildly, trying to throw her off her feet. But Alex didn't stop. She couldn't. To stop now would be to give up and she couldn't do that.

What would Nick say? What would Theo and Sally tell her?

Run, Alex.

It was his voice. Not her father, not her brother. It was Nick. She knew it was Nick. His voice rippled in the air, in the earth beneath her, in the water that forced its way through the gaps and into the undercroft, trying to find its way in. Because water always found a way. And in the earth there were roots and living things. In this place of death and misery, there was still life.

The idol was still in the corner on the far side from the

steps. She skidded to her knees and grabbed it, turning as she did so.

Call on the wild wood, the old woman had said. Bury him deep, bind him and call on the wild wood.

Alex threw herself at the pit where Maeve had found the idol and Blaise's cry of fury took her off her feet. The ghosts raced in towards her, so many of them. She could make out Daisy and Rose, but there were so many others. Countless insubstantial hands tried to grab her and hold her, bathing her in that eerie ectoplasmic glow. They raked over her flesh and dug into her clothes, tore at her hair.

They were the only light down here now, the only thing she could see, eyes like old coins, and mouths which opened to the void. They were the playthings of Blaise Chambers, and nothing but food for Crom. The old god had fed on them for all those years and they were as trapped in this as she was. All of them.

Daphne would tell her she needed to send them to the light, but there was no light down here. There was nothing but darkness and misery. That was why they congregated here.

There was no light. And she was as lost as they were. That was what they were all trying to tell her, a chorus of voices, all whispering, all lamenting, all telling her to stop, to give up, to give in.

To let Blaise Chambers win. As they had. It was the only way.

No, she refused to accept that.

Alex dropped to her knees, as the strength finally left her body. She was still holding the idol, but her hands were numb and helpless now, the circlet crushed in her grip against the cold metal.

She felt Blaise appear behind her, felt his hands on her back, on her shoulders, wrapping around her throat. He squeezed until her breath almost stopped. Her eyes fluttered closed. She couldn't fight him anymore.

'*That's it, my beloved Alexandra,*' he murmured. '*Just give in. Just let go.*'

Just let go.

Alex smiled. It wasn't what he meant, but he'd said it all the same. A command. And he did so love to command her, to have her obey. She released the idol, letting it fall into the pit, and with it the circlet to bind it.

Her whole body slumped down until her hands, scratched and bleeding, hit the bare earth, her nails digging into it as deeply as she could.

'No,' Blaise snarled, his grip tightening. '*No, you stupid bitch. What have you done?*'

'What I have to,' she told him, her voice no more than a hiss, and then she called on the wild wood. She didn't have to speak to do that. It was in her blood, in her soul. And thanks to Nick, in her heart. She just reached for it.

And the wild wood answered.

The roots surged up from beneath her, and her mouth filled with the taste of leaves, and moss and living growing things. The rustling of unfurling foliage drowned out the ghosts, the creak of branches and bark. A green glow filled the darkness, the bioluminescence of verdant and growing things, of life itself, of sunlight filtering through the high canopy and dappling on the ferny floor, the shifting light of evening through the trees. It was everywhere, everything, in her and all around her. Filling her and spilling out of her, engulfing this space.

Alex slumped down and let it take her, let it fill her and the void beneath her house. Wildewood Hall shook as the storm outside became a storm at its foundations and she was the source of it. Part de Wilde, part Kilfayne, part something else entirely. Herself. Alex O'Neill, PhD. Determined, stubborn, defiant, the cynic, the rationalist, the killjoy, the great debunker, the sceptic's sceptic...

Vines wound about her body, tendrils threaded through her veins, flowers filled her eyes and leaves her mouth and she was lost in the wild wood. She was never coming back. She knew that. She was part of it now. She was gone.

A hand took hers, strong as oak, but gentle as a newly unfurled leaf. Another touched her face, cradling her cheek. He tilted her head up from the ground, from the pit and the endless dark, like a flower turning to the light.

'Alex?' Nick murmured. His voice carried a strange reverberation, as if it was so much bigger than it sounded, as if the whole forest filled it. And perhaps it did. 'Alex, *a chuisle mo chroí*, look at me.'

She blinked and her sight returned to her. Nick was kneeling before her, where the pit had been, his smile so perfect. The one sight she craved above all else.

He was safe. He was here.

Or else, the more obvious thing struck her, they were both dead and this was some kind of afterlife which she had never really believed in.

Nick gave a soft laugh as if reading her thoughts. Because he had always seemed able to do that. 'We aren't dead, *mo stór*. Far from it. We have never been so full of life. Come on, let's get out of here, you and me.'

'How are you here?' she murmured, as he lifted her from the dirt floor which now was covered in green and growing things, all entwined together. The pit was gone, buried in a mass of vegetation, criss-crossed with roots and branches, still moving, reclaiming this place. Trees had torn through the ceiling and had burst through up into the study, and were still forcing their way onwards through the floors and walls of Wildewood Hall. One of the unused bedrooms above it was no doubt gone as well, along with part of the attics.

'Nick, answer me.'

'The wood sent me back. For you. Hush now. We'll talk later. Let me get you to safety.'

Nick carried her up the stairs, and out into the hallway, and from there to the kitchen. He always gravitated to the hearth. Alex stared at the remains of the Hall as they went, the devastation from the broken windows, the deadwood and broken stonework in the drawing room, and the very much living wood which had erupted in the study behind her, and she wondered how on earth they would explain any of this to the insurance company.

But for now, Nick held her. Nick was there. Real and solid, and he felt so very human. As exhaustion took her, she decided that she would just be happy with that.

CHAPTER 50

ALEX

Nick made tea. Of course he did. What else was there to do in a crisis? Or at least, in the aftermath of one. When Alex woke again, he'd pulled on some clothes and, but for his dishevelled hair tied back in a loose knot, and the leaves still tangled in it, she wouldn't for a moment have guessed that anything supernatural had happened at all. That he hadn't been swallowed back up into the forest, that he hadn't been the oak at the heart of the wild wood. That he was just a man and she was just a woman and there had been a terrible storm.

Because all of those things were in fact true.

As well as all the rest of it.

The dream, or nightmare, whatever you called it, it was all real.

After they had drunk all the tea in the pot, Alex realised she was still covered in dirt and blood and God alone knew what else so they made their way upstairs by torchlight. Her room was still and quiet and the oppressive atmosphere was gone. The painting was just a painting now, and Blaise Chambers was a man long dead and buried.

'I can get rid of it if you want,' Nick said when he caught her glance. 'I can take it outside and burn it right now.'

Alex smiled at him. It was still raining, the dawn barely breaking through the clouds. 'Good luck starting a fire in that,' she told him.

All the same, he took the painting off the wall and hurled it down the corridor towards the stairs. They listened to it bang and crash down the stairs until it fell to the hall floor.

It was almost dawn, and the wind had died down. The rain was just rain now and Nick was here with her. He paused at the doorway to the bedroom, hesitant, so Alex threaded her fingers through his and tugged him inside.

'Are you sure?' he asked.

'Absolutely sure,' she told him, without hesitation. 'Take off those clothes. We need to wash and warm up.' And then she realised what she had just said, the other implications that might come from those words, and her commanding manner. 'Nothing else. Not unless you want to.'

His hand closed on hers, warm and gentle, but firm. He managed a smile. 'Of course I want to, Alex.'

After what had happened earlier, she decided that was far more than she had hoped for. Too many lines had blurred and Chambers' malign influence had been so strong she was barely sure what had been real and what had not.

Alex swallowed hard and Nick lifted her hand to his lips, kissing her tense knuckles carefully.

'Let's revisit this later,' he murmured. 'Go and shower. I'll see you in a—'

He was leaving her? No. She couldn't let him do that. She pulled his hand to her chest and held it there. The sudden terror that swept over her at that thought made the world spin sideways.

'Don't. Please, don't go.'

She was safe with him. She would always be safe with him. And right now, she needed to be safe.

Nick nodded, still watching her cautiously, and led her into the ensuite where he turned on the shower. There was still hot water, by some kind of minor miracle, and soon the little tiled room was filled with steam. The two of them shed their clothing and stepped into the shower together, taking it in turns to scrub each other clean. It wasn't sexual, not really. This was cautious and gentle, a study in care for each other. He cleaned each cut and scrape on her, and she did the same for him. And finally, she stood with him, arms around his body, his around her, and the water cascaded over them both.

They took their time drying each other, and finally, fell into the bed together, swaddling themselves in the blankets, bodies wound together. It was warm and animal, and perfect. All Alex could have wanted right now. It wasn't like before. Not this contented embrace, his arms so strong and gentle around her, their legs tangled together.

In the morning – well, *later* in the morning – they would have to talk and make plans. They would have to assess the damage to the house and the estate. But more than that, they would have to try to untangle their experiences and see if there was some kind of way forward, knowing what they knew. And they would need to address reality itself and whether that had changed.

But right now, Alex didn't care. Couldn't care.

Bone-deep weariness swept through her and she pressed her face into Nick's chest, felt his heartbeat beneath his skin, listened to the rise and fall of his chest and let his warmth wrap itself around her. He still smelled of the woods, of cedar, and cloves, and something else she couldn't place. The wild, perhaps. Or just Nick.

'Alex?' he whispered.

'Yes.'

'I was lost. I was part of the wild. I wasn't human anymore.'

It sounded so normal. Perhaps it was to him. At the same time it sounded like a dream that dispersed on waking like morning mist.

'But you came back.'

'You brought me back. Your love. Our love.'

'You came when I called, when I needed you most. You came back to me.'

His lips pressed a kiss to the top of her head, the hair still damp. 'I'll always come when you call, Alex, *a chuisle mo chroí.*'

She smiled at the lyrical sound of the Irish. She loved the way he spoke it, like music remembered from long ago. 'You said that before. What does it mean?'

He took her hand gently and pressed it to his bare chest. She could feel his heart beneath his ribs, the rhythm steady, strong, and so very alive. 'It means that you are the beat of my heart, Alex. And always will be.'

Sleep took her effortlessly, safe in his arms.

'Oh no, Granny!' Maeve's voice rang out through the house, appalled. 'Look at the mess!'

The sound brought both Nick and Alex to wakefulness as if they'd just been hit with an electric shock. They were together in bed, naked, and any second now—

'We've got to get dressed,' Alex hissed and Nick stared at her helplessly. His clothes from last night were still a wet and muddy mess on the floor. So were hers. But at least her other clothes were all here to hand. Anything clean he owned was in his own room, down the corridor. 'Run,' she said. 'I'll hold them off.'

He wound a sheet around himself and made for the door, a very hesitant Greek god indeed. Alex threw on fresh clothes, and made her way to the stairs as quickly as she could to inter-cept their visitors.

Patricia looked up from the hallway, her hand very firmly holding Maeve back.

'Well, you certainly had a night of it,' the older woman said and then winced as her own words registered. She carried on in a rush, determined not to dwell on what had very definitely happened but couldn't be admitted right now. 'The *storm*, I mean. Are you all right? No one was hurt?'

The storm. Of course, the storm. And the damage to the house.

Nothing else. She couldn't possibly know about anything else.

Except she had probably heard the doors and the running footsteps because Dr Patricia Neary was no fool.

'We're fine,' Nick called, emerging from his own room wearing a t-shirt and jeans as if nothing had happened at all and he had been there all night, sleeping soundly. He hadn't managed shoes, Alex noticed. Patricia did not look fooled for an instant. 'The storm took out the power, and we've taken some damage but we're both okay. Best stay out of the study though.'

Patricia fixed her knowing gaze on him now and nodded. 'I saw. It must have hit much harder here than in the village. We should call Jimmy Óg and his brothers, get them to have a look.'

The talk turned to the builders and insurance, and how they were going to make safe the building, while Nick lifted Maeve in his arms and held her close.

Maeve chattered on about what had happened in the village, about losing power and the tree branch coming down and blocking the road, and how they couldn't get an answer from his phone. But Granny had said it would all be all right, because her daddy wouldn't let anything bad happen, and now it was.

Nick listened to her, holding her close, while Alex and

Patricia made tea, and found a cache of his biscuits in one of the tins.

'I've never seen this place so quiet,' Patricia said at last. 'Nor him so at peace. It's all worked out then?'

Alex hesitated. 'I think so,' she said finally. There was no point in denying any of it. Not to Patricia. 'It was... it was almost too much. And I thought I'd lost him. There were things the woods showed us, both of us, which will take some figuring out. But...'

She glanced at the man and his daughter. There was no mistaking that bond.

'I know my daughter made... questionable decisions,' Patricia said after a long and thoughtful pause. 'Always did. She was headstrong and always thought she knew best, even as a child.'

Questionable decisions. That was a phrase for it, Alex supposed. But that meant Patricia knew. Alex didn't know how much, but Patricia knew enough of it.

'I think she did what she thought was right,' she replied cautiously.

Patricia was still watching Nick. 'She made mistakes, no doubt about that. And it cost her dearly. But she always did what was right for Maeve. We don't like to talk about magic much around here, but it's very much part of our lives. Sally reached out to the wild wood for a guardian for her daughter, and it sent Nick. Where he came from, what he was... I don't know. But he is one of the best men I have ever met. And if he was a changeling, he isn't now. He's human, flesh and blood. And he is our Maeve's father, in every way which matters. Always has been. Always will be. He raised her, he loves her. And as far as I'm concerned, as far as *Maeve* is concerned... The paperwork says the same thing, just so you know. And now the house is safe, he's free.'

Alex just nodded. Patricia knew. She probably knew everything. She didn't miss a trick.

And as she said, Nick was free now. He could go wherever he wanted, be whoever he wanted to be. There was nothing to hold him here anymore. His so-called duty was done.

She ought to be happy for him. And she was. She really was. It shouldn't have felt like loss.

The repairs on the house were not as extensive as they had all feared. The study and the undercroft were the worst part. No one asked why there was now half a forest where that section of the building had been and the architect that Nick called had the bright idea of creating an orangery around it instead of trying to remove it. There was some evidence that there had been one somewhere in the house, at some point in the past. Alex wasn't so sure but everyone insisted that had been the case, and that there were plans for it somewhere in the records. Well, there had been records, in the study. But there had to be another copy somewhere, everyone agreed on that. This was a listed building. The National Archives were mentioned. So was Trinity College. Then the debate ensued about who to contact first.

Somehow the structure itself and the first floor were still sound. There might even be a grant to do the restoration work, she was told, given it was storm damage and they'd only be putting the house back as it had been a hundred years or more ago. Add to that the insurance money which would no doubt be forthcoming. And God, she hoped that was the case, although it seemed that the builders were happy enough to begin the work. People from Kilfayne, it seemed, dealt with the evidence of the supernatural as a daily fact of life, something commonplace and not worth dwelling on, much as Patricia had said. They all pulled together in times of crisis. The Big House, as Jimmy the builder referred to it, was part of Kilfayne. Part of their heritage. They couldn't just let it fall down, now could they?

'After a while, it's just easier to go along with it,' Nick told her with a smile. He was at peace with himself now, she realised, and with Kilfayne. 'Trust them. Besides, Jimmy says you're one of their own now. They won't see you left in the lurch.'

'One of their own?'

'No longer a runner-in,' he replied, and ruffled her hair affectionately. 'The estate employs a lot of people locally. Could employ more as well.'

'So could a hotel.'

He gave a laugh which surprised her. 'Still got that bone to chew on then?'

Alex shook her head. In fact, the lawyers had said the chain had taken one look at the damage and run screaming so that idea was well and truly past now. Besides, she couldn't hand over Wildewood to someone who would tear it all down given half a chance. Not anymore. She couldn't take that risk.

'I guess we're back to Theo's plan then,' she told him. 'God help us.' Theo had been terrible at planning anything. Luckily he'd had Nick for practicalities. 'We could let out rooms, like a guest house. Just on a small scale, all right? If we ever get it fixed up, that is. We could even open it up for ghost hunts. At least I have the contacts for that.'

'Alex? You sound like you're thinking of staying here.'

She huffed out half a laugh. 'Perhaps I am. I think this place might need me.'

Besides, she had promised.

The smile that spread over his handsome features made his eyes shine and she was suddenly struck again by the beauty in them. The flecks of green and gold in their dark brown. All the colours of the forest.

He swept her up in his arms and spun her around until she

gave a squawk somewhere between shock and delight. 'Not just this place. *I* need you. You're staying, *mo chuisle*. That's the best news ever.'

Nick set her back on the ground again, but he didn't let her go.

'Yes, but... but you don't have to,' she told him. 'You're free, Nick. You can do whatever you want, go wherever you want, you and Maeve. You have family out there. Arnold said. Ariadne and Jason Walker. Tell them you're a long-lost cousin or something. You are, after all. And it sounds like they'd understand some of what happened here if the stuff on his podcast is anything to go by.'

A frown crept down his forehead, drawing his eyebrows together. 'I might, I guess. Family's important. But I'm not leaving. Where else would I want to go, Alex? This is my home. My place. I belong here. With you.'

The breath in her lungs came out in a rush of relief.

'Really? I thought... I thought...'

She didn't know what she thought, so she pushed herself up on her toes and kissed him.

Behind them, Maeve gave a whoop of delight and Patricia shushed her, but right now neither Nick nor Alex cared.

They were together, and finally, with the wood safe and quiet, Wildewood Hall could be a home.

Three days later, Gabe, Daphne and the rest of *The Ghost Patrol* team turned up, ready to investigate in spite of every protest Alex had thrown at them. But to be honest, she was never so happy to see them, and to prove, once and for all, that there was nothing supernatural about her new home.

Even if that was not entirely true.

Nothing supernatural *anymore*, perhaps. Not the house anyway.

Or at least nothing evil. There were still moments, whispers and breeze. It was an old house of course, and it carried so many memories. Alex knew that. But there was no malice now. Just echoes. Beyond the house, however, the woods were as alive as ever. Perhaps more so.

Daphne gazed at the line of trees, a curious expression on her face. Longing and suspicion and... something else, something like need.

'What about the trees?' she asked. 'They're... they're...' She didn't finish. She didn't seem able to find the words. Her eyes shone with excitement.

'Yeah,' Alex murmured, then thought better of agreeing with any adventures her friend had in mind. 'You can do what you want in the house but maybe stay out of the woods.'

Gabe instantly got that light in his eyes and she knew it was going to take another miracle to get him to stay away.

Nick kissed her neck, completely distracting her from the argument she was about to launch into.

'Don't worry,' he murmured in her ear. 'I'll keep them safe. Let them have their fun. We all need the odd mystery in our lives, don't we?'

A LETTER FROM JESSICA

Dear reader,

I want to say a huge thank you for choosing to read *Wildewood*. If you did enjoy it, and want to keep up to date with all my latest releases, just sign up at the following link. Your email address will never be shared and you can unsubscribe at any time.

www.secondskybooks.com/jessica-thorne

I hope you have enjoyed sharing this adventure with me and if you loved *Wildewood* I would be very grateful if you could write a review. I love hearing from my readers – you can get in touch through social media or my website. I'd love to know what you think, see these characters and locations through your eyes, and of course, say hi.

Thanks,

Jessica Thorne

KEEP IN TOUCH WITH JESSICA

www.rflong.com/jessicathorne

instagram.com/Jessthornebooks
facebook.com/JessThorneBooks
tiktok.com/@ruthfranceslong

ACKNOWLEDGEMENTS

I always wanted to write a haunted house story. I've loved them for so long. I am also slightly obsessed with ghost hunting shows – I don't know what might have given that away. Shows such as *Ghost Adventures, Most Haunted, Uncanny,* and *Help! My House Is Haunted* all combine here, with others, to create *The Ghost Patrol.* I have spent so many happy hours watching them all. There may also be elements of *Scooby Doo.* That's inevitable.

Bringing that together with my love of Irish folklore and the history of the Big House in Irish culture was just a wonderful adventure. Wildewood Hall and Kilfayne are entirely fictional, as are the various legends I have woven around them. But they do have threads of truth buried in them, seeds of stories from long ago. Alongside complete fabrication. Because that's the way folklore tends to work.

I would particularly like to thank Joe Doyle and everyone at Dunsany Castle for a truly inspirational tour. It is such a special place and parts of it echo strongly through Wildewood Hall, though that is largely accidental. Long may the rewilding continue. And long may that magical library be protected. May your ghosts always be benign.

I would also like to thank my wonderful partners in crime— I mean *fiction*: The Naughty Kitchen – Alison May, Jeevani Charika, Janet Gover, Imogen Howson, Sheila McClure and Kate Johnson; and my Lady Writers' Social Club – Sarah Rees Brennan, Susan Connolly and Catie Murphy. You are a constant support and inspiration and I honestly don't know what I would do without you. Every writer needs a writerly support network and I am blessed with both of mine.

My agent Sallyanne Sweeney and my editor Natalie Edwards are always there for me. I did promise Natalie she would learn more about Crom Cruach than she would ever want to know. And behold...

And finally, my family who have been on many fact-finding missions with me, research trips, etc., which have made this possible. My kids might be adults now but a lot of our Saturday and Sunday afternoons past are bound up in this story.

And to my husband Pat, I really couldn't do any of this without you. You remain my hero, my strength, and my guardian, *a chuisle mo chroí.*

PUBLISHING TEAM

Turning a manuscript into a book requires the efforts of many people. The publishing team at Bookouture would like to acknowledge everyone who contributed to this publication.

Audio
Alba Proko
Melissa Tran

Commercial
Lauren Morrissette
Hannah Richmond
Imogen Allport

Cover design
Lisa Horton

Data and analysis
Mark Alder
Mohamed Bussuri

Editorial
Natalie Edwards
Melissa Tran

Copyeditor
Rhian McKay

Proofreader
Liz Hatherell

Marketing
Alex Crow
Melanie Price
Occy Carr
Cíara Rosney
Martyna Młynarska

Operations and distribution
Marina Valles
Joe Morris

Production
Hannah Snetsinger
Mandy Kullar
Nadia Michael
Charlotte Hegley

Publicity
Kim Nash
Noelle Holten
Jess Readett
Sarah Hardy

Rights and contracts
Peta Nightingale
Richard King
Saidah Graham

Dear Reader,

We'd love your attention for one more page to tell you about the crisis in children's reading, and what we can all do.

Studies have shown that reading for fun is the **single biggest predictor of a child's future life chances** – more than family circumstance, parents' educational background or income. It improves academic results, mental health, wealth, communication skills, ambition and happiness.

The number of children reading for fun is in rapid decline. Young people have a lot of competition for their time, and a worryingly high number do not have a single book at home.

Hachette works extensively with schools, libraries and literacy charities, but here are some ways we can all raise more readers:

- Reading to children for just 10 minutes a day makes a difference
- Don't give up if children aren't regular readers – there will be books for them!

- Visit bookshops and libraries to get recommendations
- Encourage them to listen to audiobooks
- Support school libraries
- Give books as gifts

There's a lot more information about how to encourage children to read on our websites: **www.RaisingReaders.co.uk** and **www.JoinRaisingReaders.com**.

Thank you for reading.